The Palace

of Sweets

Salvatore Coppola

To Frances and Teddy Terlizzi

and to

Major Dunne
and all those who fight the
interminable battle in the
theater of the mind

1967-1969

Gravel popped and skidded beneath the tires of the tightly packed station wagon as it lumbered down the driveway. Tall weeds sprung up like cowlicks as the car traced over the deeply gutted paths. Byron rolled his palm from side to side, and then raked his whitening hair off of his forehead. His granddaughters turned and pressed their faces into the side window, waving as the car peeled into the road and was quickly lost in the narrow, forested blade of asphalt.

He turned away and walked into the kitchen, anticipating some cups or plates in need of washing would be there, but his daughter-in-law, in her goodness, left the kitchen in perfect order. He stood alone and wondered what the next days would bring. Surely there is someone he hasn't thought of yet who is reflecting on his loss and is moved to sit for a time with him and wait and watch how the trees, no longer porous with the lightness of May, quickly shadow his shallow backyard and steal up the day's light before its time. Certainly the clatter of crunching gravel will announce the arrival of someone to relieve his loneliness and share his sorrow.

He reached into the stereo console and started the music again, raising the volume before stepping into the large, enclosed porch with its knotty pine paneling dulled with age. He turned back to the stereo and stared at it, recalling the argument they had over it, she insisting on a fine piece of furniture and he only that the sound be flawless. She won, he thought, as he ambled to the porch windows. And now it was special because she wanted it, a tactile piece that holds a place. It's something of her that remained. He opened the draw curtains fully to look out into the back yard that rose quickly to the forested mountain. It seemed like only last week he could look out and see distances and height and depth. He remembered how spring arrived slowly until it dropped a dense, deciduous curtain and his vision was cut short.

A clarinet rested over the metal folding chairs. Byron picked it up and raised it to the windows on an outstretched arm. He fluttered the keys with his thick fingers and watched for light winking through worn corks and springs that failed to snap back with urgency. He noticed an odd dent on the ligature and puzzled over the condition of one of the corks.

He scanned the porch for his tool belt, finally spotting it rolled up under one of the several metal chairs with a trombone hopelessly disassembled over them. But he turned back and lowered himself on to one of the wooden chairs. No, he thought to himself, there is still a duty to be done, one or two days' worth, whatever it is. He reached down and dragged his toolbox between his legs and flipped the top back. He turned on the free-standing lamp over his chair and fingered through the box for the proper sized cork and put it between his lips while he worked off the old cork, then slipped in the new, working the action furiously, and then set the instrument on the chair beside him.

Cumiskey pressed himself against the car, flattening his barrel chest against its dusty door as the tractor-trailer lurched by, its gears straining, with a slow, deafening thunder.

"Stay there Laddy, stay there," he bellowed over the whining diesel climbing Main Street. He scraped his way to the end of the car and clutched Michael's hand in his calloused palm. The tight stitching of his white shirt was plated with dusty brown grime from his car. He cupped his free hand over the boy's eyes, guiding him between the parked cars, into the pebbled wake of grit and eyes that creased his face to deep folds.

"Where is it, Grandpa?" he asked, reaching up and pulling Cumiskey's hand from his eyes. "Are we there yet?" Cumiskey pulled him up the curb and released him to dart up the sidewalk and spin back to his grandfather.

"Down there, Laddy," he called to Michael as the boy skipped down the sidewalk. He looked back and stopped unexpectedly, causing a woman laden with two shopping bags to brush his shoulder. She slid her babushka back to its proper position and gave Cumiskey an angry look.

"Very sorry, Miss," he said, ignoring her comments and deferring to genuine embarrassment instead. He grabbed Michael's hand again and flipped his errant tie back over his shoulder. Cumiskey stepped down Main Street with the boy in tow for a few yards. "Right there, Laddy," he said, pointing to the sign above the door that said 'BURNS TAVERN' in badly chipped black paint.

He pulled the boy back from the door, braced him against his legs, and opened it slowly. A crimson shaft of sunset filtered through the sugar maples over the western hills of the Valley, glinting into the worn, dull eyes of the men who lined the bar. The stark shaft of light melted somnolently into a pink nimbus of cigarette smoke that spiraled above the bar. Hollow eyed men turned a weary stare to the door with annoyed curiosity.

Cumiskey stepped over the threshold clutching Michael by the scruff of his neck. "Come along now, son," he said, turning and stooping to Michael as the door closed with a loud thud and the bar darkened once again. "It'll be all right now."

Eyes stared as silent nods filtered among the faces perched on beaten wooden stools and scarred tables.

Michael turned and buried his face in Cumiskey's belly, rubbing his eyes. "I can't see, Grandpa," he said, frightened at the sudden darkness and the wizened stares.

"Patrick!" The voice came from the dimly lit room. "Patrick, what is it, Patrick?" came the urgent words pressed with concern. Cumiskey felt a hand rest on his chest, then his tie being pressed gently over his matted shirt and a firm grip on his arm. "What are you doing here? Should be at home now, Patrick," he said as his eyes measured the grief etched in Cumiskey's red, hammy face.

Cumiskey looked down, sliding his tie between his

fingers, then flattened it against his belly again. "Aye, No Neck," he said, laying his hand on the man's cheek and patting it gently. "Been with the women fer three days now, been enough weeping to last a lifetime I tell you. Man 'as got to weep on his own, you know? The cleansing cry, it's the one ya share with men," he said, stepping beyond No Neck into the sea of faces that formed out of the darkness like Japanese lanterns over a midnight pond. "I'd be lookin' fer Thomas. Ya seen 'im?" he asked, straining his eyes beyond the pool table that had been stilled.

No Neck ran his hand over Michael's head and looked up at Cumiskey again. "You got the boy with you, Patrick. Ain't no place for a boy."

"You seen 'im, have ya?" asked Cumiskey again, ignoring No Neck's admonishment.

No Neck turned, "There, Patrick," he said with a pointed finger, "in the back there, at the table there by the cigarette machine."

Cumiskey ladled a path through the tavern, kicking up soiled sawdust under his heels. His eyes moistened as hands reached out from the dimness, patting his broad shoulders and hardening their lips into pursed knots of murmured sorrow. Michael planted his feet in fierce resistance, tugging desperately at the old man's shirttail, digging firmly into the scuffed planking.

"It's okay, son," Cumiskey said, leaning into the boy's ear. "They're my friends from the shop. It's okay."

Michael placed his arm over Cumiskey's shoulder and

cupped his hand over the old man's ear. "Why did you call that man No Neck?" he asked, riveting his eyes into No Neck's back.

"That's his name," replied Cumiskey, bending lower. "His real name is George but everyone calls him No Neck because he got no neck. It seems that God just set his head on his shoulders and left it there." Cumiskey stood and grasped the boy's hand. "Come along now, Lad," he said, stepping beyond the bar and walking towards the tables in the back. "Thomas," he cried out loudly with a voice that broke, "I'll be lookin' fer ya, Thomas."

A table of young men released their cards and rose slowly with empty hands, looking like lost boys, their faces shadowed with the belched soot of the blast furnaces. Cumiskey felt himself weaken as he measured the apprehension in their faces.

Thomas stepped forward. "Mr. Cumiskey," he asked with lips that seemed frozen, "what, what is it?" He walked around the table and stood before Cumiskey, laying his hand over the old man's arm.

Cumiskey rotated his hand and grasped Thomas' arm firmly. "I would like ya to do something fer me, Thomas," he said, casting his eyes to the floor.

"Ya knew Kevin, didn't ya?" he asked, meeting Thomas' eyes and taking his hand up into his own and turning it to examine its pink and supple flesh. It measured too young to have been calloused by the searing metals that dripped with heated oils as they were spit from deafening grinders. Cumiskey stroked his palm gently, feeling the softness that would, over time, cook slowly beneath burning metals, baking nerves to thick, dull welts.

Thomas nodded his head affirmatively, darting a concerned look at Michael. He answered quietly. "Sure, sure I knew him."

"He was a grand lad, wasn't he?"

"That he was, Mr. Cumiskey. I remember the summer he worked the shop, when we painted all the machines together during the plant shut down."

"Ya know we buried 'im today," Cumiskey said, hesitating to lift his eyes back to Thomas' face. He ran his shirtsleeve across his nose. "Well, ya know they had no pipes there for 'im. So I was wonderin' if ya would sing it fer me."

Thomas scanned the men gathered at the end of the bar for No Neck. The muted sound of traffic filled the tavern. He looked for support, only to be met with vacant, anxious faces of uncertainty. Then he looked at Michael firmly clutching the old man's hand.

"Ya went to school with 'im, right...? Ran track with 'im, didn't ya?" asked Cumiskey, leaning into young Thomas.

"Yes," he whispered. He nodded affirmatively to reassure the old man. "I was on the relay team with him when we won the states. He was only a sophomore. He was always afraid he was going to drop the baton." Thomas studied Cumiskey for a moment. The immediacy returned. The furrows between the old man's eyes seemed deeper than ever. The laugh that rolled through the shop floor was silenced. His powerful presence was diminished to desperate supplication.

"I heerd ya sing it here before. I thought maybe ya wouldn't mind today," Cumiskey persisted, squeezing Thomas' hand gently.

Thomas shook his head with a pained grimace. His words followed slowly. "Oh, I don't know, Mr. Cumiskey. It's not the same..."

"No, Laddy," Cumiskey interjected with a roar, "nothing's the same." He clutched Thomas' shoulder and let go of Michael's hand, dropping his head to his chest and raising his free hand over his eyes.

Thomas placed his arms under Cumiskey's shoulder. The old man's body trembled. He thought of the summer he worked the shop with Kevin, his work shirt, never tucked in, was soaked with sweat and hung loose from his lean, skeletal frame and the throttle of sorrel hair that hung over his collar.

"I need help," Thomas called out as Cumiskey collapsed into his arms.

A crowd of arms reached out and guided the old man to a chair that was hurriedly set in the space beside the pool table. Cumiskey's deep moans filled the tavern. No Neck turned away immediately, clutched Michael's hand, and pulled the boy to the front of the tavern. He fished out a fistful of change, all the contents of one pocket, and filled the boy's palm with it. "Son," he commanded, "why don't you run up to see Franny for a while....go have some ice cream. Your grand-daddy will be all right now, son. You go."

8

The door of Burn's blew open as Michael bolted up the sidewalk. The tail of his white shirt flapped behind him as he paced himself with oversized strides against the cars and trucks that made their way slowly in an endless queue. Soon he became distracted, moving in bursts from one parking meter to the next, flipping the red violation flags down and dodging the last strings of shoppers after they popped back up. He ran his small fingers over the old buildings, the coarseness of their brick and stone facades suspended for smooth, slick sailing seconds as he passed the clean windows of the bakery and shoe store and flower shop.

A knot of people formed at the corner of Elizabeth and Main. Michael shouldered his way to the front, rocking and scuffing the edge of his new shoes along the curved curb stone. The last, shallow breath of daylight embraced his face as the sun dropped its fireball beyond the Valley. A cop stood in the intersection, measuring the traffic with a trained eye and testing the patience of the last of the pedestrian traffic while people collected under the pharmacy's awning for the bus north to Waterbury.

Michael scanned the buildings across the street. To his left, as far as he could see, without a break, were brick and brownstone buildings, stately and handsome in aged Italianate, with scrolled cornices along rooflines that dropped in the distance as the grade of Main Street leveled to the meadows and the junction of the rivers. To his right, the Howard and Barber building expanded along the broad curve of Main Street where it met Olivia and the bridge over the Housatonic into Shelton. The street, filled with cars and trucks and busses and shoppers, entertained residents seated in their apartments, mostly elderly and gray in T shirts and thread-thin housecoats. Everywhere, lacey curtains billowed gracefully out the windows and floated gently over the flower boxes filled with impatiens and geraniums and pansies coaxed to fullness by warm, tending hands. At street level, the merchant's windows slowed the eye enough to dream lazily and be carried off beyond the scalloped lintels to the scrolled facia perfected so many decades ago with plumb bobs that hung true beneath a mason's steady hand. Proudly they stood, these broad shouldered russet titans, flanking Main Street like fearless sentries with their ingots of red clay rising mightily against the continuum of hills and mountains that insulated this place, this Valley, from the greater but lesser world.

The shrill burst of the policeman's whistle startled Michael as he hesitated at the corner and the crowd departed hastily. He stepped off the curb, fixing his eyes on the red neon lettering that formed an arch in the plate glass window that said 'Vonetes Palace of Sweets'.

He swung back the old wooden screen door, slamming it against the alcove wall and skipped to the break in the counter, between the register and the small grill.

"Hey, Michael my boy, what can I get for you?" asked Teddy, straightening from the deep sink and wiping his arms with a dish towel.

Michael walked his fingers along the black counter,

stopping before the Coke dispenser. "Can I buy a strawberry sundae with this much money?" he asked, holding out his hand to display the damp coins that glistened over his small, meaty palm.

Teddy responded without looking, turning to the mirrored wall and putting an extra roll into the long sleeves of his white shirt. His apron was folded down, covering the dress pants he wore, planked with brown wing tipped shoes that he kept to a glossy buff. "Michael," he said, turning and facing the boy with a heavy, fluted glass dish in one hand and an ice cream scoop that he used as a pointer in the other, "you can have anything you want with all that money, even a strawberry sundae."

Michael turned to the candy case opposite the counter and inventoried the nonpareils, jellies, chocolate covered caramels, crackers, toffees and nuts with his index finger.

Frances came up from the basement and locked the door for the clean-up. She placed a tray of dirty dishes on the counter near the deep sink, then looked at Teddy quizzically as he shrugged his shoulders and nodded his head unknowingly. She walked around the counter to Michael and dropped to a knee beside him. "Michael, honey," she asked, putting her arm around him, "are you alone? Who's with you?"

The boy slid closer to her and opened his hand full of change. "My grandpa is at the tavern and someone named No Neck gave me this money to buy ice cream."

"Oh," Frances exclaimed with a smile, "I see you have lots of money, don't you? And where's your mother?"

"She's at grandma's house with lots of people I hardly know." Michael spun out and faced the candy counter again, splaying his palm over the glass casing. "Uncle Kevin got buried today."

"Oh, I know, honey," Frances said gently as she rose and brushed his hair from his forehead. "I know you're going to miss him."

Frances turned to Teddy and watched him sprinkle chocolate shots over the mound of whipped cream that covered ice cream and strawberries. "I'm sure Uncle Kevin is in heaven watching you honey. Now," she said, turning him to the counter, "here's that nice strawberry sundae you ordered."

Michael lifted himself on the stool as Frances held his waist, securing him for the spin that was certain to follow. "Oh, Michael," she exclaimed, bending over him with her hands clasped between her legs, "does that look good?"

Teddy came around the counter and untied his apron. "All right, Fran, I'm going. You'll be all right," he said, unrolling his sleeves and buttoning the cuffs.

"Yeah, I'm okay. You finished the dishes, right?" she asked, glancing over the counter with a critical eye.

"Yeah, they're done," he replied laconically, pressing his palms over his thin hair, "just a few in the bottom of the sink." He stepped to Michael and tousled the boy's hair. "And Michael's dish." Teddy stood in the center of the Palace, looking at himself in the mirror and running his thumbs along his belt line to tidy his shirt. "Good night now, Michael," he said, setting his straw fedora on his head and patting the boy's shoulder.

The boy spun from his sundae that was now emptied of strawberries. "Where you going, Teddy?"

Teddy turned back and stepped to the boy's side. "Well, you see, Michael," he explained, "tonight is my card playing night. I get to sneak out a little early." Teddy turned to Frances who was dialing the phone and turned back to Michael, "Who's here with you, anyway? Who's he with?" he asked, turning his palm up with uncertainty.

"No one," she responded. "Wait. His grandfather's down at Burns'. I'm calling Virginia to find out what's going on. Hate to call on a day like this. Maybe you can drop him off."

Frances turned to the street and engaged in a muffled conversation. Car lights winked into the window and jumped off the mirrored walls. She returned the phone to the cabinet and turned to Teddy. "Virginia said the old rounder left with the boy without telling anyone, said they were frantic looking for him until they realized they were both missing." Frances shook her head and closed her eyes, "Said it's just been an awful day."

Teddy shut the neon window lights, signaling that the Palace of Sweets was closed. Frances cleared the last glasses from the counter as Michael spun successive stools at dizzying speeds, hoping to get the last one spinning before the first one stopped. The clean dishes rocked gently to the bottom of the deep sink for the final rinse. Frances collected them and placed them along the drip-counter, then dried them and placed them on the shelf.

Teddy walked behind the candy case and reached up to turn the radio off, silencing the Palace except for the last click of dishes being placed on the marble shelf along the mirrored wall.

"Oh," said Frances, balling her apron and placing it into a shopping bag full of linens, "I hired that new girl today."

Teddy guided Michael to the door and unlocked it, holding it open as Michael slipped out. "What new girl? Do I know her?"

Frances glided past him with her pocketbook over her shoulder. "I'm going to do these aprons too. Need to have Jerry leave more. He doesn't leave enough for the week."

Teddy locked the door and stood in the alcove with Michael. "So do I know her?" he asked, tapping his keys in his fingers and tilting his fedora high on his head.

Frances stood on the sidewalk and rifled through her pocketbook. "Wait, wait. Let me get my keys so mom doesn't have to get up out of her chair." She hesitated and turned away from them. "Yeah, yeah, you remember. The one that said she'll be moving with her mother down the street, oh, where is it?" she asked, trying to recollect. "Oh yes, into Manny's building."

"Okay, okay, I remember. She's the one who said she wanted to join the church choir. Mother's from Puerto Rico, no father."

"Yeah, he died. She won't start until next month. Fridays after school and Sundays," she said, stepping away from them. "Good night, Michael," she called out with a smile. "Teddy will take you to Grandma's."

"Bye," said Michael, extending his hand to Teddy. "I forgot to pay."

Teddy opened the car door for the boy. "Oh, don't worry about it. You keep it for next time." He closed the door of his mink brown Riviera and waited for the traffic to pass.

Byron sat there a moment, setting his palms over his knees and leaning forward in anticipation. He got up and changed the record, holding its sides with the lightest touch.

He walked back to the sun porch and straightened the throws that line the two day-beds along the outside wall. Near the back door he stopped to survey the instruments that littered the chairs, then lifted her picture from the mantle and found himself back in one of the hard, wooden chairs. He lifted the repaired clarinet and examined it again, touching every moving part and finally set it aside for good, its usefulness lost to him now.

But still, there are a few more days, he thinks, as he counts on his fingers, two, maybe three. It's too hard to figure. Is it from the death or from the burial? And Saturday, what do you do with Saturday, being the Sabbath and all? She would know but she's gone. Maybe he'll call the Rabbi in the morning. It hardly matters. He thinks to call him now but argues successfully against it. Tomorrow is soon enough. Why empty tomorrow of that small task now when now is present and present is quickly past? It fills his life, this waiting. So he clasps his hands over her photo and rests them on his lap. No matter. But how will he ever remember the yarhzreit? He's not good at remembering dates and things like that. She was. But he won't forget, he tells himself. Still, he'd like some certainty that he won't. He lifted himself and walked to the kitchen and took the calendar from the wall and laid it on the table. He reached over to the counter and picked up a pen and flipped the calendar to December and wrote in bold letters across the last week "yahzreit-write it in next calendar."

He returned to his chair and turned on the floor lamp standing beside him. He noticed the age spots over his knuckles and set her photo on the chair beside him. Still, he waits, and the silence of the evening arrives as planned. He crossed his leg and let his finger drop into the cuff of his pants, feeling some errant dust of unknown provenance pinched tightly along the crease. Curious, despite the discomfort, he pulled his ankle closer, inverted the cuff, then picked at the pressed crevice of dust and matter, rolled it into several small balls and set them on the chair beside him. Then he picked up the other leg and repeated the exercise, this time walking into the kitchen and dropping the tiny balls into the garbage. He returned to the chair. The night stared back at him with a biding silence. It will pass, he tells himself. But for now, this shiva calls for him to sit, with virtuous patience.

Frances walked down the curved slope of Main Street, stopping to admire the clothing that filled the Howard and

Barber window. Her eyes darted from mannequin to mannequin, finally to the clothes arranged over a half dozen trunks, as if they were an unfolding treasure. In the dark glass her eyes stopped and stared at the face of the women she knew well. She put her bag of soiled aprons and dish towels down and touched her palm to her cheek, lifting her flesh to its younger ride along the crest of what she thought, at one time, would have been endless youth. Forty-four, she thought, lifting the bag and turning from the window. Thirty-two years of knotting an apron and reaching elbow length into the deep sink, lifting hot, clean dishes to the rinse drain. Since the age of twelve when, one warm spring afternoon in 1935, Mr. Vonete, overwhelmed with customers, asked her to run home and put on a dress. And she returned and tied on a starched white apron for the first time and pressed it against her dress and felt its protective weight and dignified firmness and began this life of ice cream and chocolate and marzipan and jellies and hot chocolates and coffee dripping into countless pots. She reflected on the same walk along Main Street with the building facades beginning to wear like the blanched flesh of the bold woman who stared back at her from the dark window.

She stood at the corner of Main and Olivia and heard the distant whistle of the 9:05 freight as it threaded over the Naugatuck River to the triple trestle that spanned its joinder with the Housatonic River towards the eastern length of the republic. Along the fecund riverbanks, teeming with lantana and salvia, the train clattered and

17

rocked with impervious purpose. She looked at the lead diesel, with its beam straight and true, illuminating the narrowest band before it, so certain of its direction to the wide expanse of America, to cities named Syracuse and Saginaw and Centerville. Over her shoulder, along the trestle with its endless stream of railcars following in a dark, rhythmic staccato, she watched and wondered what distant places filled the steel bellies with the mother lode that rocked on the iron cradles and sent it here, through this simple and protected Valley, and to the world beyond.

Turning back towards the diesels, now well beyond her view, she watched their cotton billows vanish into the wooded blackness of the damp and forested hills of the Valley. Still, from the factory stacks marshaled along the twin-rivers, thick, regal columns of white and gray smoke rose, like repentant souls, into the dark glands of the evening.

Splayed before her, on infinite lengths of rail and roads and rivers, the seductive call of the Silk Road once beckoned her too, far and long from the confected days of her work. Yet she knew, even as a child, when she tied her apron on for the first time, even now, as she heeled the road beneath her, tired and aging, that beyond the bend of the rail, in the farthest reach of a dreamer's aspiration, there was nothing comparable to the bright illumination of the Palace of Sweets.

"Is this it from the grill for table nine?" Frances asked between glances out the window. She prodded the cheeseburgers with the spatula and turned back to Linda. "Is this it for that table? It's been wild tonight."

It's the center of October. September's amble from the languid pulse of August has come to an abrupt end. A round hunter's moon fanned heavy clouds in their run against the cold night with tethers of mango. The evening, born younger each day, twilled the heated breath of the factory stacks into white swills of cotton candy, pulling it in thin veils against the dappled hills of the Valley. The crest of Main Street teemed with Friday night shoppers in wool jackets and heavy skirts. At the corner, in front of the druggist with boxed candies seated on pedestals in the windows, silver coins drop noisily, like pinballs, through the glass fare boxes of lumbering busses.

Down the grade, before the meadows that slope to the rivers, the neon lights of the bars hid the thick hands of factory men in their dim spaces. Bits of leather and rubber flecked the raw oak planks as the cobbler ripped worn soles and heels from old shoes and carefully glued and tacked sharply edged replacements, brushing them to a high gloss under the whirl of belt driven brushes. Outside, the smell of fresh leather and glue rose quickly in the leavened air of River Pizza.

The engineer from corporate headquarters stopped his brisk walk through the BF Goodrich Sponge Rubber plant and halted the plant engineer, Theo Zarkas, and Flip, the maintenance foreman that accompanied him. He pointed towards the canal. "Listen up," he said over the noise of the rubber mixing machines churning in the background, "the plan is the canal water is going to be assisted by a large hydraulic pump and is guaranteed to deliver enough water to maintain water pressure for the entire plant during any interruption of public water usage. It will kick on immediately if there is a drop in pressure."

"So," the plant engineer asked, "I'm a pipefitter by trade. How does the system know if there's a drop in pressure, some kind of sensor or something? We got four hundred thousand square feet of space here. Are you going to cover all that with the back up?"

"Yes," the engineer explained, turning to the main water valve, "it's designed so the water flow is an auxiliary system. The sensor is not needed. The existing water pressure keeps the canal water out. If the existing pressure drops, the sensor reads it, the valve opens, and canal water flows into the twelve inch pipes that we plan on installing to tie into the existing main. Even with a power failure the sensor will read the system and will feed the mixers no matter what. These new Bambury machines require constant irrigation to keep them from overheating so we need the constant water flow. And, yes, we hope to tie it into all the buildings to cover all the space."

Flip stepped forward and pointed to the far wall of plant four. "So the plan is to lay the twelve inch pipe from the canal tie-in to the existing piping coming through that wall? You're not the first engineer to come up with this, you know. A few years ago they talked about doing the same thing, then BF shelved it. So when do you expect to start this? Are they actually going to do it this time?"

The engineer from corporate flipped pages back on his clipboard and read through his notes. He looked up at Flip and Zarkas. "It says here they want your drafts in a month so they can figure the cost. BF is figuring you can do the project in-house to save money. That's why they have me here tonight. I have to be at the Farrell plant next week to give them specs on the new machinery. That's why I asked you two to meet me tonight instead of tomorrow."

Zarkas turned to walk back to his office, "The twelve inch piping is being loaded today on flatbeds from Hurley Brothers Concrete. Should be arriving sometime Monday. Corporate is spending a lot of money on these mixers so it's got to go smoothly."

"Okay, Cole, see you next week," Flip called back as the group broke up and went their separate ways throughout the sprawling series of buildings.

Teddy released a scoop of vanilla into a parfait dish and looked down the counter. A stack of dirty dishes sat by the deep sink as Frances slid dollars into the register drawer at the other end. "Bye-bye, Davy, you were a good boy now." She watched and waved as they passed the window, then looked down the line at the silver freezer lids flipping open with fire and fury. "Did anyone get the order from that last bunch that came in?" She eyed the parlor with concern. "I really wish those kids would settle down instead of ganging up and moving the chairs all over the place." She rotated two milk shakes as she eyed the Palace in the mirrored wall. It finally seemed to be lightening up. Three tables were emptied and cleared. Teddy stacked more dishes and cups and glasses by the deep sink while more idled on an empty table, then stepped to the parlor register and let the cash drawer spring into his stomach. "Good night now and thank you," he said with a smile.

It happened each year, it seemed, that the chill of the October night sparked rapid movement along Main Street. Late shoppers with children in tow stopped in for the promised ice cream cone or hot chocolate while the high school set, like an army in garrison, occupied the parlor in the Friday night ritual before the Saturday morning game. They pulled the spindly legs of the wooden chairs over the tiled floor with an unnerving screech to sit in clusters while children spun any unoccupied stool and pleaded for shots on their cones to relenting mothers.

Teddy palmed cherry syrup over the ice cream filled Coke glass and placed it under a fountain that rose over the center of the counter. He stirred the stream of seltzer water vigorously with a long spoon, encouraging a heady froth that spilled over the top. "Linda got it," he said shallowly to Frances. "She got the kid's order. This soda is part of it."

Linda reached down into the ice cream tub and dug out the last scoop as a welt of hair worked its way from her bowed ribbon and fell forward over her shoulder. She slid two banana splits on the tray and slapped the freezer cover down with a solid thud, then wiped her hands on her apron that appeared to be finger painted with chocolate sauce and ice cream and searched the back counter for spoons. "Are we out of spoons?" she asked Teddy with raised eyebrows.

Teddy bent to the lowest shelf. "Here you go, Linda," he said with a quick smile, placing several spoons awkwardly over the edge of the full tray. "That's where we keep the reserves."

She lifted the tray and stepped towards the parlor. A spoon dropped to the floor and bounced noisily across the tile. She glanced down and continued to the back tables.

"Excuse me," she said as she reached between them and placed the tray on the table. She lifted the banana split and studied the dozen faces around the table before asking, "Who had the banana split?"

A tall girl with long, flaxen hair leaned forward and flicked her hair over the outside of the chair. "We all did," she said, laughing along with the others. "Yeah," called out another, then a third. "We're all sharing." A roll of laughter rippled from the table until the blond spoke out again. "We need lots more spoons too," she said, with an accompanying laugh.

Linda cleared the tray and turned from the table. "And water. Can we have more water?" asked another as Linda tripped over a loose pocketbook strap. She leaned against an empty table to prevent her fall, then stopped to pick up the spoon she had dropped.

"What do you need?" asked Teddy as he dug dishes from the deep sink.

"Spoons," Linda replied as she bent over and returned

with a fistful, "and water, lots of water."

"I'll get the water," Teddy said, "how many?"

"I don't know," she said, looking back over the parlor, "maybe ten."

Teddy dried his hands and shook his head, "Well, I'll bring five.They'll only drink three anyway. You watch."

Linda smiled and brought the spoons to the table. She cleaned the empty tables and straightened the chairs, then walked to the front of the Palace where Frances was cleaning the grill. "What's next, Fran?" she asked, looking out the window at the car lights staring in from Elizabeth Street.

"Yeah," Frances responded, looking up and around before looking to the raised, display window loaded with pumpkins and cattails and a scarecrow seated with a trick or treat bag full of chocolates, "could you get that lemon ice sign out of the window? I've been meaning to get it but I keep forgetting."

"Sure," Linda said, slipping between the opening of the counter and the grill. She folded her arms tightly to ward off the chill and stepped outside to locate the sign in the cluttered window. She winced and smiled as she read it and then repeated it out loud, 'Lemon Ice Sold Here-All Flavors.' She came in and slid the window, allowing her to climb in. "Kind of tight in here," she called back to Frances as she bent over between the pumpkins and straw and lifted the lemon ice sign out. She stepped out and slid the window closed, smiling as she handed Frances the sign.

"Is something funny?" Frances asked, returning the

24

smile.

"No," Linda answered, making her way in back of the grill, "it's just that the sign says lemon ice sold here, all flavors."

Frances started to the back of the candy counter. "That's right," she said, spinning her free hand in a circular motion, "we sell all flavors, you know, chocolate, raspberry, pina colada, everything. They know what we mean. I forgot to take it out when we decorated the window, should've been out by the end of September." She placed the sign by the candy counter and returned to wipe down the grill.

The street traffic thinned as the evening grew late and the merchants were closing. Suddenly, a stick figure under a long coat walked by quickly with his hand flattened against the window.

"Frances," he called out without breaking stride, exposing a glimpse of a smile.

Frances waved back to the figure now gone. "Okay, Charlie," she said with an amused smile.

"Who's that?" Linda asked.

Frances bent to the grill again. "Him," she said, "that's Charlie. He walks around a lot. Sometimes he stops in for coffee in the morning. Mostly he walks around, rain, snow, cold, it don't matter. Everyone calls him the Greek because his family is from Greece."

"He doesn't drive?" asked Linda.

Frances shook her head. "Charlie, no, he doesn't drive, because of the injury or something, he can't drive. He knows everyone. Always waves like that when he passes by."

Linda walked to the rinse sink and turned on the hot water. She rolled her sleeves above her elbows and reached to the bottom of the clean water, its fresh heat sending a quick shiver down her spine. She turned to Frances with a perplexed look. "So, where does he walk to?"

"Nowhere in particular, he just walks, sometimes over the bridge to Ansonia, crosses the river over the other bridge and heads back, sometimes to Shelton." Frances moved to the wash sink beside Linda and scrubbed the dishes in the hot soapy water and then dropped them into the rinse sink.

"So that's it?" asked Linda, turning to stack the cleaned dishes against the mirrored wall. "He doesn't stop or talk or anything?"

"Oh, yeah," responded Frances, shaking her head emphatically, "he talks. Likes to talk, just not when he's going somewhere, that's all. He has lots of friends, knows everyone. He'll stop in sometimes and stay and talk, if something's happening. But mostly we just hand him his coffee and he keeps walking.

The sound of chairs screeching along the floor broke the conversation. Jackets and sweaters swirled like matador capes in the mirrored walls, soon followed by a noisy trail of pocketbooks and bags clustered at the register.

Teddy stood behind it, his half frame glasses sitting at the edge of his nose. He worked the register with two hands as the dollar and cents flags rose in the window and the cash drawer popped into his belly.

Teddy followed them as they filed out. The sidewalk locked into a scrum of animated conversation that gunned with loud laughter before they piled into cars and drove off in a caravan of horns and megaphones and colorful shakers.

Teddy reached into the window, between the pumpkins and gourds and cattails that fanned like monochrome peacocks, and turned off the red neon lettering. Then he placed his glasses into the pocket of his white shirt. "Well, girls," he said, tossing his soiled apron into the box behind the candy case, "it's about time for my card game."

"Teddy," scolded Frances, bending into the wash sink again as Linda brought the last of the dishes to her side, "how about the chairs? Just help Linda stack them before you go."

Linda walked to the small bathroom at the rear of the parlor and filled a metal bucket with hot, steaming water, then rolled it out, steering it awkwardly with a heavy spaghetti mop. "Where's the Star Water, Fran?" she asked, searching in the bathroom closet.

"Oh, I bought a new bottle. It's under the register," replied Frances as she gathered the receipts of all the registers, bundled them separately and stuffed them into a worn, cloth bank envelope.

The high finance of the Palace of Sweets required three cash registers. The counter register, beside the grill, tallied the takeout and counter orders. The parlor register, seated at the other end of the counter, kept track of everything eaten at the tables, while the candy register was used to tally the freshly made chocolates and jellies weighed in an old, dented brass bowl that sat on a weighted axle with a wheel that spun the confections into balance. Easter was the biggest season for the candy register, often causing the routine to retreat to abandon and use whatever register was available to handle the volume of currency racing in.

Both hands were needed to operate the registers, one for dollars and one for cents, depressed simultaneously, to raise the price flags in the window. The arithmetic of adding the price of the items was done on small white scratch pads that sat beside each register with long columns of numbers scribbled and then crossed out to clear the way for the next order.

"Okay, Fran," Teddy said, looking into the mirror and buttoning his tweed sport jacket with one hand and fixing his fedora with the other, "I'm on my way."

Frances walked to the back of the candy counter and shut the radio that was near an autographed picture of Sinatra. "What about mom?" she asked, bending down and sliding the door of the candy counter to the side to count the napkin packages. "I'll be downstairs awhile with the inventory." She turned to the shelf behind the candy counter and counted the available linens. "We're running out of everything. Hot chocolate, I think we're just about out of hot chocolate."

Teddy shook his head in disbelief. "Okay, I'll stop in and check on her," he responded, holding the door open with his foot. "Night, Linda," he called back with a smile, "it'd be nice to get to the card game before it breaks up."

"Night, Teddy," she responded, lifting her head from beneath the counter. "Hey, Fran, what register?"

"What register? What do you mean, what register?" asked Frances, lifting the trap door behind the candy counter that led to the basement.

Linda laughed. "The Star Water, you said you bought a new bottle."

"Oh, the bleach," cried Frances. "Here, it's here," she said, lifting the bottle from the floor. "Oh, just a little crazier than usual tonight, Linda, I meant under this register." She placed the bottle on the tile floor and started down the stairs to the basement. "Close the door after me so you don't fall down while you're mopping. I'm always afraid someone's going to fall down here."

The piercing odor of the bleach filled Vonetes as Linda rolled the heavy pail brimming with hot water to the far corner of the Palace, spilling steaming puddles along the way. She dropped the heavy spaghetti mop into the water, wrung it into the pail and dropped it to the tiles, bearing down as the steam rose and fogged the mirrors, her own refection whitened to a distant ghost. She tried to secure her hair with her ribbon but gave up, letting it fall loosely from her unraveling topknot.

After several strokes she lifted the mop into the pail and rinsed it, then backed along the wall, across the five ton air conditioning unit, carefully guiding the unwieldy mop between the fine legs of the tables pyramided with yellow and pink and green pastel chairs.

Softly at first, with the mop pressed to the floor, she raised her voice with the art songs her father taught her. As her mind carried her back to the small house in the mountains, the humming gave way to a hesitant, soft voice rising above the drone of the street traffic. She lifted the mop into the pail and drained it again, letting her eyes rise to the pressed tin ceiling, and drop to the white mosaic tiles, leaning into the heavy mop in full voice. She never heard him enter, cutting a note to a short scream when she caught his image in the whitened mirror and turned, startled.

He held his hand out to ease her. "I'm so sorry," he explained nervously with a face animated with concern, "I didn't mean to scare you but you were singing so loud that I didn't know what to do. I left my jacket here. I wasn't sure if I should let you know I was here or just try to get out before you saw me."

Her face reddened with embarrassment as she recognized him as one of the group that had just left. She cradled the mop against her shoulder and pulled her hair back nervously. "Oh, that's okay," she said softly, "I didn't hear you and it scared me when I saw you in the mirror, that's all. I thought Teddy locked the door," she said.

He turned to the back of the candy counter, grabbed a chocolate covered caramel, and bounced it playfully in his palm. "I left my jacket here so I had my friends drive by to see if you were still open," he said, tugging the jacket over his shoulders. "Where's Frances?" he asked, turning to the empty grill.

She looked at him closely. His hair was dark and neatly trimmed. His eyes were soft and expressive. And his lips, when he spoke, were full and ample, causing her to hold her glance a moment too long.

"Oh, Frances," she said quietly, "she's downstairs taking inventory, counting hot chocolates or something."

The reflection of the Palace lights running off of her chestnut hair caught his eye as she spoke. Her eyes were cobalt dollops on her white porcelain skin and framed by delicate, dark crescents of eyebrows. He found himself studying her face as she spoke with such unusual clarity.

He popped the caramel into his mouth. "My name is Blake. What's yours?"

She dropped the apron, placing both hands on the mop, as if for support, and glanced at the ribbon dangling from the mop. "Linda," she said softly, then repeated it to be certain he heard her above the sound of the traffic, "my name is Linda."

"Are you at Valley High?" he asked through a full and wet mouth. The car horn sounded and voices could be heard calling him to hurry.

"Uh huh," she responded, "I'm a senior. Are you?"

"Uh huh," he replied, as the car horn sounded, "I'm a senior too." He swallowed the caramel and smiled. "Tell Frances I owe her for the candy," he said as he walked to the door. He stopped to zip his jacket and looked up at her. "You have a nice voice," he said, in a soft and sincere tone.

"Oh," Linda responded, grimacing, "it was loud, wasn't it?"

Blake held the door with his foot as he finished buttoning the jacket. "No," he said glancing at her, "it wasn't loud. It was nice." A cold wind whipped into the alcove, swirling vagrant leaves to a spiral and depositing them into the Palace. The car horn sounded impatiently. He started out, then looked at her and stepped back in, picking up the leaves. Her eyebrows raised in curious anticipation. "Hey," he said in an excited, stuttering rush of words over the calls of his friends in the car, "hey, Linda, that, that means beautiful in Spanish."

She gripped the mop with both hands and returned his smile, "Yes," she said softly as he ran out and into the waiting car. She watched as the lights of the car vanished past the window and out of her view, then looked into the mirror and watched it trail off down Main Street. She stood in the center of the Palace and realized that she hadn't moved since the moment he walked in. She glanced at herself in the mirror, wondering what she looked like and noticed how red her hands looked, even in the old faded mirrors. She flicked her eyebrows in dismay, rinsed the mop again, and continued mopping the floor singing in full voice.

"All set, Linda?" asked Frances as she rose from the basement, holding her pad in one hand and closing the door with the other.

"Just about, Fran," she responded as Frances stepped from behind the candy counter and admired the bright, clean floor.

"Oh, now I'm cold," Frances commented, placing the inventory beside the take out register. "Was someone here? Did I hear you talking to someone?"

"Oh, yes," explained Linda, wide eyed with excitement. "Could you also hear me singing?"

Frances smiled and nodded. "Just a little," Frances said, walking to the back of the candy counter and getting both of their coats, "nothing wrong with that."

"Well," Linda explained as she wheeled the pail into the bathroom and emptied it, "I was doing the floor with my back to the door and I was singing, I guess too loud, because all of a sudden I see the reflection of someone in the mirror and I screamed." Linda took her coat from Frances and swung it on. "So anyway, his name is Blake. He left his jacket here and came back to get it, practically scared me to death. He took a caramel," she said with a smile. "Said to tell you he owed you for it."

"Oh, Blake, he's a nice boy. He likes the caramels." Frances laughed as she put on her coat and they walked to the door and turned out the lights. "I know his family. His aunt comes in quite often, coffee and a muffin or something in the morning. His folks are real quiet." They stood together in the alcove as Frances locked the door. "Okay, Linda, see you tomorrow."

"Night, Fran," Linda called back, turning into the cold wind with her books held firmly to her chest.

She walked down Main Street against a wind that funneled leaves and raised them against the storefront windows until they fluttered to a rest in the alcoves. Her eyes drifted above the store windows to the black sky. She thought of the song she sang before she was startled. She recalled his words and the sound of his voice and the way he held out his hand to ease her fear. She smiled as she thought of how his eyebrows rose excitedly when he told her that linda meant beautiful in Spanish.

The rich aroma from River Pizza thickened the air when she turned and stepped up to the wooden door of her apartment building. The loose doorknob rattled as she started up the steep incline of wooden steps that creaked loudly. She smiled when she noticed her apron hanging below her coat. "Hi, mom, I'm home," she called out, as she swung open the apartment door and pivoted into her bedroom.

"Hello, Sweetheart," the heavily Spanish accented response came from the kitchen, "how's my baby?"

"I'm good," said Linda.

"Oh," her mother remarked with a laugh, "you still have your apron on! I have some dinner for you. Are you hungry?"

"Starving," responded Linda with a laugh. "We were so busy, I never had time to eat anything. Then Frances had to go to the basement and I did the floor. And when she came back up we left so the floor could dry without us tracking it up again. I just forgot to take my apron off."

They sat in the small kitchen as Linda ate and she told her mother about the evening, how busy it was, and bleaching the floor, and the jacket left behind, and her fright. She asked her mother how her day was. Her mother explained how busy the shop is and how there's overtime tomorrow since they ran low on pocketbook frames today but expect more in by the morning.

After dinner Linda went to her bedroom and let down what was left of her topknot. She shook her hair out and let it fall over her shoulders, then turned in the mirror and measured it against her bra strap, that being the length beyond which her mother would not allow. She showered and put on her pajamas and cupped her hands over her eyes as she looked out her bedroom window over the Housatonic. To her right she saw the triple trestle spanning the river with its long, diagonal splurge of steel. Turning to the left she strained to see eddies spinning off the wet lips of Hog's Island. Further still, at the edge of the moonlight, the Naugatuck rolled its lodestar to the river's joinder, giving urgency to the long flow into Long Island Sound and the great Atlantic.

Blake dashed from the car, slamming the door with a powerful thud. He raced around the house and bounded up the steps, throwing open the door and placing the gym bag over his back.

"You're late," his father growled, not bothering to look up from the newspaper.

Blake glanced at the wall clock and looked wide-eyed at his father. His mother stepped from the living room and stood in the threshold, positioning herself between them for what she was certain to follow.

"He isn't, not yet..."

"He's late," he yelled, casting a belligerent look to his wife. "You keep out of this. Come out to defend him," he muttered, "always come to defend him." She stepped towards her husband and glanced at the whiskey bottle on the floor beside him.

Confident of herself, she stepped to her husband and placed her hands over his shoulders, guiding him back into his chair. "He's not late, the wall clock's fast," she said, nodding for Blake to pass by.

"Good night," Blake said as he passed in back of his father. He felt the dull thud of his father's fist attempting to grab the gym bag as he stepped up the three stairs to his room.

"Good night, honey," his mother called back to him without looking, satisfied that the passing occurred without incident.

His father returned to the newspaper, then looked up at the wall clock and pointed to it. "He's late," he said with disdain, "don't matter what you say."

Linda wrapped her hair in a towel and walked into the living room. She bent over to pick up several pieces of lace. "Mom, you're not going to work the loom now, are you?"

"No," her mother replied without looking up, "I just want to get some of these bobbins set for tomorrow."

Linda sat on the floor beside her mother and wound some thread over the closest bobbins. "You know, I think this thread is thinner than what you usually use."

Her mother darted up and stretched over the loom to place a bobbin over its spindle. She looked at Linda with a furled brow. "I think you're right, it doesn't have the same feel as the thread from Moca. I'll make a doily from this and that should finish it. I don't like it either."

Linda finished wrapping the bobbin she held and placed it on the spindle, then walked to her mother who was now seated on the rug. She bent and kissed her, "Goodnight, mom."

"Oh, so early for a Friday," her mother responded.

Linda turned away and walked to her room, "Yeah, I'm just so tired."

"Goodnight, pleasant dreams," her mother called out after her while wrapping thread around the spindle.

Her bed was a small twin, narrow and slight of frame, with a space for books and knick-knacks along the headboard. She lay there, first on her back and then curled up, thinking of his face and all the words he said and the tone and inflection of his voice. The muffled sound of the traffic roused her and caused an alternating drift between the cadence of the street and her thoughts of Blake. Finally, with heavy eyes and long, deep breaths, she slipped off into an abiding slumber wondering if she would ever see him again.

Downtown before dawn, automobiles streamed from every direction, their tail lights reflecting in the dark store windows like bright red unspooled skeins of yarn. Main Street became a ribbon of crimson and ghost with exhaust from tailpipes expanding like genies from a magic lantern. Husky voiced men with hands clenched in their pockets held silver lunch pails tightly between their ribs and arms. Inside the factories toolmakers measured unforgiving tolerances and conversed in shouts over deafening lathes and drills.

Perched a block above the Palace of Sweets, clutches of men in tartan hats dragged on cigarettes that flared like fireflies. They gathered in ephemeral circles outside the cigar store and raised clouds of condensed breath with their animated conversations.

At the intersection of Main and Elizabeth, Teddy stacked a hand truck with boxes of candy and sugar and syrups from the trunk of his car while Frances started another fresh pot of coffee down its hissing, drizzling way. By late afternoon, in the board room of the Birmingham Savings Bank, Dennis Foley, the founder's grandson and President of the bank, continued the meeting of the bank directors.

"And, as officers and incorporators, we would have the responsibility to transition the bank from the mutual savings that Birmingham Savings has been since its inception to a bank owned by the shareholders. If we're going to get a nice parcel out of this redevelopment plan and construct a new bank building we should consider having a corporate structure that will maximize the bank's potential."

Phineas Foster, the largest depositor and owner of several Valley factories, shook his head in disgust. "I don't like it a bit. I've seen it happen countless times. We lose that community feel the bank has now. Dennis, you know, your grandfather and the other founders started this bank to encourage thrift and provide a safe place for folks to deposit and save money and have that money invested locally. Even though it appears nothing changes eventually a shareholder held bank is driven by the stock value and not by the needs of the community." He looked at Martin Small and Mark Grow and then nodded to the others at the table. "You young fellows, I know what you're thinking, I can smell your brains cooking now, figuring out how to get this damn fangled thing done so ten or fifteen years from now you can cash out. Me and Allen, Jay over there and Wilford, we built this bank up over decades to support the growth of this community. Derby was the center of commerce in the Valley for over a century. This bank was responsible for so many of the homes and factories that were built here and expanded here. Even discussing making it a shareholder bank disgusts me. The bank, the high school, the churches and the post office, why, those are the heart of any community. You start monkeying around with any of them and you risk the city losing its heart. You can forget me ever voting to allow this to happen. And like I said before, we got no business taking over the entire block on Main Street, to put up a fancy new building that is raised off the street, doesn't have an entrance on Main Street and half the block is used for a parking lot. Who the hell approved that anyway? It doesn't fit in at all. This bank will be publicly held over my dead body."

Wilford Tully, the aging owner of the pocketbook factory, buried his cigarette into an ashtray and shook his head. "We're already starting to lose the little mom and pop retailers downtown. They're either closing up or moving out. We got three banks downtown and this is the only mutual. The other two are commercial banks. They're not making home loans locally. They want big commercial loans. They're looking out for their stockholders. Like Phineas says, they don't give a hoot about the Valley."

Martin Small looked at Phinias and glanced at Wilford. "Look, we can't ignore the reality that all the mutual banks are going to make the transition at some point. No one is advocating doing that now. But if this bank is going to thrive and keep financing investments in homes and real estate and factories then it will need the added capital of a public offering. You can't deny that. It's just something to consider down the road. That's why I talked it over with Dennis and wanted it brought up here, just to get a sense of where we stand. We are going to invite Rudy Harper to the next meeting. He's on the state banking committee so he can give us some good insight into the process."

Phineas leaned over the table and rapped his palm against it several times. "Look, Rudy is in his first term in Hartford. He happened to get on the banking committee because Dennis called the chairman and asked that he be appointed. This is all by design, you moving this along and pretending this is just to give us information from the inside. He don't have anything we need to know. He's still wet behind the ears. Me and Wilford here, Allen, we won't be around much longer. Cripe, we're all pushing eighty. So when we're dead, you Young Turks can do whatever the heck you darn well please. But for now, don't even bring it up again."

Millie let out a yelp as a gust of wind whipped her umbrella and drove her from the alcove of Vonetes down Main Street. A disheveled figure in dark clothes and an unbuttoned coat appeared in the door and opened it slowly. His shoes were mat black as a puddle formed around their wide, rounded toes. Rain beaded off the brim of his pork-pie hat and dripped on the tile floor. His coat, wet and frayed at the cuffs, hung loosely from his shoulders.

"Adam, Adam, Adam," Frances sang out from behind the grill, "you're soaked."

He pulled the Evening Sentinel from the stack he carried in loose wrapped plastic that trailed him. "Yes, Frances," he said with a grin, audibly sucking air through his few remaining teeth, "Adam is soaked."

"You want a coffee?" Frances asked with her hand over the stack of paper cups.

"No, no coffee today, Frances," he responded, sucking more air through his teeth, "let's have a hot chocolate today." He ran his wet sleeve across his nose.

"All right, all right, a hot chocolate. Are you staying?"

Adam shuffled around and backed up to the radiator. "No, no, can't stay, can't stay, people already irritated at me." The sound of hot chocolate being mixed whirled through the Palace.

"You're late, Champ," Teddy said, taking the paper from Adam and looking at the floor, "and you're dripping."

Adam held out his free hand and chuckled, sucking in more air, "I'm not late," he responded, pointing to the wall clock, "I'm just not early. Not my fault either, Teddy. Press broke down. Not Adam's fault, no sir." Frances set the hot chocolate down on the counter and lidded it, then wiped off the cream that dripped down the sides. He wrapped his fingers, blackened with newsprint, around the hot paper cup and held it to his chest, "How much today, Frances?"

"Oh," she responded, turning away and bending to answer the phone, "just go, Champ. People are going to be mad that the papers are late and wet."

"They ain't so wet, just when I have to touch them. Only late because I spoiled them all to think early is on time."

The Champ. He slept in vacant downtown apartments that were increasingly available or, by choice, he slept in the connected basements of the buildings that lined Main Street, stocked with out-of-season clothes and naked mannequins. He would match up the incomplete mannequins with arms and legs or torsos he came across as he decided on a restful basement to spend his night. His clothes were selected from stock that didn't sell, items that survived two or three consecutive July Sidewalk Sale Days, a buyer's error that was his good fortune. His meals, mostly free, devolved from handouts for odd jobs he did or promised to do. He was the lightweight wrestling champ of the world in 1922, when, as he was happy to inform, wrestling was a real sport and there was honor in honor. His nose was flattened and crooked and his ears were cauliflowered from all the time spent scrunched down against the canvas. His paper route was his franchise, pedaled with feet that flared out in a clown's shuffle under round-toed shoes that tipped up like a pair of Klompens. He didn't own a car and never had a license. He had almost no teeth left and shaved only once a week or so. There was no schedule. Occasionally, someone would tell him to bathe and he would do so somewhere. He always smiled and sucked in air through the dark space between his gums and last teeth that rose like stalagmites. He was the Champion of the World and he pedaled the Evening Sentinel all over downtown every afternoon, six days a week, under the strain of great anticipation. Everyone waited for the Champ.

He wasn't late often, extraordinary events being the exception, like the day Kennedy was shot. Then the Evening Sentinel literally stopped its presses and dumped the whole run just so they could scoop the larger morning papers that came out of New Haven and Bridgeport and New York. The headlines were two inches high, with thick black lettering across the top of the broadsheet, 'Kennedy Killed in Dallas.' By the time the run was printed everyone knew but they read the article anyway. Adam delivered the Evening Sentinel that day around five-thirty, the latest ever. The Valley, as the nation, was stunned at the loss. Factory men gathered in the bars while the boys from Lakeview Terrace and Prospect Street walked down to Vonete's late that afternoon to measure a nation's grief over maple sundaes and hot chocolate.

Throughout the Valley, from Shelton and Derby and Ansonia and Seymour, right up through Naugatuck and Waterbury, as far as Torrington, people felt connected to John Kennedy because he drove up Main Street in each Valley town at one and two and three o'clock in the morning the Sunday before the election, November 6, 1960. They came out in hundreds, in each small hamlet, holding torches and railroad lanterns. They stood on the curbs and at intersections, factory workers and housewives, coats over their bedclothes, foregoing sleep to line the streets just to see him stand on the hood of his car for a moment and speak briefly in each little Valley town. It was pouring that night too.

Adam worked the lid off his hot chocolate and sucked in some warm whipped cream from the top.

"Thank you, Frances. Not my fault today. Late and wet," he said, reaching for the door, "Yeah, they're mad all right." He shuffled his wide shoes out the door and called back, "See ya, Teddy."

"Take it easy, Champ."

The gray day moved to darkness under low and pendulous clouds. On Main Street, the red neon light glowed brightly in the window of Vonetes as Frances wiped down the heavy sandwich knife with a dishtowel. "I think I see Linda coming," she called out to Teddy. He barely nodded in response as he settled into the first parlor table and opened the paper. Frances turned and sliced the sandwich, tucking in the tuna and melted cheese that squeezed out. Linda turned, backed into the heavy glass door, and spun into the Palace. "Hi, Fran," she said over a wide smile. Rain dripped to the floor from the hood of her maroon bench warmer.

"Oh, Linda," cried Frances with a twisted face, "no umbrella?" She tilted the soup pan that sat nearly empty on the grill.

"It's in my locker." She walked to the back of the candy case and flicked her hood down, then placed her books on a shelf where the linens were kept. "The girl I share it with locked it after I got my books. But I got a ride most of the way anyway, so it wasn't so bad."

Teddy looked up from the paper over his reading glasses. "What's doing, Linda?" he asked, picking apart the wet page and turning it as he got up. He held her coat as she slipped out of it. "Coat's wet." He spread it over the long radiator by the door, straightening it with his hands. "This will get it good and dry."

"How was school, Linda?" Frances asked, pointing to a box full of sandwiches and drinks. "This is Hubbell's order if they come in and I'm busy. How was school?"

"Great. The math teacher was out so I got to spend the free period in the music room. Then I went to see one of the French teachers for some pronunciation help." She took a clean apron from the shelf and stood before the faded mirror as she tied it.

"Oh, that's nice," Frances responded, walking along the counter to the sinks. "What do you do in the music room?"

Linda smiled, took clean dishtowels from the shelf, and walked to the wash sink. "Well, the two music teachers are in there. Sometimes I play the piano or we go over some of the chorus pieces. Today we talked about conservatories." She turned to her side to check her apron bow, bunched her hair into her left hand, and fastened it with a butterfly clip.

Frances prodded a hamburger on the grill, "Yeah? What's that?"

Linda started clearing the tables of dirty dishes. "What?" she asked, "a conservatory?"

"Yeah, what's that?"

"Oh, it's a school, like a college, but you only go there if you want to be a singer or a musician or an actor. It's like an art school," she explained, "for performers."

"Oh, and is that what you want to do?"

Linda carried a full dishpan to the sink. "Well," she said, rolling her eyes, "my mom doesn't have the money for that, Fran. Besides, I'd have to leave, go to New York or Boston, maybe Pennsylvania or Ohio. I really can't do that to my mom."

"Yeah," Frances said, shaking her head supportively, "she'd be alone. But you could sing at the schools around here, right? Don't they teach singing around here?"

Linda smiled and placed the dishes beside the wash sink, unbuttoned the cuffs of her white shirt, and rolled them above her elbows. "Well," she said with hesitation, "it's really not the same." She stopped her work and rested her hand on the counter and looked at Frances. "It's really hard to get into the really good conservatories. And the education you get at a conservatory is really focused on your art. I mean, my dad always wanted me to get an education as well as voice training."

Frances looked at her quizzically, "Don't you like singing in the church choir? The ladies, when they come in, when you're not here, they all say what a beautiful voice you have."

Linda started placing the dishes into the deep wash sink, guiding them gently to the bottom. She raised her eyebrows and smiled appreciatively at Frances. "Oh no, Fran, I love singing in the choir. Everyone has been great," she said with a laugh, "they all treat me like I'm their kid, you know, really watching out for me."

"Well, you're probably the youngest one, right, so, you know, it's only natural that they will watch out for you."

Linda nodded her head affirmatively and bent over the deep sink. "Yeah, that's what I mean, and I really love it. But, well, it gets kind of technical. I just have to wait, probably when I'm done with college, to take voice lessons."

The door opened and Frances turned. "Oh, Leon's here," she said, clapping her hands over her head, "it's all set. You said you'd be here in ten minutes. That was twenty minutes ago."

"Hasn't been busy all day, soon as we call in the order, they start coming in. You know the way it is."

Frances looked into the bags and shook her head, "Oh, it's all cold now," she lamented, "but that's the way it happens sometimes, I know."

Leon fished his coat pocket for money. He laid a shoehorn on the counter and continued to fish. "Look at that," he said, smiling at Linda and looking at Teddy, "my favorite shoehorn, been looking for it all day." He handed Frances a ten and glanced back down the counter. "Hi Linda, Teddy."

"Leon," they replied in unison.

"Okay," Frances said, working the two handed register and handing him his change, "all set. Hold it from the bottom," she admonished, "so the bags don't break."

Teddy laid the Sentinel near the Coke dispenser. "Nothing in this paper Linda," he said turning away and walking towards the window. "I don't know why I wait for it every day."

Linda looked up from the wash sink without responding while the water drained with a gurgle. She ran the hot water and squirted soap in before placing a stack of dirty dishes on the bottom, immersing her hands in the rising water up to her elbows. It ran a sensation down her spine and sent her thoughts to the warm Puerto Rican nights by her father's piano, the softness of his voice instructing her. She leaned deeper from the waist, lost in the euphoric sound of the Chants d'Auvergne on her lips, French folksongs he promised to teach her to extend her vocal range.

"Teddy, anyone die?" Frances asked, clearing the order pad for the next call.

"No," Teddy said, looking up Elizabeth Street at the traffic waiting for the officer to blast his whistle for a change of direction, "no one died. A few obituaries," he said, shrugging his shoulders and turning away, "but I didn't know them. No one we know died."

"Let me see it for a minute," Frances said, coming around to the front of the counter and gesturing to Teddy. "I just got to get the Penny order ready, couple of sandwiches. They're slow, too. What page, deaths, let's see. Honestly, this paper, every night you got to hunt for it, that and the police blotter. You'd think it was a big secret or something." She opened the paper and flattened it over the counter, allowing half of it to drop off, "Oh Teddy, Margaret's husband died."

"Who?" asked Teddy, looking over her shoulder. Frances pulled the paper closer to her face. She read the obituary out loud, skipping some words before putting it down on the counter.

"Margaret who?" Teddy asked again, opening the paper to the obituaries and patting his shirt pocket for his glasses.

"Margaret Shaly, Tom Shaly died," she said, moving to the grill. "Wake is tomorrow." She started scraping down the grill. "I'll have to go to that. That's what I mean, you sit there and read the paper and you don't read anything. I don't know what you read for hours. There's nothing in there except deaths and the blotter."

"What do you mean?" Teddy responded, looking up Elizabeth Street, "I read that name and I don't think of Margaret as Margaret Shaly. I don't think I know them. Do I know them?"

"Yeah you know them. She had all those kids and he spent money like water. The oldest one is probably fifteen years older than the youngest."

Teddy took the paper back to the table and opened it up to the local sports. "Oh yeah, he used to decorate the house at Christmas, had it lit up like Luna Park, kept the neighbors up all night right through to the end of January. But I don't think of her as Shaly. I think of her as a Banahan."

"Banahan," Frances cried, raising her spatula over her head, "she hasn't been a Banahan for twenty five years. That's why I have to read it for myself. You have to read the whole obituary. They tell you right in there the wife's maiden name. And the kids, who the kids are, the brothers and sisters, it's all in there. Sentinel's got nothing in it but they do a good job on the obituaries."

"I read about the redevelopment," Teddy said, carrying the paper and settling into his parlor table.

Frances waved him off. "Redevelopment, they've been talking about that for ten years. We'll be dead before that happens!"

"Well, that's the stuff that's important," he said, moving his hands in a circular motion. "Obituaries, they're important, too."

"Hi." The voice was soft and deep. He straddled a stool and leaned over the counter.

Linda remained bent over the deep wash sink scrubbing plates. She heard the adjacent faucet drip into the rinse sink as the water rippled and heard the entry note of the Chants sound in her mind. She counted the measures and heard the instrumental line of the song building softly to the entry of the soprano line. Her arms were submerged beyond her elbows. In her mind, far from the Palace of Sweets, levitated to weightless pleasure on the splendid portamento of the Bailero from the Chants d'Averegne, she imagined her voice melting into the ascending harp run. She counted the measures and imagined the dynamic markings of the vocal line.

Blake sat on the stool and leaned forward, his lips nearly touching the top of her head, "Hi, Linda."

She lifted her face from the deep sink and rolled her eyes up. "Hi," she responded, stretching out the vowel as she recognized him and stood wide eyed. She reached to her right to get a dish towel. "How are you?" she asked in a flared voice. Her eyes flashed with surprise, then her face grimaced, "Oh, you're all wet!"

"Yeah," Blake responded with a smile, "I thought the rain was stopping when I left school, but it started again. I'm fine. I think it's starting to stop." He took some napkins and wiped his face. "I've come in a few times after that night I left my jacket here, but you weren't here," he volunteered.

"Here, you can dry off with this." She thrust the clean dish towel into his hands and continued to speak at a rapid clip. "You did? I usually work only on weekends and sometimes one afternoon and night during the week. I've seen some of your friends come in, you know, some of those girls." She watched him as he ran the dish towel over his face and hair that was matted and unruly and dripping.

"Thanks," he said, handing the towel back to her and looking into her eyes. He watched her ponytail bounce as she moved to break her stare.

"What can I get for you?" she asked, realizing that she hadn't noticed a parlor table fill with customers that Teddy was waiting on. "Want some hot chocolate or something to warm you up?" She turned to stack the clean sundae dishes on the marble shelf.

"Yeah, that sounds great. And I guess I'll have a cheeseburger," he said, turning on his stool to see how many tables were full and in need of service.

"And what will Blake have today?" Frances called out from the grill, "something nice and hot?"

"A cheeseburger," Linda rubbed her hands over her apron, repeating earnestly, "A cheeseburger, and a hot chocolate." Then she looked up the counter to Frances. "I'll get the hot chocolate," she said over a laugh. "What about the parlor, Fran, is there anything I can get for them?"

"Let's see," Frances said, lifting her pad and ticking it off with a pencil, "I need one strawberry shake, a marshmallow sundae with chocolate ice cream, a lemon

52

Coke and a regular Coke." She bent and took a handful of hamburger meat from the half fridge below the sandwich counter, flattened it between her palms and put it on the grill, placing a foil plate over it to keep the oil from splattering.

"Blake," she called out, "I saw your aunt Florence last week. She came in after the mass for Kevin Cumiskey."

Blake left his stool and walked to the window, looking out into the darkened street and staring into the glare of headlights. "Yeah, my aunt said they're not doing too good."

Frances shook her head and prodded the hamburger with her spatula. "None of them are doing so good. Virginia, his mother, do you know her?"

Blake stepped to the front of the grill. "I know her to say hello to but I never really spoke to her. I used to see her at track meets. My brother was on the 440-relay team with Kevin when they won the states. We got a picture of the four of them lined up, you know, with their arms around each other. It's hard to look at it now. How about his sister, how's she doing?"

Frances shook her head. "Well, she lost a lot of weight. Virginia brought her in one day so I could make her a vanilla shake. I put two eggs in it too to bulk it up." Frances laid two slices of cheese over the hamburger and placed the tin plate back over it. "Almost done now, Blake, two slices, just the way you like it."

Blake sat at the stool in front of the register. "I guess it'll just take more time for them."

Frances bent to check the height of the gas under the grill. "Some things you just don't get over. She brought her grandson Michael in for a hot chocolate last week, very sad."

"What about his dad?"

Frances shook her head and sighed. "No, he's not doing good at all. Virginia's worried. He's depressed, won't eat or anything. Has no interest in hunting. He was a big hunter you know."

"Yeah, my dad says he doesn't say much at the shop. Said he's real quiet, missed a lot of work." Blake stood as Frances removed the tin plate and raised his eyebrows.

Frances handed him the plate. "Ketchup's on the counter if you need it, Blake. He was very proud of Kevin. He joined, you know."

"Yeah, I know."

"Feel any dryer yet?" Linda asked as he returned to his stool.

She squeezed more whipped cream into the hot chocolate.

"So, are you at Derby High?" he asked as the cheeseburger juice dripped down his fingers and into the plate.

"Uh-huh," she responded, somewhat surprised that he didn't already know that. "Why," she asked curiously, "where do you go? You don't go to Derby?"

He shook his head and held up a finger, asking for time to swallow. "No," he said finally, "I go to Valley Tech."

"What?" Linda lifted the cover off of the Coke dispenser

and strained to pour the syrup into it. "But didn't you leave your Derby jacket here that night you came back in?"

"Yeah," he said, spooning the whipped cream into his mouth and then stirring the hot chocolate, "but that was my brother's jacket."

"So," Linda said with an illuminated look on her face and reaching to replace the cover of the dispenser, "so that's why I never see you in school."

Blake's smile was curtailed by a mouthful of food. He raised his eyebrows high and shook his head affirmatively. Linda glanced towards the parlor and noticed some empty tables that needed to be bussed. "I'll be right back," she said, grabbing an empty tray on her way by. Blake took a napkin and wiped his mouth, stood, and backed away from the stool.

"I have to go anyway. My mom will have supper for me," he said, shrugging his shoulders and smiling. He took another step back and raised his eyes to the pressed ceiling, then down the faded mirrors along the walls and the neat row of stools. "What's your work schedule?"

"Wait," she said, collecting the last glass and laying the tray on the counter. She wiped her hands on her apron and spoke rapidly. "I work Friday nights, you know, like the last time, and Sunday afternoons, sometimes into the evening, if we're busy. But we close early on Sundays. We're closed by seven."

"But today's Thursday," he said with a laugh and turned his palms up in disbelief, "you don't work on

Thursdays?"

She returned his laugh and bobbed back down into the rinse sink. "No, well, not usually. But today I came in to see you," she said, laughing and feeling a blush rise into her cheeks, then shaking her head to erase the statement. "No, just kidding. Teddy's busy with the Christmas ordering and stacking the basement this week, at night, so I'm helping out for a few hours. Why didn't you ask Frances about my schedule?"

Blake tightened his face with discomfort. "I felt funny asking. Besides, I figured if I came in enough I'd find you here eventually."

"Do you live around here?" she asked, hoping to find out all she could in these final moments before he was gone.

"Couple of miles away, up above Pink House Cove," he said, glancing up at the clock above the counter. "Can I call you?" he asked, glancing at the wall clock. "I really have to go now. Can I have your phone number?" His tone turned serious as he turned to leave.

Linda stopped all motion and leaned towards him with an apprehensive look on her face. "I don't have a phone, at least not yet. Not at home anyway. But you can call me here if you want. Frances won't mind."

Blake hesitated and tried not to let his surprise show, then glanced at the clock again. "Okay, yeah, but I'll just stop in again, if that's okay with you."

"Sure," she said, stepping towards him, "here." She passed the ancient marble and brass candy scale and held a chocolate covered caramel out for him.

"Thanks," he said, "I still owe Frances for the one I stole the last time." He made his way to the counter register and paid Frances and said good-bye, pulling the door open fully and letting in a rush of cold air.

Linda walked slowly to the window and watched his image fade as he ran up Main Street, towards Pink House Cove. Frances, with her back turned, looked into the mirror and saw her leaning into the window. "Ahh, Linda," she sang out with a slurred rise of her voice, "I think Blake likes you." She turned and stepped between the counter and grill towards Linda. "He's come around a few times but he'd look around and order a hot chocolate to go, didn't stay. I couldn't figure out who he was trying to see. Sometimes the kids just meet their friends here, you know? He never said anything."

Linda walked back to the deep sink and fixed her sleeve above her elbow again. She felt a smile break over her lips. "No, I don't think so, Fran. Maybe he was just hungry."

Teddy looked up over the newspaper and smiled. "I don't think so, Linda. He wasn't just hungry."

"I don't think he was just hungry," Frances called back as she cradled the phone in her shoulder and took an order.

Teddy closed the paper and stood, thumbing his shirt into his trousers and placed it on the counter. One day last week he came in and walked past the candy counter. We were real busy. He turned like he was going to leave so I asked him if he wanted anything. I think I surprised him because he ordered a coffee to go."

Frances returned the phone to the cradle and stepped down the counter. "It's a maple nut sundae order," she said, waving the order pad in her hand.

Linda placed some rinsed plates on the drain counter. "So, maybe he just wanted a coffee or something," she said to Teddy.

Teddy shook his head. "No," he said knowingly, "he doesn't drink coffee."

Linda laughed and took the order pad from Frances. "Is that true, Fran?"

Frances turned and started to pump cherry syrup into a large wax paper cup. She shook her head in agreement with Teddy. "It's true he doesn't drink coffee. Not yet anyway." Frances walked to the Coke dispenser and turned to Linda. "I know. He's been coming in here since he was a kid. All the kids, I know them all. If he drank coffee he would have had that at the counter tonight." She reached for a long spoon and stirred the Cherry Coke, snapped a lid on and turned towards Linda. "What did he drink tonight?"

"Hot chocolate," she said flatly. She turned and grabbed a large paper cup used for sundaes to go. She flipped open the vanilla ice cream and muscled three scoops into the cup and flipped it shut, then ladled maple nut topping loaded with walnuts on it and filled it with whipped cream and handed it to Frances. She returned to the deep sink and sunk her arms in. Her mind raced. Did he have any girlfriends? How often did he come in to try to see her, once a week? It was a month ago that she saw him, did he come in only once or twice? How often, really, and when did he come in? What if he looked for her only once but came in for other reasons the other times? Did he come in with the other girls? Was he on any teams? Where's Valley Tech? Where's Pink House Cove? He has a brother, older, what about sisters? Does he have any sisters and do they go to Derby High? Does he have other brothers? What are his parents like? What kind of music does he like? What else does he like other than cheeseburgers and chocolate covered caramels? Why did he leave so fast? What's his name? She walked to Frances' side while drying a plate. "What's his name?"

Frances bit a slice of buttered rye toast and looked perplexed. "What's whose name, Blake?"

"Yes," laughed Linda, "what's his last name?"

Frances smiled and swallowed, "Oh, Teitel. Blake Teitel. That's shortened from something but I don't know what. He's nice, isn't he?" Teddy collected the last glasses and dishes and placed them beside Linda, then went to the basement.

Linda bent into the deep sink. "Yeah," she responded casually to Frances, "he seems really nice."

"Very nice," Frances added, placing the meats into the half- fridge for the night.

Linda nodded in agreement. She leaned into the rinse sink and immersed herself in the clear, streaming water, content to feel the heat over her arms and to be alone with her thoughts of him. She wondered when he would be back and if she would be there, and what if Frances was wrong, what if he really wasn't so interested in her, what if he was interested in one of those other girls. But he said he came in to see her a few times but she wasn't there and he remembered her name so that must mean something.

Frances wiped down the counter and the tables and straightened out the parlor chairs. Then she went to each register and emptied it into a bank bag, leaving just enough for the morning.

The Greek stepped from the curb and called out Teddy's name as he walked by the Palace, in and out of sight with a few quick strides. He knew the distance of cars from the sound of their tires and the patter of pebbles and stones they kicked up. He was young, although few knew his actual age. He learned the rumbling beat and revolving rhythm of the street from his paper route as a child. He earned walk-around money as a messenger of information too sensitive for phones and other modern conveniences and as a courier of light seamstress work or of slips and bets and other nostrums of vice too sensitive to be discussed over party-line phones. His discretion in the face of sin and vice was the currency on which his stride bore its marked cadence. He was everywhere and nowhere all at once, embracing the duality of a photon, a presence and an absence that defied measurement and position. And what he carried was there and gone without a trace, tidied away under a wool overcoat or tucked into dress pants or covered by the flair of a bold and bright dress shirt.

The word on the street was that he was the victim of a blunt trauma at a very young age when he darted between two parked cars and met the fender of an auto. But there was uncertainty to the story as rumor and legend congealed. And when the academics of school proved beyond his ability, his father took the boy to the tumbled old quay on the Naugatuck side of the trestle and stepped into their old boat and rowed out to Hog's Island to fish. And in the length of the day, marked by the position of the sun or the rumbling of freights running the trestle, the Greek attained his sense of position in the universe and his manner of approach and disposition to the world at large.

"The worms, keep them moist, out of the sun," his father would instruct with his long, reedy leg resting on the boat frame and other on the island.

"Always?" asked the Greek daily as he sat on his little haunches and baited the hooks, then covered the can of worms with a loose rag.

"Always, and keep the lure perfect. Son, the lure is like a woman. It attracts the eye of the fish and brings it to the bait."

"The fish like worms and lures?"

"Of course, but we're smarter than the fish." The old man would stand and squint cigarette smoke from his eyes, holding the butt inward, protected from the winds of the great seas of his origin. "We, you and I, son, we can feed the family from here, right here from Hog's Island." And the Greek's father would stand the boy on the shore of

Hog's Island and point east, towards the rising sun, and tell him long and vivid stories of the Levant, stories of great vessels and powerful navies appearing on the horizon of the eastern Mediterranean and masting towards the head of the Aegean to the Sea of Marmara and on to the Bosporus. And in the Greek's mind there came to reside generous and contented dreams of his ancestry and his destiny.

"Do they like the sinkers too?" he asked as he squinted up at his father.

"Yes, son, they like sinkers too, but not as much as they like lures."

They spoke of the Greek gods, with sons of great power and bravery and daughters of extraordinary beauty, then wrapped the day's catch in old newspaper and walked it home to their apartment, a converted storefront with the large pane glass windows still intact. And the old man held the boy's hand and they talked of the island of Rhodes and the great scholars that resided there protected in antiquity by the Colossus, erected to honor Helios, the sun god, in gratitude for a great military victory. And when the Greek climbed into his bed, nightly, a bed shared with his brother Tassos and his sister Christina, his father would bend close to him and whisper in his ear that the toppled Colossus could never be rebuilt because the Oracle had so instructed as against the wishes of the gods. And the Greek shook his head in understanding, a fact that he was charged with to the exclusion of his siblings, and dreamt peacefully of the great and mighty Levant.

62

And his father was broken for him, a child so feeble that he would never understand his own limits. In despair, one fine and splendid morning, with great and clutching pain in his chest, he posed the boy on the edge of Hog's Island, looking east, into the sun, in the stance of the Colossus. He told him to watch the harbor for all the people of the Valley and to be proud, to stand erect and to walk with confidence, and to provide sound instruction and wisdom to all who asked, as the Oracles did. Then he rowed off toward the great Atlantic, bent with chest pain, and called back to the boy that someday he would return, like the magnificent Odysseus, and that he should wait there for his brother Tassos to come to the shore to retrieve him. And the Greek fished and caught enough for the whole family that day and waited for Tassos to wave and stand on the fallen quay and finally wade out to fetch him.

He circled the area in a wide perimeter, like a sling racing around a hollow, cinching the Valley. Past stairwells, stores, restaurants and factory gates, churches and cemeteries, stopping momentarily this evening to hand Rosa the seamstress her paper bag of work from the judge's wife, the Greek cat-walked around the Valley like a sentry, observing and conveying, collecting and distributing what belonged to others and passing into the darkness. In sunlight and in streetlight, or moonlit at midnight, the Greek was an endless presence, crossing ceaselessly from shadow to light and to shadow again.

"Linda." Frances said softly, realizing that she was deep in thought. "Linda," she said again, touching her shoulder, "you can leave now that the dishes are done. Are you okay?"

"Oh," she replied, straightening slowly and holding the last of the forks and spoons. "Yes, I'm okay. I'm done." She dried the final dishes and placed them along the counter, looking at their neat reflection. "Where's Teddy?"

"Downstairs," Frances replied, motioning towards the back of the candy counter. "He's probably done too."

Linda walked to the radiator and put her coat on. It was dry and warm and enveloped her body in its captured heat. She walked to the back of the candy counter and picked up her books, then bent into the trap door. "Night, Teddy," she called down.

"Night, Linda," Teddy replied from a distant corner of the basement.

Linda walked to the door and looked outside. "I guess it stopped raining," she said, turning back to Frances.

"It's been stopped for a while now. Just cold and damp out there," she said, watching Linda open the door. "Night now."

"Good night, Fran." Linda stepped out of the alcove and walked down Main Street, holding her books tightly to her chest to insulate her from the cold wind and hold in the heat of the radiator. Past the florists and jewelers and stationers, and past the restaurant and shoemaker, she huddled herself against the cold. She glanced across the street at Burns' and smiled at the stool propping open the door to the murky tavern light. She couldn't imagine the heat emanating on the flesh of the factory men hours after leaving the crucible.

"Hi, mom," she called out, dropping her books on the couch and stepping towards the kitchen. "What's for supper?" she asked, as she unbuttoned her coat.

"Hi, Sweetheart, how was school?" came the pleasant reply. Her mother turned from the sink to the pan on the stove. Her frame was small and delicate. Her skin was dark and smooth with the hints of laugh lines along her eyes. Traces of silver filament threaded her black hair that was pulled back and bunned. Her tongue was thick and heavy with the Spanish of the Puerto Rican mountains, an accent that she apologized for to anyone she spoke to for the first time. "Uh, what, your apron, again?" she said with a smile as she scooped the dinner into the plates.

Linda laughed and slipped out of her coat. "Oh, I know." She untied the apron and laid it on the washer. "Forgot to take it off," she explained, taking her plate and leaning on the refrigerator, looking out over the river.

"Don't stand and eat, honey," her mother said, pulling a chair from the table. "So how was school?" she asked again. "I waited to eat with you. Sit."

Linda sat and spoke in between forkfuls. "School was good," she explained, "Mr. Maher was out, so no math homework. He might be out tomorrow also, really sick or something. So how was work?"

Her mother looked back at her coat, swallowed, and asked, "Where's your umbrella?

Linda looked across to her mother. "In my locker, Rene locked it and left. But I didn't get too wet." She opened the refrigerator and poured some cold water into a tall glass, drinking half of it as she stood, then poured a small glass and placed it in front of her mother. "How was work?" she asked breathlessly.

"Thank you," she said as an aside. "Take your time. You're going to choke," her mother demanded, tapping the table. "It was good, getting very busy with the spring fabrics and bags. They say they have lots of orders, might be working Saturdays for a while."

"Does this happen every year?"

"Yes, they say they need the orders ready for shipment in January. Then they said we do a lot of linings for some of the straw bags for summer." Her mother turned and pulled a ball of fabric from a shopping bag. "They also want to start making silk scarves. You like the material?" she asked, laying it on the table.

Linda ran it through her fingers and rubbed it between her thumb and fingers. "Wow," she exclaimed, "beautiful feel."

Her mother smiled with satisfaction. "Yes, so soft. Probably hard to work with, it's so fine."

"But you can do it."

Her mother nodded. "The owner came to me himself. He said he wants the best seamstresses on it because it's expensive so he can't afford too much waste."

"Nice." Linda touched the silk again, then carried her empty plate to the sink, placed it in a dishpan and ran some hot water. Her mother stood beside her and nudged her over.

"I'll do the dishes. You do enough dishes."

"Did a lot today," Linda replied, turning to hang her coat in the closet. "Teddy was busy with the Christmas candy. But really, he read the paper for the first couple of minutes I was there. When I got there my coat was a little wet so he put it over the radiator. Oh, it was like toast when I put it on." She stood at the window and looked for the moon but saw only the dark belly of heavy clouds barely perceptible in the night. Across the river, on the Shelton side, the stacks of the huge B. F. Goodrich sponge plant pumped thick white smoke into the dark sky. "The train is late," she said, glancing at the clock and picking up a towel to wipe the plates. Then she walked to the piano and started the harp run from the Bailero.

"Much homework?" her mother asked, rinsing the sink and taking the silk into the living room. She picked up a basket, carried it into the living room, kneeled beside it and searched for a particular needle.

"No, not really," Linda replied. She rose and put her books in order on the couch. "Just review some stuff for tomorrow." The center light reflected off the nearly barren walls. She sat at the piano bench and leaned over to touch the baby dress her mother was making. "The lace feels too thin."

He mother sat back on her heels. She rolled her sepia eyes to Linda who looked back with the same eyes. "They're saying B. F. is buying some new machines for the plant across the river."

Linda looked incredulous. "What? The sponge plant,

really? Teddy didn't say anything about that. He usually knows all that stuff."

"They said they heard they want to expand the building too."

"Wow, no one said anything while I was working."

Her mother shrugged her shoulders, "They say they want to concentrate on their chemical business. They want to make some improvements, buy some new machines and fix it up." She pulled a thread and looked up at Linda. "I didn't know they had a chemical business." She adjusted a bobbin and turned back to Linda. "So, you think the lace is too thin?"

"No," she said, taking the thread between her fingers, "just feels a little different. Maybe I've been washing too many dishes." Linda picked up a spool and wrapped her fingers around it. "No, I guess not." She turned and faced the piano, letting her fingers depress the keys lightly and humming along with the music. "Mom," she asked without turning and continuing to play, "do you know anyone at the shop named Teitel?"

"Teitel?" her mother asked. She sat at the lace loom and started pedaling it, whirling its bobbins into a dizzying spin.

"Teitel."

The bobbins stopped. "No," she replied, pulling an incorrect thread, "I don't think so." Her fingers worked feverishly again, darting around the dozens of spinning bobbins. "Why?"

"Oh, nothing really," Linda responded casually, hoping

not to arouse her mother's curiosity too much. "Just some guy who comes into Vonete's, that's all." The sound of the bobbins clicking and the piano filled the room for a moment.

"So," her mother finally asked, realizing her daughter may not offer more, "who is this guy? How old is he, this person?" she asked over the sound of the box loom.

Linda stopped playing and turned to face her mother. The Valley was small and insular, hemmed in by hills and mountains and defined by its rivers, so somewhere, through someone, he had to be connected into the pocketbook shop. "He's not like an old guy or anything. He's my age, a senior at Valley Tech."

Her mother glanced up at her and put on a serious look. She had been through this before with her older daughter. She knew how fast love blossomed in the young despite their own denials. And she recognized that her daughter's need to talk of him confirmed that he meant something to her already, however brief or innocent or sweet. The whirl of the bobbins stopped. Suddenly the room was silent except for the muffled sound of the traffic on Main Street. "He comes in to see you? Who is this person?"

Linda took some lace from the rug and busied herself straightening it. "I don't know," she responded, shaking her head. "He just comes in and I was talking to him, that's all." She leaned over and untangled the bobbins that loosened when the action stopped.

"What's his name?"

"Blake." Linda got up and walked towards the bathroom

to get ready for bed. "Blake Teitel."

The apartment was quiet for several moments. "I don't think I know anyone in the shop with that last name." The bobbins flew again.

Linda went into her room and lay on her bed, stretching her head back, trying to find the moon. In the distance she heard the sound of the diesels, late, running along the Shelton side. She glanced at the bureau with the picture of her father and her, flanking her sister on her sister's wedding day. A soft smile creased her lips as she recalled the tone of his voice telling her to pay attention to the markings of the music, to hold each note without wavering, and saw his body sway as he sat at the piano and looked at her, nodding his head to help her timing. She remembered how he would touch her when she stood beside the piano, placing his hand over her diaphragm as if to influence the release of every breath. And his voice, soft and imploring, with his fingers curled, "Sostenuto, Linda, sostenuto. Hold your notes. Let your notes ride over your breath. Give them their full value. You can't cheat your notes."

"Linda," her mother called out, glancing at the dark room, "I hope you're not lying on that bedspread."

"No," Linda responded quickly, jumping up quickly to flick on the light. "Well, just a little. I was thinking about daddy." She unbuttoned her blouse and turned sideways in front of the mirror. She took the bow and winced as the rubber band pulled and let a flood of chestnut hair fall over her shoulders and back. She put on her pajamas and stood in the doorway watching her mother manipulate the bobbins. "I'm going to bed, mom. Good night," she said as she bent and kissed her mother.

Her mother turned from the lace. "You're tired, sweetheart?" she asked. "I hope you're not getting sick from the rain."

"No, I'm not sick, just tired." She pulled back the heavy lace spread and shut the light. The weight of the blankets warmed her as the muffled sound of traffic and the comforting whirl of the bobbins spun her thoughts to the mountains of Puerto Rico. She thought of Blake and wondered how long she would have to wait to see him again. The words of Il Mio Ben Quando Verra came to her in the spinning vortex of bobbins and she imagined her father's face, kind and gentle, moving with exaggerated motions to encourage each sound, the very form of her lips. And his hands, palms up, with his fingers bent and pliant, lifting and encouraging the notes from her. The words turned in her mind and her lips moved imperceptibly, manifest in recitative, as he instructed each song she ever learned.

Max returned to his table in the club room of the Deer Run Country Club. He was home for the weekend from his second year of law school with one of his classmates, Lachlan Fox. In the crowded and boisterous club room they watched the evening news and drank beer while they waited for Marshall to pick them up for a ride to New Hampshire for the Yale game the following day.

Lachlan looked at his watch and downed his beer. "He's late again."

"Marshall's always late, but he has a nice car. I skipped my workout at the gym to be here on time. He has no sense of time. That's why I arranged for him to drive us to Dartmouth tonight and not wait for tomorrow. Last time I drove out of state my car had a radiator hose busted in Pennsylvania."

Maximilion Cruz was familiar with the club, having been raised in the pampered embrace of white tablecloths, polished silverware, and spotless stemware. He enjoyed the long, curved, tree lined driveway that rolled to a broad opening with contoured hills and manicured lawns that separated the members from the lesser world. Cruz was raised to believe it was his birthright to reclaim the sugar plantation his grandfather and father owned in Batista's Cuba. Cruz's father, a man not taken to risk, sold off the family's holdings early in the revolution and fled to Puerto Rico and finally to New Haven and waited for the counter-revolution. But to the perpetual perturbence and considerable cost to his family, Fidel Castro survived assassination attempts and anti-revolutionary invasions while the family's fortune evaporated.

He was taught manners and courtesies from his parents and treated the wait staff with respect while learning the advantages of education and privilege and status and the connective tissue the club offered to those ends. He was gifted with striking looks of black hair, blue eyes and an angular face. His deportment, even now as a young man, was measured and stylized by height and a strong carriage. He lifted weights daily, downed supplements from the health food store, and measured his strength against his peers and the mirror image he studied and admired. Despite the efforts to mold his raw testosterone into refined gentlemanliness in this finely mannered club, a modern gelding parlor of sorts, his petulance was barely in check and his ambition to attain status and position was unrelenting in an unattractive way.

Lachlan turned away from the television and opened some peanuts. "Johnson's sending another fifty thousand troops over. This thing just keeps getting worse. My deferment is up next year. It's getting scary."

"Don't worry about it. My dad knows one of the guys on the board and one of the guys he does a lot of business with, his wife is on the board. I can get you deferred again if you need it. Enroll in some evening classes after law school. That would be enough to keep you out. Don't sweat it."

"Is that what you're going to do?"

Max finished his beer and took some of Lachlan's peanuts. "Me, no, I'm planning on clerking for one of the federal judges for a year or two, one of the members here. It looks great on a resume. By that time who knows where the war will be. I'll worry about that then."

"Well, how would I have known to look here for you two?" Marshall said with a laugh. He set his beer down and pulled up a chair.

Max pointed to the wall clock above the bar. "About time

you showed up. Drink up, I want to get on the road."

Lachlan smiled and shook Marshall's hand, "Don't let him rush you. We were just talking about the war and how our deferments are going to run out."

Marshall grabbed a bunch of pretzels and drank half his beer. "Oh, that mess. At least we know someone on the board."

"Everyone knows someone on the board," Lachlan commented.

Max grabbed his jacket and stood up to leave. "Lach, I just told you, I can help. Relax. Let's go."

State Representative Rudy Harper sat at the head of the conference room table and passed out a folder with information on the state banking commissioner's office to the assembled officers and incorporators of Birmingham Savings Bank. Dennis Foley took the extra folders and held them.

"We have a few board members who couldn't make it today. Phineas and Allen are upset even discussing any plan to make a public offering. And Wilford Tully had a stroke last week."

Harper looked up from his notes and shook his head. "I hadn't heard that. How is he doing? No one told me."

Dennis frowned and opened his folder. "He isn't good. I spoke to his wife yesterday. She said they are just trying to keep him alive until his daughter returns from Europe. They expect her back today sometime."

"Oh my, well, I'm sorry to hear that. He was a great

businessman, very committed to the Valley."

Dennis pursed his lips and lit a cigarette. "It's a shame. His wife said she's just going to sell the shirt shop. No one in the family wants to run it. So that's another business we may lose."

"Well, so maybe that's why I am here today. Dennis asked that I meet with you and talk about the pending federal legislation that will eventually allow for interstate banking and restructure how the banking industry is organized and capitalized. So what I put into the folders that I just passed out are the highlights of the federal legislation and the current and some proposed state legislation that will make the mutual savings bank structure basically obsolete over a number of years."

Dennis looked up without opening his folder. "So, is your committee proposing this? Who is actually drafting the law?"

"Well, we are taking the uniform law suggested by the banker's association and we are just amending it to suit our needs and the Governor's concerns. Most of the proposals are not being touched. Of course, once we hold hearings and get feedback from the industry things can change. But for now the outline I provided, which was drawn up by the committee staff members, has all the essential information about how to go about the change and the timeframes needed."

"So how soon are they telling you the federal legislation is going to be passed and open up interstate banking?"

"Five to seven years from now. I guess the feds feel that

by having fifty states regulating banking that puts the domestic banks at a disadvantage to the international banking industry. If we don't have the ability to raise capital efficiently through the markets then over time the domestic banking industry will end up being a protected industry but unable to attract international money and enter international markets. That's just the way the industry is moving. I'm not saying they are right. I only just got into this so I don't know a lot more than you do. All I can do is make contacts in Hartford, get information for you, and smooth the process."

They turned down Main Street, conversing in animated tones about the hulking outline of the Farrell's plant. Blake described to her the scale of the Anaconda plant in Ansonia and the reason it was called the Copper City. Their feet squished through the slushy sidewalk as cars fishtailed up the grade of Main Street.

"This is it," Linda said, opening the hallway door. A single, naked ceiling bulb on the second floor landing illuminated the stairs.

"Hi, mom, we're here," she called out as they entered the living room. "Mom, this is Blake," Linda said calmly. Then she looked at Blake, "Blake, this is my mom."

Her mother put the lace down and rose from the floor, extending her hand, "Pleased to meet you," she said with a thick Spanish accent.

"Thank you," Blake replied awkwardly. "Nice to meet you too." He was surprised at her heavy accent and petite, youthful appearance. "What's that?" Blake asked, pointing to the loom.

Linda touched his arm, "I'm going to change," she said, leaving him alone with her mother.

"That is my lace loom," she responded, with her hand delicately placed over several bobbins. "It's from Puerto Rico, the village that I am from."

Blake wrinkled his nose and managed a smile. "Wow," he exclaimed, "that looks complicated. Is it hard to work?"

Her mother smiled and shook her head, "No, where I am from it is learned from childhood. So, no, I don't think it is hard. It maybe looks hard, but it isn't."

Blake shook his head in disbelief, "I don't know about that," he responded, focusing on the piano in the corner. "Who plays the piano?"

"Linda plays, and my other daughter, Carmen, she plays also. She lives in Puerto Rico. She's married. Their father taught them how to play the piano and...." She noticed Blake straining to understand her, stopping in mid-sentence while the smile dropped from her face. "I am sorry, maybe my English is not so good."

"No, no, you speak fine. I understood everything. I just didn't know all this. It's hard to talk when Linda is working because she is always so busy."

The sound of tires spinning and the blast of the train horn across the river broke the momentary silence. Blake looked out the kitchen window and saw the silhouette of the 6:10 running over the snowy banks of the Housatonic. "Wow, you can see the river from here?"

"Oh, yes, it is very nice to live here, the rivers and the trains. We like the trains," she said as Linda entered the room.

Her hair was down, brushed back over her shoulders and held in place by an ivory lace cloche made in a pattern of snowflakes. Delicate gold earrings framed her face. She wore a button down peasant dress with a floral pattern embroidered in ivory lace. The hem hit the top of her boots as she put her bench warmer on.

"Okay, I'm ready," she said.

"Have a nice time," her mother said, nodding to Blake politely, "I am happy to meet you."

Blake nodded back, "Nice to meet you too."

"Oh," her mother exclaimed, rushing to the kitchen table and handing Linda two letters, "will you mail these in the box across the street for me? I forgot to take them earlier."

"Sure," Linda responded, smiling at Blake and opening the door to the hallway. "I'll be back by nine or so, Mom."

"I am not worried. You are only downstairs. Have a nice time."

They waited for the traffic to break before crossing and dropping the letters into the mailbox. The snow swirled with the last breaths of the storm, giant flakes spinning and twisting in the wind. Linda's foot slipped out as they stepped down from the curb. She grabbed Blake's arm instinctively and gave out a quick yelp. "Oh," she cried, "I thought I was going to fall." She held his arm securely. He looked at her and smiled, placing his hand over hers. A tractor-trailer truck rumbled by and snow swirled around her face, large flakes whipping in the slipstream, landing on her cloche and cheeks and coat.

"It's okay, unless we both go down. Then that won't be so good," he said with a smile. "Hey," he continued, foregoing a chance to cross as he looked at her closely, "you never told me you were Spanish."

"My mom's from Puerto Rico," she said with wide, rounded eyes. "Why, does that matter? You never asked."

"No," he said with a laugh. "It doesn't matter at all. But the first time I met you I said linda meant beautiful in Spanish. So you knew that, right?" They stood facing each other, oblivious to the traffic spraying slush in a wide arc. The last snowflakes floated around them as the sky started to open up and stars appeared beyond the clouds. "I thought I was telling you something you didn't know."

Linda looked up into the street lights and smiled. They started across carefully. "Yes," she said clearly, "I know that but your friends were beeping the horn and you ran out so fast I didn't have a chance to respond. It actually means pretty in Spanish. But you were so excited about it, you know, the way you said it, so enthusiastically. Beautiful is okay too."

Blake looked at her and nodded. "Okay, so maybe we can leave it at beautiful. I kind of like it better."

"Sure," Linda replied as they entered the restaurant. They hung their coats and were seated at the old wooden booths with carvings of hearts with engraved names or notes that were generations old.

"This place used to be up the street a few blocks, before

they redeveloped that area and widened the bridge into Shelton. They tore down the old River but the owners took most of the old booths and brought them here when they built this."

Linda looked around the full dining area and the counter lined with customers for take-out orders. The kitchen was open revealing men with whitened arms tossing pizza dough high into the air and waitresses scurrying around with trays full of food. "It sure is busy now. My mom and I always meant to try the pizza but we just never got here yet, and it's only next door. So, what's good?" she asked, as she picked up the menu.

"Everything is pretty good." He looked at her closely as she studied the menu. Her hands were soft, with fingers adorned only with a birthstone ring. Her skin was creamy white, pinched with a hint of red blush on her cheeks. Her lips were perfectly fluted and formed deliberate patterns when she spoke.

She looked up at him. "It smells so good in here. I can't decide what to get."

Blake held his menu and read off different suggestions without hinting at a recommendation. "Do you want to split a pizza?"

Linda put her menu down. "That sounds good," she replied. "What kind?"

"You ever have white clam?"

She wrinkled her nose. "No, never heard of it."

Blake smiled at her apprehension. "The white clam pizza is great, but how about if we get a large pizza, half with cheese and the other half white clam? This way, in case you don't like it, you can still eat the cheese half. And we can split a half pitcher of soda. Does that sound okay?"

"Yes, that's sounds great," she said, closing her menu and flicking her eyebrows up as Blake ordered. "So," she asked, tapping his hands with her fingers, "what's a white clam pizza anyway?"

Blake laughed and pointed to the menu. "Let's see. It's a pizza without any red sauce. So it has clams on it and other seasonings, garlic and stuff. And it has some grated cheese but no mozzarella, unless you ask for that. But that's extra, it doesn't just come with it. You think you still want to eat that?"

"Sure, why not? So, it's so nice to sit across from you and talk to you without working at the same time. I never really get to talk to you, you know, really talk." And so they talked and recounted all the missed visits and time spent in thought of one another.

"Yeah," Blake said smiling, "I learned more about you talking to your mom than I have talking to you at work. So your mom told me you play the piano, you and your sister. She said your dad taught you."

"Uh huh," she responded, peeling the paper from her straw. "He was a voice teacher. He taught me and my sister how to play piano but he wasn't really a piano teacher."

Blake poured soda into their glasses and put on a perplexed look. "Wow, so is that why you were singing when I walked in that night?"

"Yes," she said clearly. "He taught me the basics, some of the beginner voice books, some vocal technique. Lots of diction, breath control, posture. There's a lot to know. I was young so he really focused on articulation and diction, you know, forming your words and not dropping endings. "

They both leaned back as a pile of napkins and plates and utensils were placed on the table. "So," Blake asked, sorting out the table settings between them, "where is your dad now?"

Linda looked at him and placed a napkin on her lap. "He died two years ago." She placed her straw in the soda, opened her hands, and shook her head, letting several moments pass in silence. "It's kind of a long story," she said, leaning over to make room for the pizza. "Do you want to hear it?"

"Yeah, of course I do. I didn't come here just to eat pizza. I could have gotten a take out for that. I wanted to get to know you. Is it too hard to talk about? If it is, I understand." Blake raised a slice and put it to his mouth.

Linda took a slice, flicked her fingers at how hot it was, and placed it on her plate. "Wow, that's hot!"

Blake shook his head in agreement, "Very." He placed his pizza on his plate as Linda cut a piece and raised a forkful.

She took a bite of pizza and looked at Blake. "You're right, the pizza is good. Anyway, I was born and lived in New York City until I was nine. Then my dad had a stroke and my mom wanted to move back to Puerto Rico, to Piletas. It's in the mountains, near Lares. She thought the clean mountain air there would be good for him." She took a sip of soda and continued. "That lace my mom was holding, it's called mundillo lace. It's all hand-made, from an area around Aguadillo. My grandmother is from a small village there, Moca, so when she married my grandfather they moved to Piletas where he was from but they brought the loom with them.

Blake toyed with his straw and took another bite of pizza. He closed his eyes for a moment to process all he just heard. "Okay, so your dad passed away two years ago. So how did you end up in the Valley?"

Linda sipped some soda and smiled. "Oh, that's easy. My sister Carmen, my mom mentioned her, she is three years older than me. Anyway, in Piletas, in the mountains of Puerto Rico, people get married very young. So, she fell in love and decided she wanted to get married. She was seventeen. But my mom wanted us both to have an education. So she figured she better get me out of there the first chance she could. Her brother, my uncle Luis, works at Hull Dye. So he arranged for us to get the apartment and got her a job at the dress shop. That is how we got here."

Blake looked at her closely. He was smitten with her. It was falling into place, the clear articulation of her speech, the soft refinements in the way she dressed and moved. He loved everything about her and started to think she was beyond his reach. "So, what does your mom do there?"

"She's a seamstress. She's really good with her hands. She can make anything. If you show her a dress you want she can just turn it inside out, look at the stitching and she can make it. She made the dress I'm wearing now." She broke off another slice of pizza and put it on his plate. "Eat. You're not eating. You've been listening to me talk for too long."

Blake smiled and lifted the slice. "So, what about the lace? Does she sell that?"

Linda finished chewing and wiped her mouth with a fresh napkin. "No, she doesn't sell the lace. She makes things mostly as gifts for babies or weddings."

"You know how to do that too, to run the loom?" he asked as he poured some soda into her glass.

"Yes," she responded, shaking her head slightly. "Not like my mom," she said proudly, "but I can do it. The loom that she was working on, my grandfather made that for her when she was little. Anyway," she said, feeling that she was talking too much again, "my mom likes it here because she can walk to work and we're on a bus line or train for New Haven, Bridgeport, Waterbury or the city. We like the apartment because it reminds us of New York with the fire escape out the window overlooking the river. We put our flowers and plants out there so they get lots of sun. And the wild flowers by the river, let's see, there are holly hocks and lavender, phlox and the Rose of Sharon and some others too. They're all so beautiful. And the trains, we like the trains."

Blake sat back, trying to piece it all together. There was a simple, peaceful cadence to her life that spanned a few blocks of Main Street. She looked beautiful sitting across from him in her ivory cloche over her chestnut hair and radiant skin framed by gold hoop earrings. "Where did your dad teach?"

She took a long sip of soda. "Columbia School of Music," she responded, stiffening herself against the back of the booth. "He was a professor of bassoon and associate professor of voice." She met Blake's eyes and saw his expression sink. She leaned forward and slid her soda to her side. "My dad had polio. He walked with crutches all his life and, you know, he couldn't really do much of anything physical with his legs. Everything was an effort for him. Then he had a series of strokes over a couple of years." Linda looked down at the table and shrugged her shoulders as her eyes watered despite her efforts to prevent that. "It was hard enough for him just to move, you know. So he studied really hard. He was actually a Latin teacher before he got all his music degrees. He spoke Latin fluently. Like we speak English, he spoke Latin, just like that."

"So how did he meet your mom if she's from Puerto Rico?"

Linda put her slice back on her plate and wiped her hands on a fresh napkin. She looked at Blake and managed a small smile. "My mom used to clean his office at Columbia. He was born here, in the city. His parents were Italian immigrants. So he would help her with her English and she would teach him Spanish and they started spending time together and they just fell in love. That was it. She used to call my sister Carmen and me her charquitos, her little puddles of the Mediterranean and the Caribbean. My mom's not educated."

Blake shook his head in amazement. "Wow, that's quite a story. I didn't even know they had professors of bassoon." It started to make sense to him, her confidence and diction, refined mannerisms and posture. He tried to suppress a sinking feeling as his eyes met hers. He thought she was out of reach so he may as well say what he wanted. He put his hand over hers and smiled at her. "You look really pretty tonight." He felt that he wanted to stay all night and listen to her talk and watch the way she lifted her eyebrows in animated conversation.

"Thank you." She moved her fingers into his and held his hand. She sensed his discomfort. "What about you? You let me do all the talking. You didn't say anything."

Blake squeezed her hand and smiled at her. "Sure I did. I said the white clam pizza was great. Don't you remember that?"

Linda laughed and locked his other hand into hers. She looked at his face, wanting to lean over and touch it, to brush his cheeks with the pads of her fingertips. "I remember that. And you were right. But tell me more."

Blake glanced at the wall clock, released his hands from hers and tied them in a knot in front of him. "Well, I'm not as interesting as you. In fact, the most interesting thing that happened to me was meeting you," he said softly, and felt his eyes melt into hers.

"Come on, don't be shy on me now. I remember those girls you were with the first night I met you. They were all paying attention to you. What about them? They were pretty girls."

"Yeah, they're pretty, but they're just school friends. I don't date anyone if that's what you mean."

"So, didn't you say you lived up by Pink House Cove?"

"Yes, do you know where that is?"

"No, is it far?"

"No, just a few miles up Route 34, above McConney's farm. It's real pretty up there. You can see the bend in the river and the hills of the Valley from my bedroom. My dad, he's a machinist at Teledyne. My mom, she used to work at a candy factory but that closed down. And I have an older brother but he lives in Canada now. He's against the war. He and my dad, they had big fights about it. So he just left one day."

"Oh, so it was his jacket that you came back to get that night?"

Blake smiled at her recollection. "Yeah, I wear it because it makes me feel closer to him. I don't have one of my own anyway. He gave it to me before he left."

"Wow, so that's pretty interesting. Do you miss him?"

"Yeah, I miss him a lot. He hasn't contacted us yet so we don't know where he is. We're waiting to hear from him. My mom's real upset. My dad, well, he's just mad at him."

"So, what are you doing after high school? Do you have any plans?"

Blake released his hands and twirled his straw. "Me? I joined the Marine Corps. I think I was going to get drafted anyway. I don't have any money for college and my grades aren't that great. So I joined on a delayed enlistment program. I leave sometime after next summer, in September. I didn't want to get stuck around here without a future so I figured I'd join and try to go to college when I get out."

Linda put her soda down and leaned over the table. "What," she whispered, "you're leaving?"

Blake leaned towards her and touched her hand, "Yes, but not for a while."

"So, what did your parents say?"

"Well, my mom, she's real upset. My dad doesn't really care. He just asked me why the Marines. My dad and me, we don't get along so well anyway. I'm really doing it for the education benefits later. Otherwise, I wouldn't be going to college at all."

Linda sat back against the booth and flicked her eyebrows. "Wow. How long did you join for?"

"Only three years. Not too bad. Then I'll be back. You'll be a senior in college by then." Blake saw her face go limp with disappointment. He glanced at the wall clock. "It will go by fast." He took the bill from the table and looked at her, "Maybe we should go now."

They stepped into the cold night. The clouds were gone and the sky was now dotted with brilliant stars. They walked two doors up to her apartment and stood beneath the naked light bulb in the hallway.

"Goodnight," he said. "You're going to smell like garlic all night," he warned, and laughed along with her.

"Goodnight. Thank you for everything. Will you come to

Vonete's soon?"

Blake started down the stairs. He turned as he walked down, "Sure, I'll stop in soon. You think Teddy and Frances mind?"

Linda stood at the top of the stairs and leaned against the door of her apartment. "No, they're fine with it," she said, waving her hand to him.

Blake opened the door and looked up at her. Under the naked light of the single bulb he wanted to tell her again how beautiful she looked. "Okay, see you soon. Thanks for the date," he said as he vanished into the street.

He walked quickly up the grade of Main Street, looked at the clock hanging from the jeweler's store and started to jog. He ran past the juke joints and barrel houses and rowdy saloons that lined the Barbary Coast, an eclectic collection of bars and taverns that housed all manner of vice and provocation, along upper Main Street. He ran past the dam and the Yale Boathouse, by Coon Hollow and up the river until he rounded Pink House Cove.

Car lights flashed on him as he crossed and walked up the steep hill, trying to catch his breath before getting home. He approached the house and heard loud music. He knew he was too late to get in without consequence. He walked into the small living room where his mother was seated in a worn wing chair. She spoke quietly so as not to disturb his father who was seated at the kitchen table spinning an album at the top of its volume.

"Blake, why so late?" she asked. "You know what happens."

He ripped off his coat and threw it over the couch. "I didn't realize it was this late," he said, pulling his shirt off so his father couldn't grab it.

"You're late again," his father growled, pushing himself from the table and wedging the chair against the wall to block Blake's path.

Blake tried to step over the chair. His mother stood in the living room with her hands folded with worry. The blow came, a heavy open handed slap to the side of his head that sent him over the chair and to the floor. His mother started to plead, lifting her hands to his father to try to stop him. Blake lay on the floor, using his foot to move the chair aside. The next blow came squarely on the center of his back, a blow so fierce it emptied his lungs of air. He gasped trying to catch his breath as his mother stood between him and his father. "It's okay, mom," he lipped, "I'm okay." His voice was but a whisper that could spare no air.

"No," his mother pleaded, "no more, Stanley. He's a good boy, no more. Sit down, sit down." His mother picked up the chair and set it in place.

"Someone has to teach that boy not to come home late again. You ain't going to teach him so I am," his father bellowed. He looked at her and gutted his unruly hair with his thick fingers.

Blake stood and turned to his mother. She shook her head and closed her eyes in despair at the sight of his red and welted face and back. She buried her face in her hands. "I'm all right," Blake said before entering his room and shutting the door. He turned on the light and stood before the dresser mirror. He examined his face and back. White finger marks from the blows were traced on his face and the skin on his back was raised and welted. He heard mumbled conversation from the kitchen, then the sound of a record, a woman's voice, a capella, filling the house. He shut the light as the house grew quiet except for the music. He lay in his bed with his hands folded under his head and trembled. The music jumped indelicately and he ran his fingers over the side of his face. He knew the redness would be gone in the morning. Finally, the soprano voice returned over the sound of violins for several measures until the rest, a rest that introduced calmness over the madness. And he heard the dark, peaceful sound of the cello and harp fill the house for a few measures, and again the woman's voice rising, sad and lustrous. She came to mind, the way her eyes darted with expression, how her gold earrings skimmed against her hair. He thought of her apartment, the loom in the corner and the piano against the wall. He remembered the view of the river and snow covered rail banks and the hulking B.F. Goodrich plant along the tracks in Shelton. He turned on his stomach and closed his eyes. The soft adagio of the strings soothed him while the beautiful sound of a woman's voice calmed the night.

"Hi, Teddy."

Teddy turned and put his arm over Linda's shoulder as she stepped up the curb. She hesitated on the sidewalk with him for a moment. "Hi, Linda, I didn't even see you coming. Just out here checking the weather, about ready to go back in and read the paper." He guided her with his hand on her back as they stepped to the door. "Don't really need much in this life to be happy, Linda. The Sentinel delivered on time, and a good cup of coffee. That's about it."

Linda slipped into the Palace and turned to him. "And how about a good card game?" she asked with a smile.

"Ah," he responded with a finger pointed to the heavens, "you know me too well, and a good card game."

"Hi, Linda," Frances sang out with an inflected tone. She muscled the last scoop of ice cream into the oblong sundae dish and placed it on the counter. Then, in a burst of enthusiasm, she leaned over the ice cream freezers and placed her two hands on the counter. "Oh, Linda!" she exclaimed, "you're all dressed up today. What's the occasion?"

Linda smiled at Frances and continued to the back of the candy counter. "Yearbook picture," she responded, slipping out of her coat and grabbing a crisp white apron from the stack.

Frances' smile was as broad as a field. "Wait, wait," she implored, rushing around the counter to deliver the sundae. "Turn," she said with a mesmerized grin, laying her hands on Linda's shoulders and spinning her slowly. "Oh," she continued, "these are gorgeous." She let her fingers ripple beneath the strand of pearls that hung delicately from Linda's neck. She sat back on an empty stool. "Where'd you get the pearls and matching earrings?" she asked. She leaned in to examine the fine oriental floral embroidery over the angora sweater. "Oh, that outfit is just beautiful, sweetheart. Teddy," Frances cried tersely, rising from the stool, "doesn't Linda look pretty today?"

Teddy lowered the Sentinel and looked over his reading glasses. He smiled slowly. "Linda always looks pretty to me. So I guess I missed it. Why are you all dressed?"

Linda slipped her apron over her pleated skirt. "Class picture," she said, tying it into a neat bow.

"Yes, Judy," Frances called out as she rushed to the grill. "Judy, Judy, Judy. We have to get carried away in here once in a while, right?"

"Isn't it kind of late for yearbook, Linda?" asked Teddy, still peering over his glasses.

Linda walked to the deep sink and carried on a mirror conversation with Teddy as she stacked the sundae dishes along the counter. "Yes, but I missed the class pictures last year. This was the final makeup day for new students or for people who were out that day." She tied her hair into a loose topknot and fastened it with a white barrette. She walked to Frances and Judy and touched the pearls and the earrings. "My sister sent these to me from Puerto Rico, just for the picture," she said proudly.

"They're lovely," remarked Judy, stepping forward to look at them closely.

Frances glanced at them again from the grill. "They're beautiful, Linda, just beautiful." Linda slipped into the white sneakers she kept under the counter and started to clean the tables.

Frances ambled through the late afternoon conversation with Judy and sent her away chattering with a lopsided bag just as the Greek stepped in rubbing his hands together. "Frances," he called out, clapping his hands together lightly while peering over the sandwich board to see what was still available. "All right, Frances," he said again, and hailed Teddy with a raised arm wave. The Greek's shoes were black, buffed to a shine, narrow toed and zippered on the side. He liked the feel of the soft calf's leather as it gripped his ankle and the sound rising from the sharp leather heels that could crack concrete. He held his hands over the grill to warm them. He scanned the window before calling out his order,

"Bacon, egg and cheese, Frances."

"Okay, Charlie," Frances responded, returning the phone to its cabinet, "it's going to be a minute or two." She scraped the grill down and snapped two eggs open, then winked at Linda and baited the Greek. "You got a minute?"

"Just a minute, then I have to go." He pivoted to the window, looking up Elizabeth Street and down Main, nervous energy racking his mind as he idled over the grill. The street beckons. He examined the knife blade crease he ironed in his jeans earlier. He doesn't sit until the evening, not before eight or so, because it wrecks the crease and puts unsightly accordion folds in the back of the knee, causing the hem to rise too high up on his shoes. He eyed the sandwich board again and noticed the cheese plate was empty. His voice dropped. "No American cheese,

Frances?"

Frances opened the under counter refrigerator door and peeled a slice from the stack. "No, Charlie, we got plenty of cheese, you just can't see it from there." The bacon and eggs shimmied and popped like bare feet on desert sand.

"Teddy Vonete," the Greek called out as he marched down the counter to Teddy's table. He spotted Linda behind the candy counter counting the day's receipts. "Linda," he rang out in serious tone, "you look nice today, Linda."

Linda nodded affirmatively as she counted out the last dollar and wrapped it in a paper band. "Thank you, Charlie," she said over a light smile and wrote the amount on the stack of bills.

Teddy sat back in his chair and closed the paper. "You stopped walking, Greek, you must be hungry," Teddy said pocketing his reading glasses. "So what do you hear?"

The Greek put on a serious face. He leaned on an empty stool without bending his knees. "I hear Teddy Vonete is cleaning up at the Elks." A smile broke over his face.

Teddy laughed and pulled himself out of the chair. "I don't think so, Greek. You sure you heard that on the street?" He tied his apron back on and carried his coffee cup to the deep sink.

The Greek's smile widened further. "That's the word, Teddy Vonete. Teddy Vonete is cleaning up." The Greek liked the way Teddy's name fell from his lips, clean and clear and rhyming, even if he had to appropriate Mr. Vonete's last name to make it work.

"All right," Teddy responded with a grin that couldn't betray the truth, "so I won a few good hands. So what else do you hear?"

"I heard the bank's taking the block across the street, all of it. Mary Jane says she's closing up, said she ain't waiting for them to kick her out."

Frances raised the wrapped sandwich above her head and reached for the phone, "All set, Charlie." The Greek backpedaled up the counter and took the sandwich along with a few napkins.

Teddy shrugged his shoulders, shaking his head side to side. His face sank with disappointment. He unbuttoned the cuffs of his white shirt and immersed his arms into the deep sink. "They're going to wreck this town," he called out to the Greek. "She'll be the fourth empty store. The more stores that close the fewer people come to shop. Pretty soon there's nothing left. Nothing wrong with these buildings, just need a little fixing up," he said, looking up from the deep sink. "What about B.F.? You hear they want to sell?"

The Greek stood at the door, measuring the traffic from three directions. "Rumor is they looking for a buyer, that's why they are fixing it up. Teddy Vonete, you're cleaning up, that's the word," he said on his way out. The Greek gave Frances a straight armed wave until she returned it, then he stepped to the sidewalk and disappeared, and the late afternoon became evening and the evening rolled into night.

"Okay, Blake, push now." Teddy guided the ladder

through the trap door until it cleared the floor, wrestling with its awkward weight until Blake climbed the basement stairs. "Now close the door so we don't fall through," he said with a face reddened with strain. Blake let the door bounce to a close and took the ladder from Teddy. He raised his eyebrows and smiled, "I lost a lot of good help falling through that door."

Blake lifted that ladder while Teddy guided it through the Palace to the temporary shelves over the mirrors. Linda stood tensely near the grill in a grimace expecting the worst. Slowly, through the parlor tables that were pushed to one side, they inched their way past the baskets waiting to have their green grass matted with jelly beans and bright yellow marshmallow chicks and peanut butter eggs and truffles and handsome white and chocolate bunnies.

Frances held a stirring spoon still in a bowl of melted chocolate set on the grill. "Atta boy, Blake, just go easy," she repeated. "All right," she said, turning to Linda, "now shut the window light and lock the door. Anyone comes to the window just tell them we're closed." She poured some chocolate into a tray of molds. "People come, you know?" she stated resolutely. "They're crazy. They see us in here and they think we're open." She held her arms out in disbelief and pointed to the high shelves. "Oh yeah, you could be way up near the ceiling and they'll be banging on the door. Even with the lights off, they still do it ... you know, shaking the door and trying to talk through the glass." She gave the pot a stir and let a smooth cord of chocolate fall from the spoon. "This is all set."

She took the pan from the counter and set it in a larger pan full of hot water that was set on the counter. "Okay now, Blake, how about we put on some music?"

Blake reached up to the radio and glanced at the small stack of eight track tapes. He gave Frances a perplexed look, "Radio or tapes?"

"Radio, those are mostly old tapes, mostly Sinatra," she said. "Nothing you would like."

Chocolate bunnies stacked three deep lined the counter at soldierly attention. Candy eyes filled a bowl waiting for their place in bunny orbit. Teddy set the ladder along the back wall and started to fill the baskets. Frances cut stretches of colored cellophane paper and stacked it in a neat pile on one of the tables.

Blake took a stool and turned to Linda. "So what do we do now?" He took a candy eye and popped it in his mouth. "I always liked to eat the eyes first," he said with a smile.

Linda reached in and popped one in her mouth too. "So do I. Okay, what's next, Fran?" she asked, taking another one.

"Okay... well... let's see," she responded, trying to sequence the work in her head. She continued to stack the sheets of cellophane while she spoke. "I guess you two can start putting the eyes and flowers on." She looked up at Teddy for assurance. "Teddy, they can start, right?"

"Start what?" he asked without bothering to look from the top of the ladder. "The eyes?"

"You're all set if we start, right?"

"Ready when you are," he said, climbing down.

Frances walked to the counter and dabbed the end of a lollipop stick into the melted chocolate. She moved her face close to the chocolate bunny's face, like an optometrist examining an eye, and applied the melted chocolate to the bunny. "It's easier if you put the chocolate on the bunny first. The eyes are too small to handle with the melted chocolate. You end up with chocolate all over your hands and eyes sticking everywhere but where you want them." She lifted the bunny and bagged it in a clear cellophane package. "Then, Blake, you and Linda can hand the bunnies to me. I'll set them in the basket and wrap them. Then you can get them up to Teddy. He lines them up." Frances ran her hands over her apron and looked around the Palace, thinking of anything she forgot before the bunny wrap began.

"What about the candy flower?" Linda asked, holding a large bowl of yellow and pink floret candy.

"Oh," Frances exclaimed taking one and dabbing it with chocolate. "They go right over the little basket," she said, placing the floret perfectly on an attentive rabbit.

"There, right below the paws?"

"That's it," said Frances, "that area right below the paws, that's the basket. It's not that clear in the mold but it's there." Frances glanced at Blake and pointed to the stack of aprons under the counter. "Maybe you should put an apron on."

Easter was the busiest time of the year in the Palace of Sweets. Tiered shelves set in the window were lined with

chocolate bunnies of all sizes and shapes, hollow and
solid, bleachers loaded with hares waiting to be whisked
away. Chocolate and white chocolate bunnies competed for
space in the crowded window with a very large jar of jelly
beans that rested in the corner. Children would write their
name on a small piece of paper with their guess as to the
number of jelly beans in the jar. The shelves were full and
lined with brimming Easter baskets tied with colorful
ribbons and covered in pink and yellow and blue
cellophane. Mothers toting big eyed children allowed a
hesitation in their fast pace to dream of the wonders of the
candy-eyed hares staring through colored wrappers. In the
center of the window display sat a huge, hollow chocolate
Easter egg decorated with candy ribbon and filled with all
the varieties of sweetness made at the Palace. The child
who most closely guessed the number of jelly beans won
the Easter egg.

To the left of the counter register was a large, colorfully
wrapped box that said `One Entry Each'. A pencil was tied
with a string to the box and several small white pads
littered the counter. On the Saturday before Easter,
around noon, when the shelves were stripped of anything
sweet by frantic last minute shoppers, Teddy would stop
everything and ask a customer to pick a name from the
box and make the happy call.

Linda arched her back and stretched her arms, then
dabbed a spot of chocolate on Blake's nose and placed a
candy eye on it. "Does your back hurt?"

Blake pinched the eye off his nose and ate it, "No, not so

much."

"Did you kids tell your parents you'd be here late?" Frances asked as she stapled another cellophane wrapper and surveyed the baskets that now filled the shelves above the mirrored walls.

"Yeah," Linda said, taking a sponge and cleaning off the counter of chocolate drippings, "I told her I'd be here late because we're dressing the baskets. She wanted to know what that meant. Now I can't wait for her to see all this."

Blake stepped back and crushed a few candy eyes under his feet, then bent over to pick up the rest of those that had fallen. "My mom knows," he said, glancing up at the clock. "It's better for me to get home after my dad falls asleep anyway." Blake fingered the last candy eye from the bowl and placed it in Linda's palm. "I'll help you with the floor if you agree to go."

Linda fingered the candy to her mouth and shook her head and said, slowly and deliberately, "I told you," she said slowly, "I can't dance."

Blake untied his apron and pulled it over his head. "What if I tell Frances and Teddy?"

"If you want to tell them, go ahead, but it won't change anything."

Teddy came down from the ladder and folded it carefully then laid it against the wall. "Well," he remarked, examining the shelves full of baskets, "that's a good job done."

Blake stepped to the floor and started to drag a table back into place. "That's okay, Blake." Teddy said, "We're going to mop the floor. We'll put the tables back in the morning,"

"Frances," Blake asked, sidling up to her, "what do you think of this? She won't go to the prom because she says she can't dance."

Frances lifted a box of jellybeans from the floor and set them on a chair. "Linda," she said, turning her hands in disbelief, "what do you mean, you don't know how to dance? Everyone can dance."

Linda dried her hands. She filled a glass with ice and squirted cherry syrup into it, then set it under the Coke dispenser and stirred it vigorously as the soda filled it.

"I don't know how to dance," she said, slipping a straw into the soda and taking a drink. "I know it sounds funny," she said with a laugh, "but I never learned. My dad couldn't dance." She took another drink and handed the soda to Blake, "I just never learned to dance."

Frances ran the deep sink and started filling it with the few remaining dishes that needed washing. "Look, Linda," she said over the sound of the water filling the sink, "it's your senior prom. You can't worry about dancing, that's easy. All the kids go." She lifted herself from the sink and flicked her wrist. "Don't worry about dancing," she said with enthusiasm, "it'll be nice. All the girls have gowns and have their hair all done up with flowers and curls and the boys all have on tuxedos and boutonnieres. You can stop in to show us." she said, dropping her hands back into the sink. "Everyone stops in here. All the kids come in, right, Teddy?"

Teddy leaned over the counter and took a resting breath. He caught Linda's eye in the mirror and smiled at her reassuringly. "Lots of the kids stop in, Linda. We have our camera and we take pictures." Then he turned and nodded his head confidently, "You can dance, Linda, right here, now. Frances," he commanded, "put a tape on."

Frances quick-stepped over to the radio and turned it off. "Teddy," she said, taking the stack of tapes in her hand and shuffling them like a thick stack of cards, "Teddy, we could find a song on one of these. I don't know, there's so much to pick from."

Teddy walked over and scanned the tapes, slipped one in, and turned on the tape player. "Summer Wind," he said with certainty as the song started. "It's got a beat, could be a two-step or a four, depending on what you feel comfortable with." He let the song play through as he spoke. Linda and Blake sat on stools and watched him in the center of the floor. He took his palm and placed it over his stomach and started to move, then reached for Frances and started to rock their hips without moving their feet, talking to Linda all the while, describing the beat and counting out, one, two in a slow and measured beat. Then he took Frances in a four beat and glided her around the floor until she spun out of her apron, and set it on the counter. Then she grabbed Blake's hand and rocked him in a stationary moment, until the music stopped.

Teddy extended his hand to Linda and guided her to the dance floor. "Come on, Linda. We can't dance like you kids do, but this is real dancing."

Linda shook her head in embarrassment. "I don't know Teddy, I..."

"Yes, you can," Teddy said, placing his arm around her waist and clasping her hand in his. Then he dropped her hand and waist. "Take your apron off," he said, gathering it up in a ball from her hands and throwing it to Blake. "Ready now?"

Linda flicked her eyebrows up and bit her lower lip. "I guess, she said, then jumped back. "No, wait," she said, and undid her topknot and let her hair fall to her shoulders, then shook her head to loosen it. "Okay," she said with a laugh, placing her hand over Teddy's shoulder and clasped his hand, "I'm ready. Now what do I do?"

"You just listen to me," Teddy instructed, standing her before him like a statue. "When the music starts, we're not going to move our feet. Put all the movement in your hips, to loosen them up. We'll get to the feet after."

Frances started the tape again. "Don't go too far, Blake. You're my partner," she called out as the music started.

Teddy started moving his hips to the music, counting a slow one, a hesitation, two. He put hand pressure on Linda's hip to sway with him and started to move his head to a four count. "You feel the beat?" he asked, "It's all in the base line."

"Yes, I hear it," Linda said, looking directly at Teddy, too frightened to look at Blake or Frances, "this is fine, I just can't move my feet."

Teddy winked at her and started to move her hips more deeply into the beat. "We'll be moving feet in a second."

Then he released her and stepped away. "Okay," he said, walking towards the tape player to start the song again. "By the time the song finishes this time, you'll be dancing with Blake."

The song started and Teddy stepped off with a short and slow two step. Linda laughed and looked down. "No, don't look at your feet. Keep your eyes up," Teddy said. "Never look at your feet. Just keep stepping, just like you're walking, that's all, just like a walk," he said calmly. They danced through the open area beside Blake and Frances. Teddy tapped Blake's shoulder and switched partners, floating away with Frances.

Blake faced Linda in the center of the Palace. He put his hand around her waist as she draped her arm over his shoulder. Teddy walked to the tape player to start Summer Wind again. Blake brushed Linda's hair over her shoulder and looked at her closely, clasping her hand in his. "You look beautiful," he said quietly. He felt himself tremble with excitement that she was there, in his arms for the first time. His lips were parted, as if wanting to meet hers, to taste the sweetness of her mouth right there, in that instant, before the moment turned away.

"She looks beautiful tonight, Blake. Doesn't she look beautiful, Teddy?" Frances asked with dreamy smile. "Start the music."

The music started with the instrumental introduction. Blake tightened his arm around her waist and squeezed her hand. "Just relax and follow my lead," he said.

Linda reeled back and peeled a delighted crescendo. She

laughed out loud, too self-conscious to continue. Her head canted to the right as a bale of hair, shimmering and iridescent in shades of red and sorrel and brown, pulled forward and back again. "Come on," Blake said, laughing but trying to keep his composure. He stepped off and felt her foot land on his, then slip off just as quickly.

"I'm so sorry," she said, her face serious again.

"It's nothing, don't worry," Blake said, feeling her move with him rhythmically. "Just keep moving, just like walking. You're doing great." She stepped on his foot again and looked down at her feet. Then she stopped moving.

"Can't stop," Blake said, continuing to move.

"Keep going, Linda. You got it," Frances called out as she spun by with Teddy.

Linda started to move again and tapped Blake's shoes against her toes, then looked down.

"Can't look at your feet," Teddy said, watching them move. Then he stopped dancing and stood beside Linda as she continued to sway to the music. "Look, if you look down, you should be looking at your skirt because by the time you finish a step your hem is just getting there, so it's okay to look at your skirt. Got that?"

Linda shook her head and started moving her feet again. Blake pulled her body closer to his, dropping his hand to the base of her back, resting the heel of his palm over the cleave of her buttocks. He applied pressure to her lower back, hoping to better control her motion. He was thrilled to feel of her body so close to his. She was certain that nothing ever felt this good before this moment.

"That's it," Blake whispered, watching her glance down. "Just like walking, just keep your eye on the hem." The skirt flowed freely and lightly to the music, cresting and flaring, etching the moment into their memories, counter to the movement of their feet.

They raised their eyes and looked at each other closely, saying nothing, moving to the music for minutes, unaware of anything around them except each other. When the music stopped they stood motionless in a moment that was full and satisfying and immeasurable. His knees felt weak. Her breath was shallow.

There, deep in the of the Palace of Sweets, between chocolate bunnies with candy eyes, before the two swan shaped fountains, among the three, two handed registers, in the warm interstices of callow bodies reflecting in aged mirrors, two young hearts swelled and simmered in a walk they call dance.

The heavy glass door opened slowly pushed by a gaggle of small girls. Their eyes, widened with relief from July's heat provided by the large, floor standing air conditioner, darted around the Palace in search for a place to settle. They stood, clover-like, in the center of the mosaic tile floor, between the counter stools and the candy case. Frances stepped out from behind the grill and folded her hands into her apron, bending slightly at the waist, "And can I help you girls?"

A towheaded wisp of a girl palmed hair from her face and waved a damp index card before Frances. "We're the hopscotch champions."

"Oh," Frances exclaimed with delight, "the hopscotch champions! We've been waiting for you girls."

The hopscotch champions entered the reflective walls of the Palace of Sweets with prideful joy. They are the first of a long and enthusiastic stream of winners that get free sundaes when the oppressive July heat stretches the day, like hot taffy, to interminable lengths and delivers sweated playground champs of every variety. Checkers and hopscotch, pet shows and hoola hoops, doll contests and wiffle ball, the entire team. And jump rope and double-dutch. They came, all of them, the crazy hat winners too, skipping in or huddled in shy clusters, these children of furnace builders, mechanics and welders, riggers, merchants, toolmakers, postmen and seamstresses. Their names were printed in the Evening Sentinel and sometimes their pictures appeared, too. And if they brought the article in with them Teddy taped it up on the mirrored wall with great fanfare for all to see, at least through the perpetuity of the endless summer days.

No one recalls when it started, this summer ritual. For sure, it was decades ago, when life moved at a slower pace and childhood was shortened by the call for human capital to the rolling fields that filled the street markets with fresh produce and the silos with wheat for storage, warm with summer's heat, through the long winters. Then, along the banks of the Housatonic and Naugatuck, factories grew and the whirl of belt driven grinders and hydraulic casters filled boxcars with crafted metals and rich fabrics. Proud buildings of brick and stone and milled wood rose and stores opened on the street level and people moved into the walk-up apartments above and sat by their windows as the world passed below. Slowly, the steam engines pulled the boxcars from their moorings along the riverbed and north through the stately Berkshires and west over the vast plains of the republic and southeast to the great ports of the Atlantic and finally, to the end of the rails in the west.

It was 1905, soon after the new century rounded the turn of the gun lap on its run to the millennium, that Mr. Vonete, a Greek immigrant with a wide and generous face, opened the Palace of Sweets. In those days he sat in the raised window spinning confections from heated copper kettles. And soon full and laden trolleys gave way to lumbering buses and horse drawn carriages to cars. But still, the window on Main Street became a destination and a reward. And before the age of the refrigerator his deep tubs of ice cream filled sundae dishes with whipped cream squeezed decoratively from a leather piping bag. Formal of attire, he worked in a white shirt and tie and dress pants protected by a stiff, heavy white apron, and served each sundae with a long spoon and a glass of water delivered on a tray.

But soon trolley tracks and cobblestones were paved over with glinting black diamonds as ghostly wafts of asphalt steam carried the memory to vapor. And trucks carried goods over the paved roads and the endless freight tracked through the Valley with less frequency. Still, the residents kept the day by the locomotive's horn and factory whistles, an elegy to the past that paced their lives even while the asphalt pulled them from the majestic crown of mountains. Main Street, thick with tractor trailers and cars along its grade, began to empty of dwellers, no longer bound by train, trolleys and boats. And the merchants followed to new and gleaming malls with spacious, lined parking lots. And it happened over decades, year turning upon year, the shoulders of these buildings began to stoop with neglect and abandon until the thought occurred that redemption could be found in a wrecker's ball.

But they came, these summer champs, arriving in multiples of three or four or more, spinning themselves into sweet delirium at the counter stools. They chatted and giggled and smiled brightly over milkshakes and floats and banana splits, cackling and thickening their presence, ambling confidently between their stories of conquest until Vonete's resembled a rookery during the feeding cycle.

Sometime after the war, somewhere between 1948 and 1954, no one can recall with certainty, just after a storewide privilege sign from Coca Cola was put up on the building's façade that said 'Vonetes Palace of Sweets,' Teddy installed a small grill along the counter. It was adjacent to the raised window in an effort to maintain the customer base because iceboxes gave way to refrigerators and supermarkets stocked ice cream in cardboard boxes. And with that small innovation, the commerce continued and the conversations and smiles flowed without interruption over the years because he and Frances faced the customers over the little grill or the lipstick-red Coke dispenser or the heavy tubs of ice cream or the deep sink. And the confections stacked in neat and tidy rows beneath the glass of the walnut case beckoned them all to linger and talk and taste.

"Okay, girls, just have a seat," Frances said, turning from them and pointing with the spatula. "You can sit on the stools or at the tables, wherever you like."

They returned over and over again, the young boys and girls, to the spinning stools and dizzying array of confections and the warm, gracious smile of Frances and avuncular kindness of Teddy. Eventually, the girls came in to seek employment, after school or during the summer, with time off for every activity in their busy lives. They came in alone or in pairs, the aspirants, brimming with enthusiasm to work at the apex of Main Street.

But they didn't stay long; none of them did. They were young and fearless, with hair of golden light and red sunsets and evening vespers of shimmering darkness, all tied in ribbons and barrettes with wispy tendrils. No, they didn't stay, they couldn't. Their lives were too rich and their futures so full of promise apart from the circular, dizzying motion of the Palace of Sweets. So they rotated through like carousel horses, young and colorful, with names like Chubby and Diddy, Pookie and Cookie, finely painted and of delicate structure, in constant motion. They were lithe and weightless, stringed charmers in nearly full blossom, spinning and laughing and chattering with the enthusiasm of youth, until one day they molted into womanhood and slowly stepped away from the swell, glancing back longingly into the faded mirrors of the Palace of Sweets.

The playground supervisor came in and sat the girls at the counter. Frances returned to the grill while Linda took care of the hopscotch champs. She set the sundaes before them and bantered with them about the summer and potholders they left momentarily unfinished at the playground. The girls strained on the stools to lean over the counter and lifted clouds of whipped cream with chocolate shots into the air. Then, leaning back, awkwardly fisting the long sundae spoons like hammers, they scraped the sides of the glass dishes and watched the toppings rise from the bottom like deep-sea treasures. The bashful ones polished off a hot fudge sundae, two banana splits, and a dusty rose. As they left Teddy took the newspaper photo from the supervisor and taped it with great fanfare to the mirror while making claim to know the four newest celebrities in the Valley.

Teddy scraped down the grill as the last of the customers trekked out into the humid evening. The Greek strode by the window, rapping on it twice and calling out Teddy's name with a lingering tone that could be heard as he passed out of sight. His gait was firm and rhythmic, his purpose unquestioned. No time to hesitate, not for the Greek, as the summer night, alive with restless heat, spun its dark top over the slick surface of shadowed desire. Along the riverbanks and sidewalks lined with porches, streetlights pandered, offering halos of light when the day's heat condensed to dew. They called his name out of the darkness, from crowded stoops and flung open windows, and he responded with a characteristic straight handed wave and a trailing voice. He stopped for the street girls with pendulous halters and short pants that started just above their buttocks. He hesitated just long enough to fill his head with their scented hair and the touch of their soft hands. And behind their smiles the Greek sensed that virtue's kind face and sweet voice was painted with diaphanous heat.

Linda reached up and turned off the radio. Water draining from the deep sinks pillowed the sound of the last spoons being stacked in silver canisters.

"All set?" His voice seemed to come out of nowhere, suddenly, like an unexpected fragrance.

She turned quickly and stepped from the candy counter, touching his hand and pulling off her apron. "Yes," she said, "done just now."

Frances came from the bathroom with her apron in her hand. She reached down and turned off the large air conditioner. "Blake," she asked, "still hot out there?"

Blake spun a stool with his finger. "Yeah, very" he responded as Linda sat beside him. She let her hair down, complaining that it was too tight, then fastened it up again in a loose top knot.

Teddy turned off the window lights and tapped Blake's shoulder. "How's Blake?"

"Too hot, Teddy," Blake said, spinning his stool to

Teddy. "Too hot, but it's nice in here."

"Yeah, you know, with the air pumping, keeps it real cool in here." Teddy clapped his hands and walked to the back of the counter. "So," he said, pointing to his apron, "since I seem to be the only one working, how's about a nice walking sundae? What'll it be tonight?"

Blake turned to Linda, "You hungry?"

"She had nothing all day. We were busy," Frances interjected.

"How was work?" Linda asked as she turned to Blake.

"Hot." He spent the days landscaping and repairing fences and building walls of dry stone and cinder block. He was lean and muscled. At the end of the day he went to the track to run and sprint, just as the recruiters advised. Then he showered and came here, to Vonetes, with his hair wet combed and his skin burnished, to walk her home.

And every night Frances or Teddy, whoever was aproned last, packed a sundae for them to share because the walk became an event full of quiet conversation and tightly bound hands and laughter that lilted into the alcoves and through the Green on Elizabeth Street. Their future was tenuous knowing that, shortly, these moments would still to memories. Her heart shuddered that he would return for a burial. He was certain that she would find another, smarter, with an education and a promise of a better life.

"Are you hungry?" he asked.

"Feel like hot fudge?"

"Sure," Blake responded.

They walked up Elizabeth Street, by the small J.C. Penney store and the tailors, the Elk's Club, and beyond the cigar store and dormant opera house. Often they sat on the wooden benches on the Green like indolent cats, dreaming lazily into the starlight and the life they promised each other.

This evening they climbed the wide, stone steps of St. Mary's and sat beneath its soaring steeple. Blake arched his back and ran his eyes up the brick until it tapered and disappeared from view. The white oak in the rectory yard, its leaves heavy and pendulous, washed over them with an embracing shadow.

"We have to eat fast," Linda said, handing Blake the sundae lid coated with whipped cream and chopped nuts stuck to it. "It's really starting to melt."

Blake scraped the lid with his finger and licked it clean. He watched her dig into the ice cream before he spoke, "Uh, don't I get a spoon too?"

Her eyes opened in wide surprise. "Sorry," she said, handing him a spoon. She threaded her arm through his and leaned her head against his shoulder. Cars and buses rolled by below them as walkers, distracted by their laughter, searched to find them in the darkness. In the small, decorative cardboard container of a take-out sundae, life was rich indeed.

"I think," Blake said, filling his spoon with melting ice cream and nuts, "you're eating all the hot fudge."

Linda ran her spoon to the bottom of the cup and lifted out a wad of fudge dripping with ice cream and nuts. "Oh, no," she said, feeding it into his mouth, "you just have to know where to look."

Blake reciprocated, insisting that she eat it despite her protest that he should. They laughed and whispered until the sound of the cardboard produced only empty spoons and a playful duel for the last taste. Blake reached into the bag that sat between his legs and handed her several napkins. "Frances," he said with a broad smile. "She never forgets anything."

Linda took a napkin and arched her head up as she wiped her mouth. "Teddy made the sundae. Remember, he said he was the only one working."

Blake cleaned up and bagged the spoons and cup. "Yeah, but Frances put the spoons and napkins in the bag because she says Teddy doesn't move too fast."

"You're right," Linda said with her neck still bent back to see the steeple. The glitter imbedded in the night sky seemed magnified, brightened by the stillness of its distended torpor. "Tonight the sky reminds me of Piletas."

Blake looked at her, then cast his eyes up. "Are the stars bright in Piletas?"

Linda shook her head and raised her hand up. "Oh, yes. There are no streetlights there and not many houses. So on a clear night, it's like you can touch the stars. And when the moon is full it's so bright it's like daylight."

"Really?"

"Really," she said, leaning her head on his shoulder again. "You know," she said, "this is a great church." She leaned over and kissed his cheek. "I can't wait for choir to start again."

Blake leaned into her and put his arm around her shoulder. "You miss it during the summer, don't you?"

"Yes," Linda sighed, "because during rehearsal, when we're singing and the church is empty, it's like your voice travels forever. Maybe we just sing louder when it's empty but the voices seem to fill the church, then echo back. I get goosebumps because the voices sound so beautiful and the church is so pretty. And up in the loft, it's like you're on top of the world."

Blake kissed her hair and squeezed her. "So when does rehearsal start up?"

"Right after you leave. The second Tuesday in September."

"So, I guess that's good, right?" Blake volunteered. "It'll keep you busy. You're all set with school?"

"Uh-huh," she managed quietly. "Oh, yeah, I forgot to tell you. I spoke to the advisor. It's all set. They accepted me as a music education major concentrating in piano."

"So you have to perform on piano?"

"Yes."

"And what about singing? Do they know you sing?"

She untangled their arms and sat up and looked at him. "Sort of," she said, "I said I would like to minor in voice. But I told him I haven't vocalized in a while, no scales or anything. That's real bad."

"But you'll be singing in the choir, so what's the difference?"

"Oh," Linda said with wide eyes, "it's a lot different.

Here, we practice together. You know, for most of the people in the chorus, this is all the training they get. It's more for fun, because they like to sing, than for anything else. But at school, before a jury of other music majors or the faculty, it's graded. I mean, they have to approve the music and you have to practice it during lessons at the school. I'd be doing scales every day and diction and breathing technique. You can't do it right unless your heart's in it."

Blake turned her face up to his and looked at her closely. He ran his finger along the bridge of her nose. "You know, I think you get prettier when you talk about singing. It's like, your eyes sparkle and you get all excited."

Linda smiled and tightened her hand over his. "Well, besides you, it's my favorite thing in the world." She leaned her face into his as Blake fluttered his lips over her cheeks. "Penny for your thoughts," she said mischievously.

"Not thinking of anything."

"Come on. You're thinking of something."

Blake turned to her and smiled. "Did Teddy ever tell you that he is friends with Sinatra?"

Linda snuggled closer and wrinkled her nose, "No, are you serious? Teddy never said anything about Sinatra."

Teddy never said anything about Sinatra. The autographed photo just hanged at Vonetes on the wall beside the menu board that hadn't changed in decades. Sinatra was just another friend, no different from his other friends with exotic nicknames, all, it has been said, raconteurs of sorts, weaving stories of questionable veracity in the smokefilled card-playing rooms of the Elk's Club.

"Yeah, it's true. That picture of Sinatra that's hanging in Vonete's, it says 'To Teddy, Remember the Good Times, Frank.' Teddy was best friends with Sinatra's first manager, guy named Tony Consiglio from New Haven. I think his family has a pizza place or something in New Haven, Sally's. Anyway, Teddy hung out with Sinatra, would go to the city with him when Frank was performing or when he came to New Haven to have pizza at Sally's."

"Wow, that's awesome. He never said a word about that. I'll have to ask Teddy. So," Linda said again, "you still didn't tell me what you were thinking. I know you weren't thinking of Sinatra a minute ago, that was just a diversion. Come on, penny for your thoughts."

"Okay," he relented. "I was wondering what's going to happen to us."

She placed her hands over his cheeks. "Nothing, nothing's going to happen to us. I'm going to wait right here. And you're going to come back and go to college just like you said you would and I'm going to take voice lessons and we are going to live happily ever after."

Blake managed a smile, looked down at the steps and shook his head, "You're going to college, Linda. You're going to meet lots of new people. I'll be far way. Anything can happen." Blake clasped his hands and turned to her. "I don't want to kid myself. The last year has been the best of my life. But anything can happen."

She pulled his face to hers and laid her lips gently over

his. "Nothing is going to happen, Blake. You know I love you. I'm going to be right here, singing in this church and waiting for you to come home."

Blake knotted his lips and shrugged his shoulders. "I don't know. That's easy to say now because we're together. But once I leave, who knows. I mean, for you, it's like a whole new world." Blake looked away from her and shrugged his shoulders with resignation. "You know, sometimes things just happen even if you don't intend them to."

"No," she said with certainty, "I know. I don't know what else to say. But I know. You'll see."

Blake turned to her and smiled wistfully. "I hope you're right." He stood, took her hands and raised her from the steps. "I guess it's time to go."

They walked down Cottage Street, by porches filled with quiet conversations of people sitting on chairs or steps. Large Victorian homes on small lots lined the streets in tight, neat rows. Autos parked against the curb recalled the days when factory whistles prodded lunch-pail toting men to walk faster as the day broke over the Valley. They turned down Caroline and walked by the row houses hugged tightly to the crest of the road just before its descent to Main, worn cobblestones glistening in the moonlight.

"This part of the street is so neat." Linda whispered, "How come they never paved it?"

"I don't know," Blake responded with a smile. "I just figured because it's so narrow they didn't want any cars going down it. It makes the car shake all over the place."

Linda flicked her eyebrows up excitedly, "So, when you come back we can ride down it."

"Sure. That'll be fun."

Blake turned and held her by the waist. He leaned his forehead against hers and smiled as their noses touched and her hands clasped around his neck. In the distance, just before the single trestle that bridged the Naugatuck River, the water, rising and falling in a gentle wash with the Atlantic tide, skirted Hogs Island and eased New England's ascent from the briny salt of the tidal marshes.

The lore of the Valley held that from here, at the crest of Caroline inlaid with cobblestone, before it drops to Main, the faded echo of the caulker's mallet could be heard pounding layers of cotton and oakum into ship joints built in the Derby harbor. Even now, in the humid stillness of the summer night with all sound baffled by the heavy air, the call of "frame up" ghosted the wharf with unnerving clarity. Down river, in Milford, where the rivers joined beyond Hogs Island, the common loon calls from its nested refuge.

Before the final sound of the beveler's maul scuffed over the rounded lips of cobblestone on Caroline Street, like the distant pounding of trunnels being hammered into place centuries ago, Linda felt the assuring thud of Blake's heart against her breast.

"Promise you'll come back," she whispered, taking his hand and lifting her face to his.

"Promise," he said, pressing his lips to her cheek.

And so it went on, the days turning upon each other and the leaves of the beech trees hinting to yellow as the summer aged. But the Valley, throbbing with the needs of each season, now watched the orchards sprout their fruits and the fields yield rolling acres of lettuce and corn, wheat and barley, while the foundries and factories heaped rails cars and trailer trucks full of product destined for every port and rail yard of significance throughout the nation. This commerce continued to drive the lives of the factory men and women as they pressed the pulse of the work that determined their sustenance from day to day and week to week at the hands of owners who were no longer closely tied to the Valley.

"Hey, Flip, what's doing? How are things at the shop? Keep hearing B.F. is thinking of selling out," Frances asked as she came to the back of the counter and guided the melted bacon fat to the grill drain. She bent over and squinted at the flame, working it until it glowed at just the right height and shade of blue. "Saw Joey yesterday," she offered, "starting to look better, like the therapy's working,"

"Yeah, I heard he's coming along pretty good," responded Flip. "He was down to the club the other night but I wasn't there. I don't know how these rumors start, Frances. I did hear they lost money the last few years but turned it around. We've been working overtime installing sprinklers throughout the plant and tying twelve inch pipes into the canal as a backup water supply. They're investing in the plant. They dusted off the plans Blumenthal's had for the canal water before old man Blumenthal sold out to B.F. right before he died."

Teddy snapped the lid on the coffee and handed it to him. "All set there, Flip."

Frances turned to the mirror and fastened her hair up into a French twist. Then she secured her apron with a fast tug at the bow.

"See you tomorrow. Tell Joey I said hello if he comes in again, Fran."

"Oh sure, Flip," said Frances, "He'll be in again."

"Okay," Frances called out to the clutch of customers gathered at the grill. "Who's up next on the hit parade?" She clapped her hands over her head like a string of firecrackers bursting with enthusiasm "Okay, Charlie, what's up today, Charlie? Flip, did you want something from the grill?"

Flip laid his arm over the counter and watched Frances wrap a stack of sandwiches. An amused grin lifted his rubbery face. "No, Frances, you got it all wrong. I'm just trying to pay so I can get out of here." He turned to the customers, opening his arms and spreading his large, meaty palms, "Oh brother, I don't know if I'm coming or going in this place."

Frances rippled with laughter. "Just a little coo-coo today, Flip. Nothing serious, you know?" She slapped the toaster back down again. "Gerry, you want it burnt, right?"

"Right, Fran," was the response from the back of the crowd.

"Coming to the Elk's tonight?" Flip asked as Flip excused himself through the crowd, "Well, maybe I'll catch you tomorrow."

Teddy watched Flip walk down Main Street towards the flats. Across the street, Leon worked the awning of Hubbell's with a dizzying twirl, lowering its scalloped cloth to the gracefully curved window that wrapped the block in delicate beveled glass. Teddy stepped further out into the curb and strained his neck to the narrow canopy of blue sky stretched over the buildings.

The days lumbered on until the feel of the evening touched a slight chill to the skin and hinted that the earth was tilting far from the summer solstice and further from the Valley.

The parking lot of Jimmy's of Savin Rock was an open landfill of discarded containers of French fries, fried clams, hot dogs and slick wads of cocktail and tarter sauce. Between rows of cars, people high-stepped through the garbage, dodging discarded food and trash being dropped from car windows. Customers snaked in long lines parallel with the open air grill. Rows of hot dogs waiting to be split lined the grill in smoky regiments. Behind the grill, countermen bellowed unintelligible orders to workers in back manning the fryolaters and breading stations. White T-shirts clung like wet gauze over their sweated bodies. Woodmont Point curled its sandy belly into Long Island Sound like the lone vein of a pinwheel. A flaming orange sun floated languorously over the water, casting glinting diamonds into squinting eyes.

With their arms full they walked and ate and talked, rubbing arm to arm and shoulder to shoulder, punctuating the salted air with soft talk and quiet laughter until they sat at the edge of the dry sand. Blake stopped and put the containers down, then kicked his sneakers off. "Can we sit here for a while?" He reached down and untied her sneakers as she plied them off and sat facing him, her face illuminated in the flaming sunset.

Linda smiled broadly. "Ahh," she exclaimed, "the sand is cold." She lifted her shoulders to the chill.

Blake raised his eyebrows in agreement. "Sand cools down in late August." He took her hands as she nudged herself closer to him, straddling her legs over his. Warm flecks of sun glinted in her eyes.

Linda clasped her hands around his neck and traced his face with her eyes. "You're too quiet," she said softly, brushing his cheek with her lips and laying her head on his shoulder.

He lifted her arms from his neck and distanced herself away, then placed his hands on her face and ran his finger over the bridge of her nose. "I just want to look at you this close," he said softly. He moved his hands to her barrettes and fumbled with them.

"Here," she said, reaching up and releasing the chestnut silk from its bindings. "Let me help." He took her hair into his hands and gazed at her for a long, silent moment.

"Penny for your thoughts," she whispered, putting her finger to his lips and tracing its bud.

"My thoughts," he asked, casting his eyes into the sand, "I think we're running out of time."

She shook her head in agreement and let a handful of sand fall between her fingers. "It's like an hourglass running out of sand."

Blake put his hand under her chin and guided her eyes into his. "I don't want to scare you or anything, but I want to say a few things, things that I never said before."

Linda wiped her eyes and laid her hands into his. The early evening air stilled for a moment, as the scent of summer lingered above the seriousness of the moment.

"I want you to know that, no matter what happens to me, or to us, I want you to know that you are, or you were, whatever it is, the very best thing that ever happened to me." He lowered his head into his chest to regain his composure.

"Please." Linda asked, laying her face along his. "Please don't say anymore."

Blake's throat tightened to a knot. He wiped his eyes and looked at her briefly before shaking off her request. "No," he said, struggling through in a weak and cracking voice. "No, this is too important." He raised his eyes to hers again and spoke haltingly. "I want you to know that I never thought anyone like you would fall in love with someone like me, that this whole year has been a dream, something that I never deserved. And that I love everything about you. That I love the color of your eyes and the feel of your hair on my skin, and the way it shines in the sunlight, like right now. That from the first time I spoke to you, the day I came back for my jacket, that I loved to even watch the way you speak, to watch your lips move. That I know I'll never love anyone like this in my life. You mean everything to me."

She buried her face in his neck and cried loudly, her body shaking, no longer able to hide her sadness. He leaned his face on her shoulder and cried along with her, locking her firmly against his body in a long embrace. After several minutes of stillness, when her body stopped shuddering and the tears were wiped away, he released her from his arms and guided her hair back from her face and put his cheek against hers and managed a small smile. "No matter what, Linda, no matter if I'm dead or injured or if you find someone else at college and you have to break up with me, it's okay, because I was so lucky to have all this time with you. You made me so happy."

A light smile broke over her sad face as a cool wind salted her skin to a thousand points. "Can we go?" she asked, burying herself close to him again.

Blake brushed his lips over her hair. "Sure," he said, helping her untie her legs from his, then he lifted her from the sand.

She stood and shook her legs awake. He brushed her bottom with a firm hand.

"Where do you want to go?"

"Home."

He looked at her quizzically, "Home? It's just after eight."

"I know. My mom went to my uncle's. We can be alone."

A shaft of light from the hall bulb illuminated the living room. She closed the door behind them and stood motionless in his arms as a bright river moon washed lace shadows over the room. "Don't be nervous." she whispered below the moonlight. "She won't be home. They play cards late."

Blake put his hands on her shoulders and allowed his hands to drop along the form of her body until he held her waist. "You're sure?"

"I'm sure. Besides, my uncle's brakes squeak real bad. You can hear him stopping a mile away."

Blake smiled and opened his eyes wide, "No sneaking up with those brakes?"

Linda raised her eyes to his and exhaled audibly as he lowered his lips to hers, "No," she whispered, walking him into her moonlit bedroom washed with the river breeze.

Blake moved his hands to her hair and let it fall, strand by silky strand, through his fingers. He broke their embrace and looked at her closely with eyes that wanted to stay fastened to her forever. He wanted to remember her like this, in soft moonlight, glowing with youthful passion. He cupped her face in his hands and routed his lips over her cheeks, as if to impart the memory of her beauty into his own flesh. "I love you."

She rolled her lips to his. "I know you love me," she said. She moved away from him and drank in the softness of his eyes as she traced his lips with her fingers and rested them at the center. "And I love you just as much." She stepped back into him and took small bits of his lips between her teeth before falling into a deep kiss.

Blake released his arms from her back and wedged his hands between their necks. She inched back as he opened her blouse and cupped her breasts in his hands, rolling his palms over her flesh. Then he reached down and fumbled with her pants. "I can't get that button," he said in a tone that begged for help.

"I only have a few weeks," he said under a soft smile."So could you help?"

"Sure," she said confidently. She slipped out of her blouse and stood before him in a creamy camisole that hung delicately from her shoulders. She reached down and unbuttoned her pants and let them drop to the floor with a few moves of her hips and legs, then looked at him. "So how about you, or am I the only one that has to undress?"

Blake laughed, "No," he said, slipping off his shirt and letting his jeans drop to the floor. He looked at her longingly in the pale light. Golden moonlight reflected from the river into her eyes. "You're so beautiful."

"No, Blake." she whispered as she stepped into his embrace, "You're the beautiful one."

She put her face into his neck and sucked in a long, deep breath, filling herself with his scent. She draped her hands over his shoulders, clasping them around his neck with graceful abandon. She felt the silk of her camisole slip effortlessly over her skin as they slipped into a kiss of greater weight. They fumbled with the last of their clothes and maintained a kiss as they felt their way onto the bed. He trembled. She stoked.

The 9:20 freight entered the triple trestles spanning the Housatonic under a candent plume. Its steel wheels clapped a steady percussion along the riverbanks, beneath journal bearings heated and seared like a Puerto Rican sunrise, startling in its brilliance. Into pungent moon shadows washing over her small bedroom, Blake whispered her name between seconds stolen from the narcotic rhythm that bound countless generations of human flesh before them. And in the Valley where the Naugatuck and Housatonic Rivers eddy and spin toward the great Atlantic Ocean, a Mediterranean fire burned hotly into the Caribbean night.

In the language of her infancy she murmured to him, "Te amo para siempre, te amo para siempre." *'I love you forever, I love you forever.'* Like a bubbled tide turning its white fingers back from its farthest reach, the movement of their flesh slowed to sated stillness as the clatter of the caboose rocked in the distance up the Maybrook line.

"Are you all right?" he asked, softly fingering her hair from her face.

"Yes," she whispered, "hold me close." Her body burned with heat. "Are you?"

"Yes," he said, shifting his weight to his side and running his fingers over the side of her face, "I love you."

"I love you too," she responded, arching her neck to the window. "Can you see the moon?"

Blake turned on his back, moving his head to her side and causing her head to drop off of the bed. "I see it now, but what are you doing on the floor?" he asked, smiling and pulling her up. She laughed and sat up with him, letting their lips run over each other's faces. He broke from her and ran his fingers over her face.

"Will you do something for me?" he asked hesitantly.

"Sure," she responded with a perplexed look, "anything."

"Will you sing for me"?

Her jaw slackened. She looked at him closely, being drawn into his soft look again. She closed her eyes and shook her head, "Please don't ask me to do that, Blake. You don't understand. I haven't been vocalizing or anything. It's all been too depressing. Please," she cried, "if I sing for you I want it to be perfect. Do you understand?"

Blake released her hands. He brushed her hair from her face and embraced her. "Sure," he said, trying to hide his disappointment. "If you say you can't, then I understand. It's just that I may never get to hear you sing."

She leaned away from him, clasping her hands around his neck, raising her eyebrows into her forehead. "I'll make you a promise," she said with a serious look. "When you return I'll sing for you. Anything you want. You have to tell me."

Blake looked at her blankly, "Tell you what?"

"What you want me to sing?"

He shook his shoulders. "I don't know, whatever you sing, whatever your father taught you."

"No," Linda protested, shaking her head slightly. "I want you to pick it so you will come back."

Blake placed his hands over her shoulders. "I'm coming back anyway."

She leaned into him and covered his lips with hers. "So you have to tell me what to sing."

Blake smiled at her and shook his head. "No, it's better if you pick it because I don't really know anything about this stuff."

"I know. How about that song you said your father listens to, the one from an opera. I can learn that."

"Yeah, I guess so, but I don't know the name of it."

"That's okay," she responded, stepping out of bed and picking up her clothes. She hurried into the bathroom and dressed as Blake dressed. She guided him to the piano, pinning her hair in back of her ears in a motion signaling high concentration. "You just hum it and I'll play it and write down the notes. I'll find out what it is," she said quickly, her eyes darting to his while she settled on the piano bench. "I never really studied opera. My father taught me art songs. That's what I trained on."

"Well, that doesn't matter. I don't know the difference anyway."

"Okay," she said, grabbing a pencil and looking up as he stood at her side at the piano, "now you have to hum it."

"Oh no," he said, laughing, shaking his head. "I can't hum anything."

Linda swiveled on the bench and looked at him. "Look," she said with a voice that lost all its playfulness, "you have to hum it so I can get the notes down." She turned back to the piano, sketching a rough staff on the back of a piece of sheet music. He started to hum, shaking his head like a bobble head doll. She turned back to him with a pleading look.

"You can't be playing, Blake. This is serious," she cried. Then she placed her hands over his. "Please, Blake, this means a lot to me."

He sat on the bench beside her and squeezed her hand. "I can't. I feel funny."

She turned to him with pooled eyes, "Blake, please, do it for me."

He placed a kiss on her cheek and shook his head. "Okay," he said, looking away from her. "It starts out with, like, a woman's voice singing, like alone, real high notes. Then she stops and some music starts, the instruments. Then she sings again, with the music."

Linda kept her hands on the keys and spoke without turning to him. "You still didn't hum anything. I need notes, something I can write down."

"All right, I know. I'm getting to that part. It's like, dah, dah, dah, dah, dah, dah." A silence ensued.

"That's it?" she asked, turning to him and fingering her hair back again.

"That's all I really know. That's what I pay attention to."

Linda repeated the notes to him as she played. "You have to hum it again so I can get the count of each note, sounded like the first note is held longer than the others."

Blake repeated the notes and tapped out the count of each with his hand on the piano. "I think maybe there's a violin or something in the background. It's hard for me to know for sure." Blake rose and stood at Linda's side.

"You have to hum it again."

Blake started again. Her hands followed his voice on the keyboard. She held the notes on her breath, binding the sequence into measures. He finished and stood in back of her. Her hands moved from the piano to the paper, writing down what she played, giving the notes she wrote the correct count, and making some scribbled comments about the instruments below the staff.

"I think I have it," she said, looking at the music and playing it through.

Blake turned away from her. He imagined himself lying on his bed, facing the dark ceiling and hearing the music. He ran it through his mind again. "Yes," he said quietly. "I think that's it. But I'm not sure if that's the music or the woman's voice. I don't know."

She played it through again, adding her voice to the piano, concentrating on giving the notes the right count and trying to recognize the song. He listened to her voice fill the room with full tones that floated like warm currents through the evening air. They were definitely the notes he heard from the record.

"I don't think I recognize it from anything I know," she said. She sang the notes over and over again and shook her head, "I can't place it." She turned from the piano and looked at Blake. "You're sure this is it, right?" She turned back to the piano and attempted some chords that she thought might fit with the notes. "You don't know any other notes?"

"That's it," he responded. "That's all I know of it. After that it's the woman's voice but it's too hard to remember the notes."

Linda studied the notes, playing them over without any recognition of the song they were from. "That's okay, that's all I need for now. I don't recognize it but I can figure it out from here. I'll find out the name of it and learn it. Or, maybe you can just ask your father."

Blake remained silent. He turned to the bobbins lined along the loom and the lace thread ready to spin under the power of the foot pedal. Various sized scissors and wooden forms lay neatly in a wicker basket beside it. "No, it's okay, you can figure it out from what you have there."

Linda turned from the piano and stood before him, putting her arms around his neck. "Okay."

He kissed her forehead and slipped out of her arms. He walked to the loom and touched some of the wooden dowels. "What's this going to be?"

"That," she responded with a satisfied smile, "is the beginning of a bedspread for my nephew."

Blake smiled at her warmly. Her life was so stable in this apartment overlooking the river. No loud arguments, no threats. No drunkenness, no violent blows.

"You know how to run this thing?"

Linda shook her head and smiled. Her hair had fallen forward, shrouding her face in a shimmering outline. "Uh huh," she said. "It's not really so hard. There wasn't much to do in the mountains. Study, practice the piano, sing and make lace. No streetlights, dirt roads to the small houses."

Blake looked at her and nodded his head, "Sounds

peaceful."

"After living in the city it took a while to get used to it." She put the lace down and held him. The traffic from Main Street was all that broke the silence of the room. "Some people still go down to the river to do their laundry."

"Really?"

"Really."

Blake looked at the wall clock. "I guess I better go now," he whispered.

Linda walked him to the door. They embraced under the hall bulb, trying to hold close what was certain to slip away. He kissed her cheek and whispered with closed eyes that he loved her and that she meant everything to him.

From the bottom of the steps he looked up at her. She sat on the top step as if she could stop time at the door, as if she could engage in a distracting conversation and halt fate. "See you tomorrow," she said with a smile.

"Night," he called back as he held the door to a quiet close.

Soon after that evening, in early September, 1968, the Palace was unusually quiet. Blake sat at the counter and studied the images of the Palace in the mirror. Around seven or so Teddy glanced up at the wall clock and sidled up to Frances.

"It's kind of slow. I think I'll let Linda go early. It's going to be a tough night for them."

Frances shook her head in agreement, whispering how she felt just sick to her stomach about the whole thing.

She walked to Linda and looked at Blake through the mirror, rubbing the last dish dry as if wishing for the genie to appear and grant them a deserved reprieve.

"Okay, kids," she said quietly, "it's late enough. Teddy and I can handle the rest of the night." Frances reached over and untied the bow of Linda's apron, waited for Linda to pull it over her head, and put it into the bag with the other dirty linens for the trip home.

Linda glanced at Blake in the mirror. Her face was blanched, drained of all enthusiasm. She walked to Teddy as he stood at the doorway facing Elizabeth Street. He turned to her as she buried her head in his shoulder to muffle the sound of her cry. He put his arms around her and patted her back, whispering that everything would be all right.

"Frances," Blake said in a whisper.

She wrapped her arms around him in great hug. "Everything will be just fine, Blake," she said without a waver in her voice. "You just take good care of yourself now." She extended her arms and took his hands into hers. She looked at him fully, his face down and drawn, as if all its muscles had failed at once.

He raised his eyes to hers. "I want to thank you for everything." Frances shook her head and squeezed his hands.

"No, Blake, you don't have to thank me. We had lots of fun here. We've seen lots of young couples fall in love here, you know, over all the years we been here. But this was real special, watching you and Linda. We had some wonderful times." She kissed his cheek and released his hands. "Be careful. Stay well."

Blake pulled a napkin from the dispenser and turned to the candy case. He felt like his heart was being ripped from his chest. Linda stood at the door facing the traffic. Teddy's hand was over her shoulder. The neon sign that said the Palace of Sweets distorted to a starburst of red lines running in all directions as her tears rolled from her eyes.

Blake walked to Teddy and extended his hand to him, trying to recover his composure. Teddy opened his arms and took him into a strong bear hug, "Well, Blake, my boy. I guess we say good-bye."

"Thank you for everything, Teddy," he said, "thanks for letting me hang around here all year. And for all the sundaes you made me and you never charged me for." Blake broke their embrace and looked at Teddy squarely, their eyes wet with emotion.

"It was a great year for all of us." He took a handful of Blake's cheek and squeezed it. "You be careful now. Don't be no hero, you understand?"

"I understand. I'll be real careful. I'll be all right." Blake patted Teddy's shoulder and looked into his eyes. "You look out for Linda for me, okay?"

Teddy nodded reassuringly, "Of course, of course. You just take care of yourself."

Blake turned from Teddy and took Linda's hand. They left the Palace of Sweets, its light fading from view and up the long flight of stairs to Linda's apartment.

"Hi, mom," Linda's voice was nearly inaudible as they entered. Her mother looked up from the loom and smiled at them.

"Come on," she said, rising and turning the light in the kitchen on. "I have some hot water on for coffee."

Blake and Linda sat at the table staring vacantly across the river. The room was quiet except for the sound of milk being poured into a small pan to be heated.

"Blake," Linda's mother asked, trying to break the silence. "Did you ever drink Puerto Rican coffee?"

"No," he looked up at her with a hesitant smile, "at least not yet anyway. Is it different?"

She sat at the table and tamped Spanish coffee into a silver strainer. "A little," she responded with a smile, trying to keep the mood light. "So, Blake, this is the beginning of a new life for you. Linda says you want to go to college after the Marines. What do you want to study?" she asked through her thick accent, placing cups on the table.

"I'm not really sure. That seems like a long way off right now," he responded, playing with the cup and glancing out the window.

Her mother poured the boiling water through a fine strainer as Linda brought the sugar to the table. "I heard the sponge plant might be sold. B.F. wants to sell it. That's what they were saying in the shop."

Linda shrugged and looked at Blake. "Teddy didn't say anything about that, did he?"

Blake looked perplexed. "No, didn't say anything. Haven't heard that yet."

"You know how we hear everything first in the shop," her mother said, setting a plate of coconut candy on the table. "This is from Puerto Rico. Linda tells me you like candy."

"That rumor gets around every few years that they want to sell."

Blake took a block of the coconut candy, examined it, and started to nibble at it. "Pretty good!" he exclaimed. "Maybe a new owner is what it needs." The room returned to silence as Blake looked up at the clock. "I suppose I should be going."

Linda's mother asked him to stay a moment more as she rushed to her bedroom and returned with a small package that she handed to Blake with a big smile, "This is from both of us."

Blake took the gift and looked at Linda with a puzzled expression.

"It's just something small," her mother added as she leaned against the stove.

"Well," Linda said, standing beside her mother, "you have to open it."

"Oh," Blake responded with a flick of his eyebrows. "Then I guess I will."

He peeled off the blue ribbon and peeled the tape from the silver paper, exposing a small white box. "Well," he said, trying to break the tension. "It's not a box of caramels from Vonete's, is it?"

Linda smiled at her mother then looked to Blake, "No, it's not caramels."

He pried off the top of the box and picked at the cotton padding, revealing a gold crucifix and chain. He lifted it from the box and held it up as the kitchen light reflected off its polished finish. He looked at them and turned back to the crucifix, "I don't have one. When I was a kid I had a silver one once but I lost it playing football. Someone caught the chain and it broke. Never even felt it break. Lost the game too," he explained softly. He smiled, putting the chain over his head and dropping the crucifix under his shirt. "Thank you. It's really beautiful."

"That's to protect you," Linda said under a faint smile, seeing how pleased he seemed with the gift.

Blake stepped to her mother, embraced her and kissed her, bending over her petite shoulders and feeling her delicate arms around his side. "Thank you for the cross and for letting me keep Linda out so late all these summer nights." He broke their embrace and looked down at her, her fingers squeezing his hand.

Her skin, brown and mink soft, rose into eyes that were wet with sadness. With a pronounced Spanish accent thickened with emotion she said, "You be careful and don't get hurt. Linda will be fine here so don't worry about her. Watch for yourself." She pulled him towards her again and kissed his cheek, holding the side of his face in her small palm, "Que Díos te bendiga, Blake,.... Que Díos te bediga. God Bless you, Blake....God bless you."

Blake nodded slightly to acknowledge her blessing, then walked to the hall and stood at the door, Linda at his side, her face shielded by her hands.

He swallowed hard, "I don't want you to come down the stairs with me," he said with a quavering voice. He opened the door to the hallway and stepped out, the empty gift box still in his hand, "This is way too hard."

Linda stepped into the hallway and closed the door, her face illuminated by the single bulb. She said nothing, her soft cry ascending through the hallway, a tissue pressed against her nose.

Blake took her into his arms one last time. "Look," he whispered with a voice too sad to speak. "Everything will be all right." He felt her body tremble and heard her cries grow louder. "The time will go by quickly. I'll keep the chain on."

He stared vacantly into the hallway. His sense of loss was overwhelming. He wanted to be strong even though he felt the best part of his life was ending. He always felt the time with her was just an interlude existing somewhere between the bright nebula of Vonetes Palace of Sweets and the place he stood now. Like a pleasant mirage that vanishes as you step closer, she would slip beyond his reach and he would be left with the memory of her love. He knew it was better to have been in the warm glow of her smile and have felt the silk of her hair and watched the movement of her lips shape words than to never have known those pleasures. And so he had to let her go and allow fate its rightful measure, without bitterness or anger, knowing that wherever he was her face would appear in his thoughts, forever beautiful.

Through a wan smile, he spoke in a whisper. "Just keep

thinking of all we did this year, all the great times we had, eating all those shakes and sundaes Frances and Teddy made for us. You have to find out the name of that song so you can sing it when I return. That's the promise we made. No excuses this time," he said with a soft smile. "You have to be ready."

She rested in his arms, her body no longer trembling. "I love you, Blake," she said, lifting her eyes to his. "And I will always love you." Her lips met his in a soft, gentle kiss.

He backed away from her and opened the apartment door so her mother would be with her. He stepped down the first stair and kissed her cheek one last time, her face in his palm, then walked down the stairs.

She released his hand, feeling the tip of his finger leave hers. She leaned her body against the door frame, dropping her head to her chest, her hair falling freely to the front of her face, and felt her mother's hands over her shoulders.

Blake reached the landing and looked up. Linda's body rested limply against the doorframe. Her pitched cry filled the hall. Her knees collapsed with weakness. He tried to speak but his voice failed him. He held the banister with one hand and opened the heavy wooden door. Over the sound of the traffic he called her name again and turned out of sight.

She heard the door close. The sound of the street receded and she knew he was gone. She turned to her mother's arms and rocked slowly, two metronomes swaying in the late summer evening, counting time, marking the measures until the moment is once again filled with the lovely legato of the sustained note.

Linda took her change and stopped short. Straining her neck, she clutched a carton of chocolate milk and a package of chocolate chip cookies in one hand and balanced a pile of weighty books against her body with the other. A hand, waving furiously side to side above the sea of heads in the crowded cafeteria, was followed by a small, petite body jumping up, attracting everyone's attention but Linda's.

"Linda, Linda," the elfin figure yelled over the din of conversation and piped in music from the school radio station. Linda finally spotted her and bumped her way through the crowded cafeteria.

"Oh," she moaned, "these books are killing me."

"I thought maybe you forgot," said Jennifer through the thick smoke of her cigarette. Wiry blond hair splayed over her shoulders, falling over her sweatshirt with its large, red peace sign covering the entire front.

Linda sat and slid out of her coat. She started to work on the cookie wrapper, speaking breathlessly. "No, Jen," she huffed, breaking a cookie with her fingers and putting it into her mouth, "I didn't forget. But I parked in the far lot, on Farnum. And I had to go back to get the books for my late class."

Jennifer reached down to Linda's tartan skirt and grabbed a handful of wool, rubbing the fabric between her thumb and index finger. "I really love the feel of this.

Where'd you get it?" she asked between mouthfuls of French fries that she slid over to Linda. "It's so soft."

Linda placed her straw into the milk carton and took a quick sip, "My mom made it," she responded, taking a French fry.

"Wow, it's beautiful." Jennifer lifted her books from the table, reaching down awkwardly, and dropped them to the floor, "Now there's more room to spread out. You always look so neat, Linda. I mean," she said, gulping down the last of her soda, "I was going to ask you to go to the demonstration but I figured you're not into that."

Linda laughed and shook her head, "Not really," she said, breaking off another piece of cookie. She slid the package over to Jennifer. "Maybe I should be more involved but I don't really have the time, you know, with work and all."

"So," Jennifer asked excitedly, whipping her hair away from her face and holding it in a frizzy bunch behind her head, leaning back in the plastic chair, "still no word from him?"

"No," Linda said with a dropped voice. "Nothing. I thought by now they'd allow a phone call or something, but nothing." She looked up at Jennifer, noticing the peace signs that decorated her headband and alternated with the words, 'PEACE NOW and NOW PEACE,' depending on what word you started on. "He said I wouldn't hear from him until boot camp is over. I hoped that by now they would have let him at least call."

"Oh wow, Lin! They treat them like they're in prison or

something," Jennifer said incredulously.

"Uh-huh. Not even a letter," responded Linda, arching her neck up to see the line at the food counter. "I'm still hungry, Jen. Want to split something?"

"Yeah, sure, how about a hamburger or something?"

"That sounds good." Linda reached into her tapestry bag and pulled a dollar out after a search. She turned away and sorted through the books on the desk, pulling the thick, heavy one from the pile. "I've got to do Western Civ before the tryouts," she said as Jennifer trotted away from the table, her work boots appearing oversized and odd, making a clumping sound beneath her bantam frame. "Hey, Jen," she called out, "how was applied?"

"Oh," exclaimed Jennifer, "I'll tell you later."

Linda opened the book and started reading, looking up after several minutes and spotting Jennifer talking at another table. She smiled to herself as she watched Jennifer hold the paper plate with the hamburger in her hand at the end of her fully extended arm, shaking it dangerously as she spoke with fast, clipped words, her free hand gesticulating wildly, short, reed thin fingers stabbing at the air to make a point.

"I'm back," said Jennifer. She placed the hamburger on the table, the dish spinning slightly. "Sorry I was so long. We were figuring out what to do for the next protest." She took a bite of the hamburger and looked at Linda, "Got any ideas?" she said, looking up at Linda with a smile. "Ugh," she said, looking at the hamburger. "It's kind of cold."

Linda picked up her half and took a bite, then spoke,

her mouth still full, her hand making a rolling gesture to Jennifer, "So, you were going to tell me about applied. How was it?"

"Oh yeah, right!" she exclaimed. "It was really great. York is real cool. She helps you select whatever you want to perform for the jury. They do it in, like late April and May. So, once you get it selected, she just has you practice it during the lesson. That's cool, right?"

"That's great!" she exclaimed, leaning back in her seat. "So there aren't any exams or anything?"

"No. York said she'd help us with anything. Said too many kids get all worked up about it. Said not to worry. You haven't met her yet, right?"

Linda shook her head and mumbled a no through a full mouth. "She'll be at choir tryouts tonight. I heard they take everyone. She just places your voice type so she can get a balance." A student in a military jacket stood and called Jennifer back to his table. Linda finished her hamburger and gathered her books and jacket into her arms. She walked by Jennifer who stood over the signs, leaning her small body over the table. Linda tapped Jennifer's shoulder. "Jen," she said without stopping, "I'm going to the library. I'll see you later, right, in the auditorium?"

Jennifer darted up and faced Linda as she walked towards the door. "Okay, Linda, I'll be there. Look for me, might be a lot of people."

Linda walked through the long, angled corridor of Engleman Hall. Clusters of students milled about the hallway carrying on quiet conversations that occasionally rippled with laughter. Bits and pieces of lectures, extemporaneous phrases, drifted from the lecture halls as she walked by the classrooms. She turned her back and leaned into the door that opened to the concrete walkway to the library. Her eyes squinted into a sudden gust of October wind that whipped her as she left the building. She entered the library and unloaded her books and jacket on one of the large chairs in the reading area, away from the stacks. Settling in quickly, she opened her botany text, wondering how anything to do with flowers could be so dreadful. She switched several times from the text to the handouts provided by the young, energetic professor who taught this, then moved to her class notes, trying to memorize stem parts and cell types. She returned to the library after her Western Civ class as evening arrived with sharp, crisp air. The amber glow of the lamps along the walkways outlined the sidewalk back to Engleman Hall.

The large clock above the librarian's desk said six forty-five. Linda glanced at her watch in disbelief, then stood and pulled on her coat. The sounds of instruments in various phases of tune emerged from the practice rooms as she walked briskly down Engleman Hall. Professor Avril Munk, the department chair, was alone on the illuminated stage. His ring of thick silver hair looked like a halo. He wore a yellow pullover vest stretched over a white shirt with a red bow tie. His short, portly body was stooped at the edge of the stage, making him look like a yellow ball about to roll off. He handed a manila folder to a young woman with short, bluntly chopped hair and a round, nondescript face standing before the stage.

Munk stood sharply. He turned and hammered the stage with the heels of his snakeskin boots as he made his way to the upright piano. He clapped his chubby hands several times to no one's attention, then called out, "May I have your attention. May I have your attention, please?" He darted to the microphone, trying to be heard above the voices and the tuning instruments. He spoke into the microphone again as the noise lowered to a din, then to an attentive quiet.

Jennifer moved to Linda's side, tugging on her jacket sleeve. "Hi," she said, facing the stage, speaking in a whisper. "What's going on?"

Linda turned to her, resting her books on the soft back of the chair in front of her, then stood to face Munk, who was instructing the band on practices and losing the attention of the mostly female chorus members. "He didn't say anything important yet. You didn't miss anything."

Jennifer nudged Linda, "See the woman with the short dark hair?"

"Yes."

"That's York."

A smile creased Linda's face, "I thought she was a student."

"Okay, okay, chorus members," said Munk, standing too close to the microphone. "For those trying out for the first time, which means I don't really care about your high school experience, Dr. York will be listening to each of you sing, oh, I don't know, seven or eight measures. If you feel you know your range you can tell her but she isn't bound by it. Does everyone have that straight?" Munk hesitated for a moment, as if someone may suggest they didn't quite understand. "In the meantime," he continued, "I'll be working with the orchestra in Practice Room 1. Practice will be every Wednesday at seven, right here. Are there any questions?" He allowed a few seconds to pass, nodded to York, and added, "Okay then, will the chorus members form a line in front of the stage and up the steps to the right. As you approach the piano, you will sing a few bars for Dr. York. The mic is off, so no one is really listening except Dr. York," he said.

Jennifer lined up in front of Linda, making small talk as the line moved forward along the front of the stage. Linda watched Jennifer as she approached York, her petite frame lost in the large stage, the oversized sweatshirt making her appear childlike. She heard York confirm that Jennifer was studying piano, then heard several measures from the piano and heard York say, "Soprano, okay," followed by a pleasant smile as Jennifer walked off stage.

Linda walked to the front of the piano and identified herself to York, "Citro, Linda Citro," as York flipped through several pages of names and checked her off.

"Citro?" York said quizzically. "Oh, yes, here it is," she commented, looking back to Linda. "It was in the back. You must have been a late admit."

"Yes," Linda responded with a comforted smile. "I was. I didn't register until late August," she responded. "I'm a mezzo."

York looked up from her roster. She noticed the placid, relaxed look on Linda's face. "Are you?" she asked, smiling as she looked down at the piano keys. "And how do you know that?"

"My father told me. At least that's what we practiced," she said softly, squeezing the tips of her fingers together and looking down.

York sensed her unease. "Well, we have only soprano and alto, so," she said as she repositioned her hands, "let's try this." York played a sequence from the A below middle C to the second E above middle C.

Linda sang along with the piano, quietly at first, until York said, "Louder, please," without looking up from the keyboard. She nodded at Linda, impressed with the simple, clear line of her voice and her crisp diction. She stopped playing and looked up.

"Can we try this once more?" she asked. York noticed the volume drop off on the lower notes once again. "Well," she said to Linda with a short, unconvincing smile, "I'm not about to challenge your father. If you're comfortable in the mezzo range we'll put you with the altos." Linda smiled at York and fingered her hair in back of her ear. York picked up the student list once more and found Linda's name again, "So," she said with excitement in her voice, "I see you're a music ed major. What is your instrument?"

"Piano," Linda responded.

York stood and extended her hand to Linda. "I'm Natalie

York. I handle the chorus and lots of the administrative stuff for Dr. Munk. It sounds like you studied voice."

"A little," Linda said, stepping directly in front of York. "My father was a professor of voice and he taught me to sing. But he died a few years ago. So I never took lessons from anyone, really."

York nodded at Linda reassuringly. "I'm sorry to hear that. Then you're all set here. We'll leave you with the altos and see how it goes but I suspect you may have a higher top than a mezzo. And if you have any trouble with classes or scheduling feel free to come to my office and see me."

"Thank you, Professor," Linda said as she walked off the stage and hesitated at the top of the stairs in search of Jennifer. After a few awkward moments she spotted her seated in the second row. A young man with thick blond hair was standing in back of her, leaning over and talking to her. She walked over to them, eyeing the student, his tall frame dwarfing Jennifer even as she stood to introduce Linda.

"Linda, this is Taylor. He's a phys-ed major, but is in the orchestra."

Linda gave him a cursory hello, then thought she had been too curt with him and asked, "I thought Munk had the instrumentals in the other room?"

Taylor laughed and folded his arms. "He does. I'm supposed to be there now, but," he said, waving his hand dismissively, "I'm a junior. Tonight's just orientation. Munk likes to see what he's got." He looked at Linda closely. His eyes seemed to pierce her.

"I guess that makes sense, I mean, with so many new students." Linda noticed him watching her. She turned back to Jennifer, "Is that it? Can we go?"

"Yeah, I think so," responded Jennifer, alternating her eyes between Linda and Taylor. "A bunch of us are going to the caf for something. Want to come?"

Linda looked at her watch, glanced at Taylor and back to Jennifer, "I don't know, Jen. It's getting late and I'm parked in the far lot."

"I have my car right here," said Taylor. "I can give you a ride later."

Linda thought of the long walk to the far lot, the cold and the weight of her books. She looked at Jennifer, then back to Taylor. "Well, okay, but I can only stay until nine. I have early classes tomorrow."

Chorus and band members pulled together several cafeteria tables. Students and instrument cases filled the chairs and dominated the room. They introduced each other, jumping up and down and straining their necks to make eye contact with new acquaintances, sipping hot chocolate and coffee and arranging weekend parties. Linda sat at the corner of a table with students to her right and left. She realized how different her life was than that of her peers. This was far from the quiet life she knew with her mother. She sat there with a bemused look on her face, trying to mask her discomfort. She thought of Blake and wondered if he imagined this is how her nights would be spent. She responded with a soft pleasantness to questions directed to her and courteously returned the inquiry, often repeating herself over the din.

Jennifer stationed herself beside her and darted from one friend to another, with animated conversation and ready laughter. Taylor dragged a chair behind Linda's, leaning into her view. She felt his eyes on her, even when he was speaking to others. She wanted to distance herself from him but didn't know how without appearing rude. She crossed her legs and felt his eyes on her.

"Well," she said, catching Jennifer's attention, "I really have to get going." She rose and lifted her jacket from the back of the chair.

"Why don't you stay?" asked Pat, the flute player torn between the orchestra and the chorus.

"No," Linda grimaced, "I have to go. I live at home and my mom will be worried if I'm really late. Plus, I parked in the far lot and it's pretty dark there at night."

"I said I'd give you a ride," Taylor interjected, rising and putting on his jacket. "I'm parked right in back here."

Linda looked at Taylor and smiled politely. "No, that's okay, you stay here. I really don't mind the walk." She turned from Taylor and stepped away from the table. "Good night, everyone," she said, smiling as her eyes circled the tables. "Bye, Jen. See you tomorrow."

She turned to leave and found Taylor at her side. "My car is right here, right outside."

"That's okay, Taylor, you don't have to leave now. I'll be all right." By this time he was walking with her, step for step. He put his hand on her back, guiding her towards the auditorium door. She knew he wasn't going to be

154

discouraged and decided it was better to let him have his way rather than make a scene. Anyway, maybe she was wrong, maybe he wasn't paying too much attention to her and sat beside her because most of the chairs were already taken. She filled the walk to the car with conversation about where he was from and what year he was in and pretended to be interested in what he had to say about his classes. She felt lost and out of place on the long, cushioned bench seat of the car as Taylor got in and started it.

"So," Taylor said as the pulled out of the lot, "Jennifer said you had a boyfriend but he's in the Marines."

Linda let a few seconds pass, waiting for a traffic light to turn. "Yes," she said with a clipped response. "I do have a boyfriend and he is in the Marines."

"There's a Jefferson Airplane concert here Friday night. Do you want to go?"

"No," Linda said resolutely as she turned and faced him. "I said I have a boyfriend." Her response was cold and unequivocal. She was angry. She regretted that she didn't go with her first impression and leave for home long ago.

"Come on, it's only a concert." His persistence annoyed her. He pulled into the parking lot and parked next to her car that seemed lost in the dark emptiness of the lot.

"I'm really not interested. I don't care for that style of music," she responded without looking at him.

Taylor pulled alongside her car, throwing his car into park, reaching over her shoulder and locking the door. His body leaned over hers as he pushed her books to the floor.

"What are you doing?" she screamed, turning from him to the door, trying the handle, then realizing the futility and yelling, becoming nearly frantic, "You're a jerk. What are you doing? Let me out, I want to get out!"

She was trapped. Her eyes were wide with fear. Her heart pounded beneath her breastbone.

"I just want to know why you won't go with me," he asked, releasing his hand from the door lock and placing it over the nape of her neck, pulling her tendril until they hurt.

She leaned her head away from his hand, placing her right hand on his arm in an attempt to keep him away from her. "Because I don't even know you, that's why. I don't like you!"

He scanned the lot, checking every corner. "You might get to like me," he said, rushing his left hand up her kilt, along the back of her soft, fleshy thigh, nearly to the crest of her buttocks.

"Hey!" she screamed, pushing her left hand into his face forcefully, bracing her legs against the incline of the floor and tightening every muscle in her body. She felt the wetness of his mouth and teeth against her straining palm. "What's wrong with you? Let me out!"

Gunnery Sergeant Cotton stood with his feet apart, arms folded, dominating the assembled class of recruits like Gulliver in the land of Lulliputs. The South Carolina sun glanced off his twice shaved face and warmed the December air. "Today," he stated in a melancholy tone, "is the live fire exercise." He turned his back to the platoon and stared into the sun as if to measure its distance. "The next time most of you recruits touch live rounds it won't be an exercise." He turned abruptly to Collins sitting in the front row. "You hear me, Collins?"

Collins jumped to his feet and squinted into the sun. "Yes, sir, Sergeant Cotton. The next time the recruit touches a live round in ain't going to be no exercise."

"Very well, Collins," he said dismissively. Sit down." Cotton strolled along the bleachers staring into the woods.

"Thigpen," he said quietly, "what do I mean by that, Thigpen?"

Thigpen rose slowly, looking to his left and right. In the moment the stillness of the morning seemed to filter to a softer quiet through the surrounding pines. It seemed the sound of the sun could be heard dappling the forest floor with bright, golden medallions. "Means we going to Vietnam, sir."

Cotton stepped before Thigpen and pressed his nose into Thigpen's starched blouse. "Who said anything about Vietnam, Thigpen?"

Thigpen stared into the pines. He felt Cotton's breath burning through his blouse. Thigpen's answer arrived slowly with the seasoned pace of the Georgia farmland. "Well, no one, sir. The recruit just thought that's what you meant, sir. That the next time the recruits see live rounds they going to be in Vietman, sir."

"Sit down, Thigpen," Cotton snapped, stepping back from the bleachers and addressed the platoon in a measured, pedantic tone. Somehow, he seemed to have aged before them and took on a grave manner without any hint of his characteristic arrogance or sarcasm. "Gentleman, the live fire exercise is one of our final field exercises of your training here. There is no room for mistakes or errors or any of those other dumb things you did up until now. You have been here about 10 weeks. In a few weeks you'll be graduating. You will have earned the privilege of calling yourselves Marines. Forget what you learned on the firing range. That was a controlled situation." He repeated the word controlled and let a moment pass. "You remember all that stuff about breath, aim and squeeze. All that don't mean much in a firefight. All that stuff is plain bullshit," he said, letting his voice drop to an almost inaudible level. He raised his M-16 high above his head and continued his serious tone. "In a combat situation you're going to be squeezing this baby like it's your best girl. Your eyeballs are going to be wider than a cow's ass with diarrhea. So we will assemble there," he said, turning and pointing, "and break down into fire teams. You will each get 10 rounds for the exercise."

His spoke slowly, never taking his eyes off of the recruits. "You will keep your weapons on semi-automatic, and fire one round at a time while walking forward. Do not get ahead of the line of fire. If one of these rounds hits someone it will pierce their flesh and proceed to rip through the soft organs until it hits a bone which it will break and proceed to tumble and twist and rip all the flesh along the bone line. About a half second later it will occur to you that you've been hit. Is that clear?"

"Yes, sir," the platoon responded in a single voice. After months of training they had molded into a cohesive group, knowing what was expected of them and assisting each other, responding flawlessly to commands on the parade deck, moving as one unit.

"Squad leaders, step forward and get the rounds for your fire teams. Fire team leaders, you get those rounds and stand fast with them. Do not pass them out until you are told to do so."

Kyle Sigford rose from the bleachers. He was a slight kid from the Texas panhandle, so far from nothing that he had trouble describing it to anyone who asked. He made his way past Blake and descended the bleachers. His shoulders were stooped, even when he was at attention. His eyes were pale blue and his face was long and narrow, causing his helmet to roll around his head like a bobblehead doll in the rear window of a car.

Talent placed two boxes of ammo in Sigford's hands. "Sigford," he said in his meanest drawl, "why do you always look like you just rolled out of bed, even in the field?"

Sigford looked straight ahead, holding the ammo boxes in one hand and his rifle strap with the other, keeping his weapon firmly against his shoulder. "Sir, the recruit does not know why he always looks like he just rolled out of bed, sir," replied Sigford before returning to the bleachers.

"Okay, listen up, you guys," he said, looking at his cartridge belt and pulling out a magazine. "Load your magazines with ten rounds but don't lock them in until we get to the tree line and I call up your fire team." Sigford removed his weapon and tested the bolt action. His knowledge of the weapon, comfort with its mechanics, and unparalleled skill on the range was respected by everyone in the platoon, including Cotton and Talent.

"Sigford," Talent called out, "get your first fire team over here lined up to my right. Let's get this thing moving."

Sigford lined up parallel with DeJesus, Peters and Blake. "Lock and load now," Talent commanded, leaning forward to eye their every move. The sound of the magazines snapping into place and the rounds chambering caused tension to rise along the firing line.

"When we step off the line and start firing, remember to stay in line, one round at a time. Don't rush and keep the muzzle straight out ahead of you. We ain't doing no John Wayne routines here today."

The fire team started slowly off the line as the sound of bullets pierced the air. They moved carefully, Sigford deliberately moving a half step ahead to keep his eyes on the line, watching the muzzles for any dangerous movement. After thirty seconds of walking and firing, Talent held up his arm to signal a halt to the exercise. "All right," he bellowed. "Clear your weapons."

The sound of the magazines dropping from their housing was shattered by the crack of a round going off. Talent jumped to the front of the fire team with eyes as wide as beacons. "Who fired that round?" he screamed, running to the center of the four recruits who stood motionless over twenty yards amidst the trees.

"I did it, sir," responded Blake, holding the muzzle of his rifle to the ground.

Talent rushed to Blake and slammed his forearm into the side of his head, causing his helmet to fly off and sending him rolling to the ground. "You idiot," Talent yelled, standing over him and bending over a shocked and perplexed Blake. "You're going to get someone killed. Ten weeks later and you still can't handle a weapon." He turned, picked up Blake's helmet and threw it at him as he lay there. "Sigford," Talent yelled, straining his voice as he walked out of the woods, "you better get this piece of shit unfucked. I don't even want to look at him."

Sigford ran over to Blake and pulled him up, then picked up his weapon and handed it to him. "What happened?" he asked with a confused look. Blake put his helmet back on and fastened the strap.

"When he said to clear your weapons I thought he meant to finish the rounds. So I aimed the muzzle into the ground and fired," Blake explained, shouldering his weapon.

Sigford took the weapon from Blake's shoulder and released the magazine. He inspected it for any remaining rounds and slipped it into its pouch on Blake's cartridge belt. Blake reached for his weapon just as Sigford slid the bolt back as an unspent round flipped out and fell to the forest floor. Sigford's pale blue eyes, now colorless in a bright sun, found Blake with his eyes closed as he realized his error.

"It's okay,Buddy," he said, handing the weapon back to Blake and picking up the round. "I think we're all set now." He slid his helmet up off of his forehead and adjusted the strap that hung loosely under his chin.

Blake took the weapon and secured it on his shoulder. pulling the strap tightly as if to control its deadly mechanics. "Oh man, Siggy," he whispered as they walked from the tree line."Thanks a lot. Damn, I would never have remembered to check the chamber just now." Blake returned to the bleachers and watched the other fire teams perform the exercise. He played the incident back in his mind countless times, repeating the thought that he had the muzzle pointed into the ground so there was no danger to anyone at that moment. It was the chambered round that no one but Siggy knew of that made him shudder.

The evenings in the squad bay were filled with endless hours of preparing uniforms for inspection. On most evenings he and Sigford sat on their footlockers talking quietly and polishing their boots with small, circular motions until the leather shined like glass. Until now there was no communications to or from home except a postcard sent announcing their safe arrival at Parris Island and that they were fine.

"Platoon, ten-hut," someone yelled, causing the platoon to scurry in front of their racks and stand at attention.

Talent stood in the center of the squad bay, his campaign hat cocked smartly over his forehead with its strap fastened tightly around the back of his head. He put his hands on his hips and walked back to the threshold and stood there with his back to the hallway, silent and still. His shoes gleamed in the light from the double row of bulbs that spanned the ceiling. "School circle," he said without intonation. He took several steps forward as the recruits gathered around him in a tight, quiet circle. Sergeant Cotton soon appeared in back of him, waiting for the platoon to fully assemble.

"Take your seats," Talent ordered, waiting again for the sea of white T shirts and oversized white boxer shorts to settle in on the floor. He folded his arms over his chest and put his head down in deep thought. He moved to the center of the floor and stood silently for several seconds. Finally, he lifted his head and spoke in a hushed, sullen tone.

"Listen up now," he said, looking down at his shoes, his arms still folded. "Orders came in today from Headquarters Marine Corps."

He looked up and glanced at Sergeant Cotton who caught his tense eyes. The recruits, appearing as if they each stopped breathing, turned boyish eyes to Talent.

"It looks like everyone here has orders for Vietnam. Everyone in this room is assigned 03-02, infantry. Sergeant Cotton and I thought some of you might not be ordered there right off, but we were wrong." Talent's voice trailed off as he started to pace the squad bay, the click of his heels on the polished but worn linoleum floor being the only sound.

Cotton stepped forward, placing himself at the center of the school circle. "Headquarters wants you men in country within 30 days from now. We have three weeks before graduation. That means there won't be much time for leave after graduation. So tomorrow, being a Sunday, we will suspend afternoon training. Being that it's close to Christmas, you will be allowed to go the PX to shop and attend to your personal needs."

Talent walked back to the center and nodded at Cotton. "You will also have phone privileges tomorrow while you are at the PX. I recommend you use your time wisely," he said, scanning the callow faces of the recruits sitting around him.

Then, in a deep and clear tone, he started the lecture. "Sergeant Cotton and I have trained you to the best of our abilities. In three weeks you will be United States Marines." He voice began to rise dramatically and he resumed his pacing, folding his hands at his back, his posture ramrod straight, and his cadence accenting his words.

"You will be carrying on the honorable tradition of this Marine Corps," he bellowed, facing a sea of white skivvies, his chest thrust out from his narrow waist and his eyes fixed straight ahead. "From Bellueu Wood to Iwo Jima and from the Choson Reservoir to the battle for Okinawa, the United States Marines have distinguished themselves in combat for their ability to perform the mission despite any and all odds."

The recruits were mesmerized by Talent's elocution and the presence he commanded without shouting or intimidation. Until this moment they were not allowed to hear or utter the words 'Marine Corps.' Until this moment they were nothing but a bunch of undisciplined civilians, referred to as the vilest of bodily parts and spawned by unrepentant whores coupling with dogs. They were unworthy of the slightest individual praise or recognition.

The fire team, squad and platoon became their surrogate. Still, until now, they were not allowed to connect those units to the Corps. Talent's voice rose to a fever pitch. "Every one of you men has proven himself worthy of wearing the uniform of a United States Marine. Sergeant Cotton and I would be proud to serve with any of you, anywhere. In the next three weeks we will continue to train you in the finest traditions of the Corps. When you go shopping tomorrow, buy your Christmas gifts for your mothers and fathers, wives and children, your brothers and sisters and girlfriends," he said as he pivoted and started out the squad bay, stopping just before the hall. "Sergeant Cotton and I wouldn't lie to any of you. Some of you won't see another Christmas. Use your time wisely."

The squad bay was silent. For a moment it was motionless. No one was surprised. Finally, quietly, they stood and made their way to their footlockers.

"Well," Sigford commented in his slow Texas drawl, as if responding to Blake's thoughts, "I just as soon get it done with anyway." He leaned his back against the bunk frame and nodded down to Blake. "You gonna do any shopping tomorrow? I don't know what to buy for my dad so I figure maybe we can help each other out. I mean, I know I can't help you but maybe you can help me," he said as he stopped rubbing the wooden stock of his drill weapon and let it rest between his legs.

Blake looked up at Sigford's narrow face. He raised his hand and put it on Sigford's back. "Sure, Siggy, and you can help me pick out something for Linda."

"Feels weird, don't it?" Sigford's eyes studied the festive display cases loaded with goods being tended to by women of all ages and proportions, women with made up faces and pleasant smiles and voices that lilted with animation.

"Who you got to buy for?" Blake asked.

Sigford shrugged his shoulders and smiled. "I suppose Sergeant Talent and Cotton."

Blake looked at him with a startled expression, then smiled back, "Yeah, right, and I'm buying for the Commandant."

A smile broke over Sigford's face. "I ain't joshing you, Blake. They taught me some stuff on the rifle range that I didn't know. And my dad and my brother and sister. How about you? You got to shop for your girlfriend, right?"

"Yeah, for her and for my folks." He shook his head in disbelief and laughed, "You know Siggy, you're crazier than I thought."

Sigford stepped to a display table and fanned a stack of holiday tablecloths. "These are nice for women. You know, they like that kind of stuff, tablecloths and stuff like napkins." Sigford picked up two identical tablecloths and handed one to Blake. "How about your dad, does he wear ties? We can look at ties and stuff."

166

Blake pressed his hand over the tablecloth and turned, asking for directions to the men's section. "Yeah, he wears ties sometimes. Your dad wear ties?"

Sigford started walking. "Not really, not for a long time now. Even then he wore one of them string ties, you know, with the metal studs on the end. I don't think a tie is good for him."

Blake stepped quickly to catch up to him, "How about a sweatshirt, Sig, he'd wear a sweatshirt, right?"

"Yeah," Sigford responded, his eyes widening, "yeah, I reckon he'd like that."

Sigford approached the saleswoman with a perfect French twist to her honey colored hair. She pointed in the direction of the sweatshirts with a broad, knowing smile over her full face.

"How about something like this, Blake?" Sigford asked, holding up a large, white sweatshirt with the Marine Corps emblem covering most of the front and the Marine Corps motto, 'Semper Fidelis,' printed on a banner being held by an eagle's beak.

"What size you got?" asked Blake, eyeing the small sweatshirt. "You know what size he wears?"

Sigford tried folding the sweatshirt before laying it over the others. "He ain't real big," he said, looking at Blake quizzically, "I never really thought of it."

"Is he bigger than me?" Blake asked, holding the sweatshirt up to his shoulders.

"No, he ain't taller than you. He got a belly though. Now that you're holding that up, it does look a little small."

Blake flipped the collar back. "It's a medium," he said, placing it back into the pile and fingering through until he pulled up an extra large. "How's this?" he asked, holding it up for comment.

"Yeah," responded Sigford, rolling it into a ball and placing it under his arm, "I think it'll fit. How about one for your girlfriend? Think she'll wear it?"

A smile lolled over Blake's face even as he tried to conceal it. "Well, I was thinking about some jewelry or something like that. I think we passed it on the way down here."

Beneath the thick, polished glass of the jewelry case laid sparkling diamond rings and wedding rings in matching sets glinting on soft, midnight blue velvet.

"Can I help you?" asked the young woman behind the counter, placing her brightly colored fingernails on the glass and tapping them lightly.

"We're looking for a present for my girlfriend," explained Blake.

The clerk folded her hands over the counter and spoke to them in an attentive, confident manner which long experience brings. She knew the drill, something pretty and durable that would kindle warm thoughts over long separations, but not too expensive, within the pay scale of a private.

"Well, let's see now," she said with a knowing smile, alternating her eyes between them. "Are you boys both looking for this gift or just one of you? Is this young lady lucky enough to be dating two Marines?"

Blake laughed and looked at Sigford whose lopsided smile made him laugh more. "No, it's for my girlfriend but he's helping me." Sigford propped his elbows over the display case with the sweatshirt and tablecloth hanging loosely from his arms.

A broad smile creased the clerk's red lips. "Well then," she said smartly, walking down the case to the less expensive necklaces and earrings and pendants, "I think between the three of us we can come up with something really nice. How about something in silver? Does she wear silver?"

Blake followed her with his hands dragging over the glass. He shrugged his shoulders and grimaced. "I don't know. I suppose she does."

"What does she wear now?"

"I don't know. Nothing, I guess. Except if she gets dressed up, then she wears this pretty pair of gold earrings. And she has a necklace she can borrow from her sister. But she's in Puerto Rico."

"I see," the clerk replied with a nodding head and pursed lips. Then, with a prosecutor's purpose, she started some questions. "How old is she?"

"Eighteen."

"Do you know her ring size?"

"No."

"Okay," the clerk responded, tapping the glass with her nails again. "Does she have pierced ears?"

"Yes."

"Long or short hair?"

"Long. But she keeps it up a lot, like with barrettes or, like, clips and stuff."

"Dark or light hair?"

"Dark."

"Does she work in an office?"

"No, she's in college and she works in an ice cream parlor that makes sandwiches and stuff."

"Does she do lots of dishes?"

"Yes."

"So maybe we stick with earrings. Do you think she would like that?"

"Yeah, I think so," Blake said with a nodded smile, "but I really don't know."

The clerk fished under the glass and pulled out a few sets of earrings, setting them on the glass. "I bet you don't know if she likes posts or hoops?"

Blake looked at the clerk and turned to Sigford who was staring into the case and started to laugh. "I don't even know what posts and hoops mean."

"Hey Blake, how about this?" he asked, flattening his index finger against the display case."That little thing on the shiny chain, with the ladies head on it."

The clerk placed the earrings back in the case as Blake slid down and peered around Sigford's finger. The clerk's fingers appeared under the case and the locator quiz began.

"Which one caught your eye?" she asked, moving her hand slowly, like an arcade claw, over the necklaces.

"Just down a little," Sigford twanged in his spacious

Texas manner.

"Here," she responded, hovering over a gold heart. "No, two over, to your left."

"I see you paid attention on the parade deck!" she said with a smile, bringing the piece to the counter to be handled. "This is very nice. It's called a cameo."

"A what?" asked Blake, resting it in his palm.

"A cameo."

"Shoot," drawled Sigford under a great smile, "I never knew they had names for all this stuff."

"Who's the lady supposed to be anyway?"

The clerk looked at them and laughed, "Okay, you boys got me stumped on that one. I don't think it's anyone in particular. But it's carved from sea shells. They come in all different sizes. We have larger ones but this is fine and delicate. It's very pretty. Your friend has very nice taste. Do you like it?"

"Yeah," responded Blake with a relieved smile. "I like it fine. How much is it?"

"Let's see," she said, turning the small ticket over. "Twenty nine dollars. Can you afford that?"

"Sure. No place to spend money in boot."

"Would you like it wrapped?"

"Yeah, that would be great."

The clerk placed the cameo in a small box. "Do you boys need anything else for your mothers or gifts for sisters? We also have men's jewelry on the other side."

"I think I'd like one for my sister too. Think she'll like it better than this tablecloth. She doesn't have too much jewelry."

"Oh, then she'll love this. I'll wrap them both."

"Then I think we're done," said Blake, pulling out a roll of money, "I think we're done with jewelry. We got to check the phone lines next."

"Okay, this will be wrapped in a jiffy. You Marines mailing them home?"

"Yeah."

"Okay, we'll double wrap them, one in Christmas wrap and then I'll package them for mailing."

"So how have you been? It's so good to hear your voice." Blake's face broadened to a smile as wide as the sunrise.

"I've been worried about you. Are you alright?" she asked, twisting the phone cord around her fingers as she spoke and turning to the wall.

"I'm fine," Blake responded. "How about you, how's school?"

"It's okay," she said, her voice sinking. "I have finals now, but they're not too bad. I just miss you so much. I can't stop thinking about you."

"Listen," he said with his eyes rolled into his head as he searched for expression. "We got orders yesterday. It looks like we're all going over to Nam, everyone, the whole company."

Linda felt a wave of weakness overcome her. She leaned against the candy case and dropped to a crouched position against the counter, out of sight of everyone.

"What?" she whispered, as if the question could move

the balance of fate in her favor. "Don't tell me that, Blake. Please don't tell me that," she implored with a voice that tapered to a whisper.

"Linda......Linda?" Blake asked, leaning into the phone. "Are you there?"

Blake heard her muffled, pitched cry rise through the phone. "I won't be able to come home first. Can you hear me? Linda, please say something."

Linda unfolded herself from the crouched position and sat on the wooden trap door with her knees against her chin. She took her apron and dried her eyes with it. Then, with halting, shaking breath, she asked softly, "Blake, can you hear me?"

"Yes," Blake responded, "I can hear you fine. Are you all right?" "I have something to tell you," she said, in a clear, unwavering voice. "I'm pregnant."

The phone went silent. "You can't be," he said finally.

For several seconds he heard nothing, then her high pitched cry and finally, words tortured by cries as she spoke haltingly.

"No, Blake, you don't understand," she said, gripping her hair into a ball. "It wasn't you. It happened at school, I was forced. Can't you come home? I need you, please come home."

A painful silence ensued. The phone went dead as the coins dropped through. "Operator, that will be one dollar and ten cents if you want to continue."

Blake was silent. He pulled coins from his pocket and poured them into the phone.

"Thank you," said the operator as Linda's cry became audible once again. More silence, until Blake broke in against the pain. "Linda, you have to stop crying."

"Can't you come home?" she asked plaintively.

"No, no, they're not giving any leave." More silence as Blake searched for something to say as only doubt filled his head. "I think I better go."

"No, Blake, no, please don't hang up," she cried.

Blake shrugged his shoulder, numbed with doubt, "I don't know what to say. I'll write to you when I get settled in country, okay?"

"Okay. I love you, Blake."

"Operator, please deposit one dollar and ten cents to continue."

"I'm finished, Operator." Blake whispered as he hung up. He remained there for a moment with his hand over the receiver, as if to possess it against the world and play back the words and hear every word she said again and again. He flipped the remaining change over in his pocket and let it fall, then did it again.

"You done?" asked a recruit standing at his side.

Blake turned away from the phone and looked at the Marine. Another boot in starched utilities and an erect posture trying to connect back to a life he left behind.

"Yeah," he replied softly, aware of his surroundings once again. "Sure, sorry."

There was nothing more to say anyway. He always thought this is how it would be. She would find someone else in college and he would be without her. He never dreamed it would happen like this, only that it would happen. But she said she loved him and the operator broke in and he never responded. The Marines and the war were bigger than him and Linda and the entire Valley. The sediment of twelve weeks of their lives had been condensed into three short minutes timed by an operator. And what had he neglected to say? That he loved her. That she was the first thing he thought of when he woke and his last thought at night. Maybe it didn't matter anyway. He was going to Vietnam. And he didn't tell her that he loved the way her lips formed when she spoke. Maybe it happened just as she said. Nothing made sense at the moment. And it didn't matter because he couldn't recall the sequence of their words and the sequence didn't matter anyway. Nothing could undo what was done or change the fate he anticipated from the beginning. She was beyond his reach.

Blake felt a hand drape over his shoulder. "Something wrong, buddy?" Sigford planted himself in front of Blake.

Blake shook his head and closed his eyes, "Everything, Sig. Everything's wrong. She's pregnant." He shook his head side to side and breathed deeply in stuttered fashion. "I can't believe it."

Sigford guided them out of the phone area and stood under a wreathed window. "Shucks, Blake, that ain't so bad, is it?"

"I don't know, Sig." Blake stared out the window, trying to distance himself from the vortex of emotions he felt. "It's not mine, Sig. I don't know. I guess it happened with someone at school or something." He turned to Sigford and took his package from him, looking at him with a pained expression. "I don't know what to believe, she was everything to me."

"Look, you can't figure all this out right now. We got to be back in the bus in twenty minutes. The post office is right there through them there doors." Sigford put his hand on Blake's back and moved him along in a slow shuffle down the lobby to the connecting building and into another line of Marines laden with packages of every shape and size.

"I don't know if I should mail this," Blake said, turning to Sigford for an answer. "I don't even know if she loves me anymore."

"She tell you she don't love you no more?"

"No. No, she said she loved me. I don't know, I can't hardly remember what she said."

"You got to mail it to her. You bought it for her because you loved her, right? Like Gunny Talent says, we might not see another Christmas. Heck," he continued, "the worst thing that can happen is that she doesn't wear it because she don't love you no more. I figure, where we're heading, that ain't that bad. You might never even get to know that, right?"

Blake glanced back to Sigford and firmed his place in line, "I suppose." He addressed the package at the counter and wondered if she would think it was pretty when she opened it.

The phone deadened in Linda's ear. She pulled her hair clip out with her other hand and held it limply. He said he would write when he got 'in country' and what if he didn't and what did that mean, 'in country' anyway? What if something happened to him and she never spoke to him again? Would he know that she loved him? Did he remember the promise he made to return and the song she promised to sing for him? Maybe for him it didn't matter anymore. And she told him that she loved him, she remembered that at least, the words on her lips and the sound in the phone, but what did he say? She couldn't remember what he said.

Frances picked up the phone behind the grill, heard the sound of an open line and motioned to Teddy with a serious face.

"Linda," he whispered. He dropped to one knee, taking the phone out of her hand and letting it slide on the floor as he wrapped his arms around her.

She moved her arms around him and cried into his shoulder, her voice trembling and her lungs gasping for air. "He hung up, Teddy. He hung up."

"No, no, Linda," Teddy whispered again as his embrace strengthened and he rocked her gently. "Everything will be all right, honey. You can't do this to yourself, it's not right, it's not right."

"He's going to Vietnam, Teddy. He's not coming home."

"Frances," Teddy called out. "Linda, come on, Honey." Teddy lifted her off the floor and hung up the phone. "Let's get you to a chair."

"What?" Frances asked confusedly. "What is it, what happened?" She took a chair beside Linda and put her arm around her. "Get some water, Teddy. What happened, Sweetheart?"

"He hung up," Teddy said, setting a glass of ice water on the table. "Take some small sips, Linda," he said as he rubbed her back and shook his head at Frances. "He's going over."

"Teddy, shut the window lights and lock the door. We're closed."

"No," Linda protested, taking a sip of water, "I'll be okay. Don't close, please."

"We're closing," Frances said with a tone that left no space for differences. She brushed Linda's hair back and put her barrette on the table. "You have to settle down now, Linda. You have to think of the baby. Things will work out, you'll see. Everything works out."

"Please don't close. Please," Linda pleaded as she squeezed Frances' hand.

"Okay," Frances responded, "as long as you settle down."

Linda sat with her shoulders rolled forward and her elbows supporting her. Frances sat beside her, rubbing her back and encouraging her to sip more water even after she was calm. She thought of Blake and wondered if he would call again. Maybe tomorrow, maybe he would call when she was in school and she would miss him. Or maybe he would wait, wait until he was there, 'in country,' and he would call from there but it would be the middle of the night and the phone would ring but no one would be here to answer and say Vonete's Palace of Sweets and tell him that she loved him like the night they lay beside each other while the journal bearings seared an August night. Drained, as if her body went through some medieval bloodletting, she wondered how everything got so mixed up.

She turned to the faded mirror and closed her eyes to the girl who looked back with the disheveled hair and beet red cheeks and eyes wet with sadness. She looked down at the tile floor and remembered the dance, the unforgettable feel of his hand around her waist and the flair of her hem in the syncopation of sensitive flesh and spiraling hearts. It all seemed so distant now, though it was just months ago.

In the following weeks and months Blake and Sigford were transferred to several temporary duty assignments as they made their way to Vietnam via Camp Pendelton and Travis Air Force Base and finally to Da Nang and more temporary assignments. They spent countless days and nights together with other unattached Marines finding their way to a permanent company or what was left of a permanent company after months in I Corp. And they filled the time with speculation of the where they were headed and talk of the life they left behind.

Sigford raised the mosquito netting and crawled from his rack. He pulled his sweat soaked green T shirt from his chest and walked out of the hooch to the uncovered bunker.

"What you doing, buddy?" he drawled.

Blake turned and pointed. The southern sky glowed with the dusted flame of a half moon.

Sigford sat beside Blake and lazied out his questions. "You can't sleep? You thinking about home?"

"Yeah, I'm just laying here sweating my ass off. I figured maybe it'd be cooler out here." Blake pulled on his T shirt so it hung from his chest like a wet sack. "Now I got the shits too."

"Shit, everyone got the shits. Your stomach cramping up?"

"Yeah."

"I think it's the water. That bug juice in the mess hall been tasting like piss too."

Blake looked down at his T-shirt hanging off of him like a wet towel. "I'm shitting so much I'm losing weight."

Sigford looked back at the empty airstrip. "At least the airfield is quiet." He put his hand on Blake's back and patted it. "You think of home a lot, don't you, buddy?"

Blake dropped his head between his knees with fatigue, "All the time."

"We ain't going to be here forever. Someday you'll go home and everything will be okay."

Blake shook his head between his knees. "No Sig, nothing will ever be the same. I can't kid myself. I never really thought it would last anyway."

Sigford lay down and folded his hands under his head. "Didn't she love you?"

180

Blake lifted his head and gave Sigford a glance. "Yeah, I suppose so, but I never thought it would last," Blake responded, leaving a breath of silence to wilt in the heavy air. "She was different from me."

"So what do you mean by that? How different could she be anyway?"

Blake lay back beside Sigford. "It's hard to describe. Her father was a professor of music or something like that. I don't know. I didn't even understand that stuff when she talked about it. You know, she was raised different than me and you. She was smart. Like her parents expected her to go to college."

Sigford adjusted his head in his hands and put some chewing tobacco under his lip. "So what's that got to do with anything, anyway. I don't really get it."

Blake shrugged his shoulders. "So my dad worked in a factory, you know. I mean, if I worked in a shop that'd be okay, that's just what was expected. She even talked different than you and me talk. Like, she talked clearly. Even her lips moved different than us."

Sigford locked his eyes into his forehead and drew his neck back. He studied the moon while he spoke. "So, even if she talked funny, so what does that matter so much anyway?"

Blake closed his eyes. "I don't know. It's hard to explain, but I always thought she would find someone else when she went to college that was educated like her. So when she said she was pregnant, I just figured, you know, it's over. I guess I felt like she deserved better than me."

At the back of the airfield the keen pitch of a Cobra gunship revving up broke the silence. Blake opened his eyes and turned to the silhouette beside him. He studied Sigford for a moment as the chopper lifted off.

"Sig?"

"Yeah?"

"You ever think of home?"

Sigford shook his head and responded in a shallow voice. "Yeah, course I do. I ain't got no girl or nothing like that. But I think of my dad and Becka and my brother, and my friends. You know, I wonder what they're up to, still shooting rats at the dump and stuff."

"You ever think about your mom?"

The Cobra disappeared beyond the mountains. "Yeah, but it's kind of hard because I hardly remember her, except how soft her hands felt when she touched me," he responded. "That sound funny?"

"No, it don't sound funny. But how do you remember that if you hardly remember her?"

Sigford pointed to the moon veiled with scuds. "You see them there clouds, Blake? I remember, when I was a little boy, maybe when I was four or five, I can't be sure, my ma would hold me in her arms and rock me real slow on the porch. When I couldn't sleep I'd just go to the screen door and she'd call me out, like she knew when I was standing at the door, and she would hold me in her arms and talk to me, real low, like she was whispering in my ear so no one could hear except for me. She'd be telling me about the sandman coming around. Or she would sing real soft and pretty, trying to settle me. And when she saw them thin clouds pass the moon like that she'd point to them and say, 'Kyle, sweetie, you look at that honey. You know what that is, sweetheart?' She'd say, 'Why, that's the breath of angels running by the moon coming down here to look after little boys and girls, breathing close to them, right there on their pillows and watching over them. Ain't them clouds just beautiful, Kyle?' she'd say and smile like she was real pleased with her life. And she'd be running her fingers through my hair, real soft like. Thing I remember best was how soft her hands were. Think that's what I remember most about her, how sweet her voice was and how soft her hands felt when she held me."

Blake gave Sigford a fish-eyed look, "Sig?"

"Yeah?"

"How old were you when she died?"

"Five," responded Sigford without expending any breath. "I was five. My sister Becka, she was fifteen then, she kind of raised me and Travis after that." He dug a fistful of dirt into his hand and let it drop slowly through his fingers, as if his memories, like a load of rock dropping through a sifter, were refined at that moment in I Corps. "You know, Blake, it's kind of funny, but, except for pictures, I don't really remember her face at all."

The deep thud of the twin CH-46 rotors sliced the morning fog that hung over the verdant hills of the A Shou Valley. Piercing shards of sun, glinting from the east on its milk run over the South China Sea, illuminated the Quang

Tri River like a brilliant silver ribbon.

Along the walls of the chopper the marines sat silently on suspended canvas benches. Their weapons, muzzles down, rested casually between their legs. The pungent odor of sweated bodies salted the hot air as their heads bobbed in the light sleep that listless uncertainty allows.

Sigford, gaunt from dysentery that affected everyone, raised his helmet above his forehead, left his bench seat and stood beside the gunner window. He straddled his feet above the catnapping gunner and looked out into the serene beauty of the Vietnamese countryside. He thought of how far DaNang seemed from here. Its runway, undulating beneath Vietnam's punishing heat, teemed with the serious business of war. The deafening thunder of fighter jets, towed quietly from their revetments, was constantly punctured by the nimble urgency of gunships ferrying the wounded with field dressings hastily applied. In the looted time of war, the dead, their corpses rotting and smelling, and the near dead, drugged to make their last breathes as painless as possible, waited for their ride to eternity while those who had a chance to make it were ferried away.

All the while, the narrow, dusty streets of Da Nang throttled with the robust commerce of war. Still, from here, beneath the thinning haze and far above the rattled, thin, dirt roads, the mountains rolled seamlessly into valleys and rice paddies laboriously tended by Vietnamese in conical non la hats. Tiny villages of thatch roofed homes dotted the lowlands in peaceful solitude. So where was the war, he thought to himself?

He felt a palm grasp his shoulder, "We're coming down, sit down," the crew chief said as he roused the window gunner.

Sigford rapped Blake's helmet with his knuckles as he passed and pointed down. "We're landing."

Blake opened his eyes and nodded as the Marines stirred to alertness. His head ached with a dull, rounded pain. They were in country twenty-two days now, maybe twenty-three. Better to think twenty and save the pleasure of learning it was more for another day. It didn't matter. It was too soon to start counting and too many to forget. Sweat soaked through his camouflaged utilities and darkened his flak jacket to sharkskin black. Anyway, why count at all? Da Nang wasn't so bad.

Apart from some poorly aimed mortar rounds and a few ineffective snipers, the base was secure. He was learning to live with diarrhea. Even when it ran down his legs when he sprinted to offload a damaged medevac chopper, it didn't bother him. The fever and the cramping, the jungle rats that scooted around the hooch, the insects as big as rodents, they were all quite tolerable after hearing the numb moaning of limbless boys. Those closest to death didn't even moan. Or the sickening feeling he had when he and three other marines lifted a tagged body bag from a CH-46 and found it contained rocks along with some small, unidentifiable body parts of a colonel atomized into a cranberry spray by a direct rocket hit. And they realized the rocks were put in to keep the bags from being whipped up into the blade wash. Or the vomiting wretch he became when a tied poncho slipped from a headless corpse. The threshold of comfort is very low indeed when the unforgettable odor of rotting corpses infects the nose with its insidious, glandular presence and takes up residence in the mind with sickening clarity.

Linda sat at the counter drying the tray of washed salt and pepper shakers. The Palace was closed and quiet. Teddy sat beside her and started to fill the shakers with her. He tried to engage her as Frances scraped down the grill.

"So what's doing in school, Linda? I thought last semester you said you were joining the chorus. What happened to that anyway?"

Linda looked down at the tray of shakers and shook her head. "Just didn't work out with my schedule. You know, they have evening rehearsals," she said, rolling her eyes to Teddy. "I just couldn't do it."

Teddy twisted the cap on a full shaker. "So, what does the chorus do now, you know, in the winter?"

A shallow smile creased Linda's lips. She shook her head slowly, her loss palpable. "Tonight," she said, glancing up at the wall clock, "tonight they massed the choirs of all the New Haven area colleges for a Mozart concert at Battell Chapel at Yale. It's such a neat thing to do, to mass the choirs." Linda got up and returned with the pepper funnel. "I just couldn't continue with that, not now anyway."

Teddy shook his head and started to place the clean, full shakers on the tables. "Better days are coming, Linda. You'll see. Things will get better."

Linda nodded in agreement and continued to fill the salt and pepper shakers. She imagined the massed choirs in black robes performing in the chapel, stately and uniform, practiced and disciplined, erect with the music before them. She rubbed dry a sugar container and tried in vain to stop the chill that went down her spine as she thought of the soprano line from the Requiem's introduction. She looked at the clock and wondered what Blake was doing at that moment, somewhere in country. She remembered Jennifer telling her they were singing the Ave Verum Corpus as an encore.

"I got it," Blake yelled out over the deafening noise of the Huey. Wind driven rain stung the faces of the Marines as they grabbed the corners of the body bag from the small chopper laden with death. Dusk had set in over the airfield making the somber moment darker. In Battell Chapel, half of a world away, the massed choirs started the encore. Blake saw the dampness of the material on the corner Sigford grabbed, body fluids mixing with the teeming rain in a slick cocktail making the body bag impossible to grab. The chopper lifted. Propeller wash whipped the bag violently causing Siggy to slip, his knees in the mud, the corner of the bag sucked from his grip. Blake instinctively reached up, stabilized the whipping bag and lifted Siggy from the back of his shirt as the four Marines started their bent and stumbling run from the chopper. The bag was unbalanced and light, the deceased a victim of an explosion where body parts were not recovered, dismembered pieces of a soldier going home to his loving family. They placed the bag under a canopy with the others and continued the macabre exercise of running damp body bags to an available revetment so nothing further could happen to them.

When they were done Blake looked at Siggy and shook his head in despair. Siggy looked down, disconsolate and shaken, and put his arm around Blake.

Linda screwed on the salt shaker cap, glanced at the clock again and closed her eyes. She saw the chorus standing erect and somber and heard the final, repeating bars of the Ave Verum Corpus, Mozart's mournful chorus of consolation.

"Just about done now?" Teddy asked, collecting the shakers on another tray to place on the tables and counter.

Linda looked up at him with watered eyes. She shook her head. Her voice was silenced by sadness as she rose to help him distribute the remaining salt and pepper shakers to the tables and the counter.

In early May, 1969, Quang Tri Provence of South Vietnam was a tropic welted with irony, lush with life but rich in death. The humidity and heat of Da Nang's air strip, heaving beneath the Asian sun, seemed mild compared to the steamy density of the Vietnamese jungle.

They lined up along a grass matted path in the jungle. "Shoot man," said Sigford, his voice full of the anger fear breeds when fate has paralyzed your options. "I don't like riding in them choppers. You hear them rounds coming through?"

Blake closed his eyes in agreement and shook his head. "Man, I was squeezing my ass so tight it started to cramp up."

Sigford glanced back and gave Blake a crooked smile as he recalled their encounter with the admin clerk up at Battalion Headquarters.

"Don't call me sir," the corporal at the processing desk said without looking up. His black-framed military issue glasses seemed to pinch his nose too tightly. "What's your last name again?" he asked, flipping the papers on his clipboard and scanning them for Sigford's name.

"We got to Travis a few days early and they just put us on the flight, said it wouldn't matter."

"You and who?" responded the corporal, finally looking up.

"Me and him, Private Tietel," said Sigford, pointing to Blake.

"What'd you say your name was?"

"Sigford."

"Well," the corporal intoned, "I'll write you two in for now. Put you both into the staging battalion for now until the paperwork catches up with you all. Just report back there to the warehouse to get jungle utilities."

"Any chance we can stay together?" asked Blake. "We're the only people we know here."

The corporal handed Blake's orders back to him and rolled his chair to a file cabinet. "Can't tell you that."

"They said we'd be able to stay together. Does it happen, sometimes, that they keep people together?" Blake persisted.

The corporal rolled back to his desk. "Next," he yelled, motioning the next Marine to step forward. "Happens all the time, some of these platoons are down to eighteen people, some down to thirteen. Shit, that ain't hardly enough for one squad. We send them up in bunches. Go get your jungle gear," he said dismissively.

Lieutenant Kelly called out to Sergeant Perez, holding the hand set out and tangling himself in the battered, cork-screw cord as he turned to face him. "The CO wants a recon patrol tonight. We got the people to cover it? First Platoon had it but they're down so many and they got perimeter tonight."

Perez walked to Kelly, looking at the heavy, charcoal colored clouds that hung low, draping the tree line in darkness. "Yes sir, Lieutenant, Hilgado's squad can cover it. They haven't pulled anything in a few days." Perez surveyed the sky again, turning in a complete circle, a slow, plodding pirouette in jungle boots, hands over his hips, assessing the wind, the cloud cover and the density of the jungle. He checked his watch and reached down to take a fistful of dirt, letting it drop through his fingers, clumps at a time.

"Okay, Captain." Kelly replied, unscrewing himself from the tangled cord and looking at the radio pack as he spoke. "We can do it. You got coordinates for the hill?"

Bailey approached Hilgado who was sitting in his bunker, reading a letter from his wife for the third time, a cigarette, nearly exhausted, pinched between his fingers that were caked with dirt. "Louie," called out Bailey from the top of the bunker, waiting for Hilgado to lean over and make eye contact. "Lieutenant wants your squad to do a recon patrol tonight. Better go see him."

Hilgado closed his eyes and shook his head. "A recon patrol? You got to be kidding me, Chuck," said Hilgado, climbing out of the bunker. "I got short timers here. They ain't going on no recon patrol."

He walked to Kelly's bunker, sucking and flaring his cigarette before flicking it to the barren ground.

"Lieutenant, I can't take my squad out there tonight Lieutenant. I got guys who never seen their kids yet and they're short timers." Hilgado paced before Kelly, his fists pounding rock hard sandbags. "I don't want to go out there with short timers. They won't recon shit. They'll just lie on their bellies until daylight, then come back in and say they ain't seen nothing."

Kelly met Hilgado chest on, gimlet eyed. "Sergeant, the Captain needs a simple recon patrol. You got a cloud cover so it's going to be dark out there, won't be able to see anything anyway. Just make your way in a klic and listen. Captain said they got some aerial shots showing some activity in the brush, right before the next clearing. That's the only area with vegetation left. He doesn't want any engagement, just go out a klic and listen until dawn. See whatever you can, then get your asses back in here."

"Lieutenant, once we get into the boonies they won't be able to see shit, can't control them. I won't even know who's with me or where they are after an hour, probably loaded with mines."

Kelly stepped by Hilgado and climbed out of the bunker waiting for Hilgado to appear. "They had that whole area just two months ago. If they had any mines they would have had to set them when they left and they were under a lot of fire then. We've been playing cat and mouse long enough out here."

"And what about the short timers?" Hilgado asked, walking from Kelly. "You want me to order them out?" His voice lost its fire.

"If you can get any volunteers from Bailey's squad you can take them. You don't need take out a whole squad," he said. "Just take out six guys, maybe two fire teams. That should be enough."

"Yes, sir, Lieutenant," responded Hilgado, with a voice of resignation. He walked back to the bunker and pulled his jungle cover off, stretching his neck up and around, scanning the darkened sky, searching for the moon or stars, thankful for the cloud cover and Kelly's concessions.

"Chuck," Hilgado whispered, "you got anyone you think wants to do some snooping tonight? Lieutenant says I can get some volunteers."

Bailey looked over his shoulder to Sigford, his weapon

torn down and laid out before him on his poncho, practicing assembling it in the dark.

"Sigford," Bailey called out, walking towards him. "Second squad's going on a recon patrol tonight, you interested?"

Sigford never looked up, his hands assembling the M-16, its lightly lubricated parts gliding into place, their clicking and snapping the only sound from the bunker. "Yeah, Sarge. Heck, I'll go. Beats sitting in this rat hole all night."

Blake turned to Sigford. "I'll go too, Sarge."

Bailey turned to Hilgado, his face hardly visible any longer against the walls of the bunker. "You guys know you don't have to go. This is voluntary. Hilgado's got some short timers he doesn't want to take out."

"I'm going too, Sarge," Blake repeated, uncertain if Bailey heard him.

"Okay, you're in, you and Sigford."

Sigford turned to Blake, laying his weapon on top of the sandbags, "Why you going, buddy? You don't need to go."

"Yeah, I do, Sig. I want to go, better than sitting here all night."

Hilgado assembled the fire teams in Kelly's bunker, reviewing the plan under the dim light of a lantern while the Marines applied camouflage paint to their faces and hands. He gave Sigford the Starlight scope to fasten to his weapon. When Hilgado was finished Kelly spoke, his tone serious, his face without animation.

"Remember, this is a recon patrol," he said in textbook fashion. "We don't want to surprise anyone or engage anyone. Just get out there, listen and get back in here by dawn." Kelly hesitated for a moment before releasing them. "You won't be able to see each other out there, so the sounds you hear will probably be each other. If you must talk, of course, do it quietly. Be careful and watch out for each other. Now let me look over you guys."

The fire teams stood silently as Kelly stopped before each of them to check their faces and hands for unpainted flesh, the glint of any rings or eyeglasses, then shaking each for the rattle of dogtags or metal pieces.

"Gaines," he said, removing three of six grenades from his rifle belt, "you won't need all these. It'll only get in your way. If you're close enough to throw this, then you're too close. You want to get out there, listen for while and come back in."

"Yes, sir," replied Gaines, removing another grenade from his belt.

Kelly moved on to Blake, turning to him and looking over his uniform and feeling his cuffs to be certain they were tucked into his boots. Then he shook him. "What's the rattle, Private?"

"My dog tags, sir, and my cross."

"Secure the cross private. This is a recon patrol, rattles against your dogtags. It's just in the way."

Blake removed his helmet and opened his shirt, exposing sheathed tags and the gold chain dulled from body oils and sweat mixed with dust and dirt. He lifted his dogtags over his head and put them in his pocket, turned from Kelly, distracted by the next marine, and buttoned up his shirt.

When Kelly was finished Hilgado led them to the tree line and spread them abreast, Sigford, with his Starlight scope that was nearly useless without some light to amplify, to his left. Blake positioned himself to Sigford's left and waited for the remainder of the marines to set up. Simple, quick gestures of 'set' passed down the line to let Hilgado know they were positioned. He immediately passed down the word to move and stepped into the tree line, entering the jungle black with the heavy canopy of trees and brush.

They heard vines snapping, an occasional gasp as someone got stuck with something sharp or had to find their way around an especially thick growth. After several minutes Hilgado passed the word to stop the advance and took a count, each relaying the presence of the other to the center, knowing that control was essential yet impossible, knowing that too much noise would compromise their stealth. They couldn't see each other and almost couldn't hear each other, having gone a hundred meters into the jungle. Word then passed to continue. The rhythm of the jungle was filled with insects calling to each other in ancient mating calls.

The flash filled the blackness with blinding white light. The ancient insect calls stopped. Then there was blackness again and silence, and then, seconds later, the sound of moaning from somewhere on the jungle floor.

The patrol froze. They waited for the staccato of small arms fire, waited, with the sounds of their hearts thumping in their ears, for some movement, some indication that the bad guys knew where they were and fixed their positions. Silence continued for what felt like the interminable seconds, then the moan again, muffled and weak, and the unavoidable conclusion that one of them, somewhere in the unforgiving darkness, was injured.

The stillness continued, uninterrupted except for the moan and then familiar bursts of small arms fire shredding the night. Frozen by sightlessness, the Marines readied their weapons and searched the black jungle for the enemy. They were desperate with the fear of being an inch from a detonating blast and unable to fire back as bullets ripped through the jungle. And then the moan again and Blake knew.

He dropped to his knees and swept his arms out slowly. His body shuddered with panic. He slipped out of his flak jacket and peeled off his blouse so he would be warned of the trip mine by its feel on his skin.

He stuffed his blouse into his trousers and leaned back with his arms out before him, moving in a slow sweep, to the floor of the jungle. Digging the heels of his boots into the thick, slippery, thick jungle floor, he pushed himself forward, on his back, his neck arched, anticipating the blast that would shred his brain, knowing that if he felt the pressure release mine under him it would be too late to save himself, his torso would be atomized and his legs blown off. And the moan continued.

He called Sigford's name, inching forward as sweat streamed over his face and burnt his eyes.

"Siggy, Siggy," he whispered, hoping for a response that would resolve the darkness to clarity and the desperation to some form of hope. The firefight erupted around him with bullets running through the jungle with deafening points. Tracers raced by him and directed fire at nothing in particular, just more fire power into the same blackness.

Hilgado's voice rang out, "It's coming from our three o'clock, coming from our three o'clock!" and the firepower redirected into his path.

Then, another command, "Hold your fire, hold your fire," and the ensuring silence except for a distant enemy moving somewhere in the blackness. And the moan and Blake's voice cracked in the night as he tried to call out to Siggy.

The chain was choking him, wedged between his back and the jungle floor. He stopped his movement and put his hands to his throat, slowly and deliberately, then pulled the cross around to his chest and placed it into his mouth. The moan again sounded, and he heard labored breath and the moan louder still, in the exhausted rattle of impending death. He inched forward again, finally gripping Sigford's boot.

"Okay, buddy," he whispered, as if the falsetto would somehow provide comfort as Sigford's blood poured out over the jungle floor. "I'm here, buddy," he said into the dense blackness. His hands climbed up Sigford's leg and groped along his body. He tested for trip wires as the firefight erupted again. He knelt over Sigford and let the cross swing freely in a warm cocktail of saliva and sweat.

In the darkness he could see nothing, not even the outline of Sigford's face. The moans became thinner, shallow breaths of an expiring Marine. He called out softly, "Siggy, Siggy, Siggy," then his own crying betraying any lingering hope and his jaw trembled as he rocked on his knees. He reached down to feel Sigford's face and rested his hand on the wet pulp of blasted flesh and shattered bone. He moved his other hand to Sigford's head and cradled his exposed brain in his palm.

The hollow thunk of an illumination round leaving its tube silenced the firefight. Stillness prevailed as its flair ignited above the jungle and whitened the clouds in bas-relief, beginning its descent under its parachute canopy.

Slowly, with a sway that washed great shadows across the jungle floor, darkness altered with light, as the smell of gunpowder filled the night in wafts of white coils.

He looked down at Sigford, pressing his hand against his matted hair and saw the blood still streaming from his head, his face half blasted away. And a final moan came, weak and barely audible. He lifted Sigford's limp body close to his own, whispering his name into the thinning shadows as the flair licked the darkness with its last light. All that remained was the sound of his crying, continuing to whisper Sigford's name into the darkness, unaware of anything around him except the lifeless body beneath him.

His death fouled the air with the odor of the body's gentle surrender. Sigford's shattered bone fragments rolled between Blake's fingertips and Sigford's exposed brain.

Blake pulled his blouse from his waist and placed it under Sigford's head. His cry keened into the darkness. He leaned over Siggy and slipped his cross over Siggy's blasted head. They had found the war in the sightless pitch of an operation called Virginia Ridge. He rocked on wet knees in the darkness with his fingers pinched by the bone shards of Sigford's skull. He ran his hand over the undamaged side of Sigford's head hoping his touch could comfort his dead friend as tracer rounds ripped the leaves to shreds and the rat-a-tat of small arms fire continued.

It didn't matter. Not now, maybe not ever. It was too dark to see so why bother to hide. No, let the firefight rage with its leaded brilliance. There was no returning now.

Linda swung the door open and walked to the counter.

"No, Bertha. No, the black and white is it for Arthur?" Frances smiled into the receiver as she heard the confusion at the other end while Bertha yelled back to Arthur, then she laughed out loud.

"Oh, Linda," she called out with surprise, looking up at the clock. "Oh," she recalled without explanation, "that's right." She cut back to the phone without finishing her thought. "Okay, okay, tell Arthur I'll take care of it. Fifteen minutes. Don't be late. The froth will dissolve....never mind....don't be late." She hung the phone in the cabinet under the counter and rapped her palm over her forehead.

"They make me dizzy over there," she said, engaging Linda in mirror talk. "You got an exam today, right?" She looked down the counter to Teddy plating his bacon and eggs over a slice of toast. "Need a tuna melt for Jerry and a steak and cheese for Marty."

Teddy covered his eggs with an empty plate and set it on the counter. "Man could starve in here, Linda," he said with a smile.

"Want me to make it?" Linda offered, walking towards the grill.

"No, just kidding. I'll get it. Cold bacon and eggs, nothing like it!"

Linda turned and straightened the bow of her jumper in the full-length mirror near the candy counter. Her face was full and pink cheeked with her jumper cresting just below her breasts. "I'm going to use the phone to call a friend at school."

"Of course, of course," Frances said as Teddy waved off the request with assurance.

Teddy took the end stool, uncovered his plate and looked up into the mirror. He watched Linda lower the radio volume. "What are you doing here anyway?" he asked with a frown. "I thought you had an exam or something today?"

"I have my jury today," Linda said quickly, holding her hand over the receiver and angling to catch Teddy's eyes in the mirror.

Mirror conversations. They happened regularly at Vonetes, between the counter sitters, perched like sparrows on a telephone line, unable to see each other over the other birds beside them. Talk transported with reflection and light, and timed glances into the faded mirrors. All year long, in the dead of winter when whipped cream melted into hot chocolate, and in the height of summer, when refreshing ice cream floats are lofted on long spoons into the dead heat, the patter of talk binds the seasons. This angled speaking takes some practice to get used to the cadence of the voice and the fleeting eye that not everyone can master. Like a camera shutter, they are conversations captured in distinct frames of sight, a wink of illumination tied by voices full of inflection.

"Jury," Teddy said with a mouthful of eggs and toast. "What's that again?"

Linda glanced into the mirror. "It's like an exam......"she replied, hesitating between phrases while she searched for an answer Teddy would understand, "except you have to perform..... before the professor." She adjusted her shoulder bag and turned, facing the mirror behind the candy counter. "Jen?" she asked excitedly, "I thought you left."

"No, I told you I'd wait, Lin. Where are you?"

"Vonetes. Are you going to school?"

"Yeah, soon, but I've been waiting. You want to meet me there?

"I told Jim I'd meet him in front of the library. They're holding a protest. I'll be in front of the library. I think some of the guys want to shut it down."

"Okay, but look for me. I don't like the protests. They

make me nervous."

"Yeah, don't worry, I'll be there, in front of the bike racks. I'll meet you there. What's going on anyway?"

"I'll tell you there. I've been working on something for a few months now," she said cryptically. "You think Munk will be there?"

"Are you kidding? He'd never cancel," Jennifer said with certainty. "You've been doing what?"

"Never mind, I'll see you in about half an hour." Linda hung up, turned up the radio volume and walked to Teddy's side.

"So what's doing, Linda?" he asked, turning his stool half a rotation and placing his hands over his lap.

"I got to go," she said quickly, tapping his shoulder as a good- bye gesture.

"Wait, you didn't eat," Frances said, walking to the grill. "I got a nice toasted corn muffin on the grill for you."

Linda rolled her eyes and fished her keys from her shoulderbag. "You guys are getting me fat."

Teddy got up and walked to the grill. "You got to eat," he insisted.

"I don't want to sing on a full stomach," she protested.

Somehow, they had come to a collected wisdom. In the mountains of Piletas the female eye is sharp sighted and dense with wisdom, recognizing the smallest changes in young women, glimpsing pregnancy in the nuanced flush of the cheeks or uncharacteristic fatigue. And so it was with her mother, in the sleepless nights after the rape and the countless baths that failed to cleanse, that she concluded what Linda feared. They sat at the kitchen table and spoke in quiet and gentle tones of what occurred and cried through the painful recollection of the event. Then they sat with Frances and Teddy, one night after the Palace closed, just before the call from Blake, and told them what fate arranged and bad luck delivered.

"You have to eat," Teddy repeated.

"All set," Frances chirped, turning the muffin in a tight wrap of paper. "What about a drink?"

"Water," Linda responded, pulling some napkins from the counter dispenser and grabbing the muffin. "No ice. Keep my throat moist," she called out as she swung the door open.

"Good luck on the test," Teddy called out.

"Yeah, good luck," Frances said as Flip entered for his order. She glanced at Teddy and said in an undertone, "It's not a test."

"Whatever," Teddy responded in a frustrated tone. "What's doing, Flip?"

Linda drove to New Haven between buttery swallows of the corn muffin and sips of water. She turned into the library parking lot but was greeted by two campus security police who stood behind a row of yellow police horses. She could hear the wild applause and shouts of the protesters although she couldn't see them. "No one can park here," one of the officers called out.

"Oh, please," she said, her window half rolled down, "I have an exam today. I have to park here. I'm running late."

One of the officers removed his sunglasses and leaned

on the wooden horse. "Sorry, miss," he said, "there's a protest going on in front of the building. We have to keep the area clear for emergency vehicles."

"Is the building closed? Is Engleman Hall open?" Linda asked, hearing the protestors respond enthusiastically to the ranting of a voice booming from a garbled loudspeaker.

"No. It's open but they're blocking entry to the main door." He turned over his shoulder and looked at all the open spaces beyond the horses.

"I'm supposed to have a jury before Professor Munk and Professor York today. Do you know if he's in there?" she asked, pointing to Lyman Auditorium.

The other officer stepped up to the door of Linda's car and looked down at her, nodding his head towards the buildings. "I just saw him walk from the side door of Lyman into Engleman." He turned toward the officer leaning on the wooden horse and nodded without a word. "Look, I'll let you in. Okay, just park over by the portable buildings there on the right, out of the way."

"Thank you so much." Linda shifted into first while the officers pivoted a horse out of the way and called back as she drove in, "Thank you so much."

On the steps of Engleman Hall, Lenny Wakeman, in faded green battle fatigues and a bush hat, stood in defiance of anyone attempting to enter. Linda picked her way through the throng slowly, towards the library, clutching her manila folder against her chest. She strained to find Jennifer as she approached the bike rack that was occupied by students standing on the frame to get a better view.

"Linda, Linda," Jennifer called out, waving frantically from the knoll above the bike rack.

Linda looked up, turning towards the voice, and saw Jennifer, her wiry blonde hair tied back in a ponytail like a thatch of hay. A big, satisfied smile creased her face. Linda stepped towards her, reached out and grabbed her hand.

"Oh, Jen, I can't believe you found me. I can't believe the crowd. This is serious."

"Yeah," explained Jennifer. "Lenny's got all the entrances blocked so no one can get in. Some of the faculty is still in there but mostly they're gone too. They postponed some of the exams."

"Do you think they're cancelled?" Linda asked, turning towards the blocked entrance of Englemen.

"I don't think so. No one said that yet."

Linda turned back to Jennifer, "You think Lenny will let us through?"

Jennifer stepped down and scanned the building.

"Where'd Munk say he was holding it?"

"The schedule says Practice Room A."

Jennifer grabbed Linda's hand and pulled along. "Come on," she said, cutting a seam in the crowd like a rudder. "I think York said it might be in Lyman. Munk's afraid he won't be able to hear because of all the noise outside practice room A."

At the steps of Engleman, with the crowd at crushing density, Jennifer turned to Linda and instructed her, "Wait here. I'll go talk to Lenny."

Jennifer waited for Lenny to stop yelling into a chipped and dented bullhorn. Linda spoke to some students she recognized from her botany class the previous semester and occupied the minutes with idle speculation whether exams would be cancelled or not. Then she stepped forward as Jennifer bounced down the stairs.

"Can we go in?" she asked over several heads.

"Yeah," Jennifer yelled, pointing towards the parking lot. "But he said to use the side door because these doors are chained. "Come on," she said, turning Linda around and darting in front of her.

The crowd thinned as they approached the side door. "Here, Jen," Linda said, handing Jennifer the manila folder.

"What's this?" she asked, tucking it under her arm.

They walked several steps before Linda responded. "I need a favor," she responded, stopping as Jennifer turned to her. "I need you to accompany me today."

Jennifer looked at Linda oddly. "What do you mean? Is it like a duet or something?"

"Let's keep walking," Linda responded, stepping forward. "I'm not doing the Rachmaninoff piece. I'm going to sing."

Jennifer stopped short, screwed up her face and opened the manila folder. "Sing?" she asked, perplexed. "How can you sing? What did York say?" She pulled a dog-eared copy of sheet music from the folder.

Linda placed her hand on Jennifer's shoulder and pulled her along, "Come on, I don't want to be late. You know Munk, he'll just flunk me." They walked towards the double doors with a serious looking student standing inside. "She said it's at Munk's discretion."

Jennifer opened the door and held it as Linda entered the vestibule. "I thought you just needed help getting into the building," Jennifer said, shaking her head in disbelief.

"No, Jen. When I called you I didn't even know there was a protest going on. I prepared for both in case Munk says no, but it's not what I want to do. I really need you to play for me."

Jennifer opened the second set of doors and wedged herself between the door and the frame. "Are you Jim?" she asked confidently.

"Yeah," he responded, placing his frame against the door so it couldn't be opened any further.

"We have to get in. Lenny said to tell you it's okay." She moved aside and motioned for Linda to come through.

Jim nodded and pulled the door open as Linda slipped through. Jennifer followed, "She has to go to the bathroom, then we have to see Professor Munk."

"Yeah," Jim said without concern. "I'm not sure if he's in here, but you can look."

They walked down the deserted hall towards the auditorium. The sound of Jennifer's clogs clacking over the tile echoed through the entire length of the hallway. "I would never have gotten in here without you," Linda whispered as they turned out of Jim's sight.

York was standing at her window observing the protest when the sound of the clogs stopped. She continued to look out the window, trying to read the writing on the sheets hanging from the library windows.

"Professor York," Linda said in a tone of deference. "I'm here for my jury."

York walked to her desk and picked up her student schedule. "Yes, Linda," she said with a surprised look. "I was wondering if you might show up." She glanced at her watch and commented, "you're even on time despite everything going on out there. How did you manage to get in?"

"Jennifer got me in. She's friends with Lenny."

"Then we had to get by this guy Jim at the side door here. I think he took a look at Linda and didn't want to give her a hard time."

"Is Professor Munk here?" Linda asked.

"Oh, yes," York responded with certainty. "You know him. They'd have to burn the buildings before he'd leave. But we're going to have to walk over to Lyman. He said Practice Room A is too noisy. Are you ready?"

Linda nodded her head and tugged on her purse strap, "Yes."

"Well, okay then, why don't you and Jennifer go to the auditorium and I'll be right there. It will be just Professor Munk and myself. No peers."

They turned to leave. The sound of the clogs filled the hallway again. "I'm really nervous, Lin," Jennifer said, tugging at Linda's arm and stopping her. "I've never even seen this music before."

"Here," Linda pulled a clean, fresh copy from the folder. "The one you pulled out is my dad's copy. It's ancient." The sound of York's footsteps stopped their conversation.

"Dr. York," Jennifer asked as she walked a few strides with York, "could you ask Professor Munk if we can have five minutes? I just saw this music for the first time."

"That shouldn't be a problem. I don't think anyone else will be showing up anyway."

"Great!" Jennifer exclaimed. "Thanks." She walked back to Linda and sidled up to her. "I really don't know about this, Lin."

Linda held the music out before them. "Look, Jen, you're the best sight reader in the class. Everyone knows that. Look at these piano lines, they're basic. It's an art song that my father taught me years ago."

Linda put the music back into the folder and started to walk. "Come on, she said, opening the door to Practice Room A. "I'll play a few measures for you. It's really nothing."

The chants of the protestors filled the room. Linda sat at the piano while Jennifer stood beside her. She started to play the simple line of notes. "You see, Jen, its real simple. Mostly quarter notes. It's about six and a half minutes long, but it doesn't get any harder than this."

Jennifer sighed and nudged Linda off the bench. "Let me try," she said with resignation as Linda walked to the door. "Aren't you going to sing?" she asked as she started playing fluidly.

"I'm already late. I don't want to keep Munk waiting," Linda responded as Jennifer clogged down the hall, catching up with her at the stage door.

"Wait," she asked, putting her hand against the door. "Where did you learn to sing?"

Linda put her hand on the door, as if keeping it closed could deliver her from the fate she couldn't avoid. "My dad taught me. He was a voice teacher."

Jennifer twisted her face in confusion and whispered, "I thought he taught you piano?"

Linda released the door and started to pull in open, "He did."

"How come you never said anything before?"

Linda shrugged and winced. "I guess it never really came up," she said peering through the small window of the stage door.

Jennifer clogged to her side. "I'm scared. Munk could flunk you for this."

Linda cast her eyes to the floor. She looked down the empty hallway and turned to Jennifer as they stopped. "It doesn't matter, Jen."

Jennifer released the door and put her hand on Linda's shoulder. Her eyes narrowed as she spoke, trying to make some sense of all this. "He could drop you from the program."

"It doesn't matter," Linda said resolutely.

"Of course it matters. I don't understand."

"I'm not enrolling for the fall." The words rolled from her tongue without hesitation or inflection. "There's just no way I can continue here and work and raise a baby, I just can't." She reached into her pocketbook and pulled out some tissues, handing one to Jennifer as well. Then she spoke in halting words as she tried to regain her composure. "I just want to finish this out so my record is okay if I want to come back someday."

Jennifer shook her head and responded slowly as Linda opened the door into the darkness of the back stage. She pulled off her clogs as they started walking. "I didn't know it was so bad for you, Lin. You never said anything."

"It will be okay, Jen," Linda said calmly. "It just wasn't meant to be."

The stage seemed enormous, empty except for the gleaming black concert grand standing on the left. The auditorium lights were off, making its depth drop off rapidly into a darkness outlined only by exit lights. Jennifer walked to the piano, adjusted the bench and sat, quietly positioning the sheet music.

Linda walked to the edge of the stage and stooped down as York approached. "This is what I'll be singing, Professor. It's an old art song," she explained nervously.

York glanced at the music and looked up at Linda. "I don' understand," she said with a confused look. "You're not doing the Rachmananoff piece?"

Linda remained in the stooped position and explained, "No, Professor. Do you recall that I asked you a few months ago if I sang instead since it's my minor and you said it would be at the discretion of Dr. Munk?"

York tapped the music on the stage for a moment, allowing her time to think. "Yes, well, I do remember the conversation. But I typically get Dr. Munk to approve that prior to the jury."

Linda studied York's face and met her eyes for a second before glancing at Munk. His short, stumpy body, slouched in a soft auditorium chair, seemed wrapped in the fabric. She turned her eyes back to York saying, in a regretful tone, "I've been preparing this for a few months, since our conversation. I don't know what else to say. I thought I mentioned it to you after class this semester."

York nodded with understanding. "Maybe we had a misunderstanding. Let me see what I can do," she added as she turned and walked to Munk.

Linda stood and walked to Jennifer's side. She moved the microphone away from the sound board. She stood quietly as Munk stepped into the aisle as York explained the misunderstanding. He guided York aside with a forearm sweep and stepped towards the stage. The faint sound of the protestor's chants drifted into the space. "You do realize that you will be graded as if you've practiced this with your advisor all semester long, don't you?"

"Yes, Professor," she heard herself say as the microphone picked up her words. "Dr. York explained that to me." She reached over and turned the microphone off.

Munk walked back to his seat, kicking the frame with the points of his boots before burying himself into his seat. He moved the music from side to side, unable to read the title as he reached over his head for his bifocals. "What's the name of this piece anyway? he asked, turning to York, "I can't see in the dark here."

"Il Mio Ben Quando Verra," York replied.

"Il Mio Ben Quando Verra," Linda said at the same time,

moving towards the edge of the stage. "It's an old, Italian art song my father taught me, in Puerto Rico." Then she shrugged her shoulders in confusion, realizing she said more than was necessary at a moment so formally drawn.

Munk stood and turned the music towards the stage light to read it. His knees locked against the chair in front of him, making him appear shorter than ever. "All the art songs are old," Munk said dismissively. "I don't know, the vocal line looks very simple," he said, looking up at the stage. He turned to York and repeated, "It's rudimentary. I thought you said she was a piano major."

"She is a music education major concentrating on voice as a minor." York stood and turned her back to the stage. Her seat flipped up with an audible thud as she nervously fanned herself with the music. She knew this was unnerving for Linda and felt responsible for the misunderstanding.

"David," she said curtly, "I've heard her sing before." She allowed some silence to drop between them to emphasize her exasperation. "She came to the first chorus rehearsal but never returned. When I asked her about it she explained that she had to work, so I just dropped it."

York glanced over her shoulder as Munk looked at the stage, nodding his head. "Obviously there is some problem. But when she sang, just those few notes, it was clear that she had a trained and gifted voice. She was concerned that she wasn't sure whether she was a mezzo or a soprano. You might want to hear her sing." Munk glanced at the music again and shook his head affirmatively. He slumped back in his chair as York turned and nodded silently for them to begin.

Linda turned to Jennifer and nodded. Muffled clapping filtered into the dark auditorium as Jennifer started the slow, simple introduction. Linda pivoted and faced her audience of two, losing her sight line to Jennifer. She folded her hands, resting them at her waist. She relaxed her body, looking reposed and peaceful as the piano softened and the gold framing of her cameo glinted into the darkness of the auditorium. She took a breath and let the first notes fill the auditorium when Munk popped out of his seat and into the aisle, breaking her concentration.

He shook his head apologetically, "Excuse me," he blurted out. "Forgive me Miss, er Mrs.," then turned to York for help. He shook his leg to get his pant cuff to fall from the top of his boot.

York looked at Munk and turned her palm up in ignorance, embarrassed by his behavior. "Linda," she said as she tucked her head down.

"Yes," Munk continued, regrouping. "Miss Linda, I'm very sorry to interrupt you, but I was, uh, trying to read the music and I should have known better that I can't in the darkness here. But I wasn't listening and I would like you to start again and I will listen this time. Totally my fault, I know, this is unforgivable, but could you please start over?"

Linda opened her hands and rested them on her thighs, allowing the nervous sweat to be absorbed by the material of her jumper. "Of course, Professor," she said, turning to

Jennifer who nodded assuredly, looked down and started the slow notes of the introduction. Linda clasped her hands once more, this time fixing her gaze on the illuminated clock on the back wall. Munk sat on the edge of his seat, leaning forward and draping his arms over the chair in front of him. York hunched forward, resting her elbows on her crossed legs.

The piano softened and Linda closed her eyes to the darkness. She drew air into her lungs, expanded her belly and felt her breath leave her body with measured certainty. The notes floated from her lips with perfect clarity and developed into graceful ellipses of perfectly pitched notes. In the song from the mountains, she heard her father's voice whispering. 'Sostenuto, Linda, sostenuto' 'hold your notes, Linda, hold your notes.' And the pearly luster of her voice filled the empty space with flawless serenity and beauty.

She heard Jennifer fall behind as she turned the page and then hold a fermata too long, all without consequence. For this moment, when time for her was suspended, the elegy rose from the sadness that weighed her heart. Like beads of mercury, perfect and distinct, her notes were round, plumy balloons that elevated in the narrow range on the dark side of the scale in six minutes of weightless beauty. When she released the final note she listened to her own sound trail off, diminishing into the darkness, dissipating under the soft damper of Jennifer's piano.

Munk stood slowly, moved into the aisle and eased his seat up to preserve the solitude. He stepped towards the stage, then hesitated when he saw Linda's eyes open, glistening with moisture. Jennifer rotated off the piano bench with her back towards the auditorium, a tissue pressed to her eyes. Linda looked at Munk without a word. She glanced at York, then released her hands and slid the cameo over its delicate chain nervously.

"Remarkable," Munk said, turning up the aisle. "Just remarkable."

He and York walked up the aisle into the blackness and opened the door with a loud crack, allowing a blinding shaft of light race in, then darkness again. Linda walked to the piano, collected her music and placed it in the folder. She walked to Jennifer who didn't turn to her but stood motionless. She placed her hand on Jennifer's back and walked around until they faced each other, then hugged her and thanked her for playing for her. Jennifer looked at Linda and nodded, acknowledging her gratitude and struggling to maintain her composure.

"Sorry I missed the fermata," Jennifer said, picking up her clogs.

"Don't even think about it, Jen. You were great. I didn't notice it. I kind of get zoned out when I sing that song."

"I never heard anything like that. You definitely can't quit. You just can't."

Linda shook her head, pursing her lips as they opened the door and started down the same hall they came in by.

"I have to. I don't have a choice. What you heard today was something I wanted to do for myself. I just wanted to have that feeling one more time, that feeling of being beyond all my troubles. And I was able to do it because of you. Hopefully Munk will give me the credits for it and that's it."

"But your voice, you can't just stop singing."

Linda smiled wistfully and thanked her for the compliment, then added, "My voice needs help, Jen. It really has a narrow range. I need private lessons, maybe a conservatory, but forget it."

They stood in the doorway facing the sun. Jennifer picked up the cameo and lifted it into her palm. "This is so pretty, Lin. Still haven't heard from him?"

Linda shook her head, "No," she whispered.

"He's going to be okay, Lin, and someday he'll come back."

Linda nodded as they walked through the doors into the crowd. She turned and hugged Jennifer, felt herself break down and started to walk away. Jennifer followed her, walking with her in silence until she got into her car.

"Keep in touch with me, okay. You have my home number where I'll be for the summer, right?"

Linda looked up at her and smiled as she wiped the last tears from her eyes, "I have it. Thank you again for today, Jen."

"Call me."

"I will."

"Promise?"

Linda nodded and drove off.

1975

"All right, let's begin." Hunter Biller's raspy voice emanated from a cloud of cigar smoke that wreathed his face. He picked up the phone and buzzed his secretary.

"Helen," he commanded, leaning into the intercom, "I want all my calls held until after the meeting."

He released the talk bar and walked to his desk, easing his long frame into his swiveling, rolling, leather chair. He swung his legs up and clunked his boots on the cherry desktop.

"Okay, Dave, why don't you begin?" Biller rapped his palm on his desk and gave a quick smile to the assembly of men.

David Polis of Seymour, the manager of Plant Five of the Sponge Rubber Company, rose from the sofa and nodded to Dale Pollard, the comptroller of the parent company, Prime Fabricators of Ohio.

"Well," he commented, "frankly, you guys are doing a lousy job of running the place. Forget Plant Five, if you don't get Plant Four running right we won't be in business much longer. That plant isn't close to running to capacity and it's producing too much scrap. I don't know why we keep having these meetings. I suggested you buy a new dryer and showed the numbers how you can make your investment back three times over within a year. And the DuPont chemical proposal I brought to you, you rejected that. All it took was an investment of about ten thousand dollars and you would have netted fifty thousand a year."

Biller gave Polis an annoyed look. "I thought you and I talked about that last month. And I told you I would talk to my advisors about that. Didn't we discuss that? How am I supposed to get the efficiency of the plants up if sales aren't coming in? And money, you think I have cash laying around to spend on some unproven ideas while the plants are bleeding money? Without another tap at the credit line we don't have enough cash to get us to the end of the year. Everyone seems to be paying late."

Polis stood and folded his arms. "Late payment is just one problem. Did anyone tell you that Sears cancelled their five million dollar mattress contract?"

Pollard looked up from his notes and scanned the group. "I didn't tell you about that yet, Hunter. I wanted to have a few days to call them and work out some deal, you know, maybe give them a more competitive price or talk about the quality if that was their concern. You know, Christmas and all coming up, people are not focused on paying bills. They're planning parties and buying presents, tough time of year to collect timely."

Biller streamed cigar smoke toward the ceiling and spoke as he watched it billow and roll. He seemed to be delaying to collect his thoughts and suppress his anger at learning about the Sears contract.

"How about prepayments? Are we shipping when they

still owe us for the last shipment? Is anyone paying their bills, other than me? Didn't we agree at the last meeting that we weren't shipping until we got paid?" Biller asked, dabbing out the cigar. "Sorry," he said, looking around the room. "I forget this ain't Ohio. They're used to me back there, they just tell me to put it out. Besides, I'd rather have some chew but you all out here don't like that so much either."

Ben Fiore, the acting Plant Manager of Plant Four, looked at the others and nodded his head. "It's okay, Hunter. "I don't think anyone here objects." Fiore folded his hands and glanced at the sales manager standing near the door. "The energy costs in Plant Four are eating us up. Like Dale said, this is a tough time to collect. Then in January they'll be focused on closing out last year's accounting. Nobody in sales wants to force payment up Front. Hunter, they're afraid of irritating customers. Plus, we have too much product stacked up in the warehouse and here in the plants. If we don't ship it we don't have anyplace to store it either. With B.F., we never requested prepayment."

"Ben," Biller snapped as he stood and stabbed the air with the still smoldering cigar. "I bought this business almost a year ago. Yet every time I come to Shelton I have to hear all you people tell me about how it was done under B.F Goodrich. B.F. did it this way and B. F. did it that way. What nobody says is that B. F. wanted out because they couldn't make any money here making sponge products. No one wants to talk about that." Biller sat back down and leaned over his desk. "Now I know you people had a certain way of conducting business before, but it's a different world. I can't be carrying these customers. Now, what about the debt? Will B.F. allow us an extension of the forty million to close on the buildings? Dale, you got anything on that?"

"They said they'll talk if we can come up with $5,000,000. I told them I didn't think that would work. They're talking about increasing the rent from $35,000 a month to $65,000. They want to give us an incentive to find the financing."

Biller shook his head defiantly.

"Incentive? They must be crazy. They want to put me out of business at that price. Did you remind them that I came up with almost $14,000,000 for the business and the machinery and that was financed? That was more than anyone else was willing to come up with. Every piece of equipment here is financed and covered with a lien. If they force us out of here we have 90 days to get the machinery out. But it's all financed so I don't have to pull out anything. I could just walk away from it. That would be cheaper in the end. Apparently they don't want to complete the sale of the buildings because if they did they would know I can't pay rent like that. Where do they think I can come up with the money to complete the purchase of the buildings? Don't they realize I'm their only hope? If I can't make this work no one can and they know that."

Biller stood again and walked to the window overlooking the parking lot. He put the dead cigar into his mouth and chewed on the tip. "How many employees we got here? About eleven hundred, right?"

"About a thousand," Fiore responded.

"Close enough. I said I wanted to improve the plants, put some money into them and make them competitive again. You have to convince B. F. to work with me on this. I can't get it done overnight. Tell them we're working another angle."

Biller walked over to Wade Staber who was seated on the sofa and put his hand over his shoulder.

"I want Wade to talk about the water treatment system he's been researching. It's a way to clean up the waste water and get some funding from the state."

Staber raised his hand. He reminded everyone that they may have seen him earlier in the month when he visited the plant with Hunter to view the water usage system and converting the usage to the canal outside the plant. He told them the discharge system is insufficient to meet the state of Connecticut's requirements. He looked down at two soiled note cards through oversized glasses as he struggled to read his scribbled notes. He resembled a stick man, sitting with his legs crossed and his heel leaning on the Queen Anne leg with his black trench coat unbuttoned and swagged to the rug. He was a gaunt, pallid man with hollow cheeks, tall and rangy in an awkward way. He stuffed the two index cards into his coat pocket that was already bulging with his balled up gloves.

"I been taking to the state lately," he said confidently. "We've been talking about money. Grants, money Sponge won't have to pay back."

Fiore looked down and footed the corner of the area rug into place, then looked up. "I'm a little confused, Hunter," he said, referring his comments to Hunter directly and casting a defiant eye towards Staber. "We have people right here at the plant that can get on the phone with the state and talk on a first-name basis. Why is Wade contacting the state without us knowing anything? Something like this can't be run from Ohio. I mean, if there's money available we can get it. We got two guys in the plant that are aldermen and a secretary whose husband works for the state economic development office. We can get the funding if that's what you want."

Biller leaned back in his chair and toyed with his cigar. "Ben, look, I know you all mean well, but if you had a means of financing improvements why didn't you say so when Dale and me and you talked last month? It's too late now. Wade is my spokesman for the water treatment improvements and for any funding we can find. Besides, I have arranged for Wade to be present here in Shelton on a weekly basis. You know, blueprints have to be worked out and he wants to walk every foot of the plants until he's familiar with it." Then he eyed everyone in the room. Pollard, the facility manager, sales manager, purchasing and traffic manager, plant engineers and the lead foreman. "I want everyone on the same page on this. Wade is the spokesman on this, to the state or city or any funding source. He knows the details of the plan, the necessary equipment and the timeframe we are dealing with. We want to get some immediate funding just to tide us over until the climate improves. Understood?"

Fiore nodded in agreement as well as the others. "Sure, Hunter, but I think I'm speaking for everyone in the room when I say that we have a great interest in seeing this plant succeed. After all, our careers were tied to B.F. and now they're tied to Prime."

Biller nodded, then stood and walked to Staber.

"Let me tell you fellows something that might settle you down. Maybe you should know a few things about Wade. First, he's a man of the cloth." Staber looked up at Biller and offered a half smile, then turned to Pollard and nodded his head, then nodded to the others. "Tell them, Wade, and don't be shy about it neither."

Staber stood and addressed the room. "I am an ordained Baptist minister. I may not look like that to you all because I don't have an active congregation, but it's the truth. Back in Nashville, lots of people know me there as the minister." Then Staber placed his hand on Biller's back, "Hunter and I go back a long time."

A silence filled the room as Biller looked around to measure the reaction of those assembled. "Back to 1965," he said, "I thought my life was coming apart. I had an incurable disease, they said I was a goner. But Wade came to me and we prayed on it and he predicted that things would be all right. Wade here is a psychic as well as a minister. And he was right, I'm recovered completely today. Wade restored my faith. He's been an advisor to me on many business deals. Much of my success I attribute to

Wade. This B.F. deal is small compared to what we've got back in Ohio. Wade's on the Board of Directors for that reason. He can make decisions for me."

Fiore looked at Biller and then to Staber. "That's all fine with me. Whatever you need from us Wade, you'll have. Budgets, projections, pro-formas, anything, and whatever the state needs to get the funding, just let us know."

A relieved smile broke over Staber's face. "I appreciate that very much, Ben. We're looking at May or so for the approvals. The state wants us to get some preliminary work done before that and they will be visiting the plants. I'll keep you informed as we go along. All the initial money will come from Prime as a loan for the engineering workup and the preliminary work, so I hope you won't mind if I bring in some of the men who will be actually on site working up the specs."

"No, of course not, Wade. We run three shifts so you can have access 24 hours a day. I just have to let Ray Medley, the guard supervisor, know so the guards know to let you in."

"Wade," Biller instructed, "the guard shacks are always manned, unless they're touring the buildings. So when you or your guys are going to be on the premises you have to call them and let them know. In the meantime, I'll have Helen draft a memo that we'll post through the plant that you can have any access you need."

Fiore nodded in agreement. "That sounds good, Hunter." He looked at Staber and asked, "Do they call you Reverend?"

Staber shook his head affirmatively. "Well," he said, "some people do. But you can call me Wade, that's fine."

"We don't want to be disrespectful."

"Wade's fine. Unless we pray together, you know, that changes things."

"I understand," Fiore replied with a comforting smile. "One last thing, Wade, you said the state wants to do a walk through. Do you have a time frame for that? I don't want them coming around and finding code violations. Right now we have mattresses stored in the hallways."

Staber waved off Pollard's concerns. "Early March or so, not before then. Me and the boys, we need to study the plants, get a good feel for the layout of the place before we invite the state in."

The men filed out of the room as Biller buzzed Helen and asked her to put out a memo allowing Staber access to all the buildings at any time. Then he closed the door, placed some chew into his jaw and looked at Staber. "So, what do you think?"

"Think it went fine. Makes sense to them. You know, nothing unusual about correcting the discharge system. Everyone's got those environmental problems."

Biller gave Staber a raised eyebrow and lowered his voice. "You know one of my other psychics that I consult, he told me he sees everything coming down except the smokestack and the power plant."

Staber looked perplexed, shrugging his shoulders in his oversized trench coat. "No, I got no predictions about that yet, but you know, these things just come up out of nowhere. You never know."

"Well, we got to make this plan work. You really think the meeting went okay?"

"I think it went very well. Once folks get used to me visiting they'll be okay with the changes. By the way, I did make a contact with a friend who has a soda company and has done some water treatment work."

"Well," Biller replied, "that's good. We got to move this along. Right now Pollard's telling me we're using IRS money to pay bills, you know, employment taxes, until we can catch up, and employee's Christmas club money."

Staber stood and stared into the hallway as workers filed past the door to Helen's office on their way to the plants.

"Well, I can make some more calls. I told you I'm going to do everything I can for you on this." Staber looked back at Biller and nodded his head. "You got good people here. They're going to work to get this job done. Did you and Dale talk about the insurance policies?"

Staber unrolled a print of the former B.F. Goodrich property, all twenty buildings spread over ten acres along the banks of the Housatonic River. "Where are the policies kept?"

Biller nodded his head slightly, "They're here. Pollard can probably put his hands on them. Why?"

Staber stood and nervously glanced out the office window at Helen's desk. "It might be a good idea for me to look it over. I'd like to take a copy back with me. I'll be setting up an office in New York."

Biller took a paper cup and slipped his chew into it, then ran his hand over his lips. "Yeah, that's no problem. Before we leave here we'll get that done. I know there are some extra copies of the prints in engineering. I'll get Pollard to get us a copy of all the insurance policies, you know, liability, property, everything. We might as well review all of it since the state may want to be placed on as a lien holder ahead of the equipment financing." He pulled out his cigar stub and put it between his teeth. "You got an idea what this will cost me?"

Staber looked at Biller and thought for a moment. "I'm having a meeting with Mike Fusto next week. Right now I got no idea. I'll be using my Southern Supply account to pay for the room in the city. Grand can reimburse me once the bill comes in."

"That's not a problem." Biller stood and played with an unopened bag of tobacco that he pulled from his desk drawer. "I'm leaving the whole thing in your hands. You answer to me and they can answer to you. Just let me know how it progresses."

"You don't have to know anything, Hunter. You just focus on running the plants."

Biller rose and walked to the door, opened it and turned back to Staber. "Let's go see what engineering can give us."

"Look," Max said firmly. "We can get at least eighty units into the first phase. Once they're under contract, we can start the next phase. Marshall said he can get Copper City Savings to finance the whole thing."

Lachlan scooped up the papers and tapped them on the cherry conference table until they were in an orderly stack.

"I don't know, Max. It's a swamp. Who's going to want to buy a condo on a swamp?" he asked.

Max shook his head in frustration. "Who cares if it's a swamp? You give it a catchy name, I don't know, Stillwater Suites or something. We market it right, people will buy it. Sell them to people in Fairfield County. Dress it up a little, put a nice catchy name on it and people will buy it."

He slid the leather chair over the floral carpet and opened the door of the liquor cabinet. He scooped some cubed ice into a cut, crystal glass and poured Chevas Regal over it. Lachlan stuffed the stack of papers into the case file, and then nervously fanned the edge of the paper.

"Look," Max said after a satisfying swallow, "I have five other investors who will take your place if you don't want in." His tone was all business.

Lachlan, although risk averse, was afraid of being left out of any potential gains. "Who's the general contractor?"

Max waved him off. "All of us, the investors. I'm forming a partnership that will be the general in name. We don't need anyone else. Know every sub around. We'll be the general, so all the down-side risk is there with the partnership. We don't have to commit much capital at all."

"What's the margin?"

"There's no limit. The deal will be ninety percent leveraged. That's the beauty of it, Lach. It's not our money. It's the banks. Come on, for years we've been filing motions and doing closings and preparing wills and kissing some judge's ass to get favorable rulings. I'm tired of that. We'll be doing that twenty years from now unless we go for real money. We sell out these first eighty units and phases two and three are all gravy. You know, when redevelopment comes in and we move, we still have to come up with the mortgage every month. Your dad and Martin, they won't be around forever. So it's our headache. And I got Birmingham Savings to finance the second phase. We buy the land dirt-cheap since it's worthless anyway and put up these condos like bread stacked on a shelf. It's real money. We'll be doing our own closings instead of someone else's. I mean really, doesn't some of this stuff get old?"

Lachlan walked to the liquor cabinet and poured himself Scotch, straight up. He pulled the end chair from the conference table and slouched into it pensively. He was tired, too. The enthusiasm of practicing law had drained to the tedium of feigned smiles and client drone, the endless description of want and woe that accompanied each meeting. Still, that served as backdrop and flimsy pretense as he calculated his fee.

"I think I can get Jerry to arrange non-recourse financing on the second and third phases," he said flatly. "He knows the Board of Directors has two vacancies and I'm going to be nominated for one slot. Let me see if I can get it lined up before I'm nominated."

Max smiled and emptied his glass with a long swallow. He turned to Lachlan, "So you're in?"

Lachlan equivocated. "That depends. You sure the other

investors are strong?"

Max lifted his brows and folded his muscled arms confidently. "Yeah," he said, "they're all strong."

"Is Jerry in?"

"No. I don't want any trouble with the loans and the compliance folks at Birmingham." He opened the cabinet doors again and dumped his ice into the small sink and left the glass there. "We're going to make big money on this, Lach. Anthony's in and he's going to be the exclusive broker so he's only taking two percent commission just to cover his costs. Frank's handling all the insurance and he's cutting his commission because he wants in. Marshall Storm is in because he's got his fingers into Copper City Savings and they want to do the purchase mortgages. He thinks he can talk them into a quarter-point below market if we give them an exclusive. If we make some money on this it's only the beginning," he said, peering out the window overlooking Main Street. He turned back to Lachlan, "I don't want to cut anyone else in. This is low risk, high return, split just a few ways."

Lachlan put his glass into the sink and stood beside Max. A cord of headlights reflected in the plate glass windows of empty Howard and Barber store. He had learned to live with Max's dangerous edge, which had hardened like the unnatural size of his muscles. His bursts of rage had become legendary in the office, smashing phones and tape recorders regularly. His narcissism was an embarrassment. Although he was careful to maintain a comfortable distance from anyone associated with illegal substances, his profession gave him access and the information and goods he needed. He had been through two wives already who left him without explanation or progeny, discrete as they were to whisper their grievances only to their closest friends.

"You interested in getting on the bank board?"

Max curled his lip under with disdain. "No way," he replied, turning from the window. "Too many restrictions on loans and too many disclosures you have to make. It's not for me. Particularly if you get a seat on the board, why would I need one? When they issue stock I don't want any restrictions on what I can accumulate. The big money isn't in the offering. It's years away when it gets scooped up from one of the big regional banks. That's when I want my freedom without the notices directors and officers have to give."

Lachlan picked up the case file and stood at the door. He gave Max a piercing gaze. He was uncomfortable with his unchecked ambition but knew that he had the iron stomach for risk and ability to make them both rich.

"Max," he asked hesitantly, "if the banks issue stock and you accumulate enough you have restrictions and disclosures anyway. You may as well be in a position to control things."

"Come on, between you and Martin we have enough friends on the board. And I don't intend to accumulate stock in my own name if they go public. I thought this out. I got enough friends to hold the stock for me in their names. When I cash in I'll take care of them. This way no disclosures, no one knows."

"I don't think it's that easy, Max. SEC can tie in that kind of stuff sometimes. It's risky."

Max gave Lachlan an indifferent look. "Are you kidding me? I'm not afraid of the SEC. You have to practically hand them a case before they look at it. Besides, my dad has political connections on the Senate banking committee that he can talk to if things ever got hot. Look, this is all speculation. Nothing is going public yet so why are we even discussing it?"

"No reason, I just wanted to know if you wanted to get on the board. I wasn't looking for a lecture. And while we're at it, all this stuff you take, I keep reading that stuff can have bad health consequences."

Max shrugged off the comment and pulled his pleading book from the drawer. "Nothing to worry about. I've been taking supplements since college. It's harmless. Nothing is going to happen to me, so stop worrying."

"I don't know, Max. How can you be sure it's okay long term?"

"Athletes have been taking this stuff for decades now. It's harmless. Has it affected my work yet? I like to look sharp so I can feel sharp. It's all in conditioning. Gives me confidence when I'm on trial. So stop worrying about that. Now, the condos, are you in or out? I'm getting impatient to make it big and I can't do it with house closings and wills. We can do wills and closings forever and never make it. I rather do the high risk trial work, get into some real estate investments and go for the home run."

Lachlan shook his head silently. He stood empty handed and uncomfortable. He knew there was nothing more to say and there was no arguing with Max anyway. For Max Cruz, life was meant to be lived in the comfortable belly of indulgence fueled by tireless ambition. Lachlan had heard rumors of Max's contacts in the street but never saw it. He only knew that Max was always ramped up and sometimes unpredictable.

"Yeah, I guess I'm in. Going to the club tonight?" he asked as a way to close the conversation.

"Yeah," Max responded in a relaxed tone, "of course. Got to eat that monthly fee, right?"

Max leaned over the bar, gripped Marshall's neck and squeezed it until it hurt. "Didn't expect to see you here. I thought you said your wife had some plans for you."

Marshall lifted his beer and turned to Max. "Change of plans. Good for me, right? What about you? I thought you'd be too busy with the move to show up for happy hour."

Max released Marshall's neck and turned from the bar. The fairways were crusted with a layer of hard snow that melted and refroze each day. Bare patches of green bled through in the crests of ground that dipped into the sand traps.

"I couldn't take it anymore. Martin's micromanaging the whole move, telling the movers how to pack the file cabinets into the truck. I had to leave. But I'm actually going in tomorrow to pack up the last of the files. Movers won't be done until tomorrow. We should be ready to go on Monday, at least that's the plan."

"Sounds good," Marshall said. He motioned for Max to join him at the table and watch the basketball game.

Max shook his head and begged off. "I got to make a phone call," he said as he pulled his cuff over his chunky Rolex. "I'll be right back."

"I'll hold your seat."

Linda stacked the last sundae dish against the mirrored wall and turned to Michael, glancing to the young man to his right as he spoke. "Linda," he asked, pulling his navy watch cap off, "you know Jeff?"

Jeff leaned over the stools, resting his long, lean frame over the counter. His skin was midnight black, flesh burnished by the sun that slanted on the docks as he lifted sacks of magazines into mail trucks. He wore a loosely fitted maroon sweatshirt with pulled up sleeves. His shoulders were broad and his thick forearms were irrigated by a rich supply of veins in high relief.

"How she going to know me, man? I told you I never been in here, Mike. Don't you remember I said I never been there?"

Mike turned to Jeff and shrugged his shoulders. "So, that don't mean she don't know you. That's just a way of introducing you, that's all. How do I know she don't know you? It don't matter anyway. Linda, this is my friend Jeff. He's the Moocher's brother- in-law."

Linda smiled and wiped her hands on the dishtowel she

had draped over her shoulder, "Nice to meet you, Jeff."

Jeff lifted his eyes off of the counter and looked into the mirror as he tapped the counter with his keys in sharp clicks. "Que Linda," he said in an undertone as he mirror-eyed Vonetes. He took her hand and shook it vigorously, "Nice to meet you too, Linda. Que Linda."

Linda plunged some cups into the rinse sink and set them on the drainer as Jeff lifted himself off the counter and turned to the candy counter. "Are you Spanish?"

Jeff knitted his eyebrows and allowed a wide smile to break his intensity. His mouth was crowded with teeth bunched close together. A front tooth was smaller than the rest, chipped years ago on the tar courts of the projects, but somehow it seemed natural on him.

"Who, me?" he asked in a surprised tone,."No, I ain't Spanish. Why, because I said que linda, you think I'm Spanish. Why, you Spanish?"

Linda picked up a cup to dry it. "My mom's Puerto Rican. So how do you know Spanish?"

"Because I grew up in New Rochelle, Seventh Avenue projects, you know. And there was lots of Spanish people, mostly Puerto Ricans, you know, living there and when they dressed up the little girls, like on holidays and stuff, or like for First Communion, they all be fussing and saying que linda, que linda and stuff. I know some Spanish."

Linda smiled and nodded her head. "I'm originally from East Harlem."

Jeff looked at Linda and shook his head. "You from East Harlem?" He looked at Mike and laughed. "You don't look

236

like you from East Harlem to me. You look like you from right around here. Whereabouts in East Harlem?"

"One hundred and sixteenth street, near Second Avenue."

Jeff flicked his eyebrows up in surprise and spread his hands over the counter again, "So maybe you are from Harlem." He tapped the counter again with his keys.

"You think I'm making it up?" Linda looked at Mike and laughed. "He thinks I can make that up?"

"Don't mind him. He don't believe nothing."

Jeff spun his keys on his finger and looked at Linda with a flat expression, "You know how to play cee-lo?"

Linda looked up as she dried a plate. "No, I don't know how to play cee-lo. That's gambling. I've seen it played, on the street, but no, I never played."

Jeff nodded approval, impressed that she knew the game. He rapped his keys on the counter again. "I forgot, you a girl. Girls didn't play that so much. So, how about skelzies? You know how to play skelzies?"

Linda smiled and shook her head. "Of course I know how to play skelzies. Beat my sister all the time, used to put gum in the bottle cap to give it weight."

"Que linda," Jeff laughed out loud, "damn, you are from Harlem. Ain't nobody that knows skelzies that ain't from that part of the city. Que linda."

"I'm old enough to remember the Third Avenue El. Used to ride it with my sister up to Gun Hill Road. My mom used to like to shop up there, in a little store that sold lots of Puerto Rican groceries."

Jeff backed off of the counter and stood facing the front windows. "Yeah, I don't know nothing about that, was before my time. But, okay, you convinced me you're from the city. You don't look it but you know too much not to be."

Shy walked to the door of the tenement that stood an arm's length from the neighboring buildings. It cracked and rolled and pitted the old wood planks and broken linoleum. He knocked on the wooden door of the first floor apartment. The door shook against its loose frame.

"Hey, dog, come on in," the Moocher said, backing into the room. Shy stepped in and shut the door, "Your wife here?"

The Moocher smiled, exposing a tunnel where his front four would hang. "No man, you know I's don't ever have my wife here when we do the business. She's out with the kids."

"Yeah," Shy said with a weary smile. "I know what you intend, man, but that isn't always what you deliver."

Shy Alvino was short and broad with a dark, straight ponytail bound with a rubber band. His face was pocked but a thick black beard, trimmed neatly along the cheeks and neck, made him attractive. His black leather coat and black turtleneck shirt offered a ministerial look that was complimented by his careful and mannered tone.

"What happened to your teeth?"

"Broke my bridge again, man. Getting it fixed." Vinny pointed to the sofa, "You want to sit down? You got any candy?"

Shy shook his head and shrugged. "I forgot to bring candy. Don't you ever buy your own candy?" Shy looked at the sofa. The arms and head areas were dark and stained. He remembered sitting on it once before and feeling the tacky upholstery along the length of the rolled arms. He declined to sit.

"Hey, man", Vinny laughed. "Why should I buy my own candy if I can get it free from you. That don't make any sense. We been through this before."

"Plus you could get it all for free from the vends, right?"

"Oh no, man," Vinny said with a Jamaican accent. "Never take from the vends, man. Cuts into the margin. It's all about the margin."

Vinny was witty and bright and funny. He was twig thin, moderate in height with an undersized baseball cap set on the crown of his head. He had no hair. His skull was shaved slick down to his black skin. And it wasn't a pretty head. It was knobby and bony and not round. He saw no color in people. He talked rapidly and was sometimes difficult to understand because of artifice and craft, like the tweeted Jamaican accent he employed. He asked for things that most people buy. From strangers or family or friends, it didn't matter to the Moocher. Small items, things that sold for under a dollar, like coffee or candybars at mom and pop stores, or larger items that looked like they deserved to be buried in some poorly managed landfill. But it didn't matter and no one took offense to his pestering. They often found him amusing and laughed it off with him.

"I never eat off the vends, man, that's like stealing. You know what I mean?"

"What about the damaged stuff, you know, stuff that gets twisted and crushed in the machines? You must eat that stuff."

"Oh no, man, never. Company gives me credit for that stuff. I see you don't know the vending business, man. You talking to a professional, a pro-fes-sion-al, vending machine man."

"I understand," Shy said. "Let's go to the kitchen table."

Alvino liked the Moocher. His real name was Herald, Herald Vincent Williams, but no one called him that, only his family. In his world of dark trades and hard cash, he was Vinny the Moocher, candid and light and straightforward. He said he never felt the sting of prejudice because everyone liked him, even strangers. They liked his fast talk and quick smile, with or without teeth, and his disarming self-deprecation. His conversations that bordered on racial prejudice scared some people.

"No, man. You sees, man, you don't understand, I's ain't black."

"You look black to me."

"But I's Jamaican, and that ain't black."

He usually referred to himself in the singular possessive, a nuance of his feigned accent. He married a woman from Brooklyn who insisted on moving out of there once they had children. She had some cousins in the Valley and liked the feel of the place when she visited. And she told the truth and spoke plainly and openly and corrected his lies when she could, sometimes correcting years of untruth.

"Are you from Jamaica too?"

"Me? No, my family's from Alabama but I was born and raised in Brooklyn. Why?" she would ask in an accusing tone. "Did Vinny tell you that he was from Jamaica?"

"Yeah, he said he was from Jamaica. He got that accent."

Her voice would drop an octave and she would look the questioner dead in the eye the way only black women can look when they believe they're repulsing evil. She would move her head back and forth on her neck while the rest of her body remained still.

Vinny?" she would say incredulously, "he ain't Jamaican, he's from Atlanta. He tells everyone he's from Jamaica so he can go around talking with that silly accent of his."

The questioner would usually laugh and say something like, 'but that don't make no sense, telling a lie for no reason.'

Then she would bob her head back and forth and drop her voice again. "Vinny don't need no reason to make up stories. That's the way he lives his life. He just made up a whole bunch of stories like that that don't mean nothing and he tells them. Ain't harming no one. It's just stupid. But he ain't from Jamaica, he's from Atlanta. That's why it's just stupid."

It didn't matter. The amusement of it all was usually

enough to get him whatever he needed. He conveyed no threat or sense of anger. He enjoyed life and filled each moment with laughter and fun. No one disliked the Moocher. He met the Greek soon after he arrived in the Valley, jobless and talkative in a charming way, and full of skinny energy and white lies. The Greek was a perfect find for him because the Greek knew everyone in the Valley, from the streets to the boardrooms, the perfect entre for the Moocher's nascent entrepreneurial endeavor. The Greek got the Moocher a vending machine route. And the Greek owned nothing and had nothing to mooch. Vinny told others that the Greek was moochless, 'mooch-less,' he would say with two distinct syllables but that did not matter because, eventually, the whole world wanted to buy their snacks from the Moocher. He would raise his hands to his chest and tap his fingers together. 'Why would you buy your snacks from anyone else, man? When you make your snack purchase from I, it is exotic . . . ex-o-ti-ca snacks from the Jamaican. No imitators here.' He didn't need that 'moochless Greek for nothing but friendship, just for hanging with, you see, man,' he would say, laying his hands on the Greek's shoulders. 'The Greek, he is not mooching material.'

Shy laid a cloth bag on the table. "What did you bring in?"

Vinny pulled up his sweatpants, one leg at a time, exposing his bony shins and pulled a wad of cash from each. "I's don't know, man, last time I counted was eighteen hundred and forty. That sound right to you?"

Shy pulled a small pad from his vest pocket and flipped through several pages of names and notes. "Should be nineteen hundred and twenty, that was the drop off amounts. You must of missed one of the pickups."

"No, no, no, man," Vinny protested. "I hit all them that you told me. Wasn't anything left at Pickets. State built that wall along the pond up there so I's got confused, but where I looked, you know, where they normally put it, near the well, wasn't nothing there man. Must be some mix-up or something."

"You go with the Greek? Think maybe he picked it up and didn't say anything?"

"Nah," Vinny scowled."The Greek don't make no pickups with me. You know that, man, I's do my own work. It's just a mix up. You call your people and ask them where they hid it. It's just a mix up, that's all, man. You know I'll make it up to you, right? You get your margin and I get the business."

"Okay," Alvino said without concern. "We'll get it straightened out. What do you need for this week?"

"Oh, man, business is booming for the Moocher man, boom- ing." Vinny smiled a toothless smile. "I need the regular supply of grass but I got to have more juice, man. Seems like that is the choice product I got and they want it. And I don't do that stuff so I's make a nice profit, man. You know what I mean? I be smoking up the dope margins but the other stuff, oh man, that is real money to the Moocher."

"Don't be dealing no cops, Vinny. You know the rules.

You're on your own if you get caught. I don't want to know anything."

"Yeah, yeah, man, you know you don't got to worry about me, man. Ain't nothing going to happen with me, man. I don't take no stupid risks."

"You're passing a lot of stuff, Vinny. That's serious stuff. The cops don't like the serious stuff."

"No, no, no, man" Vinny said rapidly. "I's got it all under control. My users, man, you know these are professionals. They are not street people. You know, they dress up for work every day. Bankers, lawyers, doctors, real estate people...they pro-fes- sion-als. They big dogs, man. They real careful people, don't you worry about that. It's easy work. Come on, man, they scareder than you. Don't worry about nothing."

Alvino shook his head with worry. He walked out to the living room and looked out over to the large wrought iron fence of the cemetery across the street. The old gravestones loomed ominously, leaning with age and neglect. He pulled his ponytail out and refastened it as he spoke. "I always worry. People get careless, I got trouble. I don't want any trouble. The grass, that doesn't matter so much. But the drugs, cops don't like the drugs."

"Look, man, it's like I's already told you. My people are professionals. They don't want no trouble either. I don't even meet with them. It's all done by drop and pick. I's invented that system. You know me, man, I got that entrepreneurial spirit. The Moocher is self-employed and successful. Nothing you got to worry about. Besides, some of the cops are users too. You know, they want that muscle to show man, it's good for their business."

The Moocher invented the system after the Greek introduced him to the owner of Valley Vending, a snack vending company. He talked himself into the job of driving around the Valley a few hours a day and filling the machines, collected the money and turned it in. No questions asked as long as the owner made his margins on each route. He preferred the morning hours so he could be free when the Greek started his rounds, perambulating around the beltline with that certain gait and confidence. He loaded his own truck by riding up and down the conveyer belt to save time. Once in while he'd get his butt caught because he didn't jump off the conveyer fast enough. No harm except for the severe pulls in his sweatpants that bagged them out to hysterical shapes.

Shy was skeptical. He did business with the Moocher for three years now. The Moocher kept no records, no paper, no nothing. The system worked. The Moocher took all the risk. Any shortfall of money he made up for, no questions asked.

"You sure your people aren't selling this stuff too?"

"Yeah, man, I'm sure of that. Look, the deal is that it's for the athletes, man. They procure for the athletes so they can excel, man, like in ex-cel-len-to. It isn't all for them, it's for the students."

The Moocher never disclosed who he did business with. That wouldn't be good for business and would be an unnecessary risk. Besides, it would have been a breach of confidentiality with the pro-fes-sion-al community he dealt with, the big dogs. The vending business offered him entry into offices and schools and factories. The difficulty was limiting his sales, not increasing them.

Shy stuffed the cash into his vest pocket. "Okay, you got the boxes for next week?"

Vinny rushed into his bedroom and returned with three perfectly opened boxes from the vending company. An assortment of candy bars and gum and snack crackers and cakes remained in each, along with a false bottom. Shy would fill the boxes with pills and powders and vials and meet the Moocher along rounds, swapping the boxes. Then the Moocher would truck them along his route and make his drop offs in a casual, natural fashion. To the company they were returns if anyone asked. To the Moocher it was business. He made his drop and picked up cash, very simple.

"I took some of the snack cake boxes this week since they're deeper for the dope. Ex-o-ti-ca snacks and cakes. Makes it easier to handle."

Vinny helped Shy load the boxes into his car. "Hey, man, you want to stay for the card game? We got five hands, we need one more. You want in?"

Shy turned to Vinny and smiled. That's why people like the Moocher. People were fungible items to him, each a friend without having to earn it. "No, I can't play, man. I got stuff to do. Poker?"

"Usually, hands go quick. It depends on the crowd. Poker's good, gets everyone going. Come on, man, we ordering a bunch of pizzas, wife and kids are out. We have lots of fun."

Shy thought of it as he got into the car. He looked up at Vinny and shook his head reluctantly. "No, I really can't. You'll find someone else, for the sixth, right?"

"Yeah, man. You know everyone wants to play with the Moocher. We always pick up someone. Cut Man probably be with the Greek anyway. He always wants in. Don't worry, man, people just want to have fun and it is fun with the Moocher." He returned to the apartment and answered the phone.

"Max, what's up with you, dog? I got a notice at work that you were moving to that new building across the river."

Max looked out into the club lobby to make sure no one was within hearing range. "Yeah, Monday we go into our new building in Shelton, the Towers. You still deliver there?"

"No, man," Vinny said, pulling the legs of his sweatpants down as he spoke. "That's not on my route. But don't worry, man, I can talk to Jay, he got that route. I'll offer him some of my vends up in White Hills. We can find a new drop point if that don't work out."

The phone was silent for a moment as Max awkwardly greeted some club members walking by the phone.

"You got any ideas?"

Vinny switched the phone to the other ear and strained to look out the window to the cemetery.

"I do drops anywhere, man, it don't have to be right in

the building or near the vending areas. I don't want to say where I do the drop and pick but it can be anywhere. I do a few outside now. Could you handle that?"

Max hesitated a minute and then answered in a halting tone. "Yeah, I guess, as long as it works."

Vinny got serious as he spoke. "You know where I live, right, on Hawthorne, right across from the old cemetery opening?"

"Yeah, I know where you live. I never really paid much attention to the cemetery opening."

"Well, I'm looking at the cemetery right now. It don't get too much traffic. People there been dead a long time so no one goes to visit or nothing. Even the visitors, when they do go, they look like they dead, too. Front gate gets closed to car traffic but you can always walk in, man. So how about this if I find a drop off spot in there? I'll look around there and I'll let you know."

"Yeah, but the cemetery is big. I'll never find it unless I meet you there, at least the first time."

"Yeah, man," Vinny tweeted in his Jamaican accent, "I'll meet you in there."

"But I can't take the chance of being seen with you in there. People would wonder why I was in there with you."

"Come on, man, no one will see us. I'll just be in there and you can drive in and when you see me,that will be where the stuff is. You don't have to search or nothing. I'll get it all set up. You don't have to think about nothing. When you see me I'll just walk away but that will be the drop spot. And we'll talk and I'll let you know exactly where I'll be."

Max turned back towards the pay phone. He was uncomfortable with the arrangement but he trusted Vinny to come up with a plan that would be fast and anonymous. "Okay" Max said. "I call you on Monday and you have the plan ready."

"Okay man, don't worry about nothing. We can get two or three different drops set up so no one sees you all the time. Your stuff is easy to hide. I'll get it set up and I'll let you know man."

"All right, I'll talk to you Monday," Max said.

"Monday, man," Vinny said as he hung up the phone.

"I don't think it will happen for a year or so. Some of the older guys on the board still think they're living in the depression. They remember the banks not opening and long lines and no money for the depositors. So what's the average bank stock trading at now? Is there a price range that the mutual banks fall into once they go public?"

Roland Kimball, the director of customer relations of Birmingham Savings, checked the wire service and responded without looking up. "It's hard to say, ten to twelve seems to be the standard. After a few years they might be trading in the lower teens, you know, thirteen, fourteen. The industry just needs a break out event. Right now the institutional investors are looking for a bump."

Andrew Devine, recently hired from a New York bank as the compliance officer at Birmingham, rolled back on his office chair and shook his head. "I don't see any bump coming anytime soon. They can't be paying out dividends and still grow the balance sheet and shareholder returns. If they loosen the lending standards, sure, they can get a bump in value based on the loan growth but those loans have to perform. I don't see anything dramatic happening until the feds open up the borders to interstate banking. The institutional investors know that. If they're looking for a return on investment they're in the wrong industry for the moment. And they knew that when they bought the stock. Fortunately they don't hold a big percentage of the shares yet. They're monitoring and trying to influence the legislation."

Roland reached for the phone and started dialing. "Well, I like to watch how the other mutual banks did so I know what to expect when it happens here. In the last year, including you, we hired six outside officers from banks that have gone public. I think getting you in here to tighten up the compliance for the public regulators is the last piece. You watch."

Kimball picked up the quarterly report from Devine's desk and stepped into the hallway. "That's what was described to me in the interviews. At the hiring interview the committee said they are not speaking to advisers yet but another committee is starting to look at underwriters and advisers. Right now they're just contacting the banks in the state that have gone through the IPO already."

The squeak and echo of rubber on the hardwood court and the smell of fresh sweat enveloped Max Cruz. He dove for the ball that flew to his left, caught the side wall, ricocheted off the back wall and bounced in front of him as he lay helplessly on the cold, hard floor of the paddleball court.

"Son of a bitch," he yelled to the sound of his own echo. He sat up and threw his racquet against the wall, watched it bounce and skid across the court. He took Marshall Storm's extended hand and pulled himself up then walked over and kicked his racquet against the side wall. Losing wasn't something he did well or often. Marshall pulled a fresh white towel from the bin outside the door and tossed it to Max. He gently closed the door after him knowing that Max would rip it open in anger and slam it shut with dramatic flair. Max wiped the sweat from his face and neck, ran the towel over his head and draped it over his shoulders. He kicked the racquet to the door, opened it with lightning speed and slammed it shut. "I think I need a new racquet," he said, looking up at Marshall and laughing. His rage was over. It lasted about thirty seconds, average for a Max Cruz tantrum.

Marshall turned to him and laughed. "You need a new attitude," he said, leaning into Max's face and meeting him eyeball to eyeball. "When was the last time I beat you, three or four months ago?" They were nearly the same height, a few inches over six feet, and fit. They lived parallel lives and they knew it, raised in comfort, warmth, safety and the expectancy of success.

Cruz wasn't consoled. "I don't know, who keeps track? You keep track?"

Storm smiled and shook his head. "No, no one keeps track," he said. He picked another fresh towel off the rack and turned back to Max. "You going into the sauna?"

Max took Storm's racquet and placed it in the cubby outside the sauna. He threw his into the garbage pail, grabbed two more fresh towels, glanced through the window and opened the door. "Good," he exclaimed, wrapping the fresh towels around their waists, and sprinkled water on the benches, "no one's in here."

Storm sat facing the door, swung one of his towels over his shoulders and leaned back against the wall. Max sat opposite him with his elbows on his knees and watched the sweat drip off his face. The muscles of his shoulders, chest, arms and torso rippled with every move he made.

"You beat me by two or three?" Max asked.

"Three," Marshall replied, "but no one was counting. When you lose we don't keep score, remember?"

Max gave him the sly eye and pouted his lips. "Right, I forgot. How's business since the move?"

"I don't know," Max said with a relaxed smile. "It's hard to say, too soon. Getting a lot more calls from Fairfield County contractors. And it's a lot easier for the clients without the stairs. We're getting a lot more upscale work, you know, bigger business deals, commercial real estate, bigger estate work."

When redevelopment took the north side of Main Street Manny Dimes and Martin Short decided it was time for a generational shift as well. They purchased ten acres south of the center of Shelton and built an eight story office tower overlooking the Valley but squarely in the north end of Connecticut's gold coast, Fairfield County. The view from their new offices was wide and expansive, going on without limit, to distances as far as the affluent, rolling hills of Greens' Farms and Weston and Easton. Max did all the thinking and planning. He said the demographics were right for a firm growing in sophistication and value-added work. The four partners each owned a piece of it, to the extent of their equity, having financed the remainder with a non-recourse loan. He advised Lachlan and Manny and Martin that he was no longer doing any pro bono work unless it was high profile work that delivered favorable press. He limited his trial work to personal injury actions with clear liability on the defendant's part and generous insurance coverage or contract actions against non-performing insurance companies where he assessed the risk of loss against a contingent fee win. He demanded an hourly fee as well in the event of a loss, then credited his client with the hourly fees earned against the contingent fee won. He was fair and professional, abrupt and skillful. His professional life was centered on the club and client development until he realized there were other ways of making money. His personal life was focused on the gym and his physical development. His wives were basically social props contrived to support his insatiable ego. He limited his real estate practice to commercial developers with multi-million dollar plans.

Marshall toweled his face and looked at the door. He leaned towards Max and spoke just above a whisper.

"I'm going to tell you something but if someone walks in, we start talking about how I just whipped your ass on the court, you understand?"

Max cocked his closest ear to Storm and shook his head affirmatively.

"Copper City Savings is planning on issuing stock."

Max looked at Marshall speculatively. "Copper City? Really? You guys talking about it at board meetings?"

Marshall shook his head silently and closed his eyes, as if the walls had ears and no more could be said of it.

"Well, first we have to get the bank structured as a holding company. Then we do a public offering of the holding company. We formed a committee a few weeks ago to study it, hired an advisory board. Of course that's not public yet but we've already started looking into it. I talked to Senator Betts' office already. He said most of the mutual banks are going that way."

"How soon?"

"We'll announce within three months. Probably take another nine months to a year to get it done."

"So who ends up with control?"

Marshall flicked his eyebrows and patted his face with the towel. He leaned forward like a priest in a confessional straining to hear the penitent's whispered transgressions.

"It gets pretty spread out. The officers will definitely buy up shares and hold them because their jobs are tied to it. The way I figure it, we got Jerry on the board and we get all the inside information. The depositors get to purchase shares. Then we follow the SEC filings and see who's buying and selling, you know, the inside trading disclosures. So we always know where the big blocks are. I figure we don't need to control yet but we need to know where the control is."

"They figure out an offering price?"

Marshall shook his head and felt beads of sweat drip off his chin. "Too soon. But whatever it is right now everyone inside wants to support the offering price and you have the underwriters lining up investors for the initial shot. Everyone on the inside has to support this so there's pressure to keep a stable offering price."

Max looked up and stared at the wooden slats lining the ceiling. He wondered how all this could be going on and he hadn't heard a word of it until now. "How long did you say this will take, to do the offering and stuff."

"Maybe a year or so. You know, lots of regulatory approvals, investor relations stuff, due diligence and all. But that timeframe works fine. Just listen to me on this one. We can make a ton on this if we play it right, you know? Just be patient and pick up your shares without making any noise. With Jerry and me as incorporators we are in on everything. This isn't the big deal. That happens when the shares of the holding company gets scooped up by some regional player."

Max nodded his head in agreement. "So, is Birmingham Savings looking at it too?"

Storm shook his head and wiped the sweat from his face. "I haven't heard. But you got Lachlan and Martin on the board. They would know."

Max shook his head in disgust. "Yeah," Max said with a one sided smile, "they would know. But they're too passive. I mean, Martin's all right but Lachlan, you know, he never sees the big picture and he doesn't open up. He thinks serving on the board is an honor. That he does it for the community. You know, he's into giving back and all that stuff."

Marshall shrugged. "Ask him. Or ask Martin. The officer and board members get incentive options. So they have a lot to gain if it goes through. If Birmingham hasn't considered it openly I'm sure they have privately. You guys represent the bank so it's not like they're giving you information that you won't come across anyway. Maybe you can be an incorporator, get in on the bottom floor."

"No, not me," Max replied, as he stood. "I don't want to be an officer or director or even a major shareholder if they go public. Long term, I want to be able to buy and sell shares without any disclosure requirements. We got enough pull on the board that I'll have all the information I need. I just don't like showing my hand on anything speculative. I'd rather pick up shares but fall under the disclosure requirements."

Marshall stood and opened the door. His body cooled as he stepped from the sauna to the hallway. They gathered their belongings and headed to the locker.

Max whispered as they passed several other members. "I'm going to talk to Martin and Lach. They are somnambulant. You got to put it in front of them and spell it out. They're small thinkers."

256

"Oh," Frances exclaimed, glancing up Elizabeth Street through the steam of traffic and rapping the spatula on the grill with greater enthusiasm, "there she comes now." Linda glanced towards the window. She placed her tray of dirty dishes on the wash counter and walked to the door, stepped aside and allowed Roy to enter. She looked up Elizabeth Street, to the fist-full of papers approaching the corner.

"Hey, Fran, how's everything? What's new, Teddy?" Roy asked, tucking his Racing Form securely under his arm.

Linda grabbed her heavy cardigan from the coat hook and walked out to the curb, wrapping herself in the sweater and folding her arms tightly to insulate herself from the cold February air.

A tiny fistful of papers skipped across the street at the police officer's direction as Linda stooped and embraced her and they exchanged kisses, "Hi, sweetheart," she said, then rushed them both back into the Palace.

Frances came from the back of the grill and stood at the stools, waiting for her coat to come off. "Hello, Tori," she sang out. "And how was school today? Let's see all your papers."

Tori, short for Victoria, Spanish but shared by the English and strong but just Tori because it was easy and crisp and Linda liked it. The namesake of Linda's grandmother, far from the father Tori would never know. She carried his blond hair, golden in the summer sun and a shade darker in winter, and her mother's dark eyes, setting her features in striking contrast.

Frances sat her on the stool and spread her schoolwork over the counter. She selected the big bright red valentine heart Tori cut out and pasted white lacey paper border to, taping it on the mirror behind the counter register. "Isn't this beautiful, Roy?" Frances asked as Linda slipped Tori's coat and hat off and hung them in back of the candy counter.

"Who made that?" Roy asked, standing between stools and feigning ignorance. Tori sat on the stool, spinning it slowly, looking as if she might slip off at any moment, as a wide smile broke over her face. Her thick blonde hair was wedged at her neck, framing the apple red cheeks she carried in from the cold walk. "You made that?" he asked incredulously.

She shook her head up and down, affirming the masterwork belonged to her alone, then pointed to the snowman on the opposite wall and the Santa that should have been taken down but wasn't. "I made those too!" she exclaimed. Teddy called her to the table in the parlor. "Your hot chocolate is ready," he said. "Do you want to squeeze the cream?"

"Yes, wait" she shouted as she jumped off the stool and ran to the table set with a napkin and spoon, with hot chocolate steam rising from the heavy ceramic cup.

"I'll hold the bag, okay, honey. You squeeze," said Teddy as she squeezed the leather piping bag filled with whipped cream and piled it high into the cup. "Vera," Frances yelled back, "Your toast will be right up." She handed Roy his double bagged coffee and toasted hard roll.

"How's work, Roy?" asked Teddy, returning the cream to the refrigerator. "Is the plant still busy?"

Roy clutched the bag against his red check hunting jacket. "I don't know, Ted," he said with an unsettled look as he dropped his change into his pocket. "Yesterday I go in and we find this notice that from now on all the lights have to be turned off in the plants on the weekends once everyone's gone. They want us guards to do our rounds with just our flashlights." Roy shook his head in disgust. "You can't see in them plants with just a flashlight, it's pitch black in there. But I guess they're trying to save money or something. We been running overtime for so long and now the mattresses and pillows are just piled up all over the place. They're lined up in the hallways and in trailers parked out in the yards, like they're storing them for something. I don't know, it was never like this with B. F. Goodrich owned the plants. There's talk they got to do some water treatment stuff so they need the backup inventory because they have to interrupt production. Then there's this guy, he's on the Board of Directors or something, some friend of the owner. He's walking around saying he got a vision that something's going to happen to the plant and only the smoke stack will be left standing. He says he's a psychic or something." Roy shook his head and grabbed the door. "Got everyone all worked up over there."

"Yeah, Raffie was in yesterday and said the same thing, that the owner's friend had a vision or something. People are crazy, you know?"

Frances scooped up the toast from Teddy and ran it back to Tori. Roy looked across the street to the sleek white stone and smoked mirrors of the new Birmingham Savings Bank building and the parking lot that consumed the block on the north side of Main Street. He shook his head in disgust. "They really screwed up this redevelopment thing. That building got no place here, it don't fit, the new bank building. It don't look like any of the other buildings."

Teddy closed his eyes and shook his head. "I tried to tell them but it didn't do any good. See you tomorrow, Roy," he said. He lopped a dishtowel over his shoulder and walked back to Tori. "Almost finished?"

"Yes," Tori responded brightly, asking over a swallow of toast, "are you ready?"

Teddy sat beside her and scratched his head thoughtfully. "Ready?" Teddy asked with a confused look. "Ready for what?"

Tori smiled knowingly over the noise of dishes being stacked on the counter. "You know," she said confidently.

"Slap Jack?" he asked, putting his arm around her chair. She shook her head with a wide grin.

He leaned his frame closer to her. "Magic tricks. You want me to do magic tricks?"

"No!" she protested beneath a giggle, "you know."

Teddy scratched his head again and smiled at the customers leaving. "No, I really don't know." He lifted his hands helplessly. "I really don't know. And even if I did know once, I forgot. You have to remind me."

"You know! The string."

Teddy laughed, "What string?"

Tori slurped some now tepid hot chocolate from her spoon. She tugged on his pocket. "You know, the string," she said louder.

Teddy raised his eyebrows in a surprised look. "Oh," he said, fishing a tangled loop of string from his pocket along with sundry items of dust balls, change and toothpick wrappers."Do you mean this string?"

Tori smiled widely and jumped in front of him as he tied his thick fingers into delicate stretches and twists and binds of string and lashed a frame from the taut fibers. With her tiny fingers she pinched the intersections and twisted out, creating another box of string. Teddy grabbed the cross strings with his meaty fingers and rotated his wrists through and under, then snapped it tight into more intersections. And Tori walked around the contraption with her fingers to her lips. She bent down and looked up from under it and laughed out loud at her dilemma. And when she tired of that it was Slap Jack for the quick handed and then Old Maid and finally back to the taut parallels and intersections of string.

Linda craned her head into the front window and looked up into the narrow strip of sky over Main Street. Heavy gray clouds were visible in the space between the aging buildings. She turned to her right, facing the meadows and the gritty, oily windows of Farrell's plant. She heard a little girl's giggle and glanced back to Teddy and Tori, then met Frances's eyes with a satisfied smile. This is a wonderful place, she thought, a beautiful flow of rivers and hills and buildings, though beyond their prime, rising gracefully above the curve of the Housatonic. Even as they faded, like the tail of a comet, they were lustrous enough for her.

She stepped out into the alcove and looked back into the Palace. Frances was slicing a sandwich and Teddy was being scolded for letting the string droop. She watched Tori stand and face him, pulling his large hands apart with her tiny fingers until the string was taut again. The chatter along the counter stools reflected off of mirrored nods. She rolled her eyes up to the pendulous clouds and felt contented. This Valley was Tori's home now, a place without pretense though full of warmth. In her heart, she knew that because of its narrow sky and small dreams, Tori was safe here, away from the infectious ambitions of the larger world. That may come in her life, at another time. For now, in a slot- canyon that allowed a glimpse of heaven between aging buildings, there was the careful pull of the string and the weightless joy of tiny fingers.

In the depths of winter, at a splendid crest of roads where Elizabeth slopes to Main, between columns of brick buildings shouldering in the past, just as the eastern states of the great republic settled into evening, the child's game twisted and looped with delighted spasms of laughter. The moments spent in the thoughtful pull of stringed intersections tied those two lives with a profound and abiding pleasure. Linda looked up to the sky and held her smile, satisfied to offer her child the immeasurable joy of the Palace of Sweets. Then she looked west, searching for the last glimmer of sunlight as it spun brightness into a new day over the Pacific on the delicate web of the cat's cradle.

Max Cruz was late for the conference. He took the closest seat to the door. His black hair was water-slicked back, having just showered after his workout. He folded his hands on top of the cherry wood table and fingered his shirt cuff over his watch.

Martin, Manny and Lachlan sat opposite each other along the sides interspersed between most of the senior bank officers and incorporators. Bacchus Bandis, the local state representative who sat on the Connecticut Banking Committee, sat at the other end of the table outlining the likely legislation.

"So I see it opening up, the interstate banking, in the next few years. The Banker's Association is pushing it hard. There is little or no opposition except for some community activist groups whose only real concern is that they want free checking for the world." Bandis looked up at Max and seemed to address him directly. "They really don't count for much, those types. They don't vote in great numbers and have no financial muscle."

Max looked around and shrugged his shoulders. He didn't want to start asking questions that may have already been covered by the presentation.

"So what's the plan? I don't want you to cover the same

information that you already went over. But you seemed to be talking about federal legislation. What happens at the state level, the Banking Commissioner? What's his posture on this? I mean, I thought that is what you were going to discuss here."

Bandis smiled widely and held up his palms in relief. "That is why I'm here Max. We didn't get to that yet but since you brought it up we can talk about it now. The commissioner has to at least give the appearance of concern for the affected community. That's what the state statutes call for. Of course, for those of you who are attorneys, you know that already. So the banking regulations say you have to have some opportunity for community involvement in the process and you have to at least try to address their concerns. But remember, you're not reinventing the wheel here. There have been over a dozen of demutualization proposals in the past two years and the Commissioner's Office hasn't objected to any of them."

Lachlan looked up from his blank notepad. "So what has been the experience of those other banks? I mean, I remember some of them going through the process. What were the biggest problems?"

Bandis put on a look of disbelief and shook his head. "The biggest problem is that the depositors didn't really understand what's going on. They wanted to know if their deposits are still insured. You have to remember, many of these people lived through the Depression. At that time there was no deposit insurance. So it took them a long time to trust banks again. For them, all this talk about stock ownership and demutualization is confusing. They want to know if their money is still insured, can they still get it out when they want, and will they still get toasters or dishes and stuff if they open a new account or start a CD. That's it. That's their biggest concern."

Don McCann, the chairman who succeeded Dennis Foley, reached up and tightened his tie. He was tailored and tall, impeccably dressed and gracious in all social settings. He was the first non- family member to run the bank. In a bloodless coup the Young Turks deposed the family and installed an eminently qualified CEO with a broad vision for Birmingham Savings. McCann made a quick and careful study the Valley and the Birmingham depositors, wanting to deliver to them a successful public offering which would allow him to attain his personal ambition to move on to a larger, regional bank.

He stood and turned his head to make eye contact with everyone in the room, addressing them in a polite, professorial manner. "As all of you know, most of our depositors are mom and pop types. They're the factory men and the tradesmen. They have five or ten or twenty thousand in the bank, a little five room cape somewhere in the Valley and, if their kids go to college, they go to the local state schools for two hundred dollars a semester, refundable if the kid gets good grades. This is the American dream. People get small pension, Social Security, and some money in the bank. They think they're rich, and they are. At least that's my impression. You know, they don't understand this stuff and they don't want to. Like Representative Bandis said, all they want to know is if they will still get toasters when they open an account. They want to know if their money is insured and if they can get it out when they want to. That's my concern too. I don't want these folks confused or upset over the process."

Martin Dimes palmed his comb-over and leaned over the conference table. "So," he asked, "since you sit on the state banking committee, does that help us? What I mean is, do we need an advocate up in Hartford or does this stuff just kind of get approved as a matter of course?"

Bandis looked around the table and then settled back on Martin. "Look, you know that I always look out for you guys to the extent that I can. But really, for this process, it's not something that gets a lot of objections. In most cases the banks hire one of the big New York firms who guide you through the entire process."

"Is it expensive for the bank?"

Bandis pursed his lips and thought for a moment. "No," he replied flatly. "So much cash comes in from the sale stock that they're just about giddy with cash." Bandis let a wide smile meet the smiles of those who sat around the table. His eyebrows flicked up knowingly. "It's easy money. It's a no lose. The depositors,who used to own the bank, get nothing for their ownership,just an opportunity to buy shares. They still have their deposits intact. The new shareholders have an opportunity to get in on the investment at the ground floor and now can control the bank by having the power to elect board members and influence the business and maybe make money when they sell their shares."

Max cast Bandis a stern look. "I thought the depositors had an opportunity to object to all this. Don't they have a say in it?"

Bandis scanned the room and half smiled. "Well, yes and no. The statute says they get to vote but the regulations also provide that the board can request a waiver from the commissioner's office. And I'll tell you what, since I've been on the banking committee, I have never seen the Commissioner turn down a request for a waiver. But it doesn't matter anyway. Last year when Shorleline went through this the board never asked for a waiver and so it had to go to a vote of the depositors. Well, the literature put out by the board, who was advised by one of the big New York firms that I am not allowed to name, was so positive that the depositors voted for it overwhelmingly anyway. This is going to happen. Believe me, nobody loses. There is little downside."

Max looked up again and directed his question to Bandis. "What are the incentives for the board and officers to get this done? How are they compensated? And what happens to all this money that pours into the bank as capital stock? What have the other banks done with it?"

"Well," Bandis started, rocking back and forth on his toes, "to answer the first part of your question, there's usually ten to fifteen percent of the stock that's put aside as incentives for the officers and board members. So, for instance, once the bank is public, then the options gain value as the stock price rises. They basically get to buy the stock for little or no money. As for the second question, it varies. Some of the banks use it to expand their branch operations, some get aggressive and make more loans or get into other lending areas. Every demutualization is different. Don't forget, the bank becomes a holding company. That is by design so it can get into other lines of business and not risk their required capital. But they have been getting into all kinds of high margin activity."

"Like asset leasing?" Martin asked as he toyed with a pen.

Bandis shook his head knowingly. "Yeah." he said through a smile. "Just like asset leasing."

McCann squirmed in his chair and rested an elbow on the table. He looked around the room and removed his eyeglasses. "Well, this asset leasing, isn't that for the advanced class?" he asked with a smile. "I mean, aren't we getting a little ahead of ourselves here?"

"It's a new wrinkle in all this, Don. You know, when you're a mutual you live in a very small world. But once you get into the real business of banking, you know, once the New York guys get involved, they get the holding company into financing things like airplanes, main frame computers, rail cars. Stuff like that. Asset leasing. Eventually you are going have to compete in the big world of interstate banking."

McCann whispered to his assistant who sat beside him with a confused look. He didn't want to look anxious to shed the local image of the bank. "Well, I'm not so sure the

268

bank will go in that direction. I really do want to look out for the depositors and for the community. I'd rather invest our assets right here in the Valley like we have for the past hundred years."

Around the table there were polite nods of affirmation. McCann seemed relieved at the support and felt compelled to comment further. "You know, I think the presentation was great up to about the process of issuing stock. Interstate banking, asset leasing, we're just not ready for that yet."

Baucus Bandis shook his head in agreement. "You're right, Don. If we just focus on the immediate concern of changing the capital structure of the bank we'll be just fine. The only thing to keep in mind is that long term all this is just to prepare for interstate banking. We envision a day when major banks will be bidding up the share prices for the assets of smaller banks like Birmingham Savings. That's when the real money is made. That's the key to making money in these deals. Demutualizing is just laying the groundwork. And it's easy because the depositors are mostly unsophisticated. So you get large amounts of newly issued stock into the hands of a relatively few people and they get to control the holding company. Now the holding company owns the bank as you know it today. But the shareholders own the stock of the holding company. It can either be an acquirer or be acquired at some point in the future. That's when you make a killing."

McCann nodded in agreement. "You say this will take a year or so, correct?"

"Well, in my experience, it takes about eighteen months or so. Lots of investor relations stuff, due diligence and all. Just make sure you pick up all the shares allowed. It will be a great investment once interstate banking is opened up."

"You know, I could have taken them pillows down here to the city for you. You didn't need to go."

Pollard caught Paully's eye in the rearview mirror. "Hunter wanted them delivered by an officer of the company, you know, to give Staber a sense that we're really serious about the project. He needs the pillows for a client, all ten of them, you know, maybe they want to see the quality, see more than one." He leaned against the stack of foam pillows and rested his head. He didn't want to answer any more questions.

Paully glanced at his side view mirror. Headlights surrounded him, reflecting off of the glistening black body of the Lincoln Continental. He flicked his blinker and glided into the line of traffic streaming towards the Bruckner Expressway.

"I thought you would want to go over the West Side," Pollard said from the back seat. He sat up and looked around at the traffic shooting past the car and the flashing of brake lights ahead of them.

"No," Paully responded, glancing into the rearview mirror to catch a glimpse of Pollard. "I only take that if we go on the Parkway. While you was snoozing I heard the traffic report say they got too much traffic on the bridges and to avoid the Cross Bronx. This way is better. We can take 3rd Avenue or the FDR. Said the FDR was clear. Pretty busy down here, even for a Friday night."

Pollard looked down and straightened his tie. He looked to his left and placed his hand over the shoebox sealed with fabric reinforced tape. "Where did you say this McAlprin Hotel is?"

"Yeah," Paully said, checking his side view mirrors again, "it's right there like in lower Midtown, towards the East Side. You see, Broadway don't go straight down. It cuts over on a diagonal. So by the time it gets to 34th Street, its close enough to the East Side that it's better than going down on the West Side." He studied his rearview mirror until he found Pollard's eyes staring back at him. "We ought to make it there by seven or so. That's what you told Staber, right?"

"Yeah, he said he'll be in the room all night anyway so it doesn't matter but this was such short notice. Going to be late before we get back to Shelton."

"We could have left earlier but the dispatcher said he was waiting for a call or something from New Haven."

Pollard looked out the side window. "Yeah, I had to wait for some funds to get into Tweed on the company plane."

"What?" Paully asked in confusion. "So why didn't they just fly it into LaGuardia?"

"I don't know. Hunter told me to come into Tweed."

Paully drove on, over bridges and through jammed side streets. Pollard started to feel car sick with the twists and turns on the city streets. "Ok, boss, this is it."

Pollard tucked the shoebox under his arm and picked up several pillows. "You going to stay here? I got to come back down for the rest of the pillows."

Paully looked up and down the block. "You want me to come up? I can leave the car for a minute if you want."

Pollard looked up the narrow street. Cars and cabs darted quickly in and out of traffic and double-parked cars. He hesitated for a moment then stepped away. "No, you stay here. I don't want to leave the car unattended. If a cop comes just go around the block. I'll come down for the rest of the pillows." He stood in the lobby until he spotted the elevators, pulled out a scrap of paper from his coat pocket on the way up, and knocked on Staber's door.

"I thought you forgot about me!" Staber exclaimed. Pollard entered the small, New York City suite, a room with a bed and more than one closet. But it was clean and spare with an old gray file cabinet with hints of rust on the exposed side, situated near the window. "Come on, Wade, we could never forget about you. Not now anyway. Hunter wanted this to be delivered personally, but I suppose you know that already?" He handed Staber the shoebox and looked around the room. "I got more pillows in the car. We can get them after we settle the money."

"Yeah, that's fine. How was the ride?" Staber asked as Pollard unbuttoned his coat.

"A little bumpy. Kind of feeling sick to my stomach right now. The boss didn't want to use the company plane but we wouldn't have made it if we didn't. Had to wait for Hunter to deliver the goods."

"Well, I really appreciate you coming down here, Dale. I'm supposed to have a meeting next week in Pittsburgh and I told them I'd have some money for them."

"So I heard. The plan has to move fast."

"Well, let's see, it's early February. So yeah, we got a lot to put together with the money tight and all."

Staber stepped back to give Pollard more space, sensing that he was crowding him between the door and the bed and the bureau. "You want something to drink or anything? I don't have much but I got some soda and stuff around." He rolled up the blueprints that were flattened over the bed and stood them up in the corner beside the window that overlooked trash compactors and discarded bed frames.

"No, no," Pollard said, looking around the room. "You living here now?"

"Yeah," he responded sullenly. "I just figured it's easier to control things from here than from Memphis." Staber opened the nearly empty refrigerator and pulled out a can of soda. "Come on, Dale, how about some ginger ale or something, to settle your stomach?"

Pollard stepped back towards the door. "No, no, Wade, I don't want to keep Paully waiting."

"Oh, sure, I understand that. You still have to drive back." Staber shook the box and placed it on the bed. "Well, thank you for bringing this down. This really gets things going."

Pollard took his hands from his pockets and pointed as he spoke. "I'd like you to open the box, Wade. I'd like to count the contents with you so there's no dispute how much was delivered. Would that be okay with you?"

Staber's eyes grew wide, "Oh, sure. I didn't even think of that. But of course, if I was in your spot, well, I guess it just protects the both of us, doesn't it?" Staber picked at the tape with his fingernails. "I don't have much nails for his stuff," he said, glancing over to Pollard.

Pollard reached into his pocket and pulled out his key ring with a small knife attached. He opened it and held it out to Staber who was busy failing to pick open the tape.

"Here you go, this might do it."

Staber looked up and smiled. "Oh, yeah, that'll do the trick." He braced the box against his chest and ran the blade over the tape, then placed the box on the bed again. "Ah," he said with surprise, handing the keychain back to Pollard. "There we are." He looked down at the box and looked back to Pollard.

"You want to count it or do you want me to?"

Pollard shrugged his shoulders and folded the knife away. "You can count. I'll watch. It looks like its bundled in thousands."

"Makes it kind of easy, right? How about if I break one bundle and we count that, and then we just count the rest of the bundles? That okay with you?"

"Fine."

Staber ripped the paper band off one bundle and let it drop to the bed. He held up the bills and counted them as he placed them on the bed. They were so fresh they stuck together, causing him to dab his fingers to his tongue

274

between each bill. There were ten one hundred dollar bills on the bed when he finished.

"One thousand. You agree?"

"Looks like that to me."

Staber picked up the rest of the contents of the box and held it in his hand. He took each bundle and laid it on the bed as he counted the number out loud, looking up at Pollard after each one. "Nine, I count nine intact bundles and one that we broke and counted, ten thousand all together."

"That's what the boss said it would be. I guess I can be going now, unless you need me for anything else."

"Well, no, I can't think of anything right now." Staber stared at the bed with a confused and expectant look. "Oh, you want help with the rest of the pillows? I can come down."

Pollard stepped to the door and opened it a crack. "Okay, sure. That would help. Then I can get back."

"Oh yeah," Staber exclaimed, walking to the door and shaking Pollard's hand enthusiastically. "I expect to be spending some time at the plant in a few days, got more planning work to do. But this gets me started at least. I got a friend, Mike Fusto, he's an executive in the soda business, and anyway, we've been working on a water purification project together. He got some contacts that might be looking for some work like this. By the way, do you know where the water line runs through Plant Four? I've been looking at the drawings but I can't locate it."

Pollard followed Staber to the elevator. "Why don't you

take a room closer? They got plenty of rooms in Bridgeport or New Haven."

Staber punched the floor button and turned to Pollard. "I was hoping to catch Ayn Rand here. I heard she gives lectures here at the McAlprin. She's an objectivist you know."

Pollard buttoned his coat and gave Staber a quizzical look. "Yeah," he said, shaking his head from side to side, "I'm too far into this as it is, so whatever that is, I don't want to know. Anyway, you got to talk to the maintenance folks about that. I've been spending time between Shelton and Ohio."

Staber stepped into the lobby with Pollard in pursuit. "I expect to be up there in a few days, once I make my contacts. The money will help."

"Well, I'll be back in Ohio. Hunter might be in Shelton. But we want this to be your job."

Staber slipped out of his trench coat and into the booth, "Thank you for meeting with me, Mike, I really appreciate this."

Fusto shook Staber's hand, "It's okay, Wade, but like I said, I'm not sure you want to get wrapped up in something like this. This kind of stuff makes me nervous."

Staber set his hat to his side and scanned the area. The sound of a roaring diesel pushing a stalled tractor-trailer away from the pumps filled the diner. "Maybe this was a good choice," he said, glancing up at Fusto. "Seems like all truckers in here."

Fusto picked up the plastic coated menus from between the condiments and placed one in front of Staber. "Yeah, it's convenient, not too far from the airport but people here are just passing through, so I don't know any of the locals. They got thirty- six pumps out there. They serve hundreds of meals a day, lots of turnover so the food doesn't sit around too long, you know what I mean? Mostly long distance haulers, over-the-road types. Not another truck stop until you get to central Pennsylvania."

Staber rubbed his hands together to warm them. The waitress set napkins and utensils beside them and clacked the coffee cups upright, pouring them before asking if they wanted coffee. She pulled a pencil from her hair and told them what the blue plate special was for the day. "I'd like the roast beef well done. Is it well done?" She picked up the menus and placed them back between the salt and pepper shakers.

"Yeah, it's any way you like it, Hon."

"Two blue plate specials," Fusto responded while Staber stirred his coffee. "One well, the other rare."

"You got it, fellas," she said, pulling artificial sweetener packets from her apron and placing them on the table. Staber sipped his coffee and winced. "I hope the food is better than the coffee."

Fusto smiled. His face was aged with jowls that hung low. His hair was gray and very thin on top without even the optimism of a comb-over to conceal his baldness. He poured cream into his coffee. "It is. Truckers don't care much about coffee. They're going to drink anything. But they like their food good and lots of it."

Staber fished into his coat pocket and pulled out his little notebook. "So, tell me who you know that I can contact. I don't have a lot of time to work with."

Fusto looked up with weary eyes. "You know this is real serious business, right? I only agreed to meet you because you feel a commitment to your friend. But I don't like it."

Staber slurped his coffee noisily. "I can understand that. All I need is a crew to get the job done right. No one's going to get hurt. The big boss said he don't want no one hurt. I'm going to get the word out at the plants that I'm working on the water treatment system like the one you're planning at the soda plant."

"Okay," Fusto responded. "These two guys you're going to meet, they're two brothers I know here in the area. They can probably get the job done. Did you bring some front money today?"

"Yes, of course. I have some cash today and more will come once the plans go forward.

Two men approached the booth and sat down quickly, greeting Fusto warmly. "Wade, these are friends of mine, Ralph and Frank."

"Pleased to meet both of you. Has Mike filled you in on the project we need done up in Connecticut?"

Frank Ciero nodded at Fusto and glanced at his brother. "He just told us some buildings need to come down. That's all we know."

Staber motioned the waitress for more coffee. "Do you want to order dinner? Mike and I ordered already."

278

"No," Frank said, "we just ate. Probably just get a coffee to go. We're on our way to do an estimate."

"Okay, sure," Staber said, placing the menus back between the condiments. "So, a very good friend of mine wants some buildings down. I am leading the project for him. So I need some skilled men to get this done right."

Frank nodded and spoke quietly, resting his hands over the table. "We got a friend that can do this kind of work, but we need some money before we put you in contact with him. You know, we got to see how serious your friend is and all. This is dangerous work. You got to know what you're doing."

Staber sipped some coffee, grabbed his coat, and nodded his head to Fusto who followed him into the men's room. He checked the stalls before pulling two envelopes from his coat pocket. "There is five thousand dollars in each. You hold one for the contact and let them split the other one. I'll have the same for you once the project moves along."

Fusto stuffed the envelopes into his pants pocket and returned to the table with Staber. "Well," he said, putting sugar into is coffee, "that was fast. It's all set. I got twenty-five hundred for each of you."

Staber returned and slipped out of his coat. "Booths are too small with coats on. You boys all set now?" he asked, drinking more coffee.

The Ciero brothers rose from the booth and zippered their jackets. Fusto handed Frank the envelope. "You two enjoy your meal. Pete Jameson is sitting at the counter.

He's your contact. We'll send him right over. You can work out the details with him."

Fusto nodded his head as he swallowed some food. "These guys know what they're doing, Wade. They'll take care of everything."

"Of course," Staber responded as he raised his coffee cup to his lips.

Jameson slid into the booth with his coffee cup and introduced himself to Fusto and Staber. He was barrel-chested and burly, with a full, round face and dark ringed, sparkling eyes. His hair was an unruly thatch of gray and brown loose curls. Fusto laid the envelope on the table. "That's just to get us started today. After today you'll be dealing directly with Wade here. I won't be in the picture."

Staber watched as Jameson examined the contents of the envelope and fingered each group of hundreds. "I'll have more in the next couple of weeks as you need it but the boss says it will be in checks from my ministry company to you. My company, Southern Logistics Supply, is getting paid by check from the parent company, Grand Fabricators. Of course, we're going to cover all the materials and supplies with the checks. The cash and checks will cover the rest of the fees. Some of it will have to be paid after the work is completed."

"I'm sorry," Jameson said, "I was counting the money. So, what's the name of your company again? You said it but I forgot."

"Southern Logistics of Tennessee."

"Yeah," he responded, shrugging his shoulders, "it don't

matter how I get paid as long as the checks are good. I mean, I'm going to need to cash the checks before I make the material purchases." Jameson slipped the envelope into his coat pocket. "I can't be putting out all the money for the supplies and hope the checks clear when I get them. So who is really ordering the work?"

Staber looked at him with disbelief and shook his head. "It's best for you to know that you are working for me, for the company, Southern Logistics Supply. The comptroller meets me in New York and personally delivers the cash. They need this project to work. The checks will be good. These are substantial companies I work with." He took another sip of coffee and explained. "Southern Logistics and Supply, that's my company. That's who you're really doing the job for. It's just prep work for a water treatment facility we're going to install."

Jameson looked around the diner to see who was in hearing range. He kept his tone low, leaning over the table with his hands folded at the center. "I think I got the rest of the crew all set," he said, pulling the check from his shirt pocket and dropping it back in. "But the total cost is going to be around sixty thousand or so. That includes the ten you gave out today."

Staber glanced out the window. His cheek twitched nervously. "How many do you have in the crew? How do you know how many you need? I mean, we haven't even talked about the work."

"Right now I got six, not including the truck driver," Jameson answered, leaning back as the waitress clunked down the two dinner plates and offered more coffee. "That should do it. I do this kind of work all the time, I know what I need. But we got to make a trip up there soon. Me and Shaw, he has to see the layout so we know what kind of supplies we need. He wants to walk the place, inside and out, you know, scope it out." The waitress came and delivered Jameson's dinner.

Staber filled his fork with roast beef and mashed potatoes and held it before his mouth. "I can get you in anytime you're ready. Just keep in mind the project is officially a water treatment project."

"Yeah," Jameson said between swallows. "We won't be talking to folks or anything like that. Just want to see the layout and the surrounding area so we can plan this right."

Staber smiled and ran his napkin over his lips. "Well, I told some of the folks at the plant that I was working with a genius who invented a system to make the plant very efficient. I've been there but you're right, you need to look at it for yourself."

Jameson placed his fork on his plate and looked at Staber squarely. "So, you got any dates in mind? When you going up there again? When I told Shaw that there was four hundred and fifty thousand square feet of buildings he nearly passed out."

Staber smiled and kept eating. "Yeah," he said, loading his fork with food. "Hunter got himself a real problem with all that space. But getting your boys in there, that's no problem. We can arrange to pick you up at LaGuardia on the eleventh. Then we can meet in my suite. I have to study some of the layout myself. I want to case the plant from the other side of the river so I can see exit routes and how police and emergency vehicles can get in and out. I expect to be there Tuesday night and stay all day Wednesday."

Jameson swallowed some coffee and filled his fork. "Tuesday would work out. But during the day. We want to walk all the buildings, see everything in the daylight and at night as well."

Staber shook his shoulders casually. "No problem. Just arrange to fly into LaGuardia and I'll have Paully waiting for you."

"I'll have to get more money when we come up."

"It's okay," Staber said as he mixed the remainder of his food in the center of the plate. "I can get a check to my company and cash it for you. How do you come up with the number in your crew?"

Jameson glanced to his side, "We keep working up the list. The demo guy, he's the electrician. I got my nephew working with him. They figure they want to use gasoline barrels and that plastic explosive line to connect everything, then set off the gasoline barrels with dynamite strapped to it."

Staber sat back in the booth and thought for a moment. "How much gasoline?" he asked with a sober look as the waitress placed the bill on the table.

"They ain't sure yet. That's why we need to walk the plants. Over a hundred thousand square feet, that's a lot of space."

"Where they going to buy that much gasoline?"

Jameson gave Staber a blank look. "I got it all figured out. I got a connection at a fuel farm. I got a guy who rents out a room in my motel, he got a commercial license and he's willing to drive the equipment from Pennsylvania to Connecticut the day before. We're going to fill the barrels and then bring it in by truck, all legal, you know. One of the guys is going to rent a straight job from Avis."

Staber looked confused. He put his fork down and dabbed his mouth with his napkin. "You going to need a trailer?"

Jameson put a forkful of food in his mouth and spoke through it. "Yeah, I talked to Whitey, that's the guy with the truck license. He measured the space. He said we can do it with a straight job."

Staber's face went blank. "What's a straight job?"

Jameson smiled and put down his fork. "The truck is all one piece, not a cab and trailer. A panel truck." He finished chewing, took a sip of water and dabbed his mouth with his napkin. "So, what about the money, the other fifty thousand?"

Staber turned to look at the trucks lined up at the fuel bays before turning back to Jameson. "I'm arranging another twenty thousand in a week. I'll have to speak to the boss about the rest. I got to make him aware of the costs. Money's tight."

"It's a big job, Wade. Like I said, my electrician almost flipped when I told him how many square feet we have to take down. That means more detonating cord and more dynamite. And all that gasoline. Plus everyone needs money for the airplane tickets, hotel, car rental, meals and the truck rental."

"I understand," Staber said, sliding his plate to the center of the table. "Why don't we call the boss on the eleventh, this way if he got any questions you can get on the phone with him. That money that went to the Cieros, that was just for the contact, to set this up. Everyone wants a piece of the action and the costs keep going up."

"Don't worry," Jameson responded, pulling his coat on and standing while he struggled with the zipper. "This isn't that hard to get done. Why don't you give me a call before the eleventh and we'll work out more of the details?"

Staber looked at the check, put down money for the tip, and plucked his coat from the hook. "That's fine," he responded as he hesitated at the register and Jameson started for the door. "I'll talk to you."

"Hold still, Tori." Linda repositioned herself on the bathroom floor and gripped Tori's wiggling foot tightly against her leg. "I can't cut your nails if you're moving your feet." The sound of the train whistle, closer now, caused Tori to squirm.

"Hurry up, Mom," Tori lamented with her little hands flailing. "It's coming. I'm going to miss it!"

"Okay, okay," said Linda, as she heard Tori's feet patter to her bedroom and jump on the bed to peer out the window.

"Mom," she called back, tunneling her eyes through her hands cupped to the window, "it's coming over the first trestle. Are you coming?" She took her eyes off the trestle and looked out into the living room.

Linda's mother rose from the loom, set down her thread scissors and walked into the small bedroom. Tori's nose was again pressed against the window with her hands cupped around her eyes.

"Have you started yet?" her grandmother asked as she lay beside her and pressed her nose against the window with Tori.

"No," Tori said, squeezing her hands harder to block out any reflected light. The lead diesel's white beam made the corner and spread brilliance across the triple trestles. "Grandma, how come mommy doesn't like to count the trains? Now," Tori said with excitement as the diesel entered the second of the triple trestles, "start now."

"Sometimes mommy's busy, Honey," her grandmother explained. Then together they starting counting as the freight cars clacked over the rails, their silhouettes backlight against the light of the B.F. plants. Freighters and tankers and cattle cars rolled by, each counted with precision by the voices sounding out in unison. Until at seventy-eight Tori glanced to the single trestle over Hogs Island, spotted the red light of the caboose, and turned to her grandmother. "I don't think mommy likes to count the cars anymore."

Her grandmother kept her eyes on the train, tapping the pane with her finger and pretending to continue counting.

"Sure she does, Honey. She's just busy."

"No, gram," Tori lamented, clearing her blond bangs off her forehead to get a better press against the glass, "she hardly ever counts anymore."

Her grandmother kept her nose to the glass and spoke quietly, as if what she had to say was to stay between the two of them. "Oh, I know she does, Baby, because sometimes, when you're asleep, she comes in here and lies down next to you and I see her counting the cars while you're fast asleep."

Tori's head turned toward her grandmother as if an electric shock ran through it. She sprang from the bed and ran into the kitchen, cupping her fingers to the window and peered out. "Mom," she called back as Linda took a shirt from the laundry basket and started to fold it, "grandma said that sometimes you count the train cars when I'm sleeping." Then Tori turned to Linda with her hands still fixed to the window pane. "Is that true?" She turned back to the train.

Linda put the shirt down and knelt beside Tori. She put one arm around her and cupped her eyes with her free hand. She couldn't see much except the reflection of the ceiling light in the window. "Yes, Honey," she said softly, turning to Tori, dropping the pretense of the count. "Sometimes I count the cars when you're fast asleep."

Tori turned to Linda as the caboose started over the triple trestle. The rest of the train had vanished into the darkness heading north, along the narrow focus of the Valley, toward the Berkshires. "How come I never hear you?"

Linda smiled and ran her fingers through Tori's hair, then she rested a finger on her nose. Their faces weren't an inch apart. "Because I try to be quiet so you can sleep. But sometimes I lay down next to you after I count the cars and I whisper how many I counted in your ear."

"You do, really, Mom?"

"Really, Tor," Linda said over a wide smile.

"What do I do? Do I wake up?"

Linda closed her eyes and shook her head. "No, you don't wake up. You just lay there."

"Do I say anything?"

"Well, sometimes you murmur."

"I murmur?" asked Tori, clasping her mother's forearms in her hands. "What's a murmur?"

Linda pulled her face back a little and scrunched her nose. "It's like a little noise you make, like a little squeaking noise. Its sounds like you're satisfied. And then sometimes I think I see you smile a little, like you know I'm there. Then I stay next to you and watch you sleep and listen to you breathe."

Tori smiled and glanced out the window as the crimson light of the caboose stretched its winking light toward the nestled cottages of Birchbank. She turned back to Linda. "You lay down right in my bed and I don't wake up?"

"Of course I do, Honey. You're my precious one. Sometimes, after the train passes by and it's quiet I look out the window and watch the moonlight shine on the river and I think of my life before you were born and I think how lucky I am that God gave me you to love."

"One hundred and seven," her grandmother said, walking into the kitchen and picking up the shirt from the wooden clothes rack. "How many did you count?"

Linda stood and picked a pair of socks from the rack. Tori squeezed her fingers tighter and looked out the window. The rails were again quiet and dark except for the occasional flicker of the caboose light through the scrub. "A hundred and seven too," Tori said, keeping a vigil while the caboose rocked out of sight.

"Okay, Tori, I think it's time for bed now." Linda collapsed the now empty clothes rack and placed it against the wall beside the stove.

"Mommy, I see a man standing there, near the river. I see two of them."

"Are you done with the lunches?" Linda's mother asked as she collected the folded clothes into neat piles. "It's too cold for anyone to be out there now, Sweetheart."

"All set. Just have to get Tori's milk money ready."

"No, Grandma." Tori said again, "There are two people standing there. Come and look."

Linda took the dishes from the drainer and stacked them in the cabinet.

Her mother knelt at the window and cupped her hands against the windowpane. "Where do you see a man, Honey?"

Tori tapped the window in front of her grandmother's eyes. "Right there. Do you see him? Right where the first trestle ends, on our side of the river." Her grandmother peered out the window, saw what looked like the outline of a person, then a second, and squinted her eyes tightly.

"Linda," she said in a serious tone without turning from the window, "shut the light."

Linda reached over and shut the kitchen light. She walked to the window and stood there, leaning over her mother and Tori.

"He's moving now," Tori whispered into the darkness.

"I see that," her grandmother said.

"Yes," Linda said quietly, "I see them now, too. He has a hat on and now he's walking along the riverbank but it looks like he's looking across the river and the other man is closer to the water, down the bank. There's nothing across there but the sponge plant. Why would anyone be looking at the sponge plant at night?"

Linda's mother looked up at her and placed her hand over Tori's back. "Maybe he was counting train cars, too. I don't think we're the only people who count the train cars."

Linda smiled and changed her tone. "Maybe you're right. Maybe he just likes the river and likes to take a walk to count the cars."

Tori pulled her face from the window and looked up at her mother. "I'm scared, Mommy. How come I never saw him before?"

"Maybe he's an ice fisherman like Joe at Vonetes. You know how Joe tells you that he goes out on the ice at Pink House Cove before the fish get up in the morning. Well, I think this man probably likes to ice fish too, so maybe he's looking for a spot here."

Tori looked up at Linda and wrapped her arms around her legs. "Do you think that's true, Gram, that he likes to fish?"

"Sure, Honey, lots of men like to fish in the dark."

Linda looked down at Tori and put her hands on her head. "If you saw Joe out there now and you didn't know who he was you'd be scared. But you know that if he is ice fishing, so that's okay, right?"

Tori turned out of Linda's legs and cupped her eyes out the window again. "It looks like he's walking up the river now. But we don't get ice down here, Mom. Only up at the cove, right?"

"Well, yes, Tori, that's right because the water in the cove doesn't move too much, but maybe he doesn't know that. Maybe he just moved here and wants to see the river. Don't you remember that Joe said when he gets to the river only the cows and the milkman are up and it's still dark out, right?"

"Yes."

"So maybe that's what that man is doing. He just wants to find out where it's good to ice fish."

Linda leaned over Tori and placed her face to the window. They watched in silence as the man walked along the riverbank and out of view. Linda's mother turned and opened the light. She gave Linda a quick glance and picked up a stray sock from the floor.

"Do you have the other one?" she asked Linda with a smile.

Linda shrugged and glanced around the floor. "No, I had all pairs. It'll turn up," Linda said unconcerned, "time for you to brush your teeth and go to bed, Baby."

Tori looked at her mother and back to her grandmother. "Do you know that man?"

Linda folded the socks and stacked them neatly. "I don't know who he is, Honey. But it's not important. He left."

Her grandmother took her hand and guided her to the bathroom. "Maybe he just wanted to see the triple trestles."

"Do you think he counts train cars too?"

"Well, I don't know, Tori, but it looked like that to me. As soon as the train passed by he left."

Tori brushed her teeth and walked into her bedroom. "Wasn't too many cars tonight, Gram."

"No, not too many, Honey. But I think there's more on the 9:55."

"Do I have to go to bed?"

"Yes, Baby, you know you have to go to bed. You have school tomorrow."

"But the 9:55 is bigger."

"The 9:55 is later. You know the rule, only in the summer or vacations."

"I know the rule." Tori took out her small pad and entered the date and the number of cars in the train. "Teddy said on my birthday we're going to add up all the train cars we counted and he's going to give me a penny for every car I counted."

"Teddy's too good to you, Sweetie," her grandmother

said as she tucked her in. "Does he know how many cars we count?"

"Uh huh, I told him over a hundred for every train."

He grandmother sat beside her and smiled. "And what did he say?"

Tori smiled and held up her palms. "He said he didn't believe me!"

"Oh!" her grandmother exclaimed with her hands to her cheeks and her eyebrows raised high, "I'll bet he didn't." She leaned over and kissed Tori. "Good night, Sweetheart. Mom will be right in to say goodnight."

"Okay."

The windowless door slammed shut behind Staber. He walked through the narrow hall leading to the administrative offices of Sponge Products, stepped into the office, propped open the door with his foot and stepped on some exposed wire running along the wall. He took his fedora in his hand and stood silently, surveying the office area crowded with desks and file cabinets and exposed phone wires running over the worn and soiled rug.

"Excuse me," he said to the only employee in the office, "could you tell me where I can find Mr. Pollard?"

The woman shot Staber an annoyed look as she dropped some computer runs on a desk. "Mr. Pollard's not here today. It's Saturday. He don't work on Saturday."

Staber released his foot and allowed the door to close after him. He looked across the office and saw mattresses piled in the hallway beyond the glass wall. "Well," he said, noticing the nameplate on the desk, "Evelyn, my name is Wade Staber. I'm supposed to be doing some work here with some of my men for the water purification system and Mr. Pollard told me that the plant would be empty today. But I see they're working here."

"Yeah, we got about a hundred people in the plants doing inventory. You and Pollard didn't get your stories straight. What did you say your name was?"

Staber glanced at the wall clock and watched her take another computer run from one desk to another. "Wade," he said, stepping further into the office. "You want some help with that, Evelyn? It looks kind of heavy."

"No," she responded, resting her elbow on the pile of paper, "I don't need no help. Aren't you the guy who's a reverend or a priest or something?"

Staber smiled uneasily and toyed with his hat. "Yes, ma'am, I'm a Baptist minister. You heard of me?"

"Uh-huh, I heard of you. Ruthie showed me that book you wrote, 'You Are Psychic, The Incredible Life of Wade Staber.' I seen that book."

Staber stepped around a chair to get a direct view of Evelyn. "I have one in the car if you want it. I always carry a few around with me."

"No," she said, locking the drawer of the desk, "I probably won't have time to read it. I can always borrow Ruthie's."

"Ruthie seems like a nice person," Staber replied as he strained to watch employees with clipboards moving through the doors of Plant Four, "I'm sure she would let you borrow it once she's finished."

"Yeah, well, she's nice and all but she was plenty mad yesterday when them phone company guys you hired wanted to rewire this place and replace her phone. They wrapped these here columns with new phone wire. We never seen phone wire like that before, wrapped around a pillar like it's some kind of candy cane. She told them that she already got a phone and she don't need another one. And that phone company guy he told her to shut up and mind her own business. He wasn't very nice. But do you know why she's mad? "

Staber shrugged his shoulders and shook his head, "No, ma'am, I got no idea."

"She's mad because you had the boss move all us administrative people from the second and third floor down here. Then they had us load up with all the files from the other buildings here and they moved the important files and computers out of here into some storage place off site. Said it was because you was doing all this work but we don't see no work really getting done. So now we got no place to put stuff and we got to ask Fiore to get stuff for us. You know, it's because of you that I'm moving all these computer records. We're not happy about this, Wade. It's way too crowded down here. You know what we call this place now? We call this here place Sardine City."

"I'm real sorry about that, Evelyn, but it's only temporary," Staber replied sheepishly.

"Well, I don't know how sorry you are but they also ran

the toilet exhaust fans and the laboratory exhaust fans right over our heads in here. So not only are we crowded, but it stinks. And we can hear people flush and everything else that's going on in there." She stood in front of the desk stacked with boxes and computer runs and put her hands on her hips, then looked at Staber with a blank expression. "And by the way," she continued, "my name ain't Evelyn either. It's Geri. This here is Evelyn's desk that I'm working at but I ain't Evelyn."

Staber stood silently. He unbuttoned his black trench coat and tucked its ripped lining away. "I apologize for all your trouble, Geri. So, can I talk to Mr. Fiore? I have to know when these people will be done. My men need to work alone today. I told Fiore that earlier in the week."

Geri looked at her watch and pursed her lips. "I could call him but that won't do you any good anyway. He's at the Boy Scout sleepover with his kids. But we all ought to be out of here by twelve-thirty or one at the latest. I got to go set up the fireman's ball tonight at East End Hose. My husband's a fireman, and I can't leave until they're done with the inventory. I'm the timekeeper. I got to be out of here by noon. So they'll all be gone, except for the guards."

Staber looked startled. "The guards, what guards? I was told no one would be here at all."

"I tell you what, Wade. You and Fiore, you planned today like you planned this here Sardine City." Geri pulled out a seat and dialed the phone to the guard shack. The toilet flushed and the exhaust fan breezed in the freshness over the partition while Geri spoke to the guard and hung up the receiver. She stood beside Evelyn's desk and twisted her skirt until it was straight. "They'll be here all day and night. Nobody told them nothing. Guards are always here. And we got a regular maintenance crew in here until 2:30. They're usually in Plant Four but they're in Plant Six today fixing the Bamberry machines. But I don't have to wait for them to go."

Staber beetled his brows with concern. "How many guards did you say will be here?" Staber asked nervously.

"Two. Just two on a weekend shift. They work twelve hour shifts so the next guys come on around six, six to six. Why, is that a problem? Your guys were stringing that phone wire in here yesterday. Nobody got in their way. I told him my phone worked just fine but he said he was just following orders to get new wiring for the phones. They made a mess of the place. You the one who ordered them barrels of lime that's sitting there on the dock at building four? Guys on the dock, they turned away another shipment that came in yesterday."

Staber stepped off the wire and opened the door slightly. He looked at Geri and shrugged his shoulders, "I ordered the lime for the water treatment process. I was in here yesterday with my engineer trying to work that out. That's why I got to get some work done today." Staber peered out the far glass and around the hall crowded with materials. "Is there a pay phone around here? I have to make a call."

"Yeah, we got pay phones around. One right out near the guard shack and another in building two, a couple right in Plant Four also. But you can use these phones if you want."

Staber shook his head and placed both hands along the rim of his hat. "Oh, ah, thank you, but I have some personal calls to make. I'll just find one on the street in town. Thank you for your help, Geri." Geri walked from her desk and approached Staber. The toilet flushed again and she smiled. "Goes on all day. Say, they say you can predict the future like that Jean Dixon lady."

Staber nodded affirmatively and smiled. "Yes, I have predicted some things that came true."

"Yeah, some of the guys said that you said that Plant Four would burn and only the smoke stack would be left. Did you really say that?"

Staber nodded again and scratched his ear. "Yes, I did have a vision of that."

"So, you really think that's going to happen?"

"Well, I don't know. I only get these visions and sometimes they come true. I couldn't tell you when. But I did see it and only the smoke stack was left standing."

Geri folded her hands and shook her head. "Well, I'll tell you, Wade, I sure hope you're wrong this time. This company got enough trouble without that."

"I wouldn't worry about it, I've been wrong before. I have to be going now to make those calls."

"Oh, sure, they got a pay phone right there by the Boys and Girls Club, on Howe Avenue, it's outside. Conti's Tap Room, they got one inside, but I don't think they are open this early. Or the Rexall, across the river in Derby, it has a few of them old phone booths inside where it's warm."

Staber put his hat on and stepped out into the hallway.

"I'll be fine. I need to find one outside anyway. And thank you for your help," he said as he stepped off and out of the building.

"Danbury Holiday Inn, may I help you?"

Staber buttoned his coat with one hand and turned towards the building to muffle the sound of the traffic. "Could you connect me with room 22, please?" He lit a cigarette as the phone rang into the dark room.

Donny Betts reached over the end table and tipped the receiver to the floor, then reeled it back up by the cord. He clicked on the lamp and squinted. "Hello," he said with a morning cough while leaning on his elbow.

"Who's this?" Staber asked, speaking loudly into the phone.

"It's me, Donny. Who's this?"

"It's me, Wade, you up?"

Donny glanced at the radio clock and squinted again. "I am now, what's up, Wade?"

"I just stopped at the plant. Supposed to get the demo boys set up in there this morning. Anyway, we got a change in plans."

Donny reached back and nudged the body beside him. "Get up, Tony," he whispered, turning and shoving Barry with his free hand, "it's Wade. We got a change in plans."

Anthony Barry flipped off the covers and bounced to his feet. He stretched and scratched his chest. "What's going on?" Donny sat upright in the bed and pulled his hair from his face.

"They got two guards at the plant tonight. You guys got to take them out."

Donny repeated Staber's words to Barry. He put a cigarette to his lips and let it bounce as he responded. "Yeah," he said, looking at Barry shrug his shoulders with a screwed up face. "That ain't going to be no problem. We're pretty much prepared for anything."

"Ask him what we're supposed to do with them," Barry said. He reached down and shook another sleeping body on the floor while Donny spoke to Staber.

"I don't know," Staber said, turning from the building and looking around to make sure no one was listening. "Got to get them out of there."

Donny shook his head and sat at the side of the bed. He took the unlit cigarette from his mouth. "We can handle that. We got all day to figure it out. Don't worry, Wade, we'll take care of it."

Staber slid some coins into the phone at the operator's direction and pulled his coat tighter. "Okay, so I'll see you guys around eleven at the Howard Johnson's, right?"

Donny nodded his head and lit his cigarette. "Yeah, we'll see you at eleven. I thought you were supposed to finish the wiring this morning?"

"That's what I thought too, but they got people working in the plant today. Anyway, I got to go back and get the rest of the crew to meet us."

"All right," Donny said, "we'll see you later. By the way, where's the truck now?"

"Truck's at the Tremont Motor Inn in New Haven."

300

"Okay, see you in a few hours," Donny responded. He looked at Barry and took a long drag on his cigarette, holding the smoke in his lungs. "Shit, I wasn't counting on taking out no guards. Just complicates things."

Barry opened the door of the room to a frigid burst of March air. He squinted into the sun, turned back, and kicked Ray Corley again. "Time to get up, Bud," he said, slipping on his shoes and coat and walking outside, this time closing the door behind him.

Corley sat up on the floor with his eyes closed. He scratched his head, throwing out his arms with a loud yawn. "Why we up so early?" he asked without opening his eyes. "I don't know what time it is but it feels like it's early. I'm starving, we going to have breakfast?"

Donny stood beside the bed and pulled his pants on. "No, we got to meet Wade in the Howard Johnsons in Derby. We got a forty minute ride ahead of us and we got to find a store to pick up some supplies. You'll have to wait to eat. We got a call from Wade," he said as Barry came in and laid a stuffed duffle bag on tasseled sheets. "Seems we got to take out some guards."

Corley opened his eyes and turned to Donny. His long narrow face twisted with defiance. "Take out guards? I thought we was just doing some demolition work. That's all I told Pete I was doing. Now what guards you talking about?" Barry pulled two pistols from the bag along with several boxes of bullets.

"You ever handle a weapon before?" Donny asked.

"Yeah, course I handled weapons, but I never said I was

301

going to handle any weapons today."

Donny tossed one of the ski masks to Corley. "See if this fits."

Corley tossed it back. He lay back on the floor with his head resting on his hands. "I am not wearing no ski mask."

Donny put on an annoyed look. Barry waved him off. "That's okay. You got that turtleneck on. You can just pull it up and pull down your hat. We're going to have to blindfold them guys anyway. Now, are you willing to handle a weapon?"

Corley jumped up and walked into the bathroom. "Yeah," he said as he stood and looked at himself in the mirror. "Yeah, I'll do that. But I don't want no ski mask, cuts off your vision." He ran his fingers through his long hair and stepped out of the bathroom.

"Good," Donny responded as he gathered up his belongings and stuffed them into his small suitcase. "You got any ideas about how we're going to get these guys out of there?"

Corley sat on the floor stuffing everything into his duffle bag. "Yeah," he said, stopping to light a cigarette, "I got some ideas. But we need to talk to Wade about some back roads and stuff. We can bring those guys somewhere or something and leave them there. This way they're out of the building and they can't get hurt."

Donny stepped over Corley and into the bathroom. "So how we supposed to get them up there?" he asked as he brushed his teeth.

Corley belted his pants. "I haven't figured that out yet. We got all day to figure it out, don't we? It ain't like we're going to get them now, right? We still got to meet with Wade, right?"

Donny nodded through a mouthful of toothpaste. "Yeah, we'll figure something out."

Corley slipped by Donny and ran his electric shaver over his stubble. "This is what we do. This got to be clean. We get them guys and use one of their own cars. I seen something like that on television once."

"So what do we do with them in their own car?" Barry remarked. "Ask them to drive us to Pennsylvania?"

"No, you see, man, the trouble with you is you think I'm stupid. But I ain't so stupid. I done this kind of stuff before. One of us drives one of their cars with them in it to whatever place we're going to leave them, maybe somewhere on our way out of there. So when we get there we leave them with the keys and tell them not to move for a while. By the time they leave we're gone and it's over."

Donny looked at Corley in the mirror and turned to Barry. "That will work."

Donny nodded and lifted the duffle bag. "Yeah, it might work. We got to pick up some stuff, duct tape and stuff. We got to blindfold them."

Corley looked at Donny and smiled. "Yeah, we can go pick up that stuff," he said as he walked out of the bathroom and picked up the blankets from the floor.

Staber turned into the motel parking lot and pulled up

beside Whitey. "That's the Yale Bowl over there," he said as Whitey got into the car.

Whitey glanced to his right and made out the rim of the Bowl along the skyline. "Really, I remember they was good a few years back, when Calvin Hill played there." He shifted his head back and pointed to the rental truck. "Ain't a bad truck Pete set me up with."

Staber smiled, "Glad you like it. Pete took care of you, didn't he?"

Whitey smiled and turned on the radio and played with the stations. "Yeah, old Pete, he's pretty good to me, sets me up with these here odd jobs and stuff and I get to stay at his place for free."

Staber shook his head in agreement, pulled out his small notepad and started to flip through his notes. He was anxious, bouncing his knee up and down repeatedly. The demolitions experts had called off the job on two other occasions and he felt this attempt was falling apart also. The plant was supposed to be empty and it was swarming with people. He wasn't told about the guards. But he was going forward with the plan despite all the uncertainties. "Pete's a good guy."

"Only thing I don't get is he didn't say what the gas was going to be used for, just said it's best if I don't smoke or nothing, said something about some demolition work."

Staber turned to Whitey as they started driving towards Shelton. "It's no secret. The plant needs a water purification system constructed. So what we're doing tonight is the demolition work to prep the area. You know, being a Saturday night and all, that's the least disruptive. We were scheduled to do it tomorrow morning during church hours."

Whitey looked at the Bowl. "That guy at the motel, the Tremont, he asked how long I was staying. I just told him only one night. That's right, ain't it? I'm going back to Pennsylvania tonight."

Staber turned to Whitey and spoke above the strain of the engine as he started the truck. "Yeah, the other guys are going back tonight, right after the job's done. You can stay if you want but the other guys are leaving soon as they're done. Why don't you ride with me for now? We're going to meet the guys at the Howard Johnson's now. I want to do a dry run with you to Shelton. You can leave right after you drop the load at the plant but you can't drop it until afternoon now."

"What about you? You staying another night?"

"Me?" Staber asked, driving towards Shelton. "No, I'll be gone just as soon as the charges are set up. I'm not going to be in the area when the work goes off. I got to be in New York City later tonight. It's part of the plan." They drove on for several miles until they approached a Howard Johnson's in Derby and stopped at the traffic light.

Whitey looked over to his right and noticed a church set up on a hill overlooking the road. He blessed himself and looked at Staber. "I went to Catholic grade school. Them nuns taught us to bless ourselves whenever we go by a church." He turned back to the road and smiled a contented smile. "Them nuns," he said, "they were pretty good people." He turned to Staber and continued to grin. "I guess you didn't go to a Catholic school."

Staber looked up to his right to the church, then back to Whitey. "No, I'm a Baptist. Did Pete tell you I'm a minister?"

The light turned. "No way," Whitey exclaimed with a yelp, turning back to the church. "You're a minister? Shoot, that Pete, he didn't tell me nothing about this job, just said not to smoke."

Staber didn't respond. He didn't see the car with the others in it and was concerned. He checked his watch and had Whitey park the truck in the Howard Johnson's lot. Staber scanned the area for Shaw and the Tachy brothers, Dennis and Michael, but couldn't find them.

"You know who you're looking for?" Whitey asked.

"Only one of them, I only met one of them. I told them to meet me at the Howard Johnson's."

Whitey tapped on the dashboard and watched the driveway of the restaurant for cars with three occupants. Several minutes went by without conversation, just an occasional comment from Staber about not knowing where they could be.

Finally, after Whitey grew tired of tapping, he turned to Staber, "They know what Howard Johnson's to go to? I seen a Howard Johnson's in New Haven when I went to get some food before I got to the motel. Didn't you say they were staying in New Haven?"

Staber looked at Whitey and shook his head. "I thought I said the Howard Johnson's in Derby but I could be mistaken. Maybe I just said Howard Johnson's. You know where that other one is?"

"Yeah, I know. I was by there last night."

Staber looked at his watch again. "How long will it take to get there?"

"Twenty minutes, maybe."

Roy walked into the Palace and stood against the radiator. Frances rapped her spatula on the grill and repeated the order. "One Virginia baked ham with coleslaw, that's for Bertha and one tuna melt for Arthur and the three coffees. Is that all for now?" She turned and hung up the phone in the small cabinet under the counter.

"Yes, Roy," she sang out, "coffees?"

"Yes, Frances, and I need two toasted corn muffins for the guys in the guard shack. Went to get my paycheck and they asked me to bring them some coffee. Cold out there walking around those buildings," he replied, picking up the Evening Sentinel from the counter. "Anyone die that I should know about?"

"No, I don't think it's anyone you know. Ginny Farris died, did you know her?

Roy gave Frances a funny look, the effort of trying to recognize the name distorting his face. "No," he commented after a moment, "I don't think so. Should I?"

Frances sliced the two corn muffins and put them on the grill, weighing them down with a ceramic sandwich plate. "She was originally from New Haven. Her husband was Jake. He was a big gambler, worked at Anaconda,

Waterbury plant."

Roy sat at the counter and scanned the front page. "Oh, I know Jake. Yeah, you're right, he liked to gamble. He's dead now, right?"

"Oh, yeah," Frances said, nodding her head vigorously. "He died a while ago. She had it tough. Five kids. She was nice, but she was stuck with him. I remember one year when the plant shut down for summer vacation and she made plans for all of them to go up to Lake George for the week. It was a big deal for them because they never took the kids on vacation before. But he got his vacation pay and gambled it away before he even got home that night. It was terrible. She had to cancel the plans. And he was a tightwad, kept her two feet in a shoe."

Roy flipped the paper open and scanned the articles. "What she tell the kids?"

"Nothing, she just said they couldn't afford it so she took them over to State Park every day for a picnic."

Roy looked to the parlor area and saw Linda collecting coffee and hot chocolate mugs from the tables. He glanced up at Frances, "Teddy gone for the day already?"

Frances juggled the hot corn muffins from the grill while she waited for the cheese to soften for the tuna melt. "No, he'll be back. He stopped home to check on mom. You working tonight?"

Roy folded the paper neatly, fussing with each page to get it perfectly into place and laid it on the counter. "Yeah," he said, getting up and standing in front of the grill again. "I got to drop this off then get home and get

308

some shut-eye and be back at six tonight."

Frances lidded the two coffees and wrote Roy's name on one lid. She double bagged them and placed the muffins on top. "Okay Roy," she said as he placed the money on the counter. "Have a good day now."

"All right, Frances, thank you."

"See you tomorrow," Frances said.

Staber pulled into the Howard Johnson's Hotel parking lot at Long Wharf and spotted Shea and the Tachy brothers in the doorway. They ran into the lobby and grabbed their suitcases.

"You're late," Shea said as he placed his toolbox into the trunk and shut it. Staber handed Donald Tachy the car keys. "I was waiting at the Howard Johnson's in Derby. Whitey mentioned he saw one in New Haven last night so then we drove here. Otherwise I would still be waiting for you there. The other guys should be there waiting in the parking lot for us."

"You never said which one, so we asked at the desk and they told us there was one at Long Wharf. So we took a cab over."

Staber scrunched up his shoulders against the cold. "I was headed to your hotel next but I couldn't find my notes."

"Park Plaza," Donald said. "Can you drive us there?"

"Yeah, sure. We're stopping at the Tremont to pick up the truck. It's on the way to the other Howard Johnson's."

Whitey followed Staber and Shaw and the Tachy

brothers up Route 34 and stopped at the Howard Johnson's in Derby. He waited in the Avis rental truck for them and Corley, Berry and Betts to have breakfast. Staber told them about the guard shack and the interior stairs leading to it and the need to be certain no one was left behind in the plants. They should be empty except for the three kidnappers and the two guards. They reviewed the plans for the kidnapping and discussed which pay phone to use to call the plant to start the timer which would provide the spark to the detonating cord. Then they figured the rendezvous spot on Route 110 where they would meet up, all six of them. They would use two cars, for the ride to LGA where Shaw and the Tachy brothers would fly back to Pittsburgh and Corley, Berry and Betts would drive back to Pennsylvania.

They followed Whitey's truck to the apex of Main Street, at the intersection of Elizabeth where he stopped at the traffic light and looked to the left at that window of Vonetes decorated for Easter. He pulled the truck over and ran to Staber's car.

"We got time to stop in there real quick. I can see coffee pots and stuff near the window and them chocolate Easter bunnies. I could go for something about now."

"Not really, Whitey," Staber replied, looking at his watch. "We just ate, but I suppose you're hungry."

The light changed. Staber started through the intersection. "I'll meet you there, won't take me but a minute, Wade. You want something, coffee or a chocolate bunny or something? How about the other guys, you think

310

they want something?"

Staber looked into the mirror and saw the company car pull over in back of them. "They are all set. See you there."

Whitey dashed across the street between cars and ran into Vonetes. He stood at the counter and waited for Teddy to turn.

Staber drove around the corner to Bridge Street and made a hard left into the abandoned road parallel to Main Street. He was followed by Betts, Berry and Corley in another car. They drove through the narrow alley with ice crunching under the wheels and came to a stop across from the sponge plant, just east of Linda's apartment.

"Okay, fellows," he said, turning to the back seat. "This is where you can change into the phone company outfits."

Donald Tachy looked at Staber in amazement. "You want us to change into these again, here, outside, in the cold?"

Staber shrugged his shoulders and turned to Donald. "Look, this is the best place I could find that wouldn't attract attention. Most of these buildings are abandoned and no one ever uses this road."

Staber got out of the car and opened the trunk. He stood there as they took their outfits out and used the cars as dressing rooms. They repacked their suitcases and stuffed them into the trunk.

"What can I get for you, fella?" Teddy asked Whitey as he dried his hands. Whitey turned from the candy case and smiled at Teddy.

"Just a black coffee, large if you got it."

"Sure," Teddy said, holding up a large cardboard cup, "this okay?"

"Yeah, that'd be great," Whitey responded turning and walking to the candy counter loaded with bunnies of all sizes and chocolate crosses. He picked up two boxes of marshmallow chicks and a one pound chocolate bunny and laid them on the counter.

Teddy turned to Whitey and handed him the coffee. "You need a bag?

"No," Whitey responded, handing Teddy a five dollar bill, "I got these, too."

Teddy thought for a moment, then fingered the two handed register and gave Whitey some change. "Come with me," he said, walking to the candy register and glancing at the truck parked across the street. "We got to ring up the candy sales here. That's how I keep track."

Whitey smiled and nodded to some customers as they made their way out. He scanned the shelves lined in neat tiers with Easter baskets loaded with bunnies and chocolate eggs wrapped in colorful foil, coconut eggs and peanut butter eggs and marshmallow chicks and scattered jelly beans, all dressed with pink and yellow and green cellophane wrap.

"You sell a lot of Easter candy here, don't you?" Whitey said, turning slowly to take it all in.

Teddy counted out his change and laid it in Whitey's hand. "Yeah," he said casually, "it's our busy season. Where are you from, just passing through?"

Whitey fisted his change and put it into his pocket without counting it as Teddy bagged the candy and handed it to him. "I'm from Pennsylvania. I got a load to drop off in Shelton. We're doing some work at the sponge plant today."

Teddy nodded and smiled. "Well, you have a nice day and don't work too hard."

"What can I do for you?" Jimmy asked as he stepped out of the guard shack carrying his clipboard.

"I'm here to do some work on the water treatment system," Staber responded with a smile as he recognized Jimmy from earlier visits. He pointed to his passengers and continued, "These here men are from the phone company. We're going to swap out some of the phones and lay some new wire."

Jimmy nodded, "Some of the buildings are locked. But Ruthie said you have keys, right? The big boss said you can go anywhere you want, at least that's what I understood."

Staber smiled as he watched Jimmy record the license plate on his visitor's register. "Yeah, I thought we would have been done by now but we got delayed the other day. I talked to this woman in the office earlier today, her name is Geri, and she said that the inventory work would be done by noon or so."

Jimmy shook his head in agreement and opened the door to the guard shack. "Yeah, no problem," he said as Staber entered the grounds.

"Say," Staber called back, "I got a truck coming in real soon to deliver supplies."

Jimmy came back out of the shack and stood by the car. "Yeah, just have him stop by the shack here. What's he driving anyway?"

Staber looked up the road and saw the truck coming, "There he is now."

"Ok, I'll clear him in when he comes by. He got a bill of lading or any paperwork?"

"No, he's with me. It's not a supply drop or anything. Just some material for the water treatment process we're installing."

Staber waited until Whitey pulled along the side of him. "I got to get these guys settled in here. Just wait here a minute, workers are leaving now. We can't start unloading until the workers are done."

Whitey looked at his watch. "Okay, but it's cold. I ain't turning off this heater."

"Okay. I'll be back out in a while. Just wait here. Don't go driving off anywhere."

Whitey rolled up the window, letting it remain open a crack. He turned up the heat and finished his coffee. He rested his head back on the seat and started gnawing on the solid chocolate bunny.

The three men from Staber's car got out and approached Whitey. "How was that ride? We loaded this truck in Pennsylvania and tied down the load. Ride okay?" Dennis asked.

"Oh, yeah, you boys did a good job. Ride was smooth

and them barrels must be topped off nice because it was real tight on the road. I think I used about ten shoring straps on the barrels. Just going over all these rails here, I could hear the juice squishing around and stuff."

"I tell you it was tough loading it. All we had was hand trucks and these things like to roll."

Michael Tachy wheeled a hand truck into the truck and shimmed it under the barrel. He and Shaw tied it down on the hand truck and muscled it out of the truck and onto the dock.

He looked around the massive brick building and shook his head. "We're taking down this thing?" he asked incredulously.

Shaw took one of the hand trucks and wheeled the dynamite into the plant. Tachy followed him in with the barrel filled with blasting caps and tools. The plants were silent except for the sound of the barrels being offloaded to the dock. Shaw looked at his watch and walked the length of the plant, counting out his steps. He pointed to each pillar that was to have gasoline barrels strapped to them.

"So this is the plan. Remember the plans you showed me in the hotel? That's how we figured this. Twenty-five barrels, three barrels for each pillar set up opposed to each other. We spark the explosive wire, it hits the cap that ignites the dynamite, and the barrels go up immediately. You have a raging fire in seconds and lots of explosive force to destroy the structure on itself. The upper three floors are just going to collapse down. The two extra barrels are taking care of the canal junction."

Staber looked skeptical. "What if it doesn't go? What happens then?"

Shaw looked at him with an expression fitting a dead fish. "That's what you pay me for. I come back in and make it go."

"You can't get hurt. Nobody can get hurt."

"Don't worry about me. Been doing this stuff for years, still got all my fingers and limbs. It's going to work."

"You got enough time?"

Shaw looked at Staber and started towards the dock. Staber followed walking briskly behind. "We got plenty of time. Look, Wade, you hired me to do a job. Me and the boys, we got lots to do. Why don't you go back out to the dock? Once the truck is off loaded you can let the driver go. No sense him hanging around. So if you don't mind can you find something else to do for a while? I thought you said you're leaving early. Didn't you say you have to go and get the other guys in?"

"Yeah, I'm about on my way now. I'll get Whitey's truck out of here then I got to get the other fellows in here through the back dock after dark. That's the shift change for the guards."

"That's fine. You just don't worry. I do this work every day."

"Coming around to the back dock now," Staber said as he glided his car along the tracks down the back side of Plant Four that sat in the darkness of the March evening. Staber drove slowly along the rutted street and rail line and crossed the road along the stretch of Plant Four hard by Canal Street.

"Can we sit up now, Wade?" Corley asked, "It's getting a little stuffy down here"

Staber glanced to his right and saw nothing but darkness buttressed by the four story building that was totally dark. "Go ahead," Staber said, turning back to the road crossed with rail tracks. "It's like a ghost town down here anyway."

Staber drove around the small shipping dock on the back side of the building. "I'm going to pull up and let you guys in. I'll stay for a minute, then I'll be on my way back to the dock to check on the wiring work. I told the boss I'd be in New York when the detonator goes off. Look out for Shaw and the Tachy boys."

Corley sat up and took on a serious tone. "You boys check to make sure you got your flashlights and weapons. Put your ski masks on. I have the tape and handcuffs and the keys."

They crouched outside the massive press room and sat quietly against the wall. Shaw and the Tachy brothers were still crawling through the building fastening charges. The air was dense with the smell of processed rubber. The dusk darkened to night and cold set in. Corley spoke in a hushed tone, "Okay, we should move in now. Remember, we're all staying together behind the pillars. When the guards pass they should be walking along the aisle. Unless they hear sounds they would have no reason to enter into the press room area."

Cal opened the door of the guard shack and rubbed his hands together to warm them. "What's happening?"

Roy looked up from his Racing Form and shook his head. "No, nothing's happening if you don't count my horse didn't place today. I think I'm down for the week. Good thing it's the first of the month so I get my allowance." Cal hung his coat and peeled off his hat. "Are you making a coffee run?"

"Yeah, but I figure I'll go in about a half hour or so. Pollard left a note that we supposed to get that Staber guy coming by with some workers to do some work on that water treatment system."

"Hope it ain't outside work. It's a cold one."

Roy looked up at Cal and folded his paper. "I don't know. When I came on Tommy said that he saw Staber pull in earlier, they was unloading some supplies I guess. He might be here already. You see anyone in the plants? What can they do outside when it's cold and dark?"

Cal shrugged his shoulders and sipped on coffee. "I didn't see anything. No one's in the plants, least not from what I can see, except DeAngelo."

"DeAngelo's here? I didn't know he's here. Boiler trouble?"

"I guess. His truck is down outside of Plant Four. They must have him fixing the boiler or something."

Staber drove his car around to the guard shack. "Done for the night?" Roy asked.

"Yeah," Staber replied, taking the clipboard with the

318

sign out sheet into his car and leaning it on the steering wheel. "Just about done now."

"I didn't even know you were here," Roy explained as he noted Staber on his visitor's log. "The other shift said you might be around."

"Well, I did sign in earlier. You could check the sheets. But I've been doing some running around, you know, getting supplies and stuff. But I'm done for the night now." He nodded at Roy, "Good night now."

"Night." Roy looked at his watch and marked the time out at 8:30. He wondered if Cal had come across Staber on his rounds or in the other guard shack.

"Get me three caps from the bag," Shea said to Dennis.

He fished it out of the small bag and handed it to Shea. He fastened it to the cord and moved on. The building was growing darker now that the sun had set. Shea was having trouble seeing and asked for a flashlight.

They crawled to the next column and set up their tools. Shea rounded the corner and crouched near the bottom of the gasoline barrel.

"Don't move or I'll blow your head off." The words were as cold as the muzzle of the pistol that pressed against his cheekbone.

Shea froze in place. He felt his heart beating in his throat. "No, no!" Betts yelled to Corley. "He's with us, he's with us. They're the guys we ate breakfast with."

Danny turned his flashlight to Betts and back to Shaw.

He lowered his pistol and crawled back beside the heavy machinery. Shaw kept working, snaking detonation cord around and through machinery, weaving it over columns and barrels.

"We're wrapping this column?" he asked, examining he sketch of the floor he carried with him.

"Yes, that's it."

They raced over the floor for the final cording and fastening of the explosives through the building. "Get fresh batteries," Shaw commanded.

Betts got them and went to the floor above. "I'm connecting," he yelled down.

"Ready," Shaw responded.

Betts scrambled down. "Just about done, just got to tie in the water line."

"How many you need?"

"Four sticks. We're tying the line in two places to get through the concrete."

"Water line? Why we blowing the water line?"

"Sprinklers, to disable the sprinklers."

"Got it."

Betts followed Shaw to the water line and assisted in charging the line. "Phone is next," Shaw said softly. They walked to the pay phone near the office and opened it.

Shaw unfastened the tip and ring wires to use the ringing current to charge the timer that would tick off the moments to charge the blasting cap that tied to the explosive wire that was roped throughout the plant and around the columns and tied into the dynamite sticks that were lashed to the gasoline barrels that were set against the columns holding up Plant Four. "That's it," Shaw said.

"That's it?" asked Betts, looking at the wires attached to the combustible line.

"That's it." Shaw packed up his tools and grabbed his canvas tool bag.

Cal didn't lift his eyes from the paper, continuing to scan the bold print of the local news, settling at the sports page and reading the lengthy story of the state basketball tournament that his son's team missed out on by one game. "That Staber guy might not even bother to check in here if he comes back."

"Well," responded Roy, "if he shows up again and I haven't called you, call me so I'll know he's around."

"Cripes, the team that beat us got knocked out of the tournament the first round. We could have done better than that."

Roy finished his coffee, tossing the cup into a small brown pail near the wall that was spotted with dried coffee from the hundreds of shots it took over the years. "Hey, you never know what can happen in them tournaments."

Cal folded the paper and left it for Roy. He got up and reviewed the maintenance note again while he swung his portly frame into his hunter's jacket and fixed his matching hat with the ear flaps down. Okay, Buddy, I'm heading out to my car for a minute. Freeze my butt off again."

The kidnappers adjusted their ski masks and pulled their guns out, quietly moving through the plant and hiding in the dry room behind rows of finished sponge rubber products.

Roy heard Cal's footsteps as he stepped towards the guard shack. He glanced at the clock to prepare for his rounds and stepped to the window, looked at the half moon washing the buildings with cold light. At least there would be some illumination in addition to his flashlight. He turned back into the guard shack and heard Cal rubbing his hands together for warmth.

"Damn," he said to Roy. "Only ten to ten and I feel like we been here all night." Cal's coat was half off.

Roy took his flashlight and pulled his coat on when he heard the thunder of rushing feet run up the stairs and the cold barrel of a pistol pressed into the right side of his neck just beneath his ear. "Don't turn around or I'll blow your head off." Roy froze. He felt his knees sag. "Don't get brave. Don't get brave and no one will get hurt." A pistol dug into Cal's rib.

The kidnappers forced them down the stairs and shoved them against the wall of the press room. Their hands were cuffed behind their backs and adhesive tape and gauze were used aground their eyes.

"Is there anyone else in the plant?"

"DeAngelo," Cal said. "DeAngelo is fixing the boiler."

"We're not here to hurt the working man," one of the kidnappers said. His words were labored and measured, his actions deliberate and efficient. "Did you ever hear of

322

the Weathermen?"

"Only what I read in the papers," Roy responded timidly.

"Well, you're going to hear about them now."

The kidnappers guided them to a small bench in the nurse's office. "We're going to get DeAngelo."

Two of the kidnappers left to find the boiler room and DeAngelo. Corley stayed back with Roy and Cal, placing the muzzle against each of their necks alternately and talking about the Weathermen. He told them to relax, they had nothing to fear. They were not interested in hurting the working man. This was a mission for social justice.

"Freeze and you won't get hurt," they shouted to DeAngelo as they stuck their pistols into his ribs while he was kneeling on the floor fixing the boiler. They put his hands behind his back and cuffed him, then taped his eyes and started to lead him away.

"What about my tools? Can't I take my tools?" he asked as he leaned towards the boiler. The gun dug into his ribs with more force.

"Don't get funny, Mister. We ain't out to hurt the working man. Just stay calm and you won't get hurt."

"But my tools!" DeAngelo cried.

"Forget about your tools."

The Fireman's Ball at the Echo Hose Company was heating up across the river. The dance floor was full of couples, the men in their dress uniforms and the woman in gowns. Along the bar firefighters relayed drinks to their tables with double fisted efficiency. Others leaned over the bar with their jackets opened and conversed with anyone who stepped up for an order. Geri's decorations of streamers and balloons and glitter gave the place a magical touch and lightened the mood of the late winter night. The Shelton firefighters were on standby to respond to any Derby calls. The Sponge Products plants lay just across the river, two miles by road, but a mere half mile by the crow's flight.

The kidnapper with Roy and Hanley grew anxious. He chattered nervously to fill the silence, adjusting his navy watch hat over his eyebrows and jumping from his chair to the window at the sight of shadows washed by the momentary stare of headlights from the street. "Ain't here to hurt no workin' man," he repeated with a steady cadence as he craned his neck to look down the hallway.

"You got nothing to worry about, no siree bob, got nothing to worry about. You fellows just sit tight now and everything will be all right." He checked the wall clock, "That clock right?" Just then the sound of footsteps came from down the hall towards the nurse's station. No words were said. They felt the presence of DeAngelo being seated between them. "That clock right?" he asked again.

Cal shrugged his shoulders. He waited for Roy to respond but heard nothing. Everything was black. He couldn't tell where anyone was and he didn't hear anything. He thought it was best to say something, that one of them should say something. Just as he spoke he heard Roy respond but he continued anyway, "I guess, might be off by a minute or two."

"What time is it anyway?" Roy asked.

"Who wants to know?"

"Well, no one yet, but my wife's gonna wonder what happened to me."

"You leave at six tomorrow morning. We did our homework on you boys. The organization did some background work here. We got lots of time." Five or ten seconds passed in silence. "We'll be leaving soon anyway. Where's your car?"

The three of them sat silently, helpless, blindfolded and scared, each waiting for the other to speak. "My truck, it's down near the boiler. It's old," DeAngelo offered, hoping to discourage whatever plan was being hatched now. "The clutch slips."

"Mine's close," said Roy, turning his head to the direction of the voices. "It's right there next to the guard shack, that Bonneville with the clothes hanger antenna. It's got a lot of room."

One of the kidnappers stepped to Roy. "Where are the keys?"

"In my coat pocket, the one I got on, left pocket."

The kidnappers worked quickly. Their dialogue was spare and muted, sounding like bad actors reading mechanically from an unfamiliar script.

"You guards," one of the kidnappers asked, standing in the doorway. "We just want to confirm, you get relieved at six in the morning. Is that right?"

"That's right," they said in unison.

"No one else in the building, that right?"

"No one," Roy responded nervously.

"Yeah," Cal confirmed, "no one that we know of."

The door opened and closed quickly and Roy's car started with a strained racing of the motor and the high pitched whine of a loose fan belt.

"We're going to line you up and follow each other out of here up the stair and into the shack and then to the car. No one's going to get hurt if you just do as you're told. Understand?"

"Yeah," they all seemed to mumble at once.

"What about my tool box?" Angelo asked as they stood him up.

The kidnappers look at each other and didn't respond, deciding silently to ignore the question. "We're going into the car. We'll guide you into the back seat. You keep your heads down so no one sees you, pretend you're sleeping."

The door swung open to the frozen night air. They walked silently to the car and climbed into the back seat quickly, then leaned forward and hid their eyes from view.

"Okay," one of the kidnappers ordered. "Let's go."

The Bonneville pulled out without incident, stopping for red lights and traveling slowly along Howe Avenue. Trailing behind was the third kidnapper, following Roy's car as planned.

The car pulled up along the Bonneville at the corner of Bridge and Howe. The windows rolled down, "Follow me across the river. I got to make a call."

They made the right across Bridge Street into Derby and

stopped at the light at Elizabeth and Main. The corner was dark and quiet and looked abandoned in the frigid March night. The only sound was the clicking of the traffic lights as they changed.

They made a left and drove two blocks before pulling over in front of the Southern New England Telephone Company building. Two pay phones stood idle in the cold. The driver jumped out of the car and searched his pants pockets fruitlessly. He walked back to the other car. "You guys got a dime? I must have dropped mine when I was about to shoot that guy in the building."

One of the kidnappers got out of the car and pulled a handful of change from his pocket. He held his palm open, "Take what you need."

"Only need one," he said, lifting the receiver and hearing the coin drop in and the dial tone actuate. He slowly dialed the numbers, waiting patiently for the rotary dial to return to its original position, until the last revolution was completed and the sequencing was set. The cars went back across the river and made a right up Howe Avenue, past Indian Wells and into White Hills.

Roy, Cal and DeAngelo lost their bearings immediately. They had no idea where they were or where they were being taken. They were too frightened to speak. Nothing made sense except they were certain they were kidnapped and they were sure something was going to happen to the old B.F. Goodrich plant. They knew who the Weathermen were but couldn't understand why Plant Four was the target. They seemed to be riding forever without direction.

The timer, a five cent item, ticked off the minutes and seconds until 11:35pm, when Plant Four erupted in one brilliant flash and the explosion sent plumes of flaming orange tongues into the sky as the dynamite and twenty five exploding barrels of gasoline shattered the frozen night. Two patrons seated at Conti's Tap Room fell off of their bar stools by the force of the blast.

Jake Bailey had enough, too much food, too much liquor available even for a non-drinker like himself, and too much noise. He had to be at the guard shack at six to relieve Roy and Cal. He touched the chief's shoulder and nodded his goodbye, then slipped out without notice.

Joe Pepe's eyes were growing tired as he sat in the Hilltop Hose recreation room with three other firemen watching the end of Walking Tall.

He looked over at the refrigerator and thought about another beer. He looked at his pals, their eyes as tired as his, and decided against it. "About ready to take it home, guys," he said to their nodding agreement.

Dougy put his palms over his stomach as the catering staff collected the plates from the tables at the end of the East End Hose dinner. He picked up the complimentary cigar from the table and examined it, unwrapped it, and put it to his nose. Chief Brandt of Shelton pulled up a chair beside him. "Too much food for me," he commented. He lit his cigar and said goodnight to Brandt.

"Yeah, these banquets are for the young guys. Us old timers, we just can't eat and drink like we used to."

Dougy nodded and looked around the room. The

horseplay among the younger members was getting rowdy. The noise level began to rise until conversations were maintained by shouting into the listeners' ears. And then the building shook and the noise level dropped to a murmur.

"What the hell was that?" Brandt said in a voice just above a whisper. His eyes darted around the room and locked into those of Charley Stantz.

Dougy opened the back door of the firehouse and saw the sky tinged in orange from the flames licking the darkness. No one moved. Small murmurs of conversation picked up through heavily knitted eyebrows and wrinkled foreheads. Then the tone went in and the East End celebrants left their food and drinks, wives and girlfriends, and headed for the trucks and cars.

Pepe just turned the doorknob to enter his house when he felt it shake and he heard the explosion. Moments later his home scanner activated in a loud, continuous scream, 'B.F. blew up! B.F. blew up!' He grabbed his equipment and ran back to his car, following the first engines to the scene while he radioed for assistance and instructed Oxford to send all available equipment to Shelton to meet the disaster.

Flip heard the explosion and felt the house shake. He stood on the front porch of his Atwater Avenue home to see what happened. His wife came out beside him. There was an eerie silence and then the sound of alarms filled the air. They got into his car, drove to the top of Olivia

Street and saw the sky filled with flames. "My God, the whole place is burning!" his wife exclaimed.

Flip looked at her with disbelief. "It can't be," he said with certainty. "The whole plant can't be burning at once. It's impossible. That means the sprinklers ain't working. I put them in. I know they work. In fact, some guy the boss hired was just asking me about the water line about a week ago. Something's not right. I gotta go down there."

"You can't go there now, there's fire trucks coming in from all over. You hear those sirens. Nothing you can do."

Flip put his car in park and jumped out. "I'm going over," he said as he started to rush down Olivia Street. "You go back home with the kids."

Linda jumped from her bed and flew into Tori's room as the earth shook. The blast cracked the apartment windows facing the river.

"Mommy!" screamed Tori, "Mommy!" she cried again with the bone chilling scream that only genuine terror can induce.

"Tori!" Linda called out as she flicked on the living room light and raced to Tori.

"Mommy!" she screamed again and leapt into Linda's arms in a shaking, ripping ball of tears. The apartment flickered like votive candles in a dark church as lizard tongues of orange flames licked a dappled, mango spire along the face of the river.

Linda's mother entered the bedroom with a terrified look. Through the cracked glass she saw the final bursts of

330

explosives illuminate the river and burst light into the room. She grabbed Tori and glanced out the kitchen window to the flames licking the sky. The collapse of Plant Four created a pile of debris stacked for a bonfire that blistered the adjacent buildings.

Tori hugged Linda with knuckle whitening strength as the sound of debris hitting the building magnified the terror. Linda's eyes, like klieg lights illuminating a dark stage, were bright with purpose and urgency that betrayed her voice for fear of frightening Tori further. "Let's go! Let's get out!" she said calmly to her mother.

"Just put your coat on, Sweetheart," Linda's mother said as she coaxed Tori's arms, one at a time, from Linda's neck and slipped it on along with a knitted hat and gloves. "What about her feet?"

"It's okay. Those feet pajamas are warm enough." Linda stood her on the sofa as she and her mother slipped into their shoes and coats, gathered some belongings, and moved quickly down the stairs.

The late customers at River and Burn's and the bars along the Barbary Coast rushed to the street in confusion. Cars, with drivers standing alongside them, stopped in the center of the road, stunned with the confusion of the sound of the blasts and sight of people pouring into the street.

Like silver and gold glitter along a majestic crown, the hills and mountains of the Valley lit up as the modest homes on narrow roads woke up to the sound of the explosions. The scream of police cars and emergency vehicles soon filled the night over the bridges and fire trucks loaded with thick eyed volunteers careened through the streets. Despite the hour, phones rang to wake the sleeping who rolled from their beds and headed to the plant. 'Sponge is burning!' came the frantic all, or 'the plants are exploding!,' was the breathless news and the scramble in the night to stare hopelessly at the spectacle.

"Where, Linda?" her mother asked, trailing her and Tori as they dodged men, some holding the hand of a wife or girlfriend, running to the Derby riverbank behind Linda's apartment to watch with an unobstructed view. Traffic on both sides of Route 8 pulled over in lopsided lines and drivers got out and leaned over the rails as the cold river itself seemed to burn in decorous flames.

"We're going to Teddy and Franny's apartment," she yelled back, hardly turning and holding Tori's face into the warmth of her neck. At the corner of Minerva and Main she stopped and turned to her mother.

"What's going on?" a man asked as he walked by Linda and turning to wait for an obviously confused group that followed.

"B. F. is burning," she responded quickly with a nod of her head, then turned to her mother.

"How bad?" he persisted.

Linda shook her head resolutely. "The whole thing, it's gone and burning, just exploded like you'd see in the movies. Everything's burning. You okay, Mom?"

"Yes," her mother said, stepping ahead of her. "Yes, let's keep going."

They hurried past the Palace and waited, panting for air that was now heavy with burnt fuel and rubber, at the corner of Main and Olivia. Three fire trucks roared across Main Street and ramped onto Bridge Street where the flames, now in their full dance, sucked massive amounts of air into its furnace and whipped the frozen air into a bone chilling wind.

Linda turned to her mother with a puzzled and desperate look. "They don't even know where to start," Linda shouted as the fire trucks idled on the bridge and firemen abandoned their cars on the sidewalks and streets.

"No," her mother yelled over the noise of screaming sirens and fire whistles calling out into the night. "No one knows where to start."

Teddy's mink brown Riviera pulled over and screeched to a sharp stop along the curb. "Get in!get in!" he yelled as he leaned over and pushed the passenger door open. He saw the fear in Linda's eyes and felt Tori climb in and grab onto his arm. "What happened? Felt like an explosion."

Linda and her mother climbed into the back seat of the sedan and leancd forward to talk, as if they couldn't get close enough to Teddy and Tori. "B.F. exploded. The whole thing just exploded all at once."

Teddy checked his rear view mirror. A steady stream of blue lighted cars raced down Roosevelt Drive. He pulled off into Main Street and made the left up Elizabeth. In the distance he could see fire engines streaming down Elizabeth Street towards Shelton and he knew Ansonia was called in. But Ansonia was covering Derby and Derby was already responding and the fire was Shelton's to command. He pulled the car along the curb of Olivia in front of his apartment. Frances ran outside and escorted them in. Teddy left the car and walked down Olivia Street. The sky was bright with orange and red flames and pluming with smoke. From Roosevelt Drive he saw volunteer firefighters speeding to respond from the surrounding communities. Within two hours the streets of Shelton would be filled with hundreds of pieces of fire apparatus from Monroe and Oxford, Seymour and Ansonia, Derby and Orange, West Haven and New Haven, North Haven and Hamden, Trumbull and Bridgeport, Milford and Stratford and Waterbury, too. Bridge and Canal Streets were already starting to choke with equipment. Finally, chilled to the bone, Teddy turned and walked back to the apartment and retired for the night. He set his alarm for five thirty, a mere four hours away, knowing that the city would be full with firefighters and he would give away coffee and food to anyone who stopped in.

Fire trucks, ambulances and emergency vehicles sped to the scene, heeding the calls for mutual assistance from the Shelton fire chief, only to pull back and wait as the inferno contained itself in place. The fire consumed everything flammable in Plant Four as the vortex of flames licked at the firmament, sucking in the cold night air, sending glowing cinders high into the night sky. Everyone knew that something had gone terribly wrong, a fire so massive that was stoked by rumors of the Weathermen howling in the heat induced wind.

The Valley burned that night, a stack fully opened, leaving melted heavy machines and singed and fallen brick and concrete. Wide, frightened eyes peered through the windows of the homes dotting the hills of the Valley, watching thousands of jobs vaporize before their eyes.

The car came to an abrupt stop. "Okay guys, this is it. We're going to un-cuff you and tape your hands. The tape isn't strong because we want you to be able to break it. We're going to tie you to a tree. Don't move for a while, maybe a half hour. You're going to find the car keys on the ground in front of the car and a flashlight."

Roy was too frightened to talk. Nothing made sense. Did he say he wanted us to break free after a while? That we were going to be un-cuffed? Stay there and wait? Stay where and wait for what? He felt the kidnappers guiding him out of the car and place him against a tree. He waited breathlessly for the feel of the cold gun metal against his neck again. Instead, he felt the cuffs release and the sound of tape being pulled from a roll. He stood silently as the kidnappers worked and taped his hands without speaking. He thought they were now saving his life. Instead of a bullet to the head he was having his wrists taped like so much gift wrap. His fears started to subside. He would be dead by now if that was his fate. He felt grateful but was too terrified to express that and too confused to know if that was right. He lost trust in his own judgment, wanting to thank his kidnappers for terrorizing him, putting a gun to his head, kidnapping him and dumping him somewhere unknown. And they said they would leave the car. He heard the kidnapper un-cuff Cal and DeAngelo and listened to the sound of their breathing. No guns or threats of guns. No threat of harm. They stood there, tied to the tree, shoulder to shoulder, thinking, breathing and listening, silence and darkness. Thinking, breathing and listening. All of life remained theirs.

They never heard the kidnappers leave, slipping into the frigid darkness without a trace. More timeless minutes passed without measure. Minutes without markings except for the sound of breathing until finally, as the cold air started to make matters urgent, they spoke in whispers.

"I think they're gone," Cal speculated, moving only his lips. "No," Roy responded softly while keeping his head still, "I didn't hear no car or nothing start. They could be right outside just waiting for us to make a move."

"I think they're gone, too," DeAngelo said as he started to wiggle his hands free. He snapped the tape with his thick wrists, ripped the tape off his eyes, and checked his watch. It read ten after midnight. "I can't see nothing but looks like no one's here." He helped Roy and Cal rip their tape off. There was only darkness and the shadows of bare tree limbs etched by the moon.

Papa jumped from his car and ran to the guard shack. No sign of activity. Roy's coffee cup was on the desk, the Daily News was folded on the desk and the Racing Form was under it with Cal's lunch pail on the stool.

Walt Tracz, an off-duty guard, ran into the shack as well. "Anyone in there?" he yelled, running to the other side of the shack and watching the flames of Plant Four blow. "There are supposed to be two guards on duty tonight. We got to find them."

"They got to be around somewhere," Papa replied. "Wouldn't both be making rounds at the same time."

Tracz shook his head pessimistically. "Making rounds, they could be in the plant," he responded, pointing to the growing flames and watching fire apparatus careen down Canal Street. "Follow me," he yelled back to Bailey. "We got to search the buildings."

They ran along the perimeter of Plant Four to the opening of Plant Six. Nothing was illuminated, just as instructed, except for walls licked with the flames of Plant Four. Panting, with lungs aching from the search, they got to the far end of the buildings and saw no guards.

They started back at a walking pace when they came across a half dozen drums of highly explosive diethanoline. They enlisted the help of some of the young firefighters and rolled the drums to safety, north of the Shelton Tack Co.

DeAngelo stepped forward and looked around, "Where the hell are we? They got us lost." The gravel driveway reflected the ambient light. Roy walked to the front of his car.

"I think that's Stevenson Lumber," Manley said, pointing

down the driveway and walking back to the car.

"Yeah?" Roy asked as he walked in back of the car and looked down towards the street and spotted the keys. "Hey!" he called out, "hey!" he said excitedly again breaking into a normal tone and moving at a gallop. "Here's the keys, just like they said."

"Let's get out of here!" Cal shouted as they piled into the car.

From the distance, the sky over the Valley was covered in a gauzy, pink blanket of illumination. As they passed Pink House Cove it took on an orange tint with airy, billowing plumes of smoke filling the riverbed.

They rounded the corner at Bridge Street and saw the massive buildings licking with fire, flames reflecting off the river.

They were stopped at the beginning of the block by an old auxiliary fireman standing to the side of a wooden police horse. He flashed an oversized flashlight into their eyes. "The road is closed."

Roy rolled the window down and yelled over the sound of the idling fire truck engines. "We're the guards," he yelled to the auxiliary police officer who bent and strained to see the three men in the large Bonneville.

"What guards?" asked the old man with his face practically in the car, studying them.

"We're the plant guards," he screamed, "we got kidnapped by the Weathermen!"

The auxiliary policeman squinted towards Howe Avenue and turned his flashlight to the array of firefighting apparatus queued along the street. "You see all these here fire trucks? Well, they're all waiting for the Chief to direct them into the fire. I don't care who kidnapped you. No one's driving past this here horse."

Cal leaned down over Roy and looked at the old man. "We just want to get to the Police Station," he said, pointing straight over Bridge Street to the small sign in front of a storefront that said 'Police Station.'

The old policeman looked over Bridge Street and leaned back into the car. "Everyone wants to get to the Police Station."

"Forget it," Roy sputtered. He raised the window, turned and backed the car along Roosevelt Drive. They got out and stepped their way through the assorted array of fire trucks, civil defense vans and ambulances that littered the bridge. Beneath them a worm's nest of fire hoses crossed Canal Street, preparing to pump water from the river.

"What?" responded the desk sergeant, to Roy's statement as he completed one phone conversation and picked up another one. The dispatcher's radio toned and cracked loudly in the background.

"We're the guards from the Sponge," Roy said as the sergeant slammed the receiver on the phone cradle and buried a cigar stub in an overloaded ashtray. He eyed them warily and leaned over the desk as the phone lines rang and the buttons lit up.

"What guards?" he asked slowly.

"The Sponge guards!" Roy responded quickly, "you think we're dead!"

The sergeant picked up the phone to stop it from ringing. "Shelton police," he said wearily, then put his palm over the receiver and whispered to Roy. "Dead?" he said with furled brows, "Mister," he said flatly, "I didn't even know you were alive."

DeAngelo stepped forward and depressed the phone, hanging up on the caller. "Listen to me, god damn it!" he yelled through a neck bulging with veins as thick as ropes. The phone rang again as he gripped the sergeant's hand and jammed the receiver into its cradle. "Listen to me," he scowled, "we were kidnapped from Plant Four by three guys who said they were the Weathermen. They blindfolded us and handcuffed us, then drove us to Monroe in Roy's car. They left us the keys in the road and told us to wait an hour or so. Do you understand me? You're looking for us and you don't even know it."

The sergeant's blood flow returned to his hand as DeAngelo released him. The phone rang again. "Did you say Weathermen?"

DeAngelo turned to Roy and Cal for assurance. "Yes," he said with certainty. "They said Weathermen."

"Chief," the desk sergeant yelled into the adjoining room as the chief stepped into the doorway looking like he just got out of bed. "These three were at the plant. Said they were kidnapped by some guys said they were the Weathermen."

The chief motioned them into his office. "Call the FBI, Sergeant," he said in a deadpan voice, rubbing his palm over his forehead. "This is bigger than us."

Over Bridge Street and Route 8, equipment rolled in from adjoining towns. Roman Bailey set up a makeshift desk and chair for Chief Brandt to organize a control center and direct all the New Haven County equipment. New Haven Mayor Bart Guida showed up with his Police Chief, Ben DiLieto.

"What can we do for you?" the Mayor asked.

Brandt shook his head. "Right now I got more equipment coming in than I can keep track of. I already got some of your units on the perimeter plants."

DiLieto turned and surveyed the area. He counted over twenty fire trucks just within his sight line. Every engine was running and had hoses extended or ladders raised or had its belly in the river pumping water.

DeLieto stepped in front of the mayor and yelled in Brandt's ear, "I can get you tanker trucks to feed the engines."

Brandt looked at him with a stunned silence. In all the activity he hadn't thought of that. The engines needed fuel and the fire was still building.

Brandt looked up at Guida. Up to this point all the politicians were just taking up valuable space. "How many can you get me?"

"I can start you with three, more if you need it."

"How long can I have them?"

DiLieto looked down at Brandt seated at his makeshift desk. "As long as you need them," he yelled over the noise of the engines running. "As one runs dry we can bring in another."

"Call them in."

Radios squawked and hissed as generators groaned with their deafening drone and floodlights began to illuminate the streets. The fire engulfed all of Plant Four by now, the heart of the Sponge Rubber plants.

As equipment came on to the scene Brandt ordered their placement. Ten fire trucks were ordered to set up at the river and pump water from the Housatonic to feed other engines. Hose lines were clamped together like endless pythons, swallowing and spitting out over three million gallons of water from the river.

Brandt looked up at the scrum of men around him. They yelled into radios and competed for his ear to give him updates. Someone sketched the road layout and the plants and started to write down where the equipment was placed.

Bailey stood at Brandt's side with a radio to his ear. Brandt put him in charge of all of the Valley equipment responding to the scene.

Agent O'Donnell was young, a tall, golden haired boy with smooth skin and a hard edge in his tone. Agent Czak was shorter and older with wispy gray hair that flew up like a cloud when he walked.

"Can I call my wife?"

"No."

"No? What do you mean, no? She's probably worried."

"We're questioning you. You can all her later. You're a material witness. We have to question you."

"What's there to know? I got kidnapped by the Weathermen"

"No, you don't understand. You might be one of the bombers." Roy put his hand to his face and shook it. "Who was he?"

"I told you, I don't know."

"What did he look like?"

"I don't know that either. My eyes were taped. I couldn't see. I told you that already too. Don't you understand English?"

O'Donnell ignored him. "How many were there?"

Roy shook his head in frustration. "Three," he said calmly.

"Tell me again what they said to you."

"They said not to move or they'll blow my head off. Then I feel the cold barrel of the gun on my neck. I got a chill so bad I can feel it now just thinking about it."

O'Donnell looked at Czak and nodded.

"What else did they say to you?" Czak asked.

Roy flicked his head towards O'Donnell and spoke. "I already told your buddy over there. They said they were out to help the working man and they didn't want to hurt the working man. That's all they said. They didn't say too much. It was like they didn't want to talk or nothing."

"Did you ever see them before tonight?"

Roy looked at his watch and looked back at Czak. "Are you going to let me call my wife? How much longer is this going to last anyway?"

Czak looked at O'Donnell and turned back to Roy. "We'll

let you know when we're done. Did you ever see them before tonight?"

Roy stood up and flattened his palms on the table. "You didn't answer my question. Are you going to let me call my wife? And don't look at O'Donnell over there. He don't have to tell you what to do."

Czak shook his head and closed his eyes in frustration. "No. You can't call your wife. Is that clear? Now please answer my questions. The sooner you do the sooner you'll get out of here."

Roy sat and pulled the heavy wooden chair in. "No. I never saw them before. But like a said, they had masks on."

"But you said one of them didn't have a mask. He just had a turtle neck that was pulled up and a hat that was pulled down."

"Yeah, I said that. So what's the difference? I still couldn't see their faces." Roy put his hands on his knees and shook his head. "You guys are too much. Is this what the FBI does? They interrogate innocent people? This is stupid!"

O'Donnell folded his arms and walked beside Roy. "Look, Roy, we're not trying to give you a hard time. But you got to understand what's going on here. You got a factory out there burning up, hundreds of firefighters running around risking their lives, and information that a bunch of people who weren't employees were all over the plant wiring it up for something with phone company uniforms on. Nothing makes sense to us. We got guards who didn't see anything, buildings that have no lights on, and some guy that no one knows where he is who was saying that he has a vision of something of Plant Four blowing up. That he's some kind of a psychic. And now you're telling me that you were kidnapped by a bunch of guys who said they're the Weathermen. So nothing makes any sense to us. Why didn't they just kill you when they had the chance? You see, as far as we're concerned, you could be a suspect."

Roy folded his arms over the table and rested his head over his arms. He closed his eyes and remembered the sound of his own breathing and Al's and DeAngelo's as they waited, tied to the tree, for the courage to move.

"You got agents talking to Cal and DeAngelo?" he asked without lifting his head. "Can you tell me that? That's all I want to know. Are you guys talking to them too? Because their stories and my story will all jibe. You see. We can't all be lying to you because nothing would be, like, how do you say it, consistent?"

"Why don't you lift your head up and talk to us so we can finish up here? You know you're not helping yourself by putting your head down."

Roy kept his head down. "Yeah, well let me tell you something, Mr. FBI man, I ain't helping myself when I was looking at you neither."

Czak pulled up a chair and sat beside Roy. "Look, Roy, we want to get you out of here too. We have a lot more people to question. We like to look at your eyes when you talk to us. So could you please lift up your head?"

Roy lifted his head and apologized to the agents. "You didn't answer my question," he said as he broke a smile, "you talking to the other guys, too?"

"Of course," O'Donnell answered. "State Police are talking to one of them and we got some other people talking to the other."

"Okay, what do you want to know?"

"This guy Staber, you ever see him before tonight?"

"No, not that I can remember. Like I said, a lot of people come by the guard shack to sign in and out. You don't remember all of them."

"You said you signed him out that night. You remember that."

"Yeah, I remember signing him out. You know, later on a Saturday night, it's unusual for people to be at the plant unless they're employees or something. So I remember that."

"But you don't remember signing him in?"

"No. Maybe he came in before I got there. You know, if he came in earlier, you know, before I got there, I wouldn't sign him in, someone else would. I don't know what the other guys do." Roy strummed his fingers on the table then looked up at O'Donnell. "You got people talking to the guards on the other shift. Maybe they're involved because I sure ain't."

O'Donnell nodded and smiled. "Don't worry, Roy. We're going to be talking to everyone. Tell me more about this guy Staber. Would you recognize him if you saw him again?"

346

"Yeah, I definitely would recognize him. Like I said, we don't get too many people signing out on a Saturday night."

"But as far as you can tell, he didn't have anything to do with the guys that kidnapped you and the other guys."

Roy shook his head from side to side. "Not as far as I could tell, no. But I don't know. If you asking me, I think they were in cahoots, you know? He leaves on a Saturday night and he signs out like nothing's unusual and all of a sudden me and the other guys are kidnapped by these weather people or something, and then the plant blows up. Come on, you don't have to be a genius to start to put two and two together."

Brandt placed his radio down on the table. He stood and nodded to Bailey. "I could use more pumping equipment in the river. I think we already got everything in use by now."

Bailey put his hands over the wad of keys that hung from his belt loop. "Echo Hose got old Jumbo just sitting there in the back of the station. I bet no one got that baby out yet."

Brandt stared at Bailey with a strained face. "That thing hasn't been started since Memorial Day last year. You think they can get it going."

Bailey smiled at Brandt. "We roll that baby down the hill every year to start it for the Memorial Day Parade. She'll start up and it'll pump the river dry. Make these newer trucks look sick."

Brandt looked up and surveyed the massive fire before

him. "Yeah, radio up to Echo to get the pumper down here. Let's see what she can do."

Lights flashed and engines strained as water hoses were crossing in every direction to keep the fire contained in Plant Four. Secondary explosions went off occasionally without incident. The ladder trucks raised firefighters high to hose water over the collapsing roof and between the buildings to keep the fire contained with the firefighters kept at a safe distance. For as far as Brandt could see, trucks and hoses crossed Canal Street and the railroad tracks. The trains were diverted that night, or idled on the tracks to wait out the events in Shelton. Nothing was passing over the triple trestle.

Bailey grinned widely and released his keys. "Yes sir, Chief," he called back as he pulled a younger firefighter with him to roll Jumbo down the hill.

Czak glanced at O'Donnell and lifted his head. "You got anything more to ask?"

O'Donnell snared his nose with frustration. "No, I think we're done with him."

"I can go now?" Roy asked as he rose from the chair.

"We're finished for now but the state police want to ask you a few questions now," Czak said with a long face. O'Donnell left the room.

"Now look," Roy protested, "I ain't talking to no state police. They can talk to you."

"That's not the way it's done, Roy. They get to talk to you next. It won't take that long."

348

"Won't take long? It's already three o'clock. My wife probably thinks I'm dead. I got kids. You got to let me call home."

The door opened. A thick-waisted man entered the room with a baseball hat on that said Connecticut State Police. He extended his hand to Roy.

"Sergeant Jerry Connors, Connecticut State Police."

Roy was surprised at the friendly approach. "Nice to meet you, Sergeant. My name's Roy. Is this going to take long?"

Connors pulled up a chair and sat across from Roy. "No. This won't take too long. I got a few things I have to cover. I was just talking to your buddies in the next room. So I got some idea what's going on."

Roy folded his hands on his lap and took a sip of water, "Well that's good, Sergeant, because it's been a long night and they won't let me call my wife. Can I call my wife?"

"Not right now, Roy. Let's get started and see how we do. Is that okay with you?"

Roy shrugged his shoulders and shook his head. "I guess I got no choice, right?"

"Sort of," Connors responded. "So, can you tell me what these guys looked like?"

Roy looked up a Czak with a plaintive face. Czak walked out the door.

Roy folded his hands over the table and laid his head on his hands. "No," he said with certitude. "They had masks on, except for one who had a turtleneck on and a hat he pulled down low. If I don't say that you think I'm like one of them, right? So no, I can't tell you what anyone looked like. I was blindfolded. I couldn't see anything."

"Before they blindfolded you, did you get a look at them?"

"No. Like I said a million times tonight, they had masks on."

Connors rose from his chair and stood in back of it. "Did they all have masks on?"

Roy tuned his head and rested the other side of it down. "Oh, Mother of Mercy," he moaned.

"Okay, okay," Connors said, "tell me about earlier in the night. Staber came into the plant around six o'clock, right?"

Roy lifted himself from the desk and sat up. "No. I don't remember letting him in. I just got on duty at six so maybe he was already in the plants. I don't know."

"Who did the rounds? What's the procedure?"

"We alternate doing the rounds. But it's dark now- a - days. They told us to keep all the lights off to save electricity."

Connors looked at Roy quizzically. "When was that? Do you remember who told you to keep the lights off?"

"Yeah, it came from the big bosses. You know, it's real dark in all them buildings without lights. But they said only to use our flashlights, so that's all we did."

"Did you or Cal notice anything unusual there during the rounds?"

"No, not really, just a couple of cars in the lot but, you know, sometimes the employees, their cars don't start and stuff, especially now in the winter."

"And what about Staber? Did you see his car?"

"Well, you see, he can take the company cars. He supposed to get access to everything, at least that's what we was told. So if I seen the company cars that doesn't mean anything."

"What about when he left? Did you sign him out?"

"Yeah, I signed him out. I remember that. It was about eight- thirty."

"Did you search the car or look in it?

"No. He had the company car. We never search the company cars."

"Who was with him?"

"No one, I didn't see no one." Roy folded his arms on the table and rested his head.

"Then he left?"

"Yeah, he just left," Roy responded without looking up. "He like waved to me, said goodnight or something. I don't know, he had the windows closed. It was cold. How long will this take? Are we almost done?"

"Almost."

"What about if I call my wife?"

"We're almost done."

"Where's my car?" Roy asked.

"We confiscated it. It's evidence."

"Evidence? How am I supposed to get home?"

"Call your wife."

"Can't you give me a ride home?"

"We don't provide taxi service."

Roy lifted his head off his arms and looked at Connors. "Are you shitting me?"

Bailey stood by Brandt's side and ferried information from the site to the Chief. Hundreds of pieces of equipment were in operation by now. Long arcs of water poured over the periphery of Plant Four to contain the blaze to that one massive building. Parts of the roof had collapsed at that point and masonry columns had buckled. Machinery was destroyed and some melted as the fire was finally under control. Brandt stood at his makeshift desk and looked at Bailey.

"You ever get Jumbo down here?" he asked with a wry smile.

Bailey shook his head affirmatively and laughed. "Oh, popped her clutch and she started right up, we got her down here okay. Couple of the mutual aid towns laughed when we backed her to the river. Said there was no way she could deliver what their shiny new engines could deliver. So we turn her pump on and a few minutes later they're begging us to turn down her pumping force, seems she blew the tips off of the hose nozzles."

Brandt nodded his head at Bailey and smiled.

Blake flipped his book closed and rose from the reading carousel. He stretched and yawned before getting in the elevator. The wall length library windows reflected his gaunt figure. Another day almost done, he thought,

352

fanning his mind over the next several weeks that lay ahead of him. The tax filing deadline was just six weeks away. Tax returns and client information collected in his cubicle like corded wood, neat and tidy and waiting to be worked off. The tax partners stopped by to riffle through the work and review worksheets and schedules and to ask bizarre questions on the most obscure topics, expecting immediate answers.

He was in his first year of law school, working full time and attending classes at night. He spent last summer as an intern for one of the most prestigious tax firms in the country, despite an interview with a young partner that was less than smooth.

The elevator door opened. A squat young man with a bunch of thick, curly, black hair sat with his legs propped up on a chair. His body had the promise of major college middle guard if it hadn't stopped growing at sixteen. "Blake, where have you been?" he asked. "You study securities?"

"Yeah," responded Blake flatly. "I read the Nutshell to finish it up. You really like that stuff, don't you?"

"Uh-huh, love it," said Nick through a mouthful of pizza. "That's where the real money is." Nick's eyes glided between Blake and the TV set as he finished off his beer. "Moving capital, that's it, you're wasting your time with taxes. The real money is in moving capital. Ten years from now you'll still be doing tax returns and I'll be managing billions, keeping two percent of the principle and twenty percent of the profits, all at favorable rates."

Managing billions, it took Blake a while to figure out why he liked Nick so much. They were different in every way possible. But Nick amused him with his irreverence and enthusiasm for life. And Blake concluded that that was it. Nick made him laugh all the time with his quick wit and carefree attitude. He never worried about school or grades or interviews. 'Interviews, what interviews? Sit and answer someone's dumb questions? Screw that!' He was happy knowing he would go to work for his father's investment firm after graduation. He decided that without the hand ringing self-doubt that afflicted others with independent wealth. He didn't need the law degree. He was just getting it because his father wanted him to. He was rich, really rich, but he never displayed his wealth. "Sit down," he said, pulling a cheap plastic chair from the table and slapping its seat. "Have some pizza."

Blake placed his books on the floor and pulled the sleeves of his sweatshirt up to his elbows, "I can't stay. I have to get back to the office," he said, lifting pizza to his mouth.

"Tonight? You're going in tonight? It's Sunday. You're crazy," said Nick incredulously, walking to the TV and raising the volume. "Can't hear," he said as he stared down the darting eyes of the other students who were startled by the volume. He wiped his fingers on an oily napkin. "Couldn't hear that well," he explained, sitting back down. "They're crazy too, those tax people you work for. Tell them I said they're all crazy. Stay, watch the news. Eat some pizza. Edwin Newman's doing it tonight. Come on, you look like shit. I can't let you go back there tonight. See what Newman's got to say tonight."

"I can't. I told them I'd come back. Someone's got to work for a living."

"You mean you volunteered? It's optional?"

"Yeah, I got there at seven this morning and worked until eleven."

"Forget it, man. You work because you don't think big eno..."

"Wait....," Blake said, standing to become eye level with the wall mounted set. "Hold on ... that's it ...look ...."

The caption on the screen read 'Shelton, Connecticut.' Nick hesitated for a moment, bewildered by the riveted look in Blake's eyes. The screen filled with orange flames leaping into the night sky, illuminating the triple trestles that spanned the Housatonic. "Authorities say the radical group, the Weathermen, claimed responsibility for the blaze." Newman returned to the screen as his voice trailed off for a commercial, "There were no reported injuries."

Blake stood frozen, reflecting on a place he left years ago. "That's it, Nick" he said softly, "that's where she lived, right across the river from there." He sat slowly, placing the pizza in his hand back on the tray. His face was ashen. "He said there were no injuries?" He turned to Nick and raised his voice. "Were you listening?"

"Take it easy, man," replied Nick, picking a piece of dried leaf from Blake's sleeve and abandoning his flippant manner, "Yeah, he said there were no injuries. I'm sure he said that. It was a big explosion at a mattress factory.

What's wrong?"

"That's where I'm from. That's across the river from my home town. And she lives right across the river from there. Her building is directly across from the fire."

Nick shook his head in confusion. "Hold on. You lost me. Who lives there?"

"My old girlfriend. The girl I told Jenn about."

Nick gave Blake a shocked look, "Really? She lives there?"

"Yeah. That's right in my hometown."

"The girl that worked in that ice cream parlor?"

"Yeah," Blake whispered his thoughts distant and suffused in the warm thoughts of the small apartment with sun catchers splitting sunlight into brilliant rainbow colors on the kitchen wall. "I can't believe it. I wasn't even listening. If the caption didn't say 'Shelton, Connecticut' I wouldn't have noticed at all."

"No, if I didn't make you sit here with me and eat pizza you would be on your way to do taxes. Blake," Nick said softly, "have some more pizza, you don't look so good. Look, nobody died in the blaze. Maybe she doesn't even live there anymore." Nick bit a mouthful of pizza, "You got to be more like me. Stop thinking, man, it's going to kill you."

Blake smiled slightly and drank some soda, setting the empty paper cup on the table. "You're right. I wish it could be that easy."

Nick got up and pulled several napkins from the next table. "You see," he said with a full smile. "You're doing it again, thinking." Then he leaned over the table, into Blake's face, "Stop thinking! Let's go. Get your jacket on."

"Where are we going?" Blake asked with a perplexed look. "I have to get to work."

"You're not going to work. You got no blood in your face. It's like it all pooled in your feet or something. You look like you just saw a ghost. You won't be able to concentrate anyway."

"So, where are we going?"

"My apartment. Jenn's making supper."

"You just ate. I have returns to get out."

"You don't have returns to get out. Look at you." Nick pulled dried leaves off of Blake's hood and from his pockets. "You look like hell. I can eat again and you didn't eat at all. And you look like you haven't slept in a week," Nick said, placing Blake's books in his arms. "We'll eat again. I'll teach you what you have to know about securities and you won't teach me anything about tax because I don't want to know. Besides, you can talk to Jenn, she needs someone to talk to besides me."

Blake flung on his coat. He reached into the pocket and pulled out a handful of dried leaves, dropping them in the garbage. "I got to call my aunt. She still lives there. I want to find out what happened."

"Sure," Nick said confidently, grabbing Blake's collar playfully and pulling him to the door."You can call from the apartment." He picked some leaves off Blake's jacket. "What is it with these leaves anyway? Are you still hiding in the leaves in the fucking woods?"

Blake waved his hand at Nick dismissively. "Yeah," he replied, nodding his head without enthusiasm. "Sometimes, like earlier today. It's the only thing that calms me down." Blake stopped and faced Nick, looking frightened and confused, "I don't know if I'll make it."

Nick placed his hand over Blake's back and guided him towards the parking lot. "Yeah, you will, Buddy. How're your hands right now? Just tell me, how do they feel?"

They stopped in front of Blake's car. "It's a fight, Nick, every day it's a fight. They get numb and I feel like I don't have the strength to lift anything. Some days I feel like I can't even carry my books."

"But you're here. Come on, man, you work full time, you're in one of the best law schools in the country and you make it every da, even the bad days. You're fighting every day. It's better, way better, than not being able to fight at all. Maybe you need some one-on-one counseling. My sister's friend practices in Georgetown. How about if I set up an appointment for you with him?"

Blake turned and looked to Nick skeptically. "I don't know if I'm ready for that."

"What do you mean you're not ready? How bad does it have to get before you're ready? You're already rolling in leaves and hiding under cars and digging holes in the woods. Sneaking into Arlington at night to watch the guards and the Tomb of the Unknowns. That's crazy stuff you know. It's not normal. You hide this stuff pretty well, Blake, but this can't go on. You got to get help."

"I don't know."

"No, man, that's bullshit, Blake. You got to be ready because I can't be worrying about you all day. You're so sick you think you can handle this by yourself by burying yourself under leaves and crawling under cars. Man, that has got to stop."

"No, it's not that, Nick. I know I need help. I just don't have the money for it."

"You don't need the money. It's taken care of."

"What? I can't let you pay."

"Yes, you can. If it will make it better we'll call it a loan. Someday when I need tax advice we'll forgive it, how's that?"

"I don't know..."

"It's done. We'll call tomorrow before class. Come on. Let's go have dinner and you can call your aunt, deal?"

Blake opened the car door and threw his books on the passenger seat. He realized he couldn't go on anymore, even though he didn't know where to turn. He had to try something and this was as good as it was going to get for him. He nodded to Nick and met his eyes over the car roof. "Deal."

Tom Connelly, an Assistant United States Attorney for the District of Connecticut, walked through a scrum of reporters in the spacious hallway of the New Haven Federal District Court.

"Sir," shouted one of the reporters as he jumped up from the bench to block Connelly's way, "sir, do you know who Mr. Staber is? Is there any more information?"

Connelly stopped and turned, waiting for all the reporters to gather. He didn't want to repeat himself but felt he had a duty to inform them of any proceedings that could be made public. He waited for the clacking of leather heels on the marble floor to stop before he started to speak.

"Yes," he said, "there were a few developments late yesterday that we learned about prior to this morning's pubic session." Connelly stepped back against one of the marble columns. "We learned that the man you have identified as Mr. Drubar is really a Mr. Staber. We had the name wrong and that was not an alias or anything. In fact, I understand that Mr. Staber provided the FBI with his correct name when he realized they had it wrong. You can know that he is not one of the owners of Sponge and is not an officer but he is tied to the case somehow. All that is not grand jury information and you know that any grand jury information cannot be divulged under any circumstances."

The reporters scribbled quickly on small pads and jumped in as soon as Connelly finished. "Is the case ready to break?"

"No," Connelly said, clutching his file over his suit jacket, "the investigation is continuing."

"How many agents are on the case now? Can you tell us that? What are they anyways, FBI, AFT?" she said with a laugh, "I don't know. I can't keep track of all those abbreviations."

Connelly looked at the short, older woman who asked

the question. She appeared to be standing in a hole as she tried to elbow her way to the front of the crowd. "Over seventy," he said with an easy smile. "Seventy FBI agents, most of them here on the East Coast. Then we have some AFT and other Treasury types. I don't know, maybe fifteen or twenty of them. That of course doesn't count the state police or any local police involved."

"What's AFT stand for again?" the reporter asked without looking up from her note pad.

"Alcohol, Tobacco and Firearms. They have bomb specialists along with the FBI."

"How many state and local police?"

"I don't have that number."

"One of the newspapers is reporting that this Staber fellow is a mystic or an astrologer of some sort. Can you confirm that?"

"I cannot confirm any of that. What I can tell you is that his relationship to the Sponge plants and the parent company is undetermined."

"Is it true that he was seen in Shelton on several occasions prior to the bombing?"

"Can you confirm that he invoked the Fifth Amendment during yesterday's proceedings?"

"Did he refuse to give his fingerprints and a handwriting sample to the FBI?"

Connelly smirked and looked down at his shoes. He was tall and bowed at the waist. His hair was modestly long and his blue eyes sparkled brilliantly when he spoke with excitement. "Obviously," he said with a full smile as he looked at the reporter who asked the last question, "you and several of your colleagues were not listening closely when we brought the hearings into open court for argument."

"The courtroom was too small. Some of us weren't allowed in."

"I apologize then," Connelly said. "Yes, he refused to submit to fingerprints and provide a handwriting analysis. And now he and his attorneys are running off to the Yale Law library to see if they can come up with some precedent that says a nonprofit corporation run by an ordained minister does not have to provide business documents when they are subpoenaed. That is really the legal question before the court now since he has agreed to the fingerprints and handwriting sample under protest. That argument will take place tomorrow morning in open court as well. If we have a larger courtroom available I will suggest to the judge that the argument be heard there. This way we can have everyone in and seated."

"Legally, just what does that mean, under protest?"

Connelly laughed and shrugged his shoulders. "It means he would rather provide the information than be held in contempt of court. I don't know, I guess it means that he's not happy."

"We heard that this grand jury's term is ending soon. What happens if there are no indictments and this grand jury's term expires?"

"We find 23 more people to sit and we dismiss this group. The new group gets briefed on all the testimony and

the affidavits submitted. It doesn't jeopardize the case."
Connelly looked at his watch again. His assistant waved him on from another hallway and he stepped off with long, brisk strides. Several reporters trailed him but stopped as he entered the adjacent hallway and two marshals stared at them grimly with their arms folded over their chests.

"I do."

"Please state your name and address for the record and spell your last name for me," the court stenographer said as she took her seat.

"Anthony Shaw." He spelled his name slowly, stated his address and looked at the stenographer.

"You can put your hand down now, Mr. Shaw. Please be seated."

Shaw took his seat in the witness box. He was young and handsome with a full head of neatly trimmed brown hair and green eyes. His three piece suit looked like it was being worn for the first time, without the suppleness of expensive fabric or the comfortable wearing of an aged garment.

"Good afternoon, Mr. Shaw," Connelly said. He stood and walked towards the witness stand. "There are some things that I would like to get into the record so please bear with me."

"Yes, sir," Shaw replied, not knowing if a reply was necessary.

"You and I have spoken before, haven't we?"

"Yes, sir, we have."

"In those conversations I told you that you did not have to answer any of my questions if you felt that you could be incriminating yourself, is that correct?"

"Yes, sir. You said that I could stop answering questions at any time if I wanted to." To Connelly's surprise, Shaw did not appear frightened or diminished by the setting. His responses were clear and concise.

"And did you voluntarily offer to appear here before this grand jury."

"Yes, sir, I did."

"And I told you that no one is allowed to bring an attorney into the grand jury room but some people have attorneys who sit outside the room and that you would be able to stop and consult with him if you wanted to. Do you recall that, Mr. Shaw?"

"Oh yes, sir, I recall that real well. That's what you said."

"And did you bring an attorney with you today?"

"No, no, sir. I didn't bring anyone with me today."

"And I told you that if you can't afford an attorney that the court would provide one for you. Do you remember that?"

"Yes, sir, I do. But I said that I didn't want one. I rather just deal with this on my own."

"And then I told you that the court was obligated to appoint an attorney for you because of the serious nature of the charges that you might be accused of. And that there could be very serious jail time if you are found guilty of any of those charges and that everything you say in here could be used against you to indict you and anything you have said to the investigators can be used against you in a trial. Do you recall me saying that to you?"

"Yes, sir, I do recall that."

"And what was your response to all that?"

Shaw repositioned himself in the witness chair and straightened out his suit jacket. "My response was that I didn't want no attorney," he said as he adjusted his necktie. "Whatever I did was my own fault and I'm not going to lie about it or cover it up because I rather just cooperate and be done with it. That's what I said."

"And I just want to tell you that although you did not want an attorney appointed for you there is one sitting outside this courtroom for you, and you can ask to speak to him at any time. The government is paying for that attorney to be there to represent you. Do you understand that?"

"Yes, sir, I do. That was real nice of the government to do that for me, but I don't think I'll be talking to him."

Connelly raised his eyebrows high over the rims of his eyeglasses. "You know that some of the federal charges that might come out of this grand jury include arson, kidnapping, interstate transportation of explosive devices with the intention to commit a felony and interstate communication using phones in furtherance of a felony and felonious use of the mail. These are very serious charges with substantial prison terms for any one of them. You understand that?"

Shaw gave Connelly an exasperated look. "I understand everything, sir. Everyone's been real nice to me and respectful and everything. Whatever I did I did and if I made some bad moves well then I'll pay for it. I don't need an attorney to get in the way of things and drag things out. Let's just get on with it."

Connelly shook his head, walked back to his table and took his seat. He glanced over some notes and made some comments to his assistant.

"Mr. Shaw, what do you do for a living?"

"I'm an electrician."

"Are you licensed?"

"Yes, sir, I have a residential and commercial license."

"And how long have you been an electrician?"

"About eleven years or so."

"Now, Mr. Shaw," Connelly asked as he changed his line of questioning, "do you know the Ciero brothers?"

"Yes, I do," Shaw replied as he glanced at the grand jury members. "Ralph and Frank Ciero. They're two brothers from my area of Pennsylvania who I know from around town. Everyone kind of knows them. They run some excavating business out around Pittsburgh. I did some work for them."

"Did you ever do any demolitions work for them?"

"Yes, I did, setting up charges with blasting and dynamite." He followed Connelly with his eyes as Connelly walked to his desk. "And some detonating cord," he said as an aside.

"Did they put you into contact with a man named Wade Staber?"

"Yes, they did. Actually, they gave Mr. Staber my phone

number and he called me and asked me if I was interested in some demolition work out of state. They asked me if I was interested but that they wanted to stay out of the deal. So I guess they gave Staber my phone number."

"And what did Mr. Staber say?"

"Well, I told him that seeing that I didn't have much work through the winter I could really use the money so I said yes."

"And were you going to be working alone? Did he say that or that you would be working with other people?"

"No. He told me he was trying to put a crew together."

"A crew of demolitions people?"

"Well, not all of them were demolitions people, just some."

"Mr. Shaw, are you familiar with the Sponge Rubber plant in Shelton Connecticut?"

"Yes, I am, sir."

"Do you know what happened to that plant?"

"I blew it up. Me and the other guys, we blew it up."

"And why did you blow it up, Mr. Shaw? Did someone ask you to blow it up or did you just think of it on your own?"

"No, sir, I didn't think of it on my own. I talked to Pete Petres who said he had a job in Connecticut and this guy named Staber was putting together a crew and if I was interested because I would get paid for it. I guess Pete got my name from Ralph and Frank Ciero."

"Did you know who was paying for the job?"

Shaw shook his head and smirked. "I don't know. I

guess it was that guy Staber. I just figured it was him."

"Did he say who he was working for?"

"No, not really. All he said was that he was doing some work for the owner who lives out in Ohio and that they needed the buildings down."

"Did you know this was arson or did you think this was a legitimate job?"

Shaw tilted his head to the left and spoke directly to Connelly. "No, I knew this was not a legitimate job after I looked it over. First, you never do this kind of work in the middle of the night when you can't see anything. The demolition is usually done first thing after daybreak if it's in a populated area. Secondly, you usually have all kinds of police around and the work area is sealed off, blocked off with tape and police. No, Staber told us right from the get go that this was a job to take down the buildings and that he had some kind of vision about this happening and it would be better if we could control it anyway. And then when we were in the buildings setting up the wiring and stuff he made us put on these phone company outfits and says we were rewiring phones. He told us not to talk to the workers."

"How many times were you in the buildings before the bombings?"

"You mean not including the day that we set everything up?"

"Well, yes, how many times before March 1, 1975 did you visit the Shelton Sponge plants?"

"Me? I was there three times. Pete Petres, he was my

368

contact man in Pennsylvania. He was the man paying us. He said the buildings contained four hundred and seventy-five thousand square feet of space spread over twenty buildings. So when I heard that, I told him I would have to see it for myself."

"Did you ever hear of Pete Jameson?"

Shaw smiled and looked surprised. "Yes, I have heard of Pete Jameson."

"Who is Pete Jameson?"

"Well, that's Pete Petres. I guess when he first met Mr. Staber, he didn't want anything traced to him. He didn't know anything about this Staber guy, so he told Staber his name was Pete Jameson."

"So you know for a fact that Pete Jameson's real name is Pete Petre? Is that correct?"

"Yes, sir. That is correct."

"So, forgive me, but I digressed for a moment. We were talking about your visit to the Shelton Sponge plants and you were telling the jury about that visit and what was your impression of the buildings."

"Yes, I was saying that I made three visits to the plants before the day of the bombing. One of the visits we just cased the area, even walked the area across the river from the plant at night. My impression? My impression was that those buildings were big, a lot bigger than I expected. It took a lot of wiring to stitch it all together. That was a tough job. Plus, the night of the bombings we couldn't use any lights or anything so all we had was flashlights."

"Mr. Shaw, tell the jury how you set up the arson. Can

you describe the material you used and how the bombs were made?"

"Sure. Plant Four, that was by far the biggest building, it had columns all along the inside to hold up the other floors. So we figured if we take down the columns the interior would just collapse. We brought twenty-five barrels of gasoline that we unloaded at the plant right after noon that Saturday of the bombing and set them up against sixteen of the columns, three barrels to each column. Then we attached sticks of dynamite to the barrels. Did I say that the each of the barrels contained fifty-five gallons of gasoline? Did I already say that?"

Connelly smiled at Shaw and shook his head. "No, I don't think so."

Shaw returned his smile and continued on in his serious, business-like manner. "Well, each of the twenty-five barrels contained fifty-five gallons of gasoline. So once we got the barrels in place against the columns, we put half sticks of dynamite under the barrels and I attached blasting caps to the dynamite. Then we ran detonating cord and attached all the dynamite to the detonating cord and we ran the lead to a timing device I attached to a pay phone in the plant. Oh yeah, I forgot the two extra barrels we set over the twelve inch water pipe that was fed by the canal as a backup to the city water."

Connelly smiled and nodded his head. "Thank you. Now can you tell the jury what a detonating cord is?"

"Sure, detonating cord is an explosive cord that from a distance doesn't look too much different than white rope.

Except it is an explosive and is used to string together a series of blasts that are generated from one source, in this case the timing device on the phone."

"And how much detonating cord did you use?"

"Two thousand feet of cord," Shaw looked at the jurors who sat silently paying close attention to his every word. He wanted to clarify what he said, to give the jurors some context of the job. So he spoke to them directly. "That's a lot of cord. I never did a job using that much cord before. Not in an industrial area. Maybe in a mining area, but never in an active commercial area like downtown, Shelton."

"Can you tell the jurors how you triggered the arson? What set off the explosions once you had the barrels and dynamite set?"

"Sure," Shaw replied, turning to the jurors. "I set the timing device to the pay phone. We left the building by hiding in Staber's car. He was driving one of the company cars. He hid us in the back seat and we drove back to LaGuardia once we got together with the rest of the crew."

Connelly glanced at his watch. He had other interviews to do later that afternoon. But he pressed on, hoping to tie down details that he could later corroborate with other witnesses. "Did you forget anything there, Mr. Shaw, in that car parked at LaGuardia?"

"Yes sir, I left my tool box in the trunk of that car."

"And how did you recover it?"

"I called Mr. Staber and he went back to the airport and got it for me before they picked up the company car."

"Did you actually make the call to start the timer?"

"No, I did not make that call. We were waiting to meet up with the kidnappers to get on our way back to the airport."

"And who did make that call?"

"The way I left it, one of the kidnappers was going to make the call once they cleared the buildings."

"What do you mean by cleared the buildings?"

"Once there were no more guards left there or anyone else. They were going to make that call."

"And do you know which of them made the call?"

"No, I don't know which one actually made the call but I know he didn't have a dime on him and had to get the dime from one of the other two guys. We laughed about it over drinks at the bar in LaGuardia."

"Did you ever get picked up at the airport by the company driver with a company car on one of your visits prior to the day of the bombing?"

"Yes, one time I went up there to case the job we were picked up."

"So you met the driver?"

"Paul Stabulis,yeah. I met Paully. Very friendly guy. They told him we were engineers."

Connelly walked to the front of the witness stand and stood before Shaw. He hesitated and seemed deep in thought. He didn't want to bore the jurors but wanted to get enough facts out and clear so they could use this information to rope together the rest of the story. "So, to summarize, the buildings exploded for the effort of spending ten cents on a phone call to a pay phone. Is that correct?"

Shaw looked up at Connelly without smiling. "Yes, sir, that's how it was done."

"And how did you know the explosion happened? I mean, if you left the area it could have failed. So how did you know it went off?"

"We heard the explosion while we were waiting for the kidnappers to drive the guards to the rendezvous spot."

"And the guards never saw you leave in Staber's car, leave the plant?"

"Well, no. Like I said, we were hiding in the back seat. But the car slowed down and Staber rolled his window down and said something to the guard. But he had run of the place anyway so it wasn't like they didn't know he was there.

"And what time was that?"

"About eight-thirty."

"Thank you, Mr. Shaw."

Shaw nodded his head to Connelly and glanced at the jury. "And thank you, sir."

Cut Man opened The Evening Sentinel and glanced at Louie. He looked at Roy and flicked his eyebrows. "All right, Roy," he said with a foreboding look, "you better sit down for this one. You ain't going to like it."

Cut Man. His name derived from the time he spent in the ring at Nolan Field, in Ansonia, under the lights on summer nights when outdoor boxing pulled in a few thousand spectators in the late fifties and early sixties. He worked the corners with his uncle who taught him the urgent industry of staunching the flow of blood between rounds and stopping the insidious swelling of battered eye sockets to preserve sight for the moment the bell rings and the boxers stand for another round of battering, his skills being sharpened as an Army medic in Vietnam.

Cut Mab worked at the Derby landfill, a career that gave him unlimited capacity to feed his hoarder impulse until his wife put her foot down and limited him to his collection of old Evening Sentinels which he kept stacked in his basement on wooden pallets to prevent them from getting wet when the sewers backed up. He organized them in sequences of months and years, neatly bound and labeled. Although his real name was Leonard and the boxing matches had long ceased, everyone in the Valley called him Cut Man and he carried the tools of his trade in a small medic's pouch slung on his belt.

"It doesn't matter no how. I know the son-of-a-gun got off. I could tell by the way his lawyer was talking to the jury. They had nothing on him. Some of them there checks and stuff, that's all. That ain't enough. And that guy Shaw, the one who pleaded guilty, he didn't know nothing neither. So go ahead because I ain't going to let it bother me no how."

"Says that Biller is found not guilty of all charges. But they convicted all the other guys. You know, all the guys that kidnapped you and the other guard and the furnace guy. They're all guilty of conspiracy, kidnapping, arson,

374

interstate use of the telephone. And I don't know, some other charges too." Cut Man looked at Louie who sat sidesaddle on his stool and shrugged his shoulders.

"Interstate use of the telephone? They made that a crime too?" asked Louie with a perplexed look.

"No, no, I think if it's used to commit a crime, then they make it a crime. Something like that, it's not a crime until you use it to commit a crime."

"Yeah," Roy said, "the FBI agents had lots of phone calls between Staber and Biller's office in Ohio and the other guys. They made a big deal about that in court. I hear the state wants to charge him now, too."

Louie waved his hand in disgust. "It don't add up to me. To me, how can the jury let him off? Why would the other guys kidnap people and blow up the buildings if they weren't getting paid for it? It was fixed." He got up to fill his coffee cup. Frances was busy with a customer so he poured his own and started back to the table. "Where's Teddy?" he asked Frances.

"Linda had to go to a science fair at school for Tori. Teddy took her up. He wanted to see Tori's project. They'll be back later."

"Charge who? Who they going to charge?"

Cut Man bore down to read the paper closely. He used his finger to keep his place as he looked up at Roy and Louie. "I can't tell. I guess they can charge all of them."

"Biller, too?" Roy asked.

"Yeah, him too." Cut Man scanned the rest of the column and flipped to the following page. "Said they might have a civil trial too, says Biller will sue the insurance company to get his money."

"How can he get his money if he burned down the buildings?"

"Says Staber's attorneys had him examined by two psychiatrists, one of them lawyers filed a Motion in Limine."

Roy broke his mirror gaze and looked over at Cut Man. "Filed a what?"

"A Motion in Limine, what the hell is that? Why don't they just speak English?"

"Don't say what it is. Don't matter, right?"

"Yeah, so, who had who examined, Biller?"

"No, I think Staber was examined."

"What's he examined for? They found him guilty, right? To see if he was crazy or not, I think, before the trial?"

"They didn't say nothing about that in court. I only missed a few days and no one said anything about that motion stuff or that he was crazy."

"They said he was examined. Doesn't say he testified or anything, said they thought about using it as a defense."

"So what happened? He wasn't crazy?"

"They think he was but there's no evidence."

"I thought you said he was examined?"

"But that don't mean he's crazy. Just that he was looked at, you know, like evaluated."

"Then they say a civil trial is probably going to happen if the state doesn't charge him."

"So who's in the civil trial? I thought they already

charged him."

"No, no the civil trial is for the money, the insurance money."

"No one said nothing about money. He's already not guilty."

"So that's it? They can't have another trial?"

"Only the state trial."

"But it says the civil trial is easier to prove that Biller's guilty, it's the civil standard."

"Civil standard," Roy asked with a confused look. "What's the civil standard? They already said he's not guilty, right?"

"Yeah, but not the state."

"So I have to testify again? When? Nobody told me nothing yet."

"No," Louie said, "nobody knows nothing yet. You got to wait I think."

And so it went, at the conclusion of the federal trial, confusion layered over disbelief.

It wasn't long after that in 1978, just after Biller was acquitted of arson and interstate trafficking explosives, and Staber and the other conspirators were convicted of arson and conspiracy to commit arson and interstate trafficking in explosives and kidnapping and sent to prison. Excedpt Whitey, who didn't know what he was driving from Pennsylvania to Connecticut and just needed the money. It was soon after they all went to prison that the unimaginable happened.

The days had taken on a regular cadence and the June sun burned long and hot and seemed to undulate the pavement of Main Street. It was sometime in the middle of the night, hours before Frances was downstairs fixing breakfast for her mother.

"Teddy," she called out as she combed her mother's hair and spun it into a tight bun. "Teddy, it's almost six." She went to the sink and washed the dishes and set them in the drain rack and called out once more, then climbed the steps of the small apartment and said, as if speaking to herself, "Teddy, it's late. You're oversleeping."

At the top of the stairs she knocked on his bedroom door and was met by an eerie silence. "Ted," she uttered, pushing the door open and feeling her flesh chill in the thick humid air of the July morning. "Oh, my God!" she cried, "oh, my God!"

The Palace was dark those days. The swan necked fountains stood quietly, like honor guards, solemn and true. The stools along the counter did not spin. There were no double-bagged egg creams or dripping sundaes made. The phone rang into an empty space. There were no meat or fruits and vegetable deliveries shouldered in by Joe or Barry and causing a ripple among the crowd standing before the little grill. The two-handed registers stood silently at each end of the counter, like bookends keeping orderly all that is meaningful, and reflected endlessly in the dark, faded mirrors of Vonetes Palace of

Sweets.

Someone, maybe Joe or Leon or Chaz, took a file card that Frances wrote and taped it on the door. It said 'Closed, Death in the family.' And customers came to the heavy glass door and read the note, their fingers pressed to the glass, then pivoted and left, turning back over their shoulders with puzzled faces certain that it was their mother who had passed.

But over the next few hours the word rippled through Main Street. With the speed of an electrical current, from store to store, and office to office, to the apartments and factories and along the bus lines with patrons shaking their heads in disbelief, the word got out. Adam's delivery of the Evening Sentinel confirmed the dreaded news.

Tori, in a private moment reserved for the family, with Linda and Frances at her side, placed a deck of Old Maid cards inside Teddy's casket and stuffed the tattered string of the cat's cradle into his pants pocket.

At the end of that long day, when old friends spoke of the past in the present tense and remembrances stitched years and decades together, at the kitchen table set against the wainscoted wall, Frances sat in her black damask dress patterned with scrolled leaves. She folded her hands on her lap. Her ash blonde hair hung thin and loosely to her shoulders. Linda rubbed the last glass dry until it squeaked, put it in the cabinet and took her place at the table, having sent Tori home with her mother hours ago.

Alone, late into the thick and humid summer night,

when the rest of the family, the sisters and brothers, nieces and nephews and friends were back at home, they were left to face the unplanned silence and long moments unoccupied with words.

Linda sat expressionless, her face pasted with a patina of fleshy oils. She dabbed the sweat beads that rolled between her breasts with a paper towel. She lifted the damp dishtowel from the table and fanned herself without relief. Then she hiked her dark floral dress over her thighs and billowed it, gathering the cloth into her fists and folded her hands calmly. She looked up at Frances.

Through the silence of the evening, as the occasional rub of traffic along Olivia Street patterned the heated lacuna, Linda noticed the age on Frances' face. Somehow, without the expressive rap of the spatula on the grill or the loud clacking of heavy dishes piling at the deep sink, her face sagged, lacking tone or color. Her hair, usually fastened neatly above her neck, fell limply to her slouched shoulders.

"Fran," she whispered cautiously, "what are you going to do tomorrow? I know it's soon, but have you thought about it?

Frances remained motionless. The weight of Teddy's death had settled over her. Tomorrow, she thought, has no purpose. Death consumes the present and revives the past. But tomorrow, no, there is no tomorrow worth contemplating. Tomorrow could never arrive. Not anymore. Not like it used to. The Palace could never be the same. They were there, together, since 1934, except for the war years. They were a team, a brace, no less than the mortar and brick of the building itself, where daily interactions were celebrations of the ordinary and a respite from the vortex when life funneled difficulty into a patron's day.

Frances ran her tissue over her nose. She opened her palms over her black dress and raised her shoulders, shaking her head slightly. "I don't know, Linda. I don't know if I can go back there, not tomorrow, maybe not ever. Maybe I just need to rest for a while."

Linda glanced at the clock. She took a tissue from the box that was set on the table and ran it over her cheeks and looked at Frances. She looked weary, weary and worn and fragile. Her skin was pasty and sallow. Linda never saw her like this. Never saw her as vulnerable or sad or pained. She braced her back against her chair and placed her hands on the table. "Sure you can go back there, Fran," she said confidently in a manner that Frances always spoke. "Sure you can. Teddy would expect you to open up, right?"

Frances shook her head. She seemed unmoved. Teddy was gone. Maybe the time for the Palace was finished. The street was changing. The factories were closing. The apartments were emptying along Main Street and merchants were moving. Sponge Rubber, only across the river, not a hundred yards away, was gone. Howard and Barber's, the original department store just three doors down Main Street, had closed.

Redevelopment had already shown its hand and it was ugly. How long would it be before it came to the south side of Main Street? It all seemed futile. She took the hem of her dress and ran her hand across the stitching, amused by its feel between her fingers. It was tight and fine and secure. She sighed deeply, placed her hands on the table and looked up. "I don't think so, Linda. I feel like I have no strength left. I don't think I can do it."

Linda mustered a shallow smile and put her hands over Frances'. "Sure you can, Fran. You're just all tired out because it was such a shock and it's all so fresh. But you can do it. I'll help you. I think maybe the longer you wait the harder it will be."

Frances reached over and patted Linda's hands. Maybe she was right. Maybe I should just go back in there and start up and it will feel better, she thought. "I can't," she whispered.

She can't, Linda said to herself, stretching her arms out and leaning over the table. "Fran," she asked with a perplexed, shocked look, "you mean you might close?"

Frances shook her head slightly. Her eyes closed for a few seconds before she raised her eyebrows, "I don't know, Linda. Maybe it's too soon to know. It's too much for me alone, to run the whole thing. Everything's changing. Downtown is all different. City might decide to tear down the south side like the mess they made across the street with the new bank building and a parking lot." Frances shook her head and looked at Linda forlornly. "I just don't know anymore."

"What?" Linda asked in a whisper of shock as she shook her head in denial. "You can't close. You mean close the

Palace?" She hesitated for a second, her eyes staring with disbelief at Frances, and then narrowed them to slits of intensity. "What about the customers, Fran? You have to think of them. You can't just close. It wouldn't be the same. Nothing would be the same."

Frances dropped her face to her chest and hitched her shoulders with uncertainty. Linda sat back, gripping a fistful of dress. "Frances, you've been there for over forty years. The Palace has been there since 1905. You told me that yourself, that whenever people move away, they always stop in when they visit, just to see you. Even though they're gone for years or even decades, they know that they can come back here and nothing would be different." Her voice crimped with emotion as she leaned over the table and tried to continue, "The window, the window would be empty. There'd be nothing left. No bunnies in the window at Easter or candy canes at Christmas or pumpkins at Halloween. Nothing would be the same. You can't just close. That would be a mistake." Linda's voice trailed to a whisper as she buried her face into her arm over the table and cried, "Teddy wouldn't want you to close, and I don't want you to close either."

"Ah, Linda," she sighed impassively, "I, I just don't think I can go back in there. I can't imagine turning the key to an empty place every morning."

Linda sat up and dabbed her eyes with her damp tissue that was crumbling in her sweated palm. She looked up to the ceiling in an effort to keep from crying, and then spoke with painful, halting words. "I want to tell you something," she said between heavy gulps of breath, "something I never told you before. You see......I know it sounds stupid... but I have this dream that someday Blake will come back. When Tori was younger I would lay beside her to get her settled down. She would always count the cars as the freight passed before the trestle and write it down so she could tell Teddy. And sometimes I would fall asleep beside her and I always had this dream, the same dream, that someday he's going to show up, one day and .... he's just going to sit right down in front of the deep sink and just say 'Hi' ..and I'm going to lift up my head from the steam and my elbows will be dripping with hot water and he'll be there, Fran, ...he'll just be there... like it used to be .... right there in the Palace of Sweets."

Linda walked to the sink, pulled a paper towel from the roll and wiped her face with it, then turned to Frances with a whispered plea. "I don't want you to close, Frances. Please, don't close. I don't want you to do it for me," she said as she buried her face into the paper towel, "but please don't close the Palace of Sweets."

Frances covered her eyes with her hands. She recalled her own youth, approaching her prime, brimming with womanhood, young and beautiful. Then she looked at Linda, her face buried in her arms, resting on the table. She remembered, years ago when her life was full of love's fragrance, before the war spaded that rare flower beneath the rich soil of the Ardennes Forest. Her breath hitched and a short whimper broke from her as she thought of that day in January of 1945 when the engineer on the

384

Mayberry Line sent out a distress call and halted all the north and east bound trains. He ran across the bridge from Shelton, opened the door and stood in the middle of the Palace, a lanky man out of breath in his hobnail boots and vest with a pocket watch. He raised his engineer's hat up to the top of his head and walked up to her and said he was looking for a woman named Frances. She wiped her hands in her apron and told him that she was Frances. And he teared up and told her the news that the young caboose-man that would run over the bridge to see her and tell her stories of the huge North Platte train yard was lost when his B-26 Marauder was shot down during the Battle of the Bulge. He said he was sorry to deliver the news but that he felt it was his duty to tell her because he didn't want her to think that the young man had forgotten her. She closed her eyes and reflected on that moment thirty-three years ago when she backed herself to an empty stool to lean on as she felt a numbness grow over her. Her breathe grew labored as she tried to contain her grief all these decades later. Seconds ticked by in silence.

She rose and walked to Linda. She held Linda's hand and rubbed her back. She knew now what she thought to be all along. That for nine years Linda had guarded her deepest hope from those closest to her. "Okay, Honey," Frances said confidently, "tomorrow morning we'll open up, me and you. But I want you there. I don't want to be alone."

Linda leaned back and dried her face with the paper towel. "I'm a mess now," she said through a slight smile.

"Oh, it's been a rough week. We're both kind of drained. You get home now. Maybe Tori's still awake," she said as she took some cold water from the refrigerator and took out two glasses. "Have some water, it'll get you settled."

Linda pulled a fresh towel from the roll and wiped her face one last time. "Will you be all right?" she asked, taking the water in small sips, then setting the half empty glass in the sink.

"Yes," Frances responded reflectively, "I'll be okay. You'll be there in the morning?"

"Sure, every morning," Linda said at the door. "My mother talks about working the midnight shift at the shop. She'd get ten percent more. Maybe she'll switch shifts. Then she'll be there for Tori after school."

"Well, you do what's best for Tori," said Frances, following Linda out the door. "Want a ride home?"

"No," responded Linda from the sidewalk, "I need the walk to clear my head."

"Okay. Goodnight now," said Frances, standing behind the screen door.

"Goodnight, Fran. What time in the morning, six?"

"Yeah, six. Well," Frances said after some thought, "I have to get mom set for the day. Dougie and Louie, they said they will stop to see if we open. Six is good. They said they will be checking."

"Okay, night, Fran."

They met there the next morning, in the alcove, just as a big saffron sun burned off a thin, diaphanous haze and strained its golden threads of day through the oiled

386

windows of Farrell's. A promise of searing heat was in the air already as Frances turned the key and felt the weight of the lock's arm fall. She pushed the door open and they stepped into the silence, just the two of them, compelled by their need that dwarfed their fears. They stood for a moment, the dutiful and the dreamer.

Linda reached up and turned the lights on as Frances stood quietly in the center of the Palace, looking around as if it was a place she left at some other time in her life and now returned to. She examined the fixtures, lifted her head to the pressed tin ceiling, then ran her hand along the black counter. Her stomach was in knots. She looked into the mirror and saw herself alone in the glass, her paper bag of fresh aprons clutched tightly in one hand, relieved that nothing looked different although everything had changed. Then she looked beyond the image of herself and peered back to the decades that passed, all of them, waif, gossamer images recurring in the center of the glaces `a repetition. The mirrors, though stained and faded, their silver backing tarnished with age, still carried her back to the days of her childhood and beyond. And she wondered how it must have looked in 1905 when the Greek candy makers first opened the doors to the Palace of Sweets. How sharp the images must have been then. How clear the future was when the trolleys clacked from New Haven to Waterbury and the Palace opened to the center of the universe. Then her thoughts swept back to the present, images of the past, like Russian nesting dolls, hidden and out of sight, and she saw only herself in the faded, opposing mirrors.

"I'll start the coffee," said Linda, tugging at the bag in Frances' hand and pulling out two white aprons, sticking one into Frances' stomach. "Come on, Fran, put this on, customers will be here soon."

Frances walked to the back of the candy counter and placed the bag down. She put the bib apron over her neck and adjusted it under her collar, then slowly took its strings and pulled them to a snug knot.

"Put the radio on, Fran. Too quiet in here," Linda said. She made a racket running the water, banging the coffee pots and filling the silence until the moments carried themselves and the grill hummed and sizzled. And the morning grew long with the phone heavy from use, until the space filled with the pivot and grace of the common line and the window glowed again with the red neon lettering of the Palace of Sweets.

Martin Short and Max Cruz entered the conference room on a storm of energy. Cruz handed Julia, his secretary, the armful of legal files and fished a recorder from his pocket for her to transcribe. He peeled off his fitted suit jacket and gave his white shirt a quick tuck into his pants.

"Sorry we're late," he said to those seated. He looked across the conference table and walked to the blinds, drawing them semi- closed to avoid the blinding sun that rested over White Hills.

Max got up and closed the door of the conference room to keep out distracting noises. Martin finally sat at the head of the conference table and looked around the room.

"I guess we all don't know each other, so would it be all right with everyone if we made some introductions? I'm Martin Short. I think I spoke with one of your secretaries when we set up this meeting. I am one of the two litigators in the firm and I will be handling this case if you retain us." He turned to Max and nodded his head.

Max looked around the table and smiled. He pulled his chair out and stood. He was mature, displaying confidence, impeccably groomed and unusually muscular, with dark, striking looks. Years of pretrial work, motion arguments and successful trials prepared him for anything in open court. His muscled frame, chiseled under weights and toned to perfection, was perfectly cut under his tapered suit.

"My name is Max Cruz. I am the other litigator in the firm and I work closely with Martin on the larger cases. If there is an appeal by any party I generally do all the appeal work and argument if one is called for." He pointed across the table to young women taking notes. She looked up and waved as he spoke. "Tracy is our legal assistant. She prepares all the motions and keeps track of all the court calendars." A shallow smile creased his face as he sat and turned to his left.

"My name is John Cantell," explained the balding man to the left of Max. He sat with his fingers perched against each other. He gave an impression of competence and stability with his pugilist's nose and broad jaw. "I'm Hunter's personal attorney from Ohio. He asked me to come along so I can explain any technical information to him and he and I can try to come to a decision about whether to proceed or not with the civil suit. Right now we're in the process of interviewing a few law firms that have been recommended to us. You were one of them."

"Who recommended us to you?" Max asked.

Cantell folded his hands into a knot of short, thick fingers, "We asked a few of the stenographers at the federal court and the state court. They were coy about it but passed a few names to us. Then we would mention the names to the prosecutors. They would usually just nod or say something like 'very competent' or something like that. Then we did our own research."

Max shook his head and nodded. "Federal practice is very different than the state."

Cantell nodded in agreement and turned to his right. He pointed across the table to an older man with an unlit cigarette in his mouth. "This is Tony Cini, he's my private investigator that I asked to come up with me." Cini raised his hand and nodded several times as he glanced around the room. His face betrayed no emotion. When it was clear that he had nothing to say Cantell continued. "The big fellow to my right here is Hunter Biller. I'm sure all of you know who Hunter is by now but I'll let him introduce himself to you and we can begin the discussion."

Hunter stood and flattened his hands over the table. He looked around the room, tucked his thumbs into his belt and spoke slowly. "Like John here said, I suppose you all know me or at least know about me. One of the things I want to make sure of is that everyone here understands that I lost millions of dollars when the Sponge plants went up. I was found innocent in federal court of any crime and now they got the State of Connecticut breathing down my back. I just want to collect the insurance money that is rightly due me. I paid the premiums, even when there was no money coming in. I made sure the premiums were paid, and now the insurance company doesn't want to pay. So I'm not looking to get rich over this thing, I'm only trying to recover what's due to me." Biller pulled his chair in and sat with his long legs crossed.

Martin put his elbows on the table and leaned over. "Do you have the original insurance policy or was it destroyed in the blast?"

"We got the original back in Ohio, where we keep all the original documents. John has some copies that he can leave with you if necessary."

Martin directed his question to Cantell. "Is the coverage comprehensive? Replacement value or fair market value?"

Cantell looked over and spoke to both Martin and Max. "The coverage is not the problem. The company has never said that they were denying coverage based on any exclusion in the policy."

Martin shook his head slightly. He glanced at Max and looked back at Cantell. "So they are denying coverage based on the arson?"

Cantell shook his head and sat back in his seat. He started to speak by turning to Biller and holding up his palm to stop him from responding. "We submitted our claim on the Tuesday after the bombing. We just changed the policy to replacement value in December of 1974. But all we got was an oral commitment. Someone screwed up and we never followed through on the binder. Then the insurance company, Mutual Protection, they show up on Sunday morning, like twelve hours after the explosion when we still got flames burning and we're trying to keep the power house from going up. Anyway, they show up at the vacant school where the Governor set up the state's command center for the fire. The FBI was working off of a desk without a phone and the insurance company was all set up for business within twelve hours. In fact," Cantell said, sounding exasperated, "two days before they declared the fire under control Mutual Protection was doing business in Shelton. It's all over the local and national news so they show up and before we know it they have investigators all over the place, taking chemical samples, demanding the guard rosters for several weeks leading up to the bombing. So the Governor sets up a big room to process unemployment claims and the insurance company would be interviewing the employees about the fire."

Biller stood and thrust his hands into his pockets. He fished some change around and spoke. "Lots of those folks, you know, they were real upset over the bombing. Lots of them were mad when we bought the plants from B.F. anyway. Then the bombing happens and they're all out of work and the local newspapers are saying it was arson and I had something to do with it. Then you got this Staber talking about his predictions about airplane

392

crashes and hotels destroyed and seeing only the smoke stack left standing from Plant Four and he ain't making no sense at all and pointing the finger at me and I had nothing to do with it, just like the jury said."

"What is the claim amount?"

"Sixty-three million." Biller responded, returning to his seat.

Max turned to Cantell, "Sixty-three million? How did you come up with that amount?"

"Inventory lost, machinery destroyed, lost business, stuff like that," Biller said, leaning over the conference table. "Like I said, we amended the policy so we had replacement value. I swear the State of Connecticut is only going after me because the insurance company is putting pressure on it. The insurance companies own this state. That's why they want to see me in jail."

Max scribbled some notes and looked at Cantell. "What about the buildings? B.F. still owned them, right?"

"Yes," Cantell explained, "the buildings were owned by B.F. But we insured them for the proposed purchase price, around fifteen million or so. We were leasing them at the time. We were supposed to complete the purchase but we didn't meet the deadline so B.F. extended the lease."

"Yeah," Biller interjected, "and they wanted to raise the rent. That would have put us out of business if the fire didn't."

Martin's eyes darted between Biller and Cantell. "Well, let's make sure we all understand what happened here. You were indicted by the federal grand jury, along with nine others. One of them pleads guilty and turned government witness against the rest. Now, one of them, this driver, I think his name was Whitey or something, was acquitted because the jury believed him that he didn't know he was delivering explosives. And they didn't convict you because they felt the case wasn't proved beyond a reasonable doubt. But the state trial will be different. The state will probably make a deal with Staber and some of the others who were convicted in the federal trial. They may testify against you."

Cantell adjusted himself in his seat and leaned over the table again. "We're aware of that. But Hunter is innocent. He had nothing to do with the bombing. No one can tie him to any plot. No one, not Wade Staber or Shaw or Petres. None of them."

"What about the checks to Staber's company? Couldn't someone link Hunter to the arson based on the checks?"

Cantell shook his head and swatted his hand on the table. "No, that's just the point. Hunter thought he was buying a water treatment system like Staber's friend Fusto had at the soda plant. This whole idea of blowing up the plants, the whole thing was Staber's idea. Hunter had nothing to do with it."

Martin shook his head in agreement and looked down at his note pad. "Who else is going to be indicted with you?" he asked without looking up. "Is there anyone else out there that you're aware of?"

"Pollard," Cantell said quickly, "he was the CFO of Grand at the time of the arson. And Fusto, he's Staber's friend, some kind of soda executive familiar with water treatment plans. Word is the state is going to indict him."

Max lifted his head up towards Biller, "You ever talk to Fusto?"

"Never," Biller snarled, "and Pollard didn't either. This was all Staber's doing, the whole plan. He had this prophecy about the plant coming down and he told people. I think he just wanted to make it come true, maybe sell more books or something. Then he wants to point the finger at me. But that's not the way it happened. I had nothing to do with this."

The investigator, Tony Cani, spoke up. "All we know was what Wade Staber said and no one believed Staber because his stories were so bizarre. Look, I got information on Staber, stuff so whacked out no one will ever believe anything he says. He says he can talk to bees and knows people in the CIA. And J. Edgar Hoover, said he knows him. I got all that. He even wrote a book that he tries to sell called 'My Life as a Psychic: the Incredible Story of Wade Staber.' A lot of the stuff we know is right in there. All we ever knew is that he was working on a water treatment facility for the plant. That is all Hunter ever discussed with him. He had nothing to do with the arsonists and the guys that kidnapped the guards. Never even saw those guys until the trial. How could Hunter have hatched this plan?"

Martin shook his head at Cantell and glanced at Biller. He then turned to Max as if allowing him a moment to say something. Max remained quiet. He was more intrigued than critical of the facts surrounding the bombing. Max finally looked up and asked something that was on his mind since reading the transcripts of the federal trial.

"One thing I'm confused about. The CFO, Pollard, why wasn't he indicted in the federal trial? I couldn't figure that out from the indictments and the transcripts. It appeared that no one really focused on him."

"Pollard didn't really know anything," Biller said, looking to Cantell for permission to talk. "He was with me in Ohio most of the time. You know, he knew something about some financial difficulty at the Sponge plants but that's all. Besides, I don't even think he knew much about the plans for the water treatment facility. I don't know, maybe signed off on some checks and made a trip to give Staber some cash, but that's about all. The whole thing was Staber's idea. We had nothing to do with the arson."

Martin finally shook his head and tapped his fingers over the table. He was still turning Cantell's last statement over in his mind. "Look, John," he said with a pained face, "you paint a pretty complete picture here that Hunter was innocent of anything to do with the arson. But when you say there is no evidence that he had anything to do with the bombing, well, that is just not the case. The evidence is not direct but from what I know there is some circumstantial evidence of his involvement. All those guys who sat in federal prison for four or five years may be testifying for the state. All it's going to take is for one or two of them to tie Hunter into the arson and we'll have a problem.

"I agree," Cantell said, "but no one can. Look, I appreciate your skepticism, it's healthy. But when I tell you that Hunter had no idea of the arson plot, that's true. It's like the truck driver who was not convicted at the federal trial. He didn't know what he was driving. Hunter here was buying a water treatment system. No one can tie him to the arson." ·

Cantell stood and smiled at Biller. He stamped his foot, declaring it to be asleep. Then he smiled at Martin and Max and nodded with his hands outstretched. "That's why we're here. We don't want attorneys that think this is a cake walk. This is going to be brutal. We want the best firm available. That's why we're interviewing several firms."

Max looked at Cantell and spoke up. "One thing I don't understand. The other firm did a great job for you in the federal trial. Why are you shopping around?"

"Well, they did do a great job," Cantell responded as he took his seat again. "The problem is that they might have a conflict of interest. We aren't sure yet and I can't discuss it openly yet, but let's just say Staber's attorney for the state charges has been making some overtures about getting Hunter's attorney's cooperation."

Martin had a confused look. "What kind of cooperation? Can you tell me that?"

Cantell looked at Biller and at Cani. "Staber's attorney is proposing this hare-brained scheme to refuse to testify against Hunter and Pollard if Hunter would front his legal fees for him."

"And how much money are they talking about?"

"One hundred and fifty thousand dollars. You see, the attorney figures if he can get a good fee and if Staber won't testify. We collect the insurance money, then everyone is happy."

"So what's the conflict?"

"One of Hunter's attorneys taped the phone conversation. So he might have to testify against Staber's attorney. But then you have the problem of taping a phone conversation without adequate disclosure." Cantell shook his head and smiled.

Martin shook his head from side to side. "So that alone might be a violation of state law, the taping of a phone conversation without the consent of the other party."

The room grew silent. Martin nodded at Max. This was a case that had a national profile. It was big and would lead to the bigger insurance case if they won this. Max nodded and then asked softly, "What about Pollard, who is representing him?"

"He has some attorney out of California. He knows this guy and felt comfortable with him."

"What about Staber? Do we know he is being indicted for sure?"

"We know he is being indicted. He has some guy out of Stamford representing him. But he made that call so who knows how that will end up. Staber has no money, he's desperate. He may cut a deal, we don't know."

Tracy put her pen down and spoke up. "Now that I think about it, I did get a phone message from a Stamford attorney. I didn't speak to him but he said he was representing Staber and wanted to speak to me about the case."

Martin pursed his lips and shook his head. He had heard enough. He was satisfied that he could handle the case with Max and Tracy. The evidence against Biller was two-sided. He didn't appear to be innocent but the evidence seemed to fall below the criminal standard. He could use prosecution at the insistence of the insurance company as a defense, a large, wealthy insurance company trying to find a way not to pay claims. That would hit home with the jury. The case was fascinating and the civil trial that would follow if Biller was acquitted would be lucrative. The insurance company might just throw in the towel and pay off the claim. The only defense for Coast Immunity would be arson committed by Biller and so far there were no credible witnesses tying him to the arson. The conspiracy happened below him as far as the criminal trial showed. There were no credible witnesses that could testify against him. It would take an extraordinary effort for Coast to prevail. He could handle the Coast attorneys. This would be in the state courts where he and Max knew every judge and clerk in the area. They knew all the procedures and the motion practice. They knew the rules of evidence and the exceptions. And they knew the value of the case and the chummy, clubby atmosphere of the state courts. "I may want to put you on the stand. How do you feel about that?"

Cantell pursed his lips and shook his head. "We would entertain that. I think that would help the jury lean towards acquittal. Can Hunter handle the cross?"

"We'll prep him. If they couldn't touch him in the federal trial I don't see how cross can harm him. We'll object aggressively and tie the state in knots."

Cantell shook his head and nodded at Biller. "What do you think?"

"I like the idea. I am not afraid of them. I can't be tied to nothing to do with the arson."

Martin nodded with a satisfied approval. "We haven't talked fees," he said finally.

"So let's talk fees," Cantell responded. "What do you usually ask for?"

Martin looked up and directed his words to Cantell. "Our hourly fee is three hundred per hour for the attorneys and one fifty for Tracy's work. But we'll discount the normal fees if we have the civil case as well. That gives us an incentive to get Hunter off and it makes it more affordable to you right now. It will take years to get to a trial date for the civil trial."

"Now wait a minute here. I want to know just how much we're going to be suing for. I paid about fifteen million for the equipment and for the business. I got to recover that much at least for myself to pay the creditors."

"Max and I discussed what we would sue for. I think you said sixty three million. We're talking about over a hundred million. Do you think that covers your creditors?"

Biller sat back and smiled. Cantell turned to him and shook his head. "Multiple damages for unfair business practices?"

"That along with the time value of money, interest, and multiple counts even without multiple damages. We go for everything. If they decide to settle at least we have plenty of room to still recover our fees as well as make Hunter whole. That is the point, isn't it?"

Blake climbed the stairs to the third floor. He stood in the center of the small waiting room with slanted ceilings, being, as it was, the peak in a converted attic. He heard himself breathing and thought that he must be out of shape. Old magazines were piled on the small end table with a pedestal lamp in back of it, the same magazines that were there on his other five visits. He wondered if he was the only patient the doctor had since no one was ever sitting in the waiting room when he arrived and the doctor always let him out through a different door and down a rear staircase. Maybe that's the way psychiatrists operate, he thought. Maybe they think that their patients don't want anyone to see them, so they're offered the adulterer's furtive slip. Maybe they think their patients would feel funny coming face to face with someone else in need. Maybe they don't want the patients talking to each other anyway. Sometimes he could hear the drone of muffled voices, but nothing more. And that was the way it should be, he thought with his hands resting in his jacket pockets.

A tiny fan that lay on the rug under the end table was always on. He smiled as he reflected on his own innocence, not realizing until his third visit that the fan was to muffle the voices from the office and not to move the air at all. Out the window Blake faced the worn brick of another building, seeming to be within arms-length and thin metal bars in back of the screen to stop the impulsive.

The white wooden door suddenly opened. "Hi, why don't you come in."

Dr. Rennick stood aside and closed the door after Blake. "Hey, Doc, how you doing?" Blake asked in a soft voice, then took off his jacket and placed it over his lap as he took a seat on the sofa.

Rennick took a seat across from Blake and picked up his note pad. He immediately recognized a decline in Blake's posture and forlorn expression that was exaggerated by his unshaven face. "So," Rennick asked with an upbeat tone, "how are you doing this week?"

Blake was silent. He shook his head from side to side and felt his eyes well up. Then he let his head drop to his chest and kept shaking his head. "Not good, Doc. Not this week." Blake looked up as a tear rolled down his cheek.

Rennick put his pad aside and pulled his chair in front of Blake. In the stillness of the small room, Blake began to wail. "Hey," Rennick said quietly, placing his hands on Blake's shoulders that shook with each violent sob, "I want you to listen to me. You don't have to say anything. You can cry all you need to. Just listen. You just go ahead and let it out for now, Blake. I know you're hurting. But it had to come to this. Today we start to make it better, Blake. You have to trust me. You're my last appointment, you understand. There is no limit, no clock," he said between long pauses for gulps of breath from Blake. "No nothing, just us. At your other visits you were courteous and polite. But that didn't get you anywhere. This is what I'm after. You just take your time and tell me what hurts, and we can work on it together. Do you understand?"

Blake shook his head, acknowledging Rennick's words. "I, I, just can't take it anymore, Doc." Blake's voice trailed off into a staggered fight for breath. Rennick took several tissues from the box on his desk and stuffed them into Blake's hand. "I'm sorry, Doc, I didn't want this to happen but I just can't take it anymore."

"You have nothing to be sorry for, do you understand? This is what I do. Talk to me, tell me what you can't take anymore."

Blake looked across at Rennick. His eyes were red and swollen and his face was coursed with rivulets of tears. He took the tissue and pressed it over his face, making it redder still and leaving bits of tissue stuck on his unshaven beard. "Everything, Doc," he managed to say in a soft and halting voice, "I can't take anything anymore. It all just hurts."

Rennick sat back in his chair, allowing Blake a chance to breath freely but remaining close. "School, is school getting to you? Is it too much for you?"

Blake shook his head and breathed openly without saying anything. Then he took a breath through his wet and noisy nose and slowly let out a long and deep breath. "No, Doc, it's not school," he said, shaking his head without much energy. "We're on break this week anyway.

Maybe I got too much time on my hands. I just can't get it out of my mind."

"Okay," Rennick said, nodding his head affirmatively. "That's right, you told me that last week. You said that you were afraid of this week because you were on break and you didn't like having a lot of free time." Rennick spun his chair out from under himself and tossed it towards his desk, then sat beside Blake. "Now, tell me what you can't take. How about at work? Is everything all right there?"

Blake sucked in an uneven breath and exhaled audibly. "Yeah," he said shallowly, "work's okay. But I called in for the last two days. I can't even get myself to shave or do anything. I hardly got here."

Rennick grabbed his chair and faced Blake again. He leaned forward, bringing their faces within inches of each other. "Listen, I'm going to ask you some questions. I want you to answer them candidly. No bull-shitting me, do you understand?"

Blake looked towards the door and thought of leaving but he knew there was nowhere to go. Out the door was only unremitting pain with no relief. At least in here he had a chance, however small, at least it was a chance. He shook his head affirmatively and gave Rennick a quick glance. "Okay."

"Do you have thoughts of hurting yourself?"

Blake felt his stomach tighten. He wanted to vomit but he had nothing to vomit. He felt sick but didn't know what hurt more, his stomach, his head, his heart or his hands.

"Sometimes."

404

"When I asked you that a few weeks ago, you said no."

"I lied."

"You can't lie to me, I'm your psychiatrist."

"I lie to everyone."

"What do you mean, you lie to everyone?"

"I lie to everyone, it's how I get through the day. I lie to my friends at school, I lie to the people I work with, to my mother, I even lie to my priest."

"Why would you lie to your priest?" Rennick asked with a perplexed look. He knew the question was a distraction but thought the diversion would serve to calm Blake.

Blake looked at Rennick and managed a smile under his swollen eyes. "At confession," he said, shrugging his shoulders and nodding, "you know, you never tell the priest the big sins, only the little ones. They don't count anyway."

Rennick let out a relieved smile. "Fair enough. But when and why would you lie to your mother?"

Blake looked at Rennick and shrugged his shoulders. He shook his head as if to indicate that Rennick didn't understand and he was too pained to talk about it.

"Because she would worry about me all the time, even more than she does now. So I lie to her and I tell her everything's okay. Okay?" Blake looked at Rennick and opened his arms, extending his palms and said with a quiver, "I can't let her see me like this. It would kill her." Then he looked at the door, the door he knew he could just walk out of right now, the door that opened to freedom and certain hopelessness. "I don't want anyone to see me like this. And it's getting harder and harder to hide it."

Rennick got up, pulled his chair to the center of the room and started again. "Okay. We got distracted. I need to get some information from you. No distractions, no priest stories. Do you feel like harming yourself?"

"Sometimes," Blake responded, then nodded his head in affirmation, as if to make sure Rennick understood that sometimes he thinks of relieving the pain.

"How often?"

"Every day."

Rennick felt disquiet come over himself. He hoped it didn't show. "Have you ever acted on it?" he asked without expression.

Blake looked Rennick in the eye and shook his head from side to side. "No, never."

"Why not? What stops you? What prevents you from acting? Are you afraid?"

Blake looked at Rennick and smiled. "That's several questions, Doc. Which one do you want me to answer?"

Rennick raised his eyebrows and pursed his lip. Blake was right, he thought. That was several questions. But there would be no further humorous distractions and he couldn't let these very seconds, as they slipped by, ameliorate the tension. "Are you afraid?"

"No," Blake responded candidly and waited for the next question.

"Then what stops you? Why don't you act?"

Blake felt his lips contort despite his hope to remain calm. "Because," he said clearly, then took a deep and long breath, exhaled and breathed again, "because I can't do that to my mom or my brother. Or maybe I'm just a chicken and I'm using them as an excuse."

He felt his eyes fill again and closed them hoping to shut out the world. His lips tightened as he tried not to lose his composure. "So I'm stuck here. Sometimes I feel like I'm stuck here. And I can't take it sometimes. And now you're stuck with me. And I'm a mess."

Rennick leaned forward in his chair. "Don't worry about me," he said calmly, "I don't feel like I'm stuck with you. Now," he said, sitting back in his chair again, "just what can't you take anymore?"

Blake hesitated and looked at Rennick's watch. "I think my time is up," he said, gathering his jacket into one hand and appeared as if he was about to rise from the sofa.

Rennick unbuckled his watch from under his shirt sleeve and tossed it into his drawer. "I thought I made it clear that you were my last patient and that there was no quit time today. You're avoiding me, Blake. Just what can't you take anymore?"

Blake let his jacket roll to the floor and he folded his hands in a prayer-like fashion, placed them between his legs and started to rock gently back and forth.

"My hands, Doc, I can't feel my hands," he cried. "Sometimes I just drop my books because all I can feel are Siggy's bone fragments and then numbness." Blake rocked harder and cried louder. "I don't know what to do." He leaned up and took a deep breath, then put his hand over his eyes and cried again. "I feel slivers of bone on my

palms and the shards along his skull. And bits of
shattered bone on the ridges of my fingers, when I roll my
fingers together, so even my fine touch is gone for me. And
I smell the burnt flesh, like my nose is filled with the odor
of flesh cooking from the heat of the blast. I just want to
run from myself but I can't get far enough away because
it's in me. And I don't know what to do anymore. I don't
think you can make it go away and I can't take it."

Rennick leaned forward. He glanced at his note pad
sitting idly on his desk, then back at Blake, broken and
seeming beyond repair. Rennick finally shifted in his seat
and waited for Blake's rocking to ease. "Blake," he asked
softly, "who is Siggy?"

Blake fixed his eyes on the worn rug that needed to be
vacuumed. He knew that he didn't want to talk about it
anymore, ever, that he would like to forget it and put it out
of his mind forever. But that wasn't to be, at least not yet
and certainly not now. And it didn't matter anyway. He
was only a moment from death but he couldn't get there.
So now was a good time. He was spent. He had no more
sadness to suffer through. There was no other pain left to
hide. He lifted his eyes to Rennick.

"He was a friend of mine in the Marines." Blake's voice
was shallow but composed and even. "We were on patrol,
our squad, and it was at night and he basically walked
into a claymore."

Blake put his folded hands between his legs again and
leaned forward, nearly touching Rennick's forehead with
his own. "There was just a flash of light and then I heard

him moaning. I crawled over to him but there was nothing I could do. He was gone. So I held him in my arms, and it was dark, and I had to see with my hands because it was pitch black. I couldn't even see him inches away and then a firefight erupted around us. I couldn't see anything. Then someone shot an illumination flare and through the shadows I could see that half his face and skull was gone. But I held him to my chest and covered him and I kept holding his head, like I could stop him from dying or make his suffering stop." Blake met Rennick's eyes with a look of calm resignation. He shook his head from to side to side and felt his lower lip curl away, like he was ready to lose it again. He exhaled hard and looked at Rennick.

"He was gone. And there wasn't anything I could do to stop him from dying. I was trying to keep his brains inside and I remember patting down his hair on the other side of his head so he could feel me. I was trying to comfort him. He told me once that the only thing he remembered about his mother was the soft touch of her hands. She died when he was just a boy. So I wanted him to feel that softness again. But I don't know if he could feel. I don't even know if he knew if I was there. I kept whispering to him that he was going to be all right, that we would medevac him out of there and get him help, but nothing could have saved him."

Many moments pass in silence. Rennick wasn't sure what to say or what to ask. He thought of the medications he might be able to prescribe but he knew Blake was right, that he couldn't make it go away.

"How long have your hands bothered you?"

Blake shrugged. He didn't know, or at least he didn't want to make the effort to try to remember. Why did it matter anyway? It just appeared one day, full blown. Like the images on an optician's lens, it just appears clear one day from a fuzzy kind of discomfort. Then the memory comes back and no one knows where it was but it's here now.

"I don't know. It wasn't always there. Maybe six months now, maybe a year. I don't know, but it's worse. Now I can't function. All I do is try to get by every minute without falling apart."

Rennick sat back and made some thinking noise with his lips. "There is some medication I can prescribe. I think it might help."

Blake waved his hand dismissively. "I don't want to be walking around like a zombie, Doc. I'm already a mess."

Rennick shook his head in encouragement. "I don't think that would be your experience. It would just slow down your thoughts, might calm you down."

Blake glanced at Rennick with a skeptical look. "Will it help my hands?"

Rennick cast his eyes to the rug, then returned them to Blake. The answer was too painful to try to qualify. "Maybe not immediately," he responded. "Can you live with that?"

Blake sat in silence. There was no noise at all in the room, not even the sound from the fan in the waiting room. "Do I have a choice?" Blake asked.

Rennick shook his head with a concerned look on his

face. "No," he answered. The window behind the sofa had turned dark with evening. Rennick didn't know what time it was but he knew that Blake was spent and so was he. "I'll see you next week, right?"

Blake shook his head slightly. "I guess. I feel like I've been through the wringer today." Blake smiled at the thought. "You know, like those old washing machines that you had to feed the clothes through and they came out all flattened on the other side. That's how I feel."

"Do you want the prescription?"

Blake shook his head and clasped his hands together. "Okay."

Rennick glanced out the window. The night promised to be cold and long. "Look," he said, "I know you live alone but I would feel a lot better if I knew you could be with someone now. You know, like a friend from school or work. Is there anyone we can call? Maybe Nick. You can be with them to distract you."

Blake turned around and looked out the window. He was shocked that the daylight had evaporated to a heavy dusk. He had no feeling of the time or how many minutes he spent with the Rennick. "Yeah," Blake said, rising and dialing Nick's apartment for a ride home. Then he swung his jacket on and stood at the door, looking at Rennick seated at his desk.

"Nick's a good friend." Rennick said, recalling Blake speaking of him at prior appointments, when the conversations were courteous and light and polite and mostly meaningless.

411

"He's the best. He looks out for me. I try to look out for him too, like in school. He doesn't like to study much. But really, he does a lot more for me than I do for him."

Rennick put down his pen and rose from the desk. "It's good that he's married and good to know that you have a female to talk to, not just a guy."

"Yeah," Blake answered with an encouraging inflection in his voice. "Jenny is real nice. She's really the only female I have any kind of relationship with. I mean, I can talk to her and it's like not a big deal. I think she knows I'm about to crack up. She never bothers me about my personal life and stuff. She's just real nice to me."

"You feel comfortable talking to her?"

"Yeah."

"Do you have any other relationships with women, like someone at school or work?" Rennick asked in a conversational tone.

Blake stepped out of the door and into the back stairwell. He looked at Rennick with vacant eyes. He scratched his face and swept his hair from his forehead. He thought of just walking away. But he stood there, took a deep breath and spoke calmly. "No, I get along with everyone, but I can't function on a personal level. I hide all this stuff. Only you and Nick see the real me."

Rennick shook his head in understanding. "I'll see you next week. No cancellations."

"Okay."

The February morning cold whipped through the three

sets of outer church doors, rocking the inner doors slightly and sending a sliver of arctic air into the nave. "I wasn't sure I was going to make it today, Linda," Virginia said, turning from the votive candles and straining to look up. She moved back a few steps, resting her arms on the large pedestals holding the life size figures of St. Anthony and Our Lady of Guadalupe. Then her head moved back down and she glanced across the aisle to the statuary facing her from a distance.

"You know, just that little bit of snow and the church steps get so slippery. But it's a long day inside, Linda."

It began this way, nearly every Sunday, Virginia stopping to say a few words to Linda as the church emptied. They were usually short conversations, a matter of few thoughts or comments about the weather, except for the first time, the one that took Linda by surprise.

It was a Sunday remarkable only because it was so ordinary, without a great event that brought in the lapsed to fill the pews. The pastor shut the church lights and pulled the chains to open several of the stained glass windows. Warm spring morning air wafted in and sunlight shunted in from the east. Linda remained in the choir loft sifting through some sheet music and started practicing for the First Communion that would happen in May. Over the sound of the piano she heard her name being called, a thick voice raised only to a conversational level from a distance, cautious and diffident, afraid of disturbing the quiet space of the choir loft.

"Linda," the voice called out again. "Linda, it's me,

Virginia Cumiskey. Can you hear me?"

Linda rose and leaned over the choir rail and smiled. "Oh, hi, I'm sorry, Mrs. Cumiskey. Have you been calling me for a while?"

Virginia strained to look up. The arthritis made her hunched and unable to lift her neck. She took several steps back down the aisle to get a better angle and relieve the pain. She kept one hand on the pew for stability and the other in the pocket of her large, heavy cardigan sweater

"No, Linda. I just called your name a few times," she said gesturing to the now empty and dark church and making a stutter step towards the pew to lean her heavy frame against it. "I waited until everyone left."

She looked towards the shafts of sunlight streaming through the windows, far from where she stood in the dark aisle.

"It's a beautiful day, Linda, isn't it?"

Linda leaned over further and rested her elbows on the choir rail. She reached back and pinned her hair behind her ear to keep it from falling over her face. "Oh, it's just a glorious day today. I told my daughter that I'd take her up to the park before I go to work later. She loves to ride her bike and, you know, it's a long winter for the kids, being cooped up inside and all."

Virginia managed a wide smile and raised her hand from her pocket.

"Oh, I'll bet she'll just love that, Linda."

She planted her cane and strained to look back up.

"I was going to ask you for a favor. But if you can't do it I understand. So you just tell me and I'll understand."

Linda leaned forward and put on a serious expression.

"Sure, Mrs. Cumiskey," she said. "What is it?"

Virginia smiled and glanced up. Her jowls hung low, worn with grief.

"I would prefer it if you would call me Virginia. I know I'm a lot older than you but I would like that better."

Linda pinned back the other side of her hair and smiled easily. "Okay, I guess I can get used to that. I might make a mistake sometimes. But, sure, I can call you Virginia."

Virginia rolled her eyes up toward Linda. "Do you know the song, 'I Have an Angel in Heaven'?"

Linda squinted and thought back.

"Yes," she said cautiously. "I know that song. I haven't played it in a while but I know it."

Virginia raised her head fully. She fought the pain in her shoulders and didn't allow it to show on her face.

"Today is my son Kevin's birthday. He would have been twenty-seven years old today. I was wondering if I asked you if you could sing that song."

Linda raised herself off of the rail and felt her jaw slacken. Over the years she has been asked to sing many songs that had special meaning to someone. But that was always in the context of a service or a mass. She shook her head in what looked like a shudder wondering why it took Virginia this long to ask.

"Of course I can do that. When? Now?"

Virginia was facing the floor. The weight of her head was

415

too much for her aching shoulders. She tried to look up but she couldn't so she spoke to Linda as she looked down.

"Yes, now. I don't want to make a scene during the mass, you know, with all the people around. Sometimes I get too emotional."

Linda shook her head up and down, not quite hearing what Virginia said.

"So I'll sing it now?"

"I can pay you," came the reply.

Linda was shaking her head from side to side but couldn't get the words out. The church was silent except for the sound of cars passing on Elizabeth Street.

"No," she said finally, "of course you can't pay me. Don't even say that again, Virginia. I won't even consider that. I can do it for you, do you understand? And I'm going to put it in my calendar and every year, on the Sunday closest to Kevin's birthday, I'm going to sing it for you. Okay? So you don't have to ever ask me again. It'll be in the calendar and that's it."

Virginia's head turned slowly. She couldn't raise it to meet Linda's eyes. "Thank you, Linda," she said softly.

Linda disappeared from view and sat at the piano bench. She placed her hands over the keys, remembering the words and the tune. She knew the notes would follow naturally. She started playing and heard the sound of Virginia's coins falling at the votive candles. The church was silent except for the sound of the piano and her voice, perfect and true and firm and clear. And she knew where

416

Virginia was and what she was doing and she struggled to keep her mind on the music. She did it for Virginia and for Kevin although she never knew him. But Blake did and he spoke of him and so did Frances and Teddy. And that was years ago but she felt a connection to Kevin because of Blake, and Virginia's need was reason enough. So she sang, that year and every year thereafter, on the Sunday closest to Kevin's birthday, after the 9:00 mass, when the church was dark and empty and Virginia prayed holding the toes of the saints, their statues raised on pedestals, and found peace and a connection to what she lost.

Her boots remained open at the top because she couldn't reach down to fasten them. But they were warm and stable in the snow. She fastened only one coat button, the one over her chest, allowing the coat to fall open and whip her in the wind. It was tweed and pilled and hung off of her like a heavy cape. She walked with two canes now, as she said, to prevent a fall in the snow, denying that the arthritis was worsening. Her head was draped in a black woolen shawl that she folded down once inside the church.

Linda would hear her coins drop into the votive box and would wait a few moments before resting her elbows on the choir rail and conversing with her, "Very slippery out there today, Linda."

She shook her head in agreement. "Yes, I know. I almost fell walking up Main Street coming in this morning, right outside my apartment. No one bothers to shovel. It's just all ice under the snow. You really have to be careful."

"Yes, you do," Virginia replied as she tried to fold down

her shawl to lay flat against her shoulders. "I liked that new song you did at communion today, Linda. It was really pretty. But you can make anything sound good."

"Oh," Linda said quietly. "Thank you, Virginia. I went to a conference last week with some of the other music directors from around the area and I picked up some new music. You let me know if you like it, okay?"

"Oh, sure, I will," Virginia said, resting her canes against the statuary. "I made something for your daughter, Linda." Virginia reached into her coat pocket and pulled out a wad of tissue paper and held it up to Linda.

"Oh, Virginia," Linda exclaimed, "you didn't have to do that. Wait, I'll come down." She hurried down the narrow, spiral staircase and walked to Virginia who handed her the gift.

"You can open it. I wrapped it up and taped it real good in case I fell, I didn't want it to break."

The pastor turned off the lights from the sacristy. In the dark and quiet church Linda unrolled the tissue paper and held a small porcelain doll in her hand. It had short, cropped blond hair and was dressed in a jumper made of wool and held a baby in her arms.

"Mrs. Cumiskey," Linda exclaimed, holding the doll up towards the single light in the center aisle, "this is beautiful. It's just beautiful," she said again. "Tori will love it."

Virginia couldn't help smiling at Linda's reaction. "I hope you like it. One day I heard Frances talking to her about her dolls a while ago. That's where I got the idea."

Virginia continued to smile and brushed down a fold in the tiny jumper. "I made it. One of my neighbors in the apartments makes these dolls. She has a kiln for them and everything. You have to bake it in the kiln overnight. So she helped me with the painting on the face because my fingers aren't so good anymore. You know, I can see some mistakes but I hope no one else can."

"Mistakes?" Linda cried, "oh, no, Virginia, it's, it's just perfect. She'll love it with the cat in her arms and all."

"We made the clothes, too. The jumper and the blouse, Everything. We made it all. My neighbor helped me. I was able to do the stitching. It took a while because I had to wait for good days when my fingers moved." Virginia smiled widely and straightened her posture the best she could.

"Oh, my goodness," Linda cried and wrinkled her nose in disbelief. She placed the doll in Virginia's hands and turned up the tiny jumper, examining the stitching and running her fingers over the material. Her eyes darted between Virginia's and the doll. "I can't wait to show my mother. She sews, you know. But she never sewed anything this tiny. It's so adorable."

"I didn't know your mother sewed, Linda. Of course, I don't see her much. Do you think she'll like it?"

"Oh," Linda said with a pitched voice, as she took the doll and held it up again, "she'll love it."

Virginia reached up and touched the doll's hair. "I even put in a little braid in the back of her hair, just like Tori has. My granddaughter did that for me. See," she said, taking the doll and holding it so it faced Linda, "it's supposed to look like Tori." Then Virginia turned the doll and looked at it one last time, as if to reassure herself that the effort succeeded. "Do you think it looks like her?"

Linda's nose wrinkled again and she put her hands up to her mouth in surprise. "Ah, it looks just like her. I can't belief it. The blond hair and the braid and she has brown eyes. It's beautiful, Virginia, just beautiful."

The wind whistled and blustered its way into the nave again, rocking the doors slightly, just enough to remind them that a world existed outside. Virginia placed her hands on the pedestals as they spoke of the paints she used and the temperature of the oven.

"So, you said you bake it?" Linda asked.

"Oh yes," Virginia responded, cupping her hands in response. "For that finish, they call it a satin finish to the porcelain, it has to bake overnight in the kiln. The temperature has to be 2,235 degrees. The kiln glows white hot. And you have to get up every two hours to check it. My neighbor let me sleep on her couch that night because I wanted to say that I did it."

Linda held the doll in her outstretched arms and asked who cut the material and where the pattern came from for the jumper and tiny turtle neck shirt and the type of stitch needed to keep the material from looking puckered or harsh. And the minutes clocked on silently and there, in a colloquy among the saints, they wove meaning from need into the frigid morning until, along the far aisle, just before the statuary, a parishioner stamped in and whipped off his watch hat, arriving for the next mass.

Linda shook her head with gratitude and narrowed her eyes. "You didn't have to do all this, Virginia. I don't want you to work that hard. I mean, it's beautiful and all, but you don't owe me anything. I sing for you because I want to. I don't want you to do anything in return. Do you understand?"

"I know that, Linda," Virginia said with a shrug of her shoulder. "But it's just a little something. There's nothing I can do for you but at least I can do that for your daughter." Virginia reached into her coat pocket and put on her wool gloves. She smiled as she slipped into them, "Good thing this coat has deep pockets." Then she took hold of her canes and steadied herself on them before stepping out from between the pedestals. "Well, I should get along now, Linda."

"Yes," Linda exclaimed, rolling the doll back into the tissue. "I have to get ready for the next mass. What do you have planned for the rest of the day?"

"Not too much," Virginia said as she walked to the swinging doors. Linda stepped into the vestibule and held the door for her. "My daughter's got a basketball game out of town for her son Michael. So I'm going to go home and open up a can of niblets or something, maybe cut up a hot dog and fry it. Nothing fancy," she said, allowing her eyes to dart up as Linda released the swinging door and shuddered in the cold vestibule. She helped Virginia place her shawl over her head securely and then held open the heavy outside door.

Virginia moved as quickly as she could to grab the frozen railing and stepped down on the first of the twenty stone stairs. "You go in, Linda. I'll be all right. It's too cold to be out here without a coat or gloves."

"You sure you're okay to walk in this cold?" Linda asked.

Virginia turned, planted her cane down, released the rail and turned around on the stairs. She rolled her eyes up to Linda and she placed her right hand on the rail. "I'm fine Linda," she said, breathless in the cold air. She looked back and stepped down. "Don't mind me. You go in. It's too cold out here. I have to go down backwards." She held both canes in her left hand and continued to step backwards. "It doesn't hurt my knees as much going this way."

Linda released the door and slipped back into the cold vestibule. She peeked out again and watched Virginia. She stepped out and folded her arms over her chest tightly, holding the tissue paper firmly in her hand. "Thank you again, Virginia."

"You're welcome, Linda," Virginia said without looking up. Then her motion stopped and she spoke, looking down at the steps. "It's for your daughter, Linda. But someday I'm going to do something nice for you, to pay you back. I'm not sure what yet. But it'll come to me. You go in now, Honey."

The heavy wooden door closed as Linda slipped through the rocking doors and rubbed her arms to warm her body. She ran up the spiral stairs and unrolled the tissue paper once more, placing the doll on the piano and shivering, rocking herself as she sat on the piano bench blowing warm air into her cold hands.

Blake rested his elbows on his knees. He studied Rennick's soft hands, nearly covered by the cardigan sweater that was a size too large for his frame, waiting for the probing question.

"So, tell me more about the feelings of numbness you experience."

"I thought we talked about that last week," Blake said while staring at the floor."What's there to say?"

Rennick uncrossed his legs and leaned over. "You cancelled last week. Don't you remember? You left me a message on the machine talking about some work deadline you had to meet. Do you remember that now?"

Blake nodded and pulled back into his chair. He looked at the wall in back of Rennick. It was always a plain, unbroken expanse of off-white wall space since he started therapy. Now there was a large painting of an old man in a big room with a high ceiling, a room that appeared to be in a large, ancient Southern European villa with stucco interior walls. He was lying in a four post bed covered with a single white sheet. A young woman stood at the foot of the bed. Her hair was long and dark and fell over her face, hiding her features. She was holding the post for balance and clothed in a white full slip as she lifted her foot to either put a shoe on or take it off. She appeared to be thirty or so, an age holding the alluring notion of beauty and maturity. Blake studied it without expression.

"I like the painting."

Rennick glanced at Blake and picked up his pen. He knew he would say that. He knew Blake would try to deflect the conversation from him to something else, anything else. Any distraction would do but the painting was exceptional, loaded with sexual overtones layered over the clear mortality of advanced age of the old man whose eyes were closed and whose face was turned to the side. "I got it a few weeks ago, I guess right after your last appointment, at least the last one you kept."

"You get a lot of comments about it?" Blake asked.

Rennick smiled and glanced over his shoulder as if to remind himself of what the painting contained. "Yes," he said with certainty, "it does cause a lot of conversation. I wasn't sure whether to put it up or not, you know, it might be too distracting for some people."

Blake lifted his brows and smiled again, "Like just now?"

Rennick nodded in agreement. "Uh-huh, like just now." Then he glanced back over his shoulder and continued. "Really," he said, turning back to Blake, "it has caused more good conversations than I expected. Most people try to figure out if she's coming or going, or they want to know if she's his daughter, a girlfriend, wife, maybe a caregiver of some sort. Anyway, everyone has a comment."

Blake got up and walked towards the picture, then moved to one side, then the other. "She does look a lot younger than him, right?"

"Looks that way to me," Rennick responded without

turning to Blake.

"But she has this slip on and she's putting her shoes on."

"Well, that's funny that you think she's putting her shoes on. Most people can't tell whether they're going on or off, if she's just getting there or just leaving."

Blake took his seat, crossed his arms and stared at the painting. "No, I think she's putting her shoes on, that's why she's holding the post. If she was taking her shoes off she would just kind of flick them off. What do you think?"

Rennick met Blake's eyes and smiled. "I think you're paying a lot of money for us to discuss what she's doing. See, now it is a distraction."

"You forget, I don't pay, not with this crazy arrangement you have with Nick. But that's another thing, we talked about it and now that I'm finished with school you have to bill me."

"Whatever you say. You're my patient, not Nick."

"So just tell me what you think, is she coming or going?"

Rennick shrugged. He picked up his pencil and pad and laid them on his lap. "Yeah, I really don't know. That's why I bought it. There is no answer. I just liked the painting. Now, tell me about the numbness."

"Wait," Blake said, standing again to look at the painting. "What makes her really attractive is she's only wearing a full slip and there is no dress in the picture. And the slip, it's not like fancy or anything, just a plain white full slip."

"You like full slips? Plain, full slips?" Rennick asked.

Blake squinted in thought, then shook his head and pursed his lips. "Yeah, I guess I do. The full slip, you know, it shows her form but not her body. It's really the feminine form that's so attractive."

"Oh, and flesh isn't attractive?"

"Yeah, sure, flesh is attractive, but the painting wouldn't be nearly as beautiful if she was naked. It's the slip and the way it falls over her body that is beautiful."

Rennick glanced at the wall clock and then met Blake's eyes. "Look," he said in a serious tone, "if you're going to be distracted maybe we should trade seats, this way you don't have to look at it. There's no magic to you sitting there and me here."

Blake shook his head and looked at the floor. "No, Doc, that's all right. It's not much of a distraction." he said without looking up. "Yeah, I don't know. I think I mentioned it the last time we talked, the numbness. It just comes on, like when I'm lying on the floor watching television, that's when it happens."

"How often is that?"

Blake shrugged. "Mostly on weekends. During the week I really don't have that much time. Like on Saturday nights or Sundays afternoons, I like to lie on the floor and watch television. I don't like sitting in chairs. Anyway, I just feel like, not so much numbness, I just feel like helpless, like I can't move any of my muscles."

"So this is a different sensation from the numbness in your fingers when we first started, is that right?"

"Yeah," Blake agreed, "this is different. It's all over, like I can't move, as if I'm paralyzed."

"Are you sure your muscles aren't asleep? Do they tingle?"

Blake looked at Rennick and shook his head. "No, they're not asleep, no tingling. Paralyzed, that's probably the best way to describe it. I want to move but nothing will move, even when I try. Like there is something hovering over me that prevents me from moving."

Rennick firmed his lips and wrote some notes on his pad. "You're sure you're not falling asleep and that this feeling is just the start of your sleep cycle?"

"No, it's not when I'm falling asleep because I'm aware of everything that's happening around me. I can still hear the television and stuff but it's like they're in the background."

"How about if someone knocks on the door, could you answer it?"

Blake shrugged his shoulders. "No one ever knocks on the door."

"Okay" Rennick said, accepting what Blake said but wanting more. "What about the phone ringing, are you able to get up and answer the phone?"

Blake looked up at Rennick and smiled. "I call my mom every day and I talk to my brother once a week or so. But as far as the weekends at home, it's pretty quiet."

"You're not answering my question. Did this paralysis ever happen when the phone rang?"

Blake looked down at the rug. His head dropped and he rested it in his hands. "Yes, it has happened and the phone rang."

"And what happened? Did you get up off the floor to answer the phone?"

Blake shook his head and closed his eyes. "No. I couldn't get up. I couldn't move."

"And what happened?"

Blake looked at Rennick with a blank stare. Then he shrugged his shoulders and shook his head.

"They hung up. They let it ring a few times and then they hung up."

Rennick moved around in his chair. He was getting agitated but didn't want Blake to see that.

"I should know the answer to this but I always call you at the office. Do you have an answering machine?"

Blake smiled and crossed his legs. His eyes drifted up to the woman in the painting either putting her shoes on or taking them off. No one knew.

"Actually, my mom bought one for me a while ago but I never took it out of the box."

Rennick put his pad aside and leaned over. "And why not? I bet your mom's not happy about that."

Blake shrugged and looked at Rennick squarely. "I call her every day. She doesn't have to leave me messages. I don't let her worry about me. Most of the time I'm at the office."

"So that's still no excuse for not setting up the answering machine. You're the one pushing to stop these one on one meetings and getting into group sessions through the veteran's groups, but then we come across this kind of behavior that I think tells me something about

428

your life that I have to pull out of you. That upsets me because I can make mistakes. You're not helping me help you. Do you understand that I could let you go because I made a mistake and you made me believe that you were ready? Do you understand that this is not a game and you just put in your time here and tell me everything is okay and that's it?"

Blake shook his head and sat back in his chair. He looked directly at Rennick, "I understand."

"Then why don't you set up the answering machine, Blake? Tell me the real reason why you don't set up the answering machine?"

Blake's eyes rolled up the old man in the painting. He was in bed, with his eyes closed. His shock of white hair was disheveled and his head was turned to one side, away from the women, the young, beautiful, comely woman. He couldn't be certain whether the old man was tired or near death. A white sheet covered him up to his chest.

"I don't know."

"I don't believe that, Blake. Tell me why."

Blake felt himself sink into the chair. He rubbed his hands over the brocade armrests and felt the decorative tacks that held the upholstery in place. He cast his eyes down to the floor.

"Because I don't want to be reminded of how lonely I am. I don't want to walk into the apartment and see that there are no messages, that no one called. Because that's what would happen."

Blake rolled his eyes up and met Rennick's impassive

stare. "I don't want to be disappointed," he said softly.

Rennick examined Blake's expression. He looked sad and defeated. Not pained, just defeated. Rennick allowed many seconds to pass in silence. He thought Blake might talk again but nothing came from him. He leaned forward toward Blake. "I understand that. But you have to open yourself up a little. You can't expect to just work. You have to develop some interests outside of work."

Blake shook his head in agreement. "Yeah, I know that, Doc. But I'm afraid I'm not ready yet. And I do things with the guys at work and all, it's just the weekends that are long. I've been doing a lot better, right?"

Rennick smiled and relaxed. "You're asking me?"

Blake returned his smile. "Well, you're the doc, right?"

"And you're the patient, the patient who doesn't open up enough. You think I'm Houdini or something, like I can read your mind."

Blake laughed and folded his arms.

"You want me to talk more? Okay, did I tell you what happened on my birthday?"

Rennick put his pen and pad down and looked at Blake.

"No, I don't think you told me about that. When was it anyway?"

"Let's see," Blake said, counting back the weeks in his mind, "three weeks ago."

"How old are you now?"

"Thirty-one."

"You were twenty-five or twenty-six when we started together, right?"

Blake shook his head in agreement and laughed. "Right, about that, I guess. Things haven't changed much, have they?"

"It's better, isn't it?" Rennick responded in a serious tone.

"I guess," Blake said unconvincingly.

"So you were going to tell me what happened on your birthday?"

"Yeah," Blake said. He was animated now, moving his hands and describing the circumstances to Rennick.

"So on birthdays, the women in the office, they usually bring in a cake, sometimes ice cream. And they try to make it a surprise. They never did it for me because I always managed to be out of the office on my birthday. This year I just didn't pay much attention to the calendar and I was in the office. So, they page me to the conference room. Now, you have to understand, the conference room has no windows because it's on the interior of the office. So they have the lights off and I walked in and everyone yells surprise and a few of them had flash cameras. So when the cameras flashed I dove under the table to take cover. I, I just flashed back to Vietnam. It was like I was there. I swear I heard explosions and I even smelled gunpowder."

Rennick picked up his pad and made a note. Then he looked back at Blake and raised his head, "So what happened? You actually went under the table?"

Blake leaned forward and let his eyes drift to the floor. Then he lifted his head, "Yeah. I dove right under. My heart was pounding. I was shaking. Norine was standing next to me. She realized what happened so she dropped her glasses to the floor. You know, she always wears these flip up sunglasses. So when she gets to the office every day she just flips them up and wears them around all day like that. Anyway, when she saw me drop down she dropped her glasses to the floor. She made a big issue about it, saying that someone knocked her sunglasses off her head. She tried to deflect the attention from me."

Rennick was shaking his head. Maybe Blake's issues were manifesting in a different way now. "How did you feel?"

Blake let a few seconds pass. His heart was thumping in his chest and in his ears, the way it felt in the conference room. He looked up at Rennick. His eyes spoke of disappointment that it had come to that event. He thought it was getting better once the feeling of bone bits in his fingers stopped. He hoped that the smell of burnt flesh was gone and that he wouldn't have to deal with odor of gunpowder residing in his brain again.

"I don't know. Embarrassed, scared. I thought my heart was going to come through my chest it was thumping so hard. Someone turned the lights on. I guess they realized something was wrong. But they didn't make a big deal about it. I just got up and I heard Norine ask me to get her glasses. I didn't even realize they were down there. So I knelt down and that's when I started to feel okay. I was embarrassed but I got up and they sang to me."

Rennick's hand was fisted and resting against his

mouth. He looked startled and concerned for Blake. He finally put his hand down and tried to look relaxed, "And what about the pictures?"

"Wow, you know, at the time it happened I didn't even think of that. But you did and so did Norine. So they finished singing and when she passed out pieces of cake she traded cameras for cake and had all the photos developed and got rid of the ones with the lights off."

Rennick had a flat, serious look on his face. He wasn't so upset by the incident but was concerned for Blake since he worked so hard to keep all this out of the office.

"So what happened to them? Did she give them to you, the ones that caught you reacting?"

"No, when I asked her what happened to them she just said 'what pictures? I don't know what you're talking about.' And that was that."

"Are you comfortable with that?"

"Yes, I am. She knows I struggle. I told her a little, bits and pieces. She doesn't dwell on it, but she understands. She knows I can't talk about it."

"Have you ever experienced anything like that before? Something that triggered a flashback?"

Blake scanned the room in thought, "No, nothing like that, not recently anyway."

"So it's a different feeling from when you would go into the woods and hide under leaves? Like when you first started therapy?"

"Yeah," Blake said, nodding his head. "It's different. I did that because I was anxious and it made me feel safe." He shook his head and clasped his hands tightly, "This was just the opposite. When the cameras flashed I was right back in the war. I just hit the deck and it all flooded back, the flash of the grenade in the darkness, the sound of the explosion and the smell of it all... I even saw the shadowy illumination of the parachute flair...all of it was right there, within seconds it all happened. I was out of control."

"You're quite sure this never happened before? Anything like this?"

"No," Blake said, shaking his head and closing his eyes as if he was trying to keep the images out of mind, even now. Nothing like that, ever."

Rennick sifted through several thoughts, allowing the silence to fill the space and maybe settle Blake. He finally crossed his legs and folded his hands over his lap.

"And that's why you failed to make the last appointment?"

Blake shook his head affirmatively and remained silent.

"If it happens again I want you to call me immediately. I don't care what day it is or what time of day it is. If you can't reach me call my pager and I'll call you back."

"Does it usually come back, the flashbacks?"

Rennick tightened his lips and shook his head, "To tell you the truth, we're just getting some results of studies done by the VA. They're treating thousands of guys just like you who are experiencing this kind of thing. But it's only in the last few years that they recognized it as a separate illness related to a stressful experience. Before this, in other wars, they just said the guys were shell shocked. So to answer your question, yes, it often is a pattern of sorts. But most people get them sooner after the incident. It often drives them into therapy. With you it's, what, almost ten years later for the flashbacks. That's unusual."

Blake leaned forward, propping his elbows on his knees and tapping his fingers together in a prayer-like pose. "Is this related to the numbness? That started a while ago."

Rennick gave him a quizzical look. "It's hard to say. I can't tell you for certain. I think we have more work to do. It wouldn't be right to let you start into group settings yet. How does that sound to you?"

Blake shrugged. "It's okay, I feel like I've been coming here forever anyway."

He looked up over Rennick's shoulder and let the faint of a smile crease his lips.

"I kind of like looking at the painting."

He returned his eyes to Rennick and smiled broadly.

"Bet you didn't think it would make patients come back?"

"No," Rennick replied as he smiled and nodded towards the painting. "That I never considered."

Blake sat back in his chair and felt his eyes glisten. Rennick looked at him and waited for a comment but Blake said nothing. He allowed a few seconds to pass then asked Blake what was on his mind.

Blake shook his head from side to side, holding out for a few more moments until he could compose himself.

Then he nodded up towards the painting, "Sometimes I

feel like that old man looks, tired and half dead, like I'm just too beaten to enjoy anything anymore. Could that be it? Do you get patients that just don't ever get better?"

Rennick leaned forward, closer to Blake where their eyes met and his earnest tone commanded attention. "No," Rennick replied with certainty."Not with patients like you. I see some very sick patients, patients with a break from reality. Some of my severely depressed patients have some difficulty, but even they get better, at least not so severe, and manageable. A lot of patients are just not compliant. They don't take their meds. You, you'll recover fully. A day will come when all of a sudden it occurs to you that you can't remember the last time you had that numbness. And the flashback, we'll have to wait that one out a while. See how often it happens. But even if it occurs again, several times, it too will work its way out. We can try some other medications. We're not without remedies. All this will be better, Blake."

Blake sat motionless. He was satisfied not to talk anymore. He wasn't sure where it was getting him anyway.

"You told me a few years ago that all this would get better. But it's all still with me."

Rennick sat back in his chair, then walked to his file cabinet, pulled out a file and opened it up. "Stand up, Blake. Do me a favor and stand up."

Blake stood, then stepped to the back of his chair and looked at Rennick. He was eye level with the old man in the bed.

"How tall are you, Blake?"

"Five-eleven, why?"

"How much do you weigh?"

Blake looked confused but answered Rennick. "I don't know, about a hundred and sixty-five pounds or so."

"How old are you?"

"Thirty one, we just talked about that."

"Do you know how much you weighed when you first came here?"

"No." Blake said, nodding his head as if it didn't matter. "I forgot."

"Let me remind you." Rennick flipped a page in the file and scrolled down it with his finger. "One hundred and thirty-one pounds. Now you tell me, how much did you weigh when you started seeing me?"

Blake looked at Rennick and repeated his words, "One hundred and thirty-one pounds."

"Do you remember those days, Blake? The days when you came in here and broke down week after week, and you had trouble carrying your books because you would feel bone fragments in your fingers? When you would crawl under cars at night or run into the woods to cover yourself in leaves because it made you feel safe? When you wouldn't shave because you couldn't stand looking at yourself in the mirror? Do you remember that you had no furniture, just a mattress to sleep on? Tell me how you felt then. Looking back from here, tell me how you felt then. Did you feel like that old guy in the painting?"

Blake lifted his jacket from the back of his chair and put it on. He stood, glanced at the old man in the painting, and stepped to the door. Rennick had never done this to him before, had never reminded him of the broken man he once was and hoped to leave behind.

He shook his head from side to side, "No, I felt much, much worse than that guy in the painting. He's lucky, he's only half dead. I was much worse off."

Rennick closed his file and returned it to the cabinet. "I'll see you in two weeks."

1985

"When they going to get a crew to fix them lights? There must be ten bulbs out." Joe stood in front of the grill and cast a perturbed look at Frances. He leaned into the window, careful not to disturb the terrace of neatly strung candy canes and counted the burned out Christmas bulbs strung over Main Street.

Frances stood behind the grill and gave him an unconcerned smile. "I don't know Joe, the Mayor was in here the other day and noticed it too."

Izzy turned his stool and secured his shoe horn into his back pocket. "Used to be different, Joe, you know, when Howard and Barbers was still open. Used to have Santa down there for the kids, the street would be packed with people, there weren't any empty storefronts. Nice lights because the merchants would put pressure on the city. All the store windows would be decorated. Now everyone goes to the malls. They don't need to come downtown anymore. I remember when the street would be filled with people with bags they could hardly carry." He stood beside the register and continued, "Stop in here for a bite or something hot to drink. Carol," he asked, "you remember that?"

Carol unbuttoned her coat and stepped away from the

439

radiator, stabbing the air with her lipstick smudged cigarette. She pointed towards the window, examining the abundance of candy canes of every size imaginable. She counted the brown and white miniature reindeer placed between the candy canes and the colorfully wrapped popcorn balls.

"Of course I remember that," she responded, running her eyes from Izzy to Joe while handing Frances two dollars. "Hey, Fran, how come you got only seven reindeer this year? Didn't there used to be eight?" she asked. "Place is getting to be a ghost town, except for the traffic. The redevelopment killed it. The only window on the street that's decorated is Fran's and the shoe store and the jeweler's. The flower shop used to have its window all lit up and decorated. Now it's just empty." She looked into the street with the endless sequence of car lights.

"What is all this traffic tonight, anyway?" she asked in her smoker's voice, turning back to Frances. "And what about the eighth reindeer, Fran?" she asked with a wink to Joe. "I want to know what happened to that reindeer."

Frances reached under the counter and picked up the phone, answering Carol at the same time. "I don't know, I don't know," she said, shaking her head. "Maybe they can't find the other one. We used to have eight, right, Linda, we had eight reindeer last year? Hey, Joe, what happened to the other reindeer?" she asked, then laughed into the phone as she explained. "No, no, Carmy, I wasn't talking to you. We're trying to figure out what happened to the eighth reindeer. I only got seven in the window."

Joe rasped in under lidded eyes, "They got that construction down the street in front of River." He turned and held the door for three women with a shopping bag filled with shoe boxes from Hubbell's. He looked at Carol as she took two candy canes and laid them on the counter. "How come you don't know that and you work there? They're digging up the street. Water main problem or something. They been working all day. Said they'd be done by one," he said, glancing to the wall clock. "They started filling the line a while ago." He flipped the visor of his red plaid hunting cap up, exposing a face cured with deep, leathered creases. "I don't know how there could be no pressure in the buildings. Old man Lasky's gone, shoemaker's closed. Manny's apartments are almost all empty. Anyway, they say the main ain't broke, you know. Just trying to fix the pressure." He walked to an empty stool and sat with his back to the counter. "Ain't hardly nothing left."

"You going in early tonight, Carol?" asked Frances as she hung up the phone and took the money for the candy canes.

"Yeah" she said, buttoning her coat and turning to the door. "Penney's is having their Christmas party in the back room at five."

"I'm leaving, Mom," said Tori, pulling on her black and red mittens and filling her arms with books. She made her way past Joe and Carol, excusing herself as she passed, hearing her mother call out to put her hat on.

"You leaving, Honey?" asked Carol as she drew on her

cigarette. "I'll walk down with you. Want me to carry something for you?"

Tori laid her books on the counter and pulled out a matching knit hat. She reached back and tossed a bale of hair out of her coat, exposing a narrow braid that ran down her back as thin as a lisle. She collected her books and turned to Carol. "I think I got it all."

She was tall, several inches taller than Linda, with fine, delicate bones sheathed in alabaster skin. Her eyes were all her mother's, Asian brown, expressive and rich. Her hair was long and light as Iowa corn silk, all golden over blaze. In whispered conversations the speculation of who her father was filled countless hours. But the provenance of the beauty, the seed of the golden hair and long bones, remained unknown.

"Put your hat on, Tori," Linda commanded as she rose from the deep sink. Tori tugged at her hat and rolled her eyes with an annoyed look.

"Come on, Hon, you'll need it," said Carol as she opened the door and she and Tori slipped out. "It's cold out here."

Frances wiped down the counter, glanced at Linda and smiled. "She has a mind of her own."

Linda stood at the back at the Coke dispenser with one hand on her hip. "Sixteen." She lifted her chin towards the door and shook her head. "You know they know everything by the time they're sixteen. You should hear us in the morning, before school. Between her friends calling and getting her packed up, it's just chaos. Thank God for my mother. At least she listens to her."

442

"Well," commented Frances as she waved out the window to the Greek, "they got to rebel I guess, right?"

Linda took a damp sponge and wiped down the toppings containers. "I don't know," she said after a moment without a hint of amusement. "I don't remember being difficult. She doesn't really argue with me, she just likes to discuss things."

Joe came in from the street, clapping his hands and rubbing them over the radiator. "Tony says they had to call the gas company to River, said they smelled gas in there."

"Gas?" asked Frances tapping on the grill, "what kind of gas? You mean cooking gas?"

"Yeah," said Joe impatiently, thrusting his arms down and pointing to the ground. "Gas, where they were digging up the street, like in the pipes in the ground."

"So what happened?" asked Linda, repeating a grill order to Frances.

"Nothing," he said, clapping his hands together for warmth. "Gas company came in with the testers, said nothing's wrong. Nothing's wrong." Joe thundered another clap over the radiator and pivoted to the center of the floor, speaking to no one in particular. "Could you believe it? Everyone's saying they smell gas. I even smelled it, but gas company says there ain't nothing wrong."

It happened then, on the evening of December 6, just as early darkness brightened the Christmas lights that were strung over Elizabeth and Main streets. The blast, a rocking, shuddering explosion split the brick walls of River Restaurant. Shards of glass rocketed up the worn cobblestone of Caroline Street. The ground along Main Street and a mile around shook, from the flats to the Yale Boat House and beyond. Customers and employees crawled out of the blasted doors and windows. The endless snake of traffic stopped its slow belly crawl up the grade of Main Street. Everything fell silent for a second until screams for help could be heard through the flames. Injured arms reached out from behind the broken walls and stretched into stranger's hands eager to pull survivors to safety as wind licked tongues of flames to the street.

Linda gave Joe a terrified look and ran into the middle of the street. She leaned over a car stopped in the line of traffic, straining to see towards the flats, then ran like a frightened deer down Main Street. A crowd of faces etched with deep, confused lines of fright and confusion started to converge around lower Main.

Linda's mind turned mad with panic. "Tori, oh, my God! Tori!" she screamed as drivers abandoned their cars with the doors open and factory men streamed from Burn's into the street.

Out of the grey and white smoke that rose like a cumulus cloud from the burning restaurant, the supporting two story wall of brick buckled and collapsed like a pile of children's blocks.

"Get back," screamed one of the construction workers, prodding people away."Stand back. There's a gas leak!" he shouted as he pumped his arms out to warn people away and pushed the crowd back forcefully.

Linda raced to the front of the crowd and felt a powerful

hand grip her shoulders.

"My daughter!" she screamed in a panic, looking beyond the man in a hardhat to the darkened buildings and fighting his grip. "My daughter! I live there! I have to find my daughter!"

The worker gave a menacing glance to the flames licking into the evening air from the shattered windows of the River.

"Forget it, lady," he said firming his grip and pushing her back as sirens converged on the block and police flew from their vehicles to control the scene. "You can't go in there."

Her eyes darted to the several clutches of people bent to the ground helping the injured.

"I have to find her. Please help me," she begged, ripping away from the worker. "I have to see if she's injured." She skipped to the center of the street, then turned in an awkward pirouette when she didn't see Tori among the injured. The faces in the crowd collecting on the sidewalk mirrored her distress, blurred like an impressionist water color as she called Tori's name over the sound of police yelling instructions to drivers and the wailing of survivors in shock. Then, from across the street, over the cars that couldn't move and the police vehicles that only knotted the street further, she heard Tori's voice.

"Mom! Mom!" she screamed as she and Carol ran into the street and embraced Linda. The worker, deferring to the police, spread his arms and ushered them out of the road.

They cried and embraced as the police moved the crowd further from the site, to the far side of the street. Fire hoses uncoiled and lay like pythons as firemen began to comb through the rubble for survivors under the frozen rain of water arcing into the night.

Carol turned to Linda and rasped loudly over the chaos. "I would've been in there if it wasn't for your daughter. She wanted to look at the boots in Hubbell's window. Then we crossed to Penney's window to see a coat she likes. It blew up just as we crossed Minerva."

Linda strained to see between Tori and Carol, studying the activity surrounding River with a reposed, detached look over her face. The grade of lower Main Street, from Minerva to the flats, seemed like a place out of time, an event unfolding in her world but not part of it. She saw the flames lapping at the wall of her building but knew, somehow, it would not burn. It would be there for her to return to and life would continue as it has. She heard Carol crying loudly, calling the names of her friends trapped, her words feeding the hysteria of sirens and whistles and engines converging.

It would be many hours in the darkness of that December night before the piled brick would give up the victims to the mournful chill of dawn. Until then, all movement turned to a slow and deliberate fingertip dance over shallow breaths somewhere beneath the collapsed pile of brick and tile and wood and ovens.

Linda grabbed Carol's arm and nodded for Tori to do the same. They walked quickly up Main Street towards the

Palace.

"Your husband will be worried, Carol. You better call him. There's no sense watching."

"What about Grandma?" Tori yelled to Linda as she took Carol's arm and tugged her away from the scene. "If she sees this she'll think we're in there."

Linda glanced up at the bank clock. "It's not five yet," she said, crossing the street to the Palace at the direction of a policeman trying to clear the street of cars and people. "I'll walk to the shop to meet her."

Frances stood in front of the Palace, huddled in the clutch of her own arms.

"How bad is it?" she asked, following them into the Palace and hearing Carol crying loudly.

"Awful," Linda responded, shaking her head. "River blew up. The building collapsed. There's people lying in the street hurt and there are flames coming out. Call Carol's husband, Fran. There are people trapped inside."

"Tori," Frances demanded, "get the phone book behind the candy counter and bring it here."

She filled a glass with cold water and placed it on the counter beside Carol.

"There," she said, fanning through the phone book for Carol's number. "Give her some water. Carol, drink some water."

Joe returned out of breath. "They got people trapped inside there. They don't know how many. Someone said at least four or five are dead."

A young fireman entered, "Got to close up, Fran," he

said. "Gas leak down there, Chief wants everything closed up immediately."

"Richie, when? Now?" Frances asked, hanging up the phone from Carol's husband and looking at Joe and back to Linda.

"Yeah, got to turn off the grill and lock up. You're only a hundred yards away. We got to close up the entire road. I'll be back in five minutes, Fran. They don't know the source of the leak yet. They're shutting gas service to the area now," he said as the door closed behind him.

Linda ran for the coats. She reached up and shut the radio as she pulled her coat on and put her arms under Carol's, walking her back out to the street. Frances turned the grill off as Joe reached for the lights. She locked the door and glanced down the street as she whipped her coat on.

"Where are we going?" Tori asked as they walked up the block towards Bridge Street.

Frances turned to Linda, realizing then that they had nowhere to go. She glanced over Bridge Street to Shelton and realized the traffic wasn't moving. "Come to my house. Carol too. You can stay with me."

Linda's head spun as if it was on bearings. "I have to get my mother." She looked over the bridge and saw the traffic at a standstill. "Let's walk Carol over the bridge. Her husband can't get through anyway. We can look for grandma as we walk."

"You go with Carol and I'll take Tori home with me," Frances said, hesitating at the corner. "You go ahead to the shop and then bring your mother to the house."

Linda turned up Bridge Street to Shelton. She studied the faces in the cars that passed her, watching their confused grimaces focusing on the thick smoke rising over the river. She thought her mother may have taken a ride home after hearing the explosion. She knew the word would have already gotten to the shop. She studied the posture and cadence of figures walking as their silhouettes dropped from the apex of the bridge, hoping to recognize her mother's quick step as dusk folded into darkness.

And she recalled the sound and feel and smell of the blast that sent the Sponge plant into the thin frozen air of early March a decade ago. That was a hundred yards away, just across the river. She remembered running up the street with Tori in her arms and her mother at her side. It seemed colder that night when the blast shook her out of bed and the flames seemed to touch the sky. But there were no cries for help from under brick piled four levels deep.

Flood lights were set up to illuminate the scene. Main Street was closed to traffic which was re-routed for blocks. Generators gutted noisily into full throttle as the initial panic settled into a careful and meticulous search. Rescue workers, boys and men with hardened faces, pressed their tired thighs against buckled walls. Ambulances stood in silent vigil, waiting for the injured to be pulled from the wreckage. The firemen, some dumping their heavy gear, slid down narrow caves of collapsed brick and dropped through black space into cellars deep with freezing water.

They felt their way through the dark rubble as their fingers numbed until they reached the broken or held the dead.

Through the evening shouts would rise from the rubble for quiet and the generators went silent and the scene was stilled until a muffled cry could be heard or a whimper discerned over the sound of dripping water. And so it went, through the night, rumor spinning words to exaggerated heights as to the number of dead, the identity of the missing and the names of those surviving deep in the collapsed masonry, metal, wood and glass, were whispered.

A crowd of onlookers in heavy coats lined Main Street and terraced up the rounded cobblestones of Caroline Street. From the rolling sea of faces a supernumerary officer spotted Cut Man in the crowd and waved him inside the wooden police barricade. Cut Man stood there, alone, in the center of the Main Street, empty of traffic, surrounded by the tired and mildly injured, firemen and emergency workers cut on broken glass and shards of masonry.

Thoughts of Vietnam overwhelmed him. The supernumerary looked at Cut Man with the quiet anticipation of a man refusing to be disappointed. Cut Man blinked back his fear and turned back to the crowd. Blinded by the illumination of the flood lights and deafened by the generators, he took on a hesitant expression.

He looked back at the collapsed building and the injured pressing cuts to stem the bleeding or leaning against cars from exhaustion and burns and broken skin. He glanced to the firemen with blood rolling off of cut fingers and lacerated cheeks. Then Cut Man unclipped his medic belt, knelt in the street and applied his trade of gauze and Vaseline, adrenaline hydrochloride, Avitene, Thrombin, an enswil chilled from the cold and tourniquets to bleeding wounds.

Linda's apartment was quiet that late Sunday afternoon, just after Christmas. A Santa sun catcher floated a red ghost on the kitchen wall as the last of the slanting sunlight skipped over the Housatonic and scattered watered diamonds through the window.

"Tori, Sweetheart," her grandmother inquired. "You're not eating, what's wrong?" Tori slid her fork through the pile of saffron rice and pork on her plate. Her elbow rested on the table supporting her chin in her palm. "I made the pasteles especially for you, Honey. Why are you playing with your food?"

Tori moved her fork in listless circles until the shattering crash of debris filled the kitchen again. On the street below, working into the late afternoon, the last bricks and shards of wood that was once River Pizza were loaded into the dump truck. Manny's building stood on the block like a butte in the southwestern plains, alone on the block against the darkening winter skyline. "I'm not hungry," she responded softly, slouching over the table as her elbow slid forward. She placed her fork to the plate and slid it to the center of the table.

Linda rolled her eyes to her mother and slid the plate back in shuffleboard fashion. She waited for a response. Tori toyed with her narrow braid.

Linda locked her eyes into her daughter. "Now look here," she said in a stern tone, "get your elbow off the table and eat some dinner or you can forget about the basketball game Tuesday." Tori rose and pushed her chair in. Linda placed her fork down.

"And where do you think you're going? You can just sit right back down."

Tori looked at her mother defiantly, then glanced at her grandmother sitting at the edge of her chair with concerned eyes. "I don't want to sit down. I'm not hungry," she said slowly, stroking the braid as she spoke. She looked at her mother and placed her hands on the back of the chair. "I want to move, Mom," she said. "I think we should move."

Linda knitted her brows. Confusion and surprise seemed to spar for the same space on her face. She cast her eyes to her mother whose look advised against confrontation.

"And why do you want to move?"

"Oh, Mom," Tori responded in an exasperated tone, rolling her eyes and throwing her palms open. Her words flew rapidly, with anger and certitude. "Come on. Everyone else is gone from here. There's nothing left. All the stores have closed except for the bars and the tattoo parlor and the pool hall, if you call them stores."

"And Hubbell's?" Linda offered.

"Big deal, way up the road. There's nothing left on this block and everything else is falling apart."

"And what about Frances? She doesn't count?" Linda shot back.

"Okay. Vonetes is still here. So we can move and you can still work there. So what's wrong with that? Why can't we move?"

Linda's eyes darted between her mother and Tori as seconds clicked audibly from the wall clock. Her mother dropped her eyes to her lap, then raised them to the dark emptiness where the sponge plant once stood. The silence only confirmed their differences.

"Look. It's safe here. You have a beautiful view of the river from here. Grandma can walk to the shop and it's easy for me to get to work. And we're right on the bus line."

"I don't care about the bus line! Nobody takes the bus anymore!" Tori yelled. Her face reddened with anger. "I don't want to live on a bus line. The paint in the hall is peeling and dirty. The roof leaks when it rains hard. The sidewalks are full of sand and dirt because no one bothers to sweep them except for us. You said yourself the heat isn't like it used to be. Even the factories are gone. Even they moved out. I'm embarrassed to have my friends come here."

"There's nothing wrong with this building," Linda shouted blindly.

"It's a dump, Mom!" Tori yelled back, "You don't see it. but it's a dump!"

Linda struck Tori's cheek with a crack that sounded like August thunder. Her eyes muscled to slits and her mouth tensed.

"Don't you ever say that again, Tori. Never." She stood before her daughter and handed her the phone. "Call Diane. Tell her you won't be going out tonight or the rest of the week. Maybe you just have too much time on your hands."

Linda stormed from the kitchen and into the living room, pulling the piano bench out and opened it as she spoke. Her words gushed out in a stream of anger and pain.

"I'm going to talk to Frances about letting you take some of my hours." Tori stood beside her grandmother with a startled expression. She had never witnessed this emotion from her mother and she was frightened by it. "I need some time for myself. I've been thinking about this for a long time." She threw a pile of music to the living room floor and spread it out, unsatisfied with the evenness of the field. "You're ungrateful! Just go to your room, Tori," Linda demanded, wiping her tears with her fingers. Tori's eyes welled. She glanced at her grandmother, stepped into her room, and closed the door behind her.

Linda wiped her eyes again and spread the pile of music books and loose sheet music over the living room floor. Her hands trembled as she took a piece of sheet music and carefully examined the front and back, then placed it neatly at her side.

Her mother stepped to Tori's bedroom door and closed it

tightly. She knelt beside Linda, quietly spreading a small pile until it too smoothed out. "Is there something that I can help you with?" she asked in a whisper, sitting back on her legs and touching some loose music sheets.

A moment passed in silence before Linda responded, making sure her anger was checked before she uttered another word to regret. The air brakes from the dump truck released into the cold evening for the final time as the truck roared away.

"No," Linda responded without looking up. "No, Mom. I'll be okay. I'm sorry I hit her. I shouldn't have. I've never touched her in anger. I, I don't know. I just lost control," she said with sadness. "But you know, she's sixteen. She's not a child any longer. She has to be more responsible instead of thinking of herself all the time. She's had the best we could give to her. It wasn't a lot but it was all we could do. I taught her the piano but she wanted to play the violin. So she had violin lessons. Then, no, the violin wasn't what she wanted either. So she wanted to switch back to piano. But not from me, from a piano teacher. So she had piano lessons." Linda handed her mother a pile of sheet music to stack.

"Yes," her mother responded softly, "and she plays beautifully. And she's happy playing it, practices every night without telling her. She's as good as you." Her mother placed the stack of music on the floor between them and turned to check Tori's door again, making certain it was closed. Then, in the small apartment muffled in wintery silence, she spoke with the rich, mossy tones of the Puerto Rican mountains.

"Linda." The word rolled from her lips with the deeply flavored Spanish vowels of Pileta's hills, in the tongue they shared but never used. In the moment when the decades reached their weary arms to the present, her language slipped into the calming, starry stillness of the Caribbean night. "Fuite demasiado dura con ella." *'You were too hard on her.'* "Tu sabes, Tori ya es una joven ahora." *'You know, she's a young woman now.'* "Ella no puede vivir tu vida." *'She cannot live your life.'* "Aunque ella siempre ha sabido toda la verdad, eso no quiere decir que la entiende." *'Even though she always has known the truth, that doesn't mean she understood it.'* As a deep silence filled the room, her mother looked at her with eyes that spoke of painful disappointment. "Fuiste muy dura con ella." *'You were too harsh with her.'*

Linda looked at her mother from a face hung with sadness. Then, with the tongue of her infancy, in the language that resided in the deepest reach of her heart, her response came with the clarity of the mountain night. "Yo lo sé," she said with hesitance, dropping her eyes to the floor, "Yo lo sé mamá." *'I know, I know mama.'* She raised her eyes to her mother again and continued, "Pero ella no puede faltarme el respeto tampoco." *'But she can't be disrespectful either.'* She picked up more music and held it limply before her, resting it on her thighs. "¿Qué quieres decir con que ella no puede vivir mi vida?" *'What do you mean, she cannot live my life.'* "Nadie le está pidiendo que lo haga." *'No one's asking her to.'*

456

Her mother closed her eyes and sighed. "Aayyy, Linda," she said, trying to avoid what she knew intuitively, "ella tiene distintas necesidades a las nuestras." *'She has different needs than we do.'*

Linda put the music down and looked at her mother. "¿Qué quieres decir?" *'What do you mean?'*

Her mother folded her hands on her lap and asked, "¿Cuando tú tenías su edad, quién era el hombre más importante en tu vida?" *'When you were her age, who was the most important man in your life?'*

Linda smiled faintly, finding warm comfort in the obvious. "Papi," she replied quickly. *'Daddy.'*

Her mother nodded approval. Then she said, with an animated expression, "Bien, y cuando tú y hermana se vestían elegantes el les hacia grandes alardes." *'That's right. And when you and your sister dressed up he made a big fuss over you.'* "Y tú parabas a su lado por horas y horas y aprendiste los cantos de amor que te entrenaron la voz." *'And you stood at his side for hours and hours and learned the love songs that trained your voice.'* "El te dió la confianza y la disciplina y tu creciste y te convertiste en ana mujer a su lado." *'He gave you confidence and discipline and you grew up and became a woman right there by his side.'* "Tori nunca tuvo nada de eso." *'Tori never had any of that.'* "Ella se hizo mujer sin nada de eso." *'She became a woman without any of that.'*

Linda looked down at the floor. She felt at a loss over what she could not give her daughter. "Yo lo sé mama. Yo lo sé." *'I know mama. I know.'* Then she raised her eyes again with a softness that begged for understanding. "Pero nadie tiene una vida perfecta." *'But no one's life is perfect.*

Her mother looked at her and spoke softly, almost in a whisper. "Quizás ella tenga razón. Quizás debíamos mudarnos." *'Maybe she's right. Maybe we should move.'*

Linda leaned over and gathered several sheets into her arms and turned them, one by one. Her lips quivered as she spoke. "Yo sé que ella tiene la razón." *'I know she's right,"* she said quietly. "Se que nos tenemos que mudar. Quisiera esperar hasta que ella se graduara." *'I know we have to move. I'd like to wait until after she graduates."*

Her mother closed her eyes and nodded, allowing the rumble of traffic to pass before continuing. "Entonces, que estás buscando con tanta urgencia?" *'So what are you looking for that is so urgent?'* her mother asked.

"Alguna música." *'Some music,'* Linda responded cryptically.

"Si, eso lo sé." *'Yes, I know that,'* her mother said through a soft smile.

Linda smirked and nodded, realizing that saying the obvious said nothing. Then she sighed with defeated resignation. "Está bien," she said, trying to suppress a cry, *'Well, okay,'* "quizás no importa de todos modos, *'maybe it doesn't matter anymore anyway.'* "Una noche, hace mucho tiempo, estoy casi segura que era un sabado, tu fuiste a ver a tu tío Luis. Fue justo antes que Blake se fuera. Fuimos a la a playa, pero como hacía frio, regresamos ala casa." *'One night, a long time ago, it was a Saturday, I'm sure. You went to see Uncle Luis. It was right before Blake left. We went to the beach and I was cold so we came home."* Linda picked up a thread of lace from the floor and busied her fingers with it. She couldn't speak. She felt the memory rise through her body with a python's grip, choking off her words.

"Trata de continuar hijita," *'try to continue my child'* her mother encouraged, "¿Qué tiene eso que ver con la música?" *'What does that have to do with the music.'*

"Pues," *'So,'* she said, twirling the tread to a ball and then unraveling it, "¿sabas, veces cuando eres joven equieres estar tan cerca de alguien que haces lo que se siente natural," *'you know sometimes, when you're young, you want to be so close to someone that you do what feels natural.'*

Her mother let a moment pass, a pause that allowed the weight of Linda's words to hang in the quiet apartment, and then, with a placid expression that conveyed profound grace and understanding, she responded simply, "Por supuesto," *'Of course'* "así que continúa" *'so continue.'*

"Así que," *'so,'* Linda sighed, "cuando se acabó y él estaba a mi lado y los dos mirabamos la luna sobre el rio," *'when it was over and he was lying beside me and we were looking at the moon over the river,'* "me preguntó si yo haría algo por el" *'he asked me if I would do something for him."* Linda rolled her eyes to the ceiling, tortured by the memory. Her voice rose to a crimped whisper and she continued. "De manera que yo no sabía que quedaba por hacer, entonces le dije que si, que cualquier cosa." *'So I didn't know what there was left to do so I said yes, anything."* The wan smile that creased her lips as she reflected on her own confused innocence at that moment gave way to a long, painful silence.

Then slowly, with enough space to clear Linda's mind, her mother asked, "¿Y entonces que te pidió?" *'And so what did he ask of you?"*

Linda clutched her hands for strength as her eyebrows rose and she reflected on the simplicity of his request, looking directly at her mother with tears streaming down her face, "Me pidió," *'He asked,* she said with a body that quaked, "me pedio que le cantára, porque si algo le pasaba, nunca me escucharía cantar," *'he asked me to sing for him because he was afraid that if something happened to him he would never hear me sing.'* Linda hunched over into a ball and buried her face in her palms as if she could block the regretful truth from herself.

Her mother laid her hands on her shoulders and rubbed her back, patting it gently, until the interlocutor, ever comforting, intoned calmly, "¿Entonces le cantastes?" *'so you sang for him?'*

Linda shook her head from side to side and sat upright, lifting her eyes to the ceiling again. *"No,"* she said through a pitched cry, "Le dije que no podía cantar porque no podía vocalizar algo que no fuera perfecto cuando cantára para él," *'I said that I couldn't sing because I wasn't vocalizing or anything and I wanted it to be perfect when I sang for him.* "Y le prometí que le cantaría cuando él regresára," *'and I promised him I would sing for him when he returned.'*

460

Her mother laid her hands over Linda's and tapped them lightly until the crying dissipated to staccato breaths punctuating the room. "Entonces, ¿qué es lo que estás buscando?" 'So, what are you looking for?' she asked, sensing something was missing.

Linda wiped her face with her palms and looked at her mother. Her voice caught a few times before it settled to a sad whisper. "Asi que, de cualquier manera, había una canción qua él le gustaba. Era de una opera. Él no sabía el nombre. *'So, anyway, there was a song that he liked. It was from some opera. He didn't know the name of it.* "Así que fuimos al piano y la tocamos mientras yo trataba de tatarearla para escribir las notas." *'So we went to the piano and I tried to write down the notes as he hummed it.* "Siete notas." *'Seven notes.'*

Her mother scanned the floor strewn with sheet music and thin music books. Then she looked back to Linda and asked, "Esas notas están aquí en algún lugar en esta pila?" *'So those notes are here, somewhere in this pile?'* And then, without waiting for the reply, without regard to the natural sequencing, but sensing, sitting amid the collection, that a turn should be relinquished, she followed up with another question. "Pero," *'So,'* ¿por qué las quieres ahora?" *'why do you want them now?'*

"Porque...," *'Because...,'* she said, stopping to let the silence comfort her.

Her mother gathered some music and then, laying it in a neat pile at her side, asked, "¿Por qué Linda?" *'Because why, Linda.'*

"Porque eso es lo único que me queda, mama," 'Because that's all I have left, Mom,' she cried as she opened her hands to the music strewn over the floor, "siete notas," 'seven notes.' And she continued, "Siete notas de una canción que ni siquiera conozco." 'Seven notes to a song that I don't even know.'

A long moment passed as her mother looked at her sadly and turned to gather some of the music. She spoke in a quiet, wistful tone. "Ay, Linda," she sighed, "sabes," 'you know,' "que el amor que pierdes sin enojo es el que queda para siempre," 'the love you lose without anger is the one that stays forever." She placed the music on the floor in front of her and slowly started to look through it.

Linda turned and took a stack of music also and spoke in a calm voice, a voice edged with exhaustion and wear. "Debe de estar detrás de un hoja impresa," 'It would be on the back of a printed sheet,' she said "lo escribí por detrás." 'I wrote it on the back.'

Her mother got up and turned on the light, stopping to peer at the outline of the swans barely visible on the river through the back window. She returned to the floor thinking of their silhouettes grouped along the river bank. Their effortless skim in the flowing waters of the Housatonic was long past. They huddled for warmth now in feathered bundles along the reeds and trumpeted their noisy hunger, nuzzling stoically through the night at Pink House Cove or Hog's Island and waited for Joe and the other ice-fishermen to throw them some catch to relieve their pressing need.

They continued to pick through the sheet music slowly, with hardly a word spoken except to question some handwritten notes that Linda dismissed with a nod.

"How about this?" her mother asked, handing Linda a sheet with a hand drawn staff and lines and illegible scribble.

Linda took it and leaned back on her heels, studying it closely before speaking. Then she nodded affirmatively, "Yes," she said in a low voice, rolling her eyes to her mother, "Yes, yes, this is it."

She stared at the notes and tried to read the scribble. "From an opera, that's what it says, from an opera." She hummed the seven notes and repeated that it was from an opera. "I didn't recall writing it so illegibly."

Her mother lifted herself off the floor and groaned at the pain in her knees. "I'm too old for this," she said softly, bending to pick up the remaining pieces of music and placing them in the piano bench.

"So am I," said Linda, rising and sitting on the stool at the loom, stretching her legs.

Her mother walked to the kitchen and surveyed a supper that was never finished. She turned and stepped forward until Linda looked up. "Mi cariño," she said softly so her words would not be heard by Tori, "Esto es lo que quiero decir cuando digo que ella no puede vivir tu vida," *this is what I mean that she cannot live your life.*

Linda looked at her mother sadly. "Yo lo sé, mamá. Yo entiendo." *'I know mama. I understand.'*

"Estonces, ¿que vas a hacer con la música?" *'So what*

will you do with the music?'

Linda shrugged. "Nada, me imagino. No por ahora."
'Nothing, I guess. Not right now.' "Solo guardarla en un
lugar que yo sepa donde esta." *'Just save it where I know
where it is.'* "Voy a comenzar a entrenarmi voz de nuevo."
'I'm going to start training my voice again.' "Necesito
mejorarla. Siempre me he sentido limitada." *'I need to
improve the range. I've always felt limited.'* "Supongo que
podría practicar en la iglesia cuando no hay nadie." *'I
figure I can practice at the church when no one is there.'*
She went to the kitchen window and looked across the
river to the barren site of the sponge plant. "Sabes, cuando
murio papi todo cambió. Luego, cuando Tori era joven todo
era dificil." *'You know once daddy died, everything
changed. Then when Tori was young it was hard.'* Linda
turned back to the kitchen and started to clear the table.
"Pero ya no me necesita como antes." *'But she doesn't
need me like she used to.'* He estado esperando por el
momento adecuado, pero ya no puedo esperar más." *'I've
been waiting for the right time but I can't wait any longer.'*
"Ya no soy tan joven." *'I'm not young anymore.'*

"Pero no tienes maestra." *'But you have no teacher,'* her
mother said as she dried the glasses.

Linda shrugged again. "Y qué," *'So,'* "no puede dejar que
eso me detenga." *'I can't let that stop me.'* "Solo puedo,
tratar mamá." *'I can only try mamma.'* "Aún tengo los
cantos de Izzye que papi me enseñó." *'I still have the songs
daddy taught me.'* "Empezaré ahí y veré que pasa." *'I'll
start there and see what happens.'*

Her mother closed the cabinet door and looked at Linda with hesitant eyes. "No se si podrás hacer eso sin una maestra, *I don't know if you can do that without a teacher.*" "Me temo que te decepciones." *I'm afraid you may be disappointed.*'

Linda cast her eyes to the river, then turned them back to her mother, watered and swollen. "No tengo nada que perder, mamá." *I have nothing to lose, Mama.*'

And in the stillness of that December night, with a flick of her eyebrows, the interlocutor nodded quiet acquiescence and a somber, "Sí."

"I don't know. Some of what I work on at the office bothers me."

Rennick uncrossed his legs and took a sip of old coffee. "Like what? Why does it bother you?"

"The corporate mergers and tax planning. I was involved in the first inversion, that's when a domestic corporation is taken over or merged with a foreign corporation and the headquarters moves off shore, usually to a country with low corporate rates. The first one happened a few years ago. We advised a domestic oil company on moving to Panama. So they still maintain offices domestically but the headquarters is legally in Panama, a low tax country. It bothers me because it erodes the domestic tax base. See, the companies love the political stability of this country but they don't want to pay taxes to support it."

"I never heard of that, an inversion," said Rennick with a smirk. "I can see where you would rather not be associated with that. I'm surprised Congress allows it."

"Well, they wrote regulations but we work around them. Most of the regulations are ineffective. The regs are always a few years behind the latest tax mechanics. By the time the regs catch up the industry is on to some other structure. These companies and the executives, the wealthy, they have the resources to get the best advice and to influence legislation. My firm has a large lobbying arm. We make a lot of money advising on legislation favorable to our client base. And I do a lot of expatriate work, citizens denouncing their U.S. citizenship and moving overseas to escape estate and income taxes here. It just doesn't feel right to me. Maybe because of my Marine experience I think about this stuff too much. The rich don't want to fight the wars or pay taxes. They want someone else to fight the wars. So it bothers me that I am part of this process."

Rennick stretched and leaned forward, resting his elbows on his knees. "You know you can do some other kind of legal work. You don't have to continue to do that kind of work."

"I know, you're right. The problem is the money is so good. So I rationalize it and figure if I don't do it someone else will, so I just keep doing it. I've been compromised."

Rennick leaned back, shook his head in agreement, and picked up his coffee cup. "So, did you remember to bring the letter from your brother? Last time you said you found it in some of the things you were cleaning out."

"Yeah," Blake said enthusiastically, fishing a folded

piece of dog- eared lined notebook paper from his pocket and peeling it open. "You want me to read it or do you want to read it yourself?"

"No, I'd like you to read it to me. When is it dated anyway?"

"Oh, that's interesting, too. It's dated December 24, 1968. I didn't really get it until February or March. You know, once you get in country they start moving you around, so it didn't find me until a couple of months went by."

"I see. So by then you had been through some rough times."

"Yeah," Blake responded ruminatively, raising his eyebrows and nodding in agreement. "Anyway, this is what he wrote."

Blake looked down at the letter, hesitated for a moment, then looked back up at Rennick and smiled. "I'm going to read it verbatim. You have to remember, my brother was the smarter one of us. He's also kinder and more relaxed than I am." Blake looked back down at the letter. "Okay, so I'm just going to read it. Are you ready?"

"Yeah, go ahead."

"Okay."

'Dear Blake,

It's Christmas Eve and I just got off the phone with Mom. It is the first time I called since I left over a year ago now. Needless to say, it was an emotional conversation. There is much I want to say to you. Now that I have your address I hope this gets to you before you leave for Vietnam. I'm sorry that I was not around to see you off when you left for the Marine Corps. Of all the difficulties my decision has cost me, that is the one that I regret the most. My life here in Canada is starting to settle down. There is an entire fugitive society up here that is supportive and has, of necessity, become my new family. They are arranging for me to call mom a few times a month so she won't be worrying so much. I miss you and her very much, and even Dad, despite our differences.

Anyway, I want to congratulate you on getting through boot camp. I never had any doubt about your ability. Mom told me in a letter I received several weeks ago that you wore my high school jacket every day during your senior year. She also told me that you took the brunt of Dad's anger at me. I am sorry if I caused him to harm you in any way. I am so moved by your continued acceptance of my position and your defending me to him, sometimes at great risk to yourself, especially when he is drunk. I want you to know that I pray for your safety every day.

Well, I'll be going now. I hope this letter finds you and, more importantly, finds you well. Please write when you have the time. I want you to know that I am very proud of you and speak of you with the highest regard to my friends here in Canada.

It is your duty to serve our country. It is my honor to be your brother.

Love always, Chase.'

Blake looked up at Rennick.

Rennick pursed his lips and nodded, "When did you say

that was written?"

"December 24, 1968."

"And you carried that around with you since then?"

Blake looked at Rennick and shook his head, "Yes. It's what I treasure most."

"I understand that entirely." Rennick studied his appointment calendar and spoke without looking up. "I'll see you in a month, Blake."

Dougy sat on a stool, spreading both regional newspapers on the counter, the New Haven Register and the Bridgeport Post. He scanned the front page of each with a finger running over each column. Cut Man looked up from an old Evening Sentinel of the same date, thirty years earlier. That was his daily routine before work since the Evening Sentinel ceased publishing a few years earlier. Cut Man's old Evening Sentinel was flatter than a folded paper bag and nearly as brown. He called out to Frances the obituaries and the town meeting news and the police blotter, then read some selected ads and aired out the dates of the sidewalk sale. He looked at Dougy with a fish-eye rolled into the mirror.

"What's new, Doug? Anything happening I ought to know?" Dougy sipped his coffee and glanced into the mirror. "Nope, nothing new in here. This here's got no local news now. Don't get good high school sports anymore. What's new with you?"

"With me? Nothing. Except I think I got toe fungus. Did I tell you that already?" Cut Man laughed into the mirror and spoke to Dougy's reflection. "Man, my head is going bad. I can't remember who I told that to already. Did I tell you that yet?"

Dougy lifted his eyes to the mirror and watched a smile brighten Linda's face. Frances gave him an eye and flipped the eggs on the grill. "No, Cut Man, I don't think you told me that yet. But I'm sorry to hear that. Is it related to the restless legs thing you got?"

Cut Man turned the page of the Sentinel and scanned the sports section, preparing to read about his school-boy friends at the top of their game a generation ago. "No, Doc said they ain't related but I don't know. You don't know who to believe anymore, you know."

Dougy shook his head in agreement, "This is true, Cut Man, you just don't know who to believe anymore. But I got some news for you here. The Register has this article about Great Nation's Bank in Ansonia." Dougy put his finger on the text and read it to Cut Man. "Says the board of directors has authorized the bank to seek professional advice to explore the acquisition of other banks to take full advantage of the new bank holding company structure. Says they want to maximize the value of the stock to the shareholders by acquiring added value holdings, whatever that means."

"Yeah, all them banks have the same idea, seems like I'm reading about that a lot. They all changed to that holding company thing. I don't know what that is. All I know is I still go and cash my paycheck and pay my mortgage."

470

"Didn't you buy any shares of Birmingham when it went public a few years ago? Seemed like everyone wanted to buy some. Think I paid ten dollars a share, now it's up to twelve or thirteen. I don't check it every day like some people."

Cut Man took a bite of his sandwich and faced Dougy in the mirror. "You know, I thought about buying some shares but, you know, me and some of the guys at work, at the dump, you know, we figured who was going to buy it from us when we want to sell it. I mean, it got the big fancy bank holding company thing but that don't mean anything. So I didn't buy any. Didn't have any money to buy it with anyway so what would I do? Have to borrow money to buy it? That ain't for me, borrowing money to buy the shares, then I don't know who I would sell it to and for what price."

Dougy turned from the mirror and put his coffee down. "I think you're missing the whole point, Cut Man. The market, you know the stock market, that's supposed to provide the market to sell the shares. So when you want to sell them the theory is somewhere out there someone that trades in the markct will be a willing buyer and will buy them from you."

"Yeah, I know that's the theory but who even knows about Birmingham Bank or whatever it's called, Bancorp or something? And you don't know what it will sell for and then you got to pay a commission or something then pay the tax if you make money. And from what I understand you can lose money. So for me, me and the guys at the dump, you know, that's not for us. You read the local papers, you know, seems like the rich people bought most of the shares, and the officers and directors, so they control everything now. That ain't for me."

Dougy turned back to the mirror and took a sip of cold coffee. "Yeah, I understand. I'm a lot older than you so I had some money hanging around so I bought some shares. It's not much but me and the wife, we figured, why not? But that was several years ago. It hasn't gone up much since then. Now it seems like it's starting to move because banks like Great Nation, they're announcing they want to make value added acquisitions. I don't know, we'll see." He met Cut Man's eyes and gave him a wink. "Must be that value added stuff."

"Yeah, I don't understand that value added stuff anyway. And another thing I don't understand. One of the guys at the dump, he knows a lot about this stuff. He says all these banks that sold stock, they were mutual savings banks. He says that means that the depositors basically owned those banks. So I don't get it how they are selling shares of stock to the depositors who own the bank anyway. It don't make no sense to me, buying something you already own."

Dougy curled his lip down and shook his head. "I never thought of it that way, Cut Man. But I think your buddy is right. The depositors might own the bank, they certainly are responsible for the success of the bank. And the officers, they have a lot to do with it too, but they get paid for that. I think they offer the shares to the depositors

472

first. Maybe that's how it works. Maybe that's how they get the advantage. They get first dibs on the shares. Then when the price goes up they can sell them at a profit. Them and the officers and directors, they get to buy in too. Course, they all hire these Wall Street advisors. They get a nice fee for doing that."

Cut Man looked at Dougy in the mirror, sipped his coffee and shook his head. "That still don't make sense to me. Maybe me and the guys at the dump, maybe we're too stupid to understand this, but the way I see it, they ought to be giving the depositors the money they collect from the shares. We talked about it a lot at the dump. We figure the value of the bank when they had public offering, it's the depositors that own that. It ain't for the bank to sell. Seems like a scam to me, to be buying what you own. And people like me, people that don't have a lot of money, we have to borrow the money to buy what we own? That confuses me. What's the bank going to do with the money anyway? Anyone say that?"

"Well," Dougy said, standing up preparing to leave, "I think most folks don't really think of it like that. I guess the bank will expand or something. Give bonuses out to the executives and board of directors, that's what they do."

"Yeah," Cut Man responded, getting more irritated, "that don't make no sense either, giving them bonuses for doing their jobs. And then trying to sell the equity of the bank to the owners. That don't make no sense."

"I don't know," Dougy said, shaking his head with confusion but acknowledging his point. "You know, the

473

real money is thinking ten years from now when they figure interstate banking will start and then some big bank will swoop in and take over these smaller banks. Then the share price goes up and people sell and make money. That's the way it's supposed to happen. Anyway," Dougy said as he laid his money on the counter, "keep me posted on that toe fungus you got."

"Morning, Cut Man, Dougy," Izzy chirped, strolling past the counter to the parlor for an empty table. "Morning, Fran," he said as a large, heavy-set man with thinning white hair falling over his ears trailed him. The contents of a canvas pouch, nearly buried under the drop of his distended belly and cinched on his low slung belt, bounced against his thigh. His arms pinned at his back as he tried unsuccessfully to slip his jacket over his broad shoulders.

The heavyset man rifled his unkempt hair with his thick fingers and studied the mirrored walls and pressed ceiling, then turned to the counter and the raised, silver fountains. "So," he said softly, pulling out a chair and causing it to squeal over the tile floor, "this is the place that you talk of always." He dropped into the seat and rested his forearms on the table. He pulled the chair in and fidgeted with it before yanking his pants up to free them from binding him, exposing drooping white socks that drifted loosely at his ankles. His shoes were worn and clumsily tied with black and brown shoelaces strung together like a line of sheets fastened for a prison break.

The end of his belt, worn and cracked, floated out over his side.

"Morning, Izzy," said Linda, sliding two cups of coffee in front of them. "Not at the counter today?"

"Good morning, Linda. No, no counter today," he responded with a cheeky grin that seemed to swell his pillowed, morning eyes. "This is my brother, Byron. He's my older brother."

Linda smiled and extended her hand as Byron began to rise, catching his legs under the chair and tipping it back until she caught it from falling and righted it. "Hi," said Linda pleasantly, while she set the chair under him. "Let me get that for you." She took his extended hand as he attempted to stand, hooking the pouch under the table. "Oh," she exclaimed beneath a laugh, "it's so tight in here. You're having some difficulty, aren't you? Nice to meet you."

"My pleasure," Byron said, swinging the pouch out to free himself. "But I'm stuck on my tools."

"He never told me he had an older brother."

"Well," Byron said in a shallow voice as he sat down, "you can't believe everything he tells you."

Izzy looked at Linda and clapped his hands over a laugh. "That's just his way of distracting you from the truth, Linda. He's older. And quieter."

"Everyone's quieter than him," Byron said with a gnarled brow. The phone rang as Frances shouldered the receiver and took the order. Linda cast a nervous eye at the customers gathered at the grill. "Well," she asked, "do you both want breakfast?"

"I'll have my usual," said Izzy as Byron studied the glass enclosed menu between the mirrors.

"I'll have pancakes," Byron mumbled with a satisfied look on his face.

"Oh," Linda frowned, "we don't have pancakes. That menu board hasn't been changed in years. Teddy used to do pancakes. Sorry. How about something else?"

"Teddy was Frances's brother," Izzy explained as Linda waited patiently with her pencil on the small white pad. "He passed about ten years ago."

"We have muffins, eggs, simple omelets, Portuguese rolls, toasted rolls, and..."

"How about a toasted Portuguese roll?" Byron interrupted.

. "Sure, buttered?" she asked, turning away.

"Fine," Byron nodded. "Toasted and buttered."

Toasted and buttered. Toasted and buttered anything was difficult for the small grill to handle once the lunch orders started calling in. Grill space was limited in an ice cream parlor. It wouldn't exist at all but for Teddy's inspirational moment when he decided to retrofit the grill into place. Like a hearth in winter, the little grill facing the customers brought them in all year. The space between the radiator and the grill filled as customers paced as if on a leash run, rubbing their hands and stamping their feet to ward off the cold in the nestled warmth of Vonetes. And Frances chatted and smiled and laughed with each of them, talking while prodding the grill items with her

476

spatula, teasing and tapping and turning it all, then whisking it off for the double bagged wrap.

"Okay," said Linda, coming to a deserved halt in back of the candy case. "So what would you like?" She turned the old scale's wheel to one pound and wiped the remnants of the last candy order from the dented brass bowl, then looked at Byron with an accommodating smile.

"I don't know," he said as he stepped back from the counter to take it all in."I guess you can just mix it all up, a little of each."

"Do you want dark chocolate as well as milk?"

"Yeah. Yeah, I guess. It's for the guys at work. Not all for me."

"Oh," Linda said as she reached down out of sight, her fingers, like a carnival game, dropping hands full of chocolate covered caramels and pecans and almonds and crackers and toffee into the brass bowl."And where do you work?" Then she rose quickly and appeared at the break between the candy case and the candy register. "How about white chocolate? Do you want some white chocolate with that?"

"Oh, sure, that'd be great," he responded as she disappeared again. "I work at Bankos."

"Oh," she said as she examined the scale and dropped two more toffees into the dented brass bowl to top off the pound. "What do you do there? I usually go to New Haven or the city for my music."

"I fix instruments. They hide me in the back most of the time. I repair instruments."

She slid the candy into a white box, then tapped it lightly to make it fall into place. "I sing at church, St. Mary's, when I'm not here." Linda glanced at the tool pouch hanging from his belt. "Is that what your tools are for?"

Byron reached down and touched the pouch. "Yes. It's troublesome, carrying this around sometimes, but it's convenient to have the little things I use most often right here."

Linda closed the box and taped the front and sides. "That's seven," she said, handing him the box and taking a ten from him and turned to the register. "You don't tune pianos, do you?"

Byron's neck hinged as he studied the inlays of the pressed ceiling. "Huh?" he responded, wrenching his neck back down.

"Pianos," Linda said, handing him his change and looking up at him. "Do you tune pianos?"

"Oh, pianos?" Byron replied as if surprised by the question, stuffing the change into his pocket. "Yes, I do. I'm sorry, I was admiring the ceiling."

"May I ask you how much you charge?" asked Linda. "The piano at church needs a tuning badly."

Byron hesitated for a second, sensing a need in her tone. "Well," he asked softly, "that depends. Who's paying for this? You or the church?"

"I am. It's for me."

Byron turned to Izzy. He stood at the door impatiently running his hand over the shoe horn sticking out of his back pocket. "I paid for breakfast," he said. "I'll meet you in the store."

"Okay," Byron responded. "I'll be right there." He followed Linda as she walked back to clear their table. "It's free if I don't have to miss any work. When is a good time for you? I work at the store during the week, and half a day Saturdays. So the weekends or evenings are better for me."

Linda stepped to the deep sink, emptying the cups in the drain and then gently dropping them into the hot, sudsy water. "Is Saturday afternoon good?" she asked, glancing at Frances handling the crowd at the grill.

"Is two okay?" he asked, stepping away from the counter.

Linda grimaced, "How about three? They have confessions until two-thirty."

"Three is fine," Byron replied with a smile as he raked his hair back. "This Saturday?"

"Do you know where it is?" Linda asked, stepping to Frances's side and pointing. "It's right up the street, about half a mile."

"I know where it is. I've driven by it before."

"How was the roll?" Frances asked as Byron wrestled into his jacket.

"Excellent," he commented, holding up the box. "Must be the grill. And I bought chocolates, couldn't resist." He rested the glass door against his foot as he pulled his jacket over his shoulder. "I'll be back again," he said as the door closed behind him.

"Don't leave the chocolates in the car for too long, they'll melt," Frances instructed as he left.

Max sat back and looked at Marshall. They had case books stacked in piles on the large table in Max's legal library and the library computer wired into electronic legal research sites. "So the dual sovereignty issue is unresolved in Connecticut. I think we have a pretty good shot at winning that argument."

Marshall looked up from the computer and nodded at Max. "Yes, we have a shot at it although the case law in other jurisdictions usually recognize the dual sovereignty of the federal government and the states so they can both prosecute separately. If he was convicted in the federal trial the state wouldn't bother. But he got off so now they figure all the co-defendants will turn state's evidence and nail him. Thing is, if you lose the dual sovereignty argument and he gets acquitted at the state trial then the insurance company might settle figuring they may not prevail on the insurance claim. So I think we also argue in pretrial that the insurance claim forms Biller completed to submit his claim of sixty million should be excluded based on his Fifth Amendment rights. The state statutes required him to answer the questions on the claim form or forfeit his right to recover the insurance claim from Protection Mutual."

"So the argument is that Biller's responses to the Protection Mutual claim should not be admissible because they violate Biller's Fifth Amendment right against self-incrimination? "

"Right, since the state insurance statutes require the complete cooperation of the insured then that is the state action that we argue is compelled testimony and must be excluded from the trial."

Max looked at Marshall incredulously. "What the hell did he say on the forms that would incriminate him anyway? That makes no sense at all that we have to argue to exclude the claim in a trial for insurance coverage. No one is going to believe that."

"Well, if we argue right no one will ever know that. We can't keep the claim and his responses out of evidence but we can have any damaging parts redacted due to Fifth Amendment privileges. What he said wasn't all that incriminating. He just talked about his relationship with Staber, the psychic stuff and the phone calls he made to him for the water treatment plant. And the money, the money he paid him for that work. His claim states that Staber, that guy who installed the water treatment system at the soda plant, wanted him to purchase an Ohio business that they would have equity in but Biller wouldn't do it."

"That's in the statement Biller made in support of the claim? Even that doesn't make any sense since he said he paid Staber for the water treatment work and his psychic advice. How much did the Campos report trace to Staber from Biller or his companies?"

"I don't know. I have it somewhere here. I think it was forty thousand in checks and cash they traced and another twenty thousand that he stiffed Staber for. So

Staber couldn't pay the arsonists since he got stiffed by Biller. At least that's what the report says. Do you have the building coverage contract here?"

Max stood to stretch. "Man, I'm getting tired sitting here doing this research. I got to get to the gym by four."

"We still have an hour or so. Do you have the building insurance contract here?"

"No, didn't I tell you? They only had an oral binder for that coverage, through some company in the city. I have a copy of the Protection Mutual policy. It's a blanket policy covering the inventory, machinery and equipment. But they're disputing everything. The limits of the policy, the liability, business interruption, everything."

"The way I see it we got a shot at recovering something if we can get Biller off on the criminal charges. You don't think Pollard will turn on him, do you?"

"Pollard? No way. He is so locked into Biller he would never turn on him. Besides, the feds never even charged him so the evidence must be weak. State's just trying to take him down in a potluck deal hoping something scares him into implicating Biller."

Marshall glanced at the wall clock. "So, the collateral estoppel argument, who's writing that up? Me or you?"

Max smiled and sat down. "You. Come on, we both know you're going to spend the time to do the brief right. As you would say, 'all you want to do is go to the gym and figure out a way to get very rich quick.'"

"Well," Marshall said with a smirk, "I guess we can both agree it's getting to be a little too late to get rich quick.

482

Maybe by the time you're forty or so. I'll do it, I don't mind. So, we never really settled on this, but what is my cut if we get the state charges dropped or get him acquitted?"

"You'll remember. I was whipping you again at racquetball and I said I didn't want Lachlan involved in the Biller case. So I asked you if you were interested and we agreed you would get thirty percent of my percentage of his insurance recovery. It could be millions if we get this right."

"Oh, yes, I remember now. You were saying if you win this and make a big hit on the Birmingham takeover you would never have to work again. I remember that now very well. And you're right, you did whip me, again."

The heavy door yawned audibly as Byron entered the dimly lit vestibule. A whisper of light creased the interior double doors as he heard the muffled sound of a voice from the choir loft. He quietly slipped through, stepping into the dark nave with votive candles lapping the ruminative silence. He leaned over the back pew and stood silently, hearing the imperfections of the piano but distracted by the natural beauty of the voice. He turned to the narrow circular steps leading to the loft but hesitated and, instead, walked slowly down the left aisle. He examined the detail of the earth-toned figures of the stations of the cross cast in high relief. The stained glass windows glittered with brilliant colors that alternated between the arched stations. At the altar were life-size marble statuary gazing from their pedestals. He looked up at the impressive height of the center aisle and wrinkled his brow at the breadth of the expansive nave accented with graceful, ribbed, arches. He turned in an awkward pirouette, examining the spandrels of angels peering down at him. The sharp sound of his tool belt striking the pew caused Linda to rise from the piano and lean over the loft railing.

"Byron," she called out into the dark nave, waving her hand to catch his eye. "I'm here."

Byron turned and spotted her silhouette back lit by the soft halo of the piano lamp behind her. "Yes" he said, walking up the center aisle. "Of course I know you are there. I've been listening to you." He stopped beneath her and looked up at her smiling at him. "You're right, that piano needs some serious attention. You know," he said with a half turn and sweeping his hand over the width of the nave, "this is a wonderful church, Linda. The artwork is spectacular. The scale and the colors, it's just beautiful."

"Yes," Linda agreed, enthusiastically."Yes, it is, Byron." She rolled her eyes through the nave and around the apse. "I love it in here," she said, her words carrying through the church with the pride of something wonderful possessed. "It's dark and quiet and beautiful. That's why I practice here. It's peaceful."

"Oh, peaceful," Byron repeated as he stepped beneath the loft and out of her sight. "Is that it?"

"Be careful coming up the steps. The lighting is bad and they're narrow and winding."

Byron slowly twisted his way up where Linda greeted him again. "I really want to thank you for coming," she said nervously, hearing him breathe heavily. "The piano is back here." He followed her across the loft, stopping before the large organ whose pipes rose to the highest point of the ceiling. "This is some instrument," he said as he examined it closely. "Does it work?"

"Oh," Linda responded smartly, "it works fine. The church pays for that. It's the piano that needs help. I'm not the organist."

Byron set his tools down and quizzed her about the action and the tone and the amount of time the piano is used. He sat at the bench and ran his fingers over the keys with a mix of chords and short riffs and scales, repeating what he heard as the most troublesome individual notes and combinations. He slid off the bench and asked Linda to hold the piano lamp over the piano as he opened it and started to tool the strings and test the soundboard. He moved deftly about the instrument despite his large size, grunting occasionally when he leaned down into the body. He seldom spoke to Linda except to ask her to depress certain notes or test the pedals. She watched him silently, anxiously waiting for his next command and executing it, then waiting anxiously for the next request as the tone of the instrument improved noticeably, wire by wire.

"Okay, Linda," Byron said, suddenly standing at her side. "May I sit for a moment?"

"Of course," she replied, jumping from the bench and watching Byron take pleasure at the improvement of the sound as his large fingers ran over the keys.

"Okay," he said, rising slowly from the bench. "Your turn. It could use some heads replaced but I left them in the car and I don't want to climb those stairs again. Next time." He moved away from the piano and collected his tools. "Play," he said to Linda who was standing with her arms folded. "See how it feels."

Linda sat at the bench, playing the sacred music on the piano. "It sounds wonderful," she said, smiling brightly, "what a difference."

"Yes," Byron commented, standing beside her. "You might feel a better bounce off the wires." He stood and listened to her for a moment, then stepped to the rail and leaned over it.

"What a difference," she cooed again as she started to hum the notes of a familiar song.

"You shouldn't be humming," Byron said without looking back at her.

"What?" she asked with a smile that confirmed she didn't hear him. She continuing to play and looking up at him as he turned to her.

"Humming," he repeated, as he faced her and lifted his tool belt. "Not good to hum too much."

Linda stopped playing and looked at him quizzically. "Why?" she asked, as she rested her fingers on the keys.

"Because we tend to do it without thinking and that leads to some bad habits," he responded, holding his throat and smiling slightly. "Not right away, but over time. It's not good. If you want to sing, then sing. Maybe that's why you're aspirating your top notes."

Linda swiveled out from under the piano and faced him. Her hands were clasped over her lap like a penitent asking for mercy. She smiled at him as he ran his fingers through his unkempt hair in a vain attempt to tame it back. "How do you know that?" she asked directly, letting her smile drop.

Byron set a tool down and folded his arms over his pendulous belly. "I know," he said cryptically, moving off the rail and letting his face drop as if his response was as complete as he would provide. "Kind of a long story." He let his eyes meet hers for a second and noticed her hands, open and limp, as if asking for more without testing his patience. "You see, my brother Izzy, he has a wonderful voice, as did my other brother Sidney. You've heard Izzy sing there, at the sweet shop of yours," he said, seeming to grope for the name.

Linda shook her head and smiled at the thought, "Oh yes, he's always singing something."

"What is the name of that place?"

"Vonete's Palace of Sweets, but we just call it the Palace of Sweets or, sometimes, just Vonetes. But there's a Vonetes in Ansonia also. It can be confusing."

Byron lifted his hand in recognition. "Yes, yes, the Palace of Sweets. How can I forget all those confections. "Well," he said, "my brother Sidney is dead now. But they both toured with some of the big bands, way before your day," he said, waving his hand as if to dismiss the time that passed as not worthy of so much as a footnote in otherwise unremarkable lives. "Anyway," he continued, "me, I can't sing. I have no natural gifts."

"Oh," Linda sighed, smiling and nodding her head, "but you fix instruments?" she asked courteously, recognizing that he hadn't answered the question.

"Yes," he responded, moving his head to the side. "I have a musical background but that is not essential. We're Jews, you see. Czech Jews. My father was a classical violinist. My mother sang in Jewish theater and taught voice. That's how I learned about voice. There was only a curtain, a heavy maroon velvet curtain, between her studio and our small apartment. So we had to be quiet and we heard everything that was said. And I would ask her about different things because I had an interest. Anyway, we fled as things became dangerous. I was studying cello and composition at the time at the university. I gave voice lessons to help pay the expenses. When we arrived here of course we had no money and there was a language barrier. So I found a job at Bankos and I learned how to repair instruments."

"And you never returned to school?"

Byron raised his eyebrows. "No," he said with resignation. "I was very angry, and bitter." He dropped his eyes to her and pursed his lips with regret. "It's not good to be bitter, Linda. My brother adapted easier than I did. I withdrew into music. It was a language that I understood. I never tried to complete school. I got married a few years later. Then my son was born and that was that. Anyway," he said, as if to dismiss his personal history as irrelevant,

"I like fixing instruments. I like to work with my hands. I'm not bitter anymore. Now I'm just old. And that's why I know it isn't good to hum. It's like sticking a mute into a horn. But brass is inert. Vocal chords are not. Over time it can change the physics of the instrument," he said with a knowing smile.

Linda glanced at her watch and back to Byron, examining his heavy fingers resting on his belly. He leaned against the rail again, seeming to be in no hurry to leave. His hair seemed whiter now, framed by the distant but fading sun that illuminated the stained glass windows high above the chancel. "So, is your wife a musician?"

"Yes," he responded, shaking his head side to side. "She was a cellist. But she passed away, let's see now, about seventeen years ago."

A reverent silence filled the loft. "Oh, I'm sorry to hear that." Then, like a doe stepping cautiously to the edge of a pond, Linda spoke softly, in the narrow glow of the piano lamp. "I come here to practice my singing. I'm trying to improve my voice, to increase the range beyond the mezzo range," she said. "You see, my father was a voice teacher. He died when I was fifteen. He trained my voice but that was so long ago, I've forgotten so much. I'm no longer sure of what I recall or what I think I recall. It's been a long time."

Linda cast her eyes to the floor and rummaged through her mind. She wasn't certain if she should bring him through the past twenty years. She wondered if it mattered why she left college. She shrugged her shoulders and fidgeted with the necklace. Then she looked up at him. He appeared unhurried. "So," she continued, "when I'm here I try to remember what he said. I seem to remember his mannerisms more than anything, the way he tilted his head, or held his fingers when he would describe what he wanted. It's been so long I don't know if I'm doing it right. It's terrible when you can't trust your memory." Linda rolled her eyes into the nave and back to Byron. "I'm looking for a voice teacher. Could you help me?"

Byron lifted himself off the rail and put his hands into his pockets. He took his time and examined her with a cold distance in his eyes, knowing how demanding he could be and how guileless her request was. "I want you to sing for me."

Linda swung her legs beneath the piano and flipped through some music. "What would you like to hear?"

Byron stepped to the piano and took her wrist in his hand. A rush of nervous energy began to pulse through her when she felt his hand grip hers. "No, I don't want you to play the piano for me. I want you to sing for me. I'll key you in but I'd like to hear you a cappella." He released her hand and stepped away.

Linda swung out and stood beside the piano. He closed the music book and looked at her. "You think you're a mezzo?"

"That's basically where I left off with my dad."

"Did you ever consider that your dad capped you at the mezzo top notes to save your voice because you were so young?"

"Well, we didn't talk about it, if that's what you mean."

"Did you study Vaccai? Are you familiar with his songbook for mezzo?"

Linda smiled broadly, comforted by his familiarity with what she knew. "Yes, we did lots of songs from his songbook. And Parisotti. We used lots of his selections as well. Are you familiar with Parisotti?"

Byron smiled at her and nodded affirmatively. "Of course," he responded, pursing his lips as he thought, "How about Giordani?"

"Sure, Caro Mio Ben, my dad taught me that."

"Did he teach you 'Must the Winter Come so Soon' by Barber? It's from the opera, Vanessa. It's a great mezzo piece, pretty new."

"No, I don't think I know that, not that I recall anyway. Would Caro Mio Ben be okay? I remember that very well."

"Yes, that's fine, not a lot of range or dynamics, but it is fine for what I want to hear," Byron replied as he played several measures to key her in, then fell silent as the sound thinned to silence in the vacant nave.

She started the song with confidence, not growing into it but carrying the first note full throated, her flawless tone and the strength of her middle notes filling the church. The beauty of her voice distracted Byron until she clipped the last note of the eighth measure. His eyebrows buckled as her shoulders rose and breasts swelled with respiration. He leaned forward and grabbed her forearm, turning her until she faced the nave. "Keep singing," he whispered beneath her notes. He rose and stood at her back with his hands lightly cupped over her shoulders, "Relax and sing through. Don't be distracted by me." He moved his hands to her ribs, then walked around her and watched her lips and mouth and neck fold and swell and heard her lower notes thin out. He stepped back from her and placed his palm on her diaphragm, just beneath her breasts. Pressing it, he closed his eyes, listening to her top notes ring out with a round but diffident sound. Finally, he placed his hands under her chin and raised his eyebrows high with concern over the tightness he felt.

Byron moved back to the piano bench and moved the lamp to its original position. He looked at her in the last reach of light. "I can help you," he said plainly. "It's obvious you have had some excellent training. You have a beautiful voice. It's also obvious that you need real work on some of the fundamentals. I have to warn you, I'm a perfectionist," he said with in a serious tone. "I'm not sure you'll want to go through this. I can be very tough." He adjusted the lamp so it didn't glare into his eyes.

Linda walked to the stairs and flicked the light on to provide more illumination. "I'm willing to work at it if that's what you mean. I could be up here alone forever doing it wrong. I need someone with a critical ear."

"You say that now," Byron retorted as he adjusted his tool belt and stepped in front of her.

She leaned and turned off the piano lamp. "How much do you charge?" she asked, draping her pocketbook over her shoulder.

"I'm going to start you from the beginning. Breathing

exercises, scales, interval work. All the fundamentals. Do you want to go through all that at this stage of your life?"

"Back to Vaccai?"

Byron nodded his head silently then nodded at her knowledge, "Back to all the dead song writers. Some Italian, French, Spanish. And some lieder."

"I don't know German at all. I've never sung in German."

Byron shook his head, "I will teach you what you have to know. But it is critical to understand the lied. There is a great tradition for expressing longing in the lied. The German romantic's call it sehnsucht. It's an essential element of song that you must learn to express, to feel."

Linda gave him a confused look. He seemed bigger, in every dimension, now that he stood beside her, all tall and wide and broad. "Byron, you didn't answer my question. How much do you charge?"

"Nothing." He held his hand up knowing the argument was coming. "We're not going to talk about money. The answer is nothing. I don't need your money. You don't have any anyway. I fix instruments for a living. Voices are free. That's it. No discussion." Then he softened his tone without changing his expression. "I told you that I could be very tough but I'll make this easy for you. I don't have a social life. My son lives in California. His kids are grown. My work is my life. It's nothing for me to charge you nothing. Do you understand?"

She looked at him closely. He was old enough to have exhausted his patience long ago. She was certain it would be fruitless to try to change his mind and might only irritate him. She broke into a warm smile. "Okay, Byron," she said. "I'm not going to argue with you because I need you. I'm grateful to you. Any help you give me I really appreciate. Maybe my mom and I can cook you some good Puerto Rican food once in a while. Would that be okay?"

"Now that sounds like a deal."

Linda smiled at him. "Thank you, Byron." Linda studied him and smiled. "I am going to call you Viejo. It's a Spanish word. Do you know what it means?

"No," he responded. "I don't think I've ever heard of it."

"It means old man in Spanish. My mother is from Puerto Rico, from the mountains. It is an endearing expression for a man who is older and whom you respect. He is called Viejo."

Byron followed her down the winding stairs. "Ok, so now I am a Viejo. An old man, no?"

Linda released a quiet laugh, "No," she said, facing him as they stood before the rocking doors. "You are Viejo. You are also a viejo, but you are Viejo. Do you understand?" she asked, contorting her face as if that would make it clearer.

Byron smiled broadly. "I think so. It's a compliment, no?"

"Oh, it's a compliment, yes," Linda said with animation.

"Good!" Byron responded with eyes that sparkled despite their age. "On the occasions that you want to curse me, I'll remind you that I am Viejo."

Linda shook her head and smiled at him. "You won't have to. I won't forget."

494

"Read the first several lessons in Vaccai for next week. No singing, reading only."

"Sure," she called back.

"So," she asked, pushing open the large door and staring down the wide stone steps with him following, "is this the best time for you?"

"This is good for me, three or so," Byron continued. "Sometimes the store is busy early in the afternoon on Saturday."

"Okay. I need to get back to work by five or so. We do a big cleaning on Saturday night."

"Oh, yes, the job. The lessons will be only forty-five minutes to an hour."

"But we can have the church for about two hours."

"Yes. Well, maybe that's another problem. You've been singing wrong for two hours," said Byron looking up at the grey canopy of clouds that appeared in the western sky that hung low and full. "Looks like rain, Linda. I'll see you next week at three. I would like that you don't sing until I see you."

"But I have masses to do," she protested.

"Okay, but no range extension. I want you fresh when I see you. Actually," he said raising his palms up to emphasize his point, "it doesn't matter. We'll probably spend the entire time on your breathing. I might not have you sing a note."

"Okay, fine," Linda commented with a smile as they stood in front of the rectory. "A voice lesson with no voice."

"Exactly," Byron said as he crossed Elizabeth Street to

his car and he watched her walk away. "Do you need a ride?" he called back.

"No," she said, cradling her music to her chest like a schoolgirl dawdling home with a group of friends. "I enjoy the walk. It's only down the street. Thank you anyway."

"Don't bring any music with you next week. You won't need it."

Linda nodded her head and crossed Sixth Street, past the druggist and the empty sidewalk tables of the Italian café. Victorian lamps illuminated the sidewalks crossing the green like sugared strudel. She took a long breath and filled her head with the late August scent knowing that autumn whispers in on these muted lips, parched and dry. Above her the leaves of the beech trees hinted to fade, flagging their lithe and fey limbs to pale yellow.

She enjoyed the walk at the bottom of the day, when the late afternoon sun slanted in at long angles and pulled shadows across the green. Her memories of Blake levitated into consciousness like a recurring dream. The park benches that faced the boarded up opera house recalled the sound of his voice in laughter when plastic spoons sparred along the bottom of the cardboard sundae dish, fighting for the last mouthful of fudge and melted ice cream, and then offering it to the other. Ice cubes swirled and thinned the soda fountain drink in the lidded cup, sweating the wax and icing his fingers and rippling her laughter when he touched her neck and nuzzled close to her. Although so much time had passed the places remained and the walk was familiar and comforting.

She stopped at the corner of Main and Elizabeth, waiting for the traffic light to change. Her eyes ran over the vacant buildings, once stately, with brick and mortar worn and aged, in need of pointing, abandoned apartments with rotted frames and window sills littered with empty, rusted flower boxes. She thought of how vibrant Main Street was just two decades ago. The light turned and silenced the rumble of the cars and trucks as she looked across to Frances leaning into the window with a grand smile, waving her spatula from behind the small grill.

State's Attorney Ronald White stood beside the jury box and continued the cross examination of Biller. "The testimony of the SNET official stated that phone records showed hundreds and hundreds of calls back and forth to Wade Staber from your Ohio office and the Shelton plant as well as many the day and night of the fire. Can you explain all those calls?"

Biller looked at White impassively and spoke slowly. "As I said a hundred times, Wade was my advisor and he was working on the water treatment system for me. I don't really remember any of the calls, been a long time."

"He called your home the night of the arson. Do you remember that?"

"He called my wife that night, not me."

"What about the $10,000 Pollard brought to Staber in a shoebox to the McAlprin Hotel. The record shows you cashed a company check the day before for $10,000."

"I don't know nothing about any $10,000 that Pollard

brought to Wade. The cash I got the day before got nothing to do with the arson or Staber."

White raised his voice and walked towards the witness stand with an agitated look on his face. "Then tell me how Staber got the $10,000 in cash."

Biller raised his eyes to White and smirked. "I don't know. I suppose he got the money from the same angels that unlocked the cell doors for him."

"That's an interesting answer, Mr. Biller. Did your attorney tell you to say that?"

Biller smiled widely. "My attorney? No, that came from me."

"Was money tight at the plants?"

"Yes."

"Then why did you give Staber a check for $20,000 at LaGuardia the day before the arson?"

"That was for the water treatment system. Staber saved me $30,000 a year by advising me to use the canal water for the plant. That $20,000 didn't mean nothing to me."

"I bet it didn't. It bounced, didn't it?"

"If you say so. Lots of checks were bouncing about that time."

"But you made good on that check the next day, didn't you?"

"I try to pay all my bills, Mr. White, don't you?"

"That's funny, Mr. Biller, because another $450,000 of checks bounced that week and you didn't make good on any of them for years. And your company was using the employees' social security and federal tax withholding to pay bills. Do you remember that?"

Biller gave White a derisive look. "I made good on all my bills, Mr. White, and you know that. Every one of them, including Staber. I felt obligated to him to pay for the water treatment system and because he saved me all that money."

"Oh, so you paid him $20,000 you really didn't have despite the fact that your plant manager told you the water treatment system was not going to work because it made no technical sense. Do you remember Leo Faraday telling you that? Or does that slip your mind also?"

"Look, that's what Leo said but that don't mean it's right. The problem with Leo and all you educated people is that you think everyone else is stupid. But I get lots of good ideas from people sweeping the floor. What Leo said don't mean nothing."

"Then why was he managing one of the plants?"

"He was there when I bought the plants, that's why."

White walked to his assistant and took some notes in his hand. His tone softened. "Really, then why did you give Staber a check for $2,500 in mid-March, after he became a suspect?"

"Because Wade needed the money and I didn't think he had anything to do with the arson at that time. A man's innocent until he's proven guilty, ain't he? That was the least I could to for Wade."

Max Cruz approached the witness stand as he reviewed his notes. "So, Dr. Sleginger, can you tell the Court what kind of doctor you are?"

"Sure," Sleginger said enthusiastically. "I am a clinical psychologist."

"Were you asked to examine and give an opinion on the mental health of Wade Staber in 1975?"

"I was. Myself and Dr. Delores Kaufmann. She's a psychiatrist."

"And please tell the Court who asked you to conduct that examination."

"His attorney, Wade Staber's attorney asked us to conduct that examination as he prepared his defense of Mr. Staber. I believe he wanted to use an insanity defense to the federal charges."

"And what were the findings of Mr. Staber's mental state at that time?"

"My examination, along with Dr. Kaufmann, found Mr. Staber to be psychotic, a paranoid who suffers from delusions."

"And how did you examine Mr. Staber at that time? That is, how much of an examination was performed by you and Dr. Kaufma?"

"Oh," Sleginger responded immediately, "we examined Mr. Staber extensively. Many interviews and tests over many days and hours. It was extensive."

"Did you testify at the federal trial, Doctor?"

"No, sir, neither I nor Dr. Kaufmann testified at that trial."

"And why was that, Dr. Sleginger? Why did you not testify as to the mental state of Mr. Staber at the federal trial?"

"Because Mr. Staber rejected our findings. He disagreed with our finding that he had no concern for what he had done and had a sense of invulnerability."

"Is there a name of this condition?"

"Well, we call it a psychopathic structure."

"Thank you, Doctor. One more question, please. Would you say this condition would cause Mr. Staber to say he can talk to flowers and animals, that he spoke to J. Edgar Hoover in a dream four days after Hoover's death, and that he can predict the future?"

"That would be consistent with his condition, yes."

"Thank you, Doctor Sleginger."

"Dr. Kaufman, you just heard Dr. Sleginger say that you examined Mr. Staber before the federal trial and did you examine Mr. Staber for this trial as well?"

"I did."

"I am going to show you a copy of that report and I would like you to verify your signature and read the date of the report for the Court, please."

"Certainly," Dr. Kaufman said, taking the report from Cruz and flipping through it. "Yes, this is my report and my signature. The report is dated March 12, 1983, about three months ago."

"Thank you, Doctor. And what did you find?"

"Mr. Staber still believes he can cause people headaches by concentrating during the trial. That indicates he still suffers from delusions and paranoia. And his belief that he talks to bees and lambs makes me believe he is still as psychotic as when he was examined in 1975. He describes a sense of being framed in this trial."

Cruz took a moment and looked at the psychiatric report. He flipped several pages until he stopped and read from one. "Is it true that in your report that I have in my hand that Mr. Staber told you he once went on a trip for the Central Intelligence Agency to Austria to keep the Russians from getting control of the Unicorn Horn because it gives power to people?"

"Yes, he did make those statements to me."

"And did he talk about angels as well?"

"Yes, he said he saw ceramic angels that had wings in a dream but because he has seen real angels and they do not have wings..."

"And is that in the report I have in my hands and that is part of the court record?"

"Yes it is."

"Did you witness any conversations between Mr. Staber and his attorney regarding the insanity defense?"

"Yes, I did."

"How would you characterize those conversations, Dr. Kaufman?"

"How would I characterize those conversations?" Kaufman asked. "Heated. Very heated."

"Thank you, Doctor. No more questions."

Martin Short handed the letter to Staber and asked him to examine it. "Did you write this letter?" he snapped.

"I did," Staber responded sheepishly.

"Who is Mary Arniss?"

"Just a friend from Memphis."

"Did you write this letter while you were in prison?"

"Yes."

"In that letter to Mary Arniss, did you tell her that you were milking the cow and preparing to sell your testimony to the highest bidder?"

Staber looked dazed. He looked down at the letter and shook his head affirmatively.

"Speak up, Mr. Staber, so the court stenographer can record your response. Did you state that you were milking the cow and preparing to sell your testimony to the highest bidder? Tell the court."

"Yes, I did say that in the letter."

"Did you agree to testify as a witness for the State of Connecticut against Mr. Biller and Pollard, the two defendants here?"

"I did."

"Thank you, Mr. Staber." Short walked to the counsel table and took notes from Max Cruz after conferring with him briefly. "Now then, Mr. Staber, isn't it true that you predicted, in writing, that a higher form of life exists in outer space? Didn't you also write that you have seen this higher form of life?"

Staber thought for a long moment, then responded, turning towards his attorney. "I did. That is, I did write that and I did see the higher form of life."

"Really," Short responded incredulously. "And what did they look like?"

"Well, they exist as a sort of a feeling, of a knowledge

they're there."

"But isn't it true that you said they visited you in your cell in Bridgeport? You remember, you couldn't post bail after you were arrested and you said they appeared to you. Didn't you say that?"

"I did," Staber answered, casting Short a defiant look.

"For the record, your Honor, at the deposition, the witness referred to the higher form of life as angels. And what did the angel tell you?"

Staber looked at Short, then turned towards the jury. He spoke clearly and earnestly. "I had prayed for days for my release. It was hot. There wasn't even a fan in the cell. I was lying on the cement floor, my feet were in the toilet bowl to keep cool. I prayed. I had just completed a book about angels." Staber turned back to Short and glanced at his attorney before turning to the judge and back to the jury. "I was thinking about the Lord's disciples and how they had been in prison and then were magically freed. I was laying there praying and thinking about that and an angel of the Lord came to me, like the Holy Spirit, and said my bond had been made and I would be released. I was thinking about the jail doors opening and then, amazingly, the 12 cell doors, electronically operated in a wing where I was, suddenly sprang open. They opened wide. It sounded like a freight train. I'll never forget that sound," he said wistfully.

Short shook his head and turned towards Cruz and the defendant's table. "And were you freed?"

"Yes."

Short conferred with Cruz again, took his note pad and walked towards the jury. "Mr. Staber," he asked, handing him a list of names, "what I have handed you is your witness list from the federal trial. Do you recognize it?"

Staber scanned the document and looked at Short. "Yes, I do."

"Please read the names of the witnesses you hoped to call on your behalf in the federal trial to the jury."

"Sure," Staber replied, looking down and reading from the list. "William Colby, former head of the CIA, Richard Helms, another former head of the CIA, Richard Nixon, Bishop Fulton Sheen, Henry Kissinger and Jack Anderson." He looked back up at Short.

"Did any of them testify on your behalf at the federal trial?" Short asked politely.

"No," Staber answered quietly. "But if they were allowed to testify they could have helped me."

Short turned his back to the witness stand and walked towards the jury box. He turned quickly and whipped off his reading glasses. "So, you believe in angels, don't you?" he thundered. The packed courtroom was stone silent.

Staber leaned forward in the witness chair and placed his hands on the rail. "I do believe in them," he said softly. "I survived in prison because of angels. Many did not. Praise God for sending me angels. Yes," he said with certainty, "I do believe in them."

Short turned his back to Staber and walked to his counsel desk. "No more questions, your Honor," he said dismissively.

Marshall walked to the side of the pool with his hands buried in the pockets of his white pants. He was neatly belted and perfectly creased, his cuffs riding casually over his boat shoes. His polo shirt had alternating lines of Kelly green and white, conspicuously selected with a prominent designer logo.

The pool area of the Deer Run Country Club is enclosed with cream-colored slat boards spaced just enough to allow the curious a view. The stucco and stone walls of the club resembled a Mediterranean resort, somewhere between the French Riviera and a Sardinian waterside mansion. The pool is Olympic in dimension but not in function, with a wading area and a kiddy area safely cordoned off. It is underused since most members have their own anyway, it being a feature left over from the seventies, before affluence became common and central air conditioning made the cooling features of the pool superfluous except to children.

Max floated along the side of the pool, luxuriating in the heated water, then turned when he noticed Marshall and rested his head on the frame. Water on the pool surface diffused the sun to thousands of liquid diamonds. He raised his muscular arms out and rested them over the pool wall, levitating his rippled stomach and broad chest to the surface. Water drained from his stomach and dripped into the pool. His hair was wet and lay back from his face, a neatly lined drape of ebony falling flawlessly to his bronzed shoulders. Dark sunglasses wrapped his eyes, shielding him from the undeserving world but allowing him to observe. Across the pool his third wife lounged with a book over her stomach, chatting amicably with other members.

Marshall stopped and stooped over. "Max, the word is starting to hit the street." He filled a palm with water and dribbled it over Max's forehead as he surveyed the area for listeners. "You ought to start to buy in now. They expect the price to start to escalate very soon."

Max broke into a smile and kicked his legs to splash Marshall, "And where are you going in the boat shoes, boy? To the marina?" he asked derisively.

"I was supposed to take Donna over to Port Jeff at noon. Then I got the call so I figured I better get to you first."

Max rolled a shaded eye towards Marshall. "And who are they, anyway?"

"Well," Marshall said, crouching down over Max, "to start with, I am getting calls from clients that are telling me that their cousins are asking them about the stock. Then the guy who picks up our garbage, he tells me he hears Birmingham's going to be put in play. Then Donna tells me that her father, who operates a lathe at Hershey Metal, says he heard that Great Nation is going to buy Birmingham. Everyone. The word is out."

Max pushed off the pool frame and dipped his head into the water, returning to rest again on the frame. "That's not everyone now, is it? Anyway, we can track the number of shares traded. I have a timetable that I wanted to keep. Sponge civil trial isn't even on the trial calendar yet. I don't have time to follow this stuff too closely. A dollar here or there won't matter so much."

Marshall leaned forward and lifted Max's arms from the pool frame, sending him gurgling under the water. His wife laughed audibly and pointed his way. He surfaced with no sign of annoyance and nothing out of place. "The bank custodian purchased a block yesterday."

Max leveled himself on the pool again and watched the water roll off his stomach except for the thimble full sitting in his naval. He tried to see his wife but couldn't without tilting his head and he wasn't about to move. His nose sculpted the final perfection of his face, symmetrical, proportional and masculine. Finally, he tilted his head back to Max. "I'll change my timeframe. I have most of the financing available already. I'll start picking up shares. I got someone on the inside approving any loans I apply for. He basically controls the committee. Some of the loans are on existing properties I have so he is just modifying them and isn't getting anyone's approval." He rotated his head to its resting position against the coping, then shook it ever so slightly, affirmatively. "Thanks, Marshall. Have fun in Port Jeff."

Byron arrived to an empty church. He groped for the light switch, slowly climbed the winding staircase, and rested over the heavy choir rail. He looked at the detail of the scarlet and gold capitals supporting the vaulted ceiling, beneath broad spandrels imaged with dozens of seraphs and cherubs. He was eye-level with the seven murals over the apse. And above them, just below the graceful dome, were seven stained glass windows telling biblical stories with brilliant detail. He lost himself for several minutes until the sound of the interior doors rocked to a close and Linda's footsteps broke the silence.

"Am I late?" she asked, glancing at her watch and dropping her pocketbook from her shoulder, then turning to face him with a wide-eyed expression of surprise and distress.

"No," he responded with a dropped voice, not bothering to check the time. "If the store isn't too busy I'll be here early. No sense in going home. This is a fine place to spend some time anyway," he said, sweeping his arm through the width of the nave. "The details of this church are just remarkable. I mean," he continued, raising both arms out before him as if they were to lift the pillars, "if you look there, the power of the columns and the sweep of the arch, they are all of one line. The architect had a great sense of proportion and balance. And the artwork is spectacular. There," he said, sweeping his hand to her back to turn her to the closest stained glass window. "There, the faces of the figures, the flesh color, it varies, somewhat mottled. So real, and yet, other than the Corinthian capitals, those fancy gold tops on the columns with the scarlet creases, there is nothing ornate here," he said, continuing the sweep of his arms and arching his neck to the stained glass high above the altar. "And the ceiling, here, above the center aisle, it's one graceful barrel arch with a long, ribbed vault where the main altar begins and the delicate ribbing over the altar, gives you a great sense of divine presence."

Linda turned to Byron and winced, "How do you know all this Viejo? I mean, anyone can see the beauty here, but how do you know so much about it? You're like my father. He just knew so much about so many things."

"Oh," said Byron, lifting himself off the railing and walking to the piano bench. "When you're as old as me you just accumulate information in your head. Just sits up there, really doing nothing most of the time. It just depends on how you spend your time. No great mystery. It's got nothing to do with intelligence." He turned the piano lamp on and moved it to the end of the piano as he straddled the bench. "Come," he said, motioning her to his side. "We should start."

Linda stood to his side with her hands folded before her. "I didn't bring any music with me," she said, squinting at the light in her eyes.

Byron dropped his lower lip to a curl of flesh and shook his head. "Good. No need. I'll provide any music we use in the future. Today you learn to breathe." He looked up at her in the obvious discomfort of the lamp. "Sorry," he said, adjusting the lamp slightly from her face. "Yes," he said with a soft exclamation, "that brings me to some ground rules. I'm going to push you to perfection. If you feel uncomfortable with what I'm doing, you have to tell me. If you feel your voice straining and I don't sense it, you have to tell me. Sometimes, particularly doing the breathing exercises, I'll touch you. If you feel uncomfortable with

510

that, tell me. We want to extend your range by a few notes. There are a few ways to get there but some of the methods would neglect the rest of your delivery. I won't do that. This is not a short term proposition. You can't be in a hurry for results. Do you understand that?"

Linda nodded in agreement. "I understand. But how long should this take?"

Byron flipped his eyebrows up with uncertainty. "I don't know," he said, planting his palms over his knees and leaning forward. "Year and a half, two, maybe three years." Then he looked at her and said, calmly, in a retreating voice, "You can't be impatient."

Linda's eyes closed for a moment as she let his words sink in. "A year and a half?"

"Yes, a year and a half. You see, you're in a hurry already."

Linda smiled and shook her head. "Sorry," she said, nodding her head. "I understand."

"Good," Byron responded without expression. "So we begin."

Linda dropped her arms to her side and stood before him. He held his palm out like a gloved traffic cop. "Wait, relax," he said. "Talk to me about the lessons your father gave you."

Linda turned, stepped back, and leaned against the railing. "Sure," she said quietly, dropping her eyes to the floor and then looking back up to Byron. "What do you want to know?"

"Well, tell me how old you were when you started, how

many years ago you stopped, what you practiced, why you stopped. Things like that."

A weak smile crept over her face. "This probably sounds funny, but it's hard to know when I actually started lessons. I mean, my father taught us piano, my sister and me, from very early age. Five or six, I don't know. So we were always around him at the piano. Maybe around eleven or twelve he started playing while I stood next to him. We practiced songs, mostly art songs. Not too demanding, nothing really too fancy. He never really pushed me hard. He would pay close attention to my diction and phrasing more than anything. I don't know. It's hard to remember," she concluded with a weak shrug of her shoulders.

"You got through all of Vaccai?" Byron asked, testing her possible range of lessons with one word.

"I guess," Linda said with a broad grin. "I really don't know if we got through all of it. I did several pieces from his song book. But I've forgotten so much."

"Don't be discouraged," Byron said, sitting on the piano bench with his hands folded over his large stomach. "It will come back to you. But continue. So you did scales and intervals?"

Linda let a moment pass as she tried to recall. The sound of the church's inner doors rocking to a close signaled someone making a visit. Byron creased his forehead in consternation. "That's just someone coming to pray. That happens all the time. Sometimes you don't even know anyone's here, if they hold the doors until they close so they don't rock. It's okay. They come and go. Anyway," she continued, "we did mostly songs. Not too much with scales. No intervals." Linda let a moment pass as the sound of coins dropping into the votive box echoed through the church. She smiled and continued, wistfully. "I was young then, anxious to sing songs. So we did mostly slow songs. You know, love songs."

Byron smiled, seeing the obvious pleasure in her eyes at the recollection. "So you like singing love songs?" he asked plainly, encouraging her to recall more.

She shook her head affirmatively. "We moved back to Puerto Rico when I was ten. My sister was thirteen then. Anyway, my father's health was failing so my mom moved us back to the little mountain town her family was from. It's called Piletas. It was sort of backward, bad electricity, dirt roads winding up to the mountains. People still do their laundry on the rocks by the river. But it was beautiful, especially at night. The only sound was the frogs and the night insects. But the stars, the stars seemed so close you could reach up and touch them. We often used kerosene lamps for light. On clear nights the moon was so bright you hardly needed the lamps. And I would stand at his side and sing. Sometimes my sister sang with me. But she was older, in high school, so she had boys coming around that my mother tried to chase away. And I would stand there for hours sometimes and sing songs, mostly Italian art songs. That's really what my lessons consisted of, mostly diction and phrasing and dynamics. Mostly songs, I guess, in the mezzo range."

Byron turned to the piano and pressed a note, letting his finger remain on the key until the sound faded to nothing. Then he pressed it again, asking over the tone, "Do you recall going much over the F above high C?"

Linda shook her head and matched the tone with a very solid voice. "No," she said with uncertainty, "although I read the music while I sang I really didn't pay too much attention to all the details. But I don't think so. He always talked about the mezzo range. You see, he was a polio victim. He couldn't use his legs. I remember him saying, just as I came to a dotted whole note or a tie, 'sostenuto, Linda, sostenuto, hold your notes, hold your notes.' He pronounced my name in Italian, which is the same as in Spanish, with a hard vowel sound, whenever he corrected my singing, 'sostenuto, Leenda, sostenuto.' And that's what I remember best. And it was peaceful and beautiful there, Viejo, so high in the mountains. And dark at night. You could look up and fill your eyes with starlight. It was heaven."

Byron smiled and nodded. He swiveled out from the piano and continued. "Tell me," he said slowly, "tell me the song you recall the best."

Linda cast her eyes up to the ceiling, then looked back at him with a wet gaze. "That's easy," she said calmly, "Il Mio Ben Quando Verra. Do you know it?" she asked.

Byron repeated the name of the song out loud as the church doors rocked, announcing another visitor. "Certainly, from the opera Nina. My mother used it all the time. It's perfect for assessing legato. Would you like to

514

sing it as part of your lessons?"

"No," Linda said softly, "it's better that I don't. You see, in Puerto Rico, after someone is buried, it's traditional that the family and friends meet every night for nine nights to pray. It's called a novena. So after my father died, on the last night of the novena, my family asked me to sing it. My sister played the piano. I remember the faces of my family and the sound of the coquis and the chills on my skin when I sang that. Anyway, it's beautiful but I only sang it once since then, at a very sad time in my life. So, no, I'd rather not sing that." Linda turned her wrist and glanced at her watch. "I think I've been talking too much."

"No," Byron responded, sitting upright and motioning for her to get closer. "I think you said just enough. Now, I want you to pay close attention to what I say." He folded his hands into a fleshy knitting ball high on his belly. His voice was slow and exacting as he lifted his eyes, heavily lidded with age, to hers. "I want you to think of your lungs as water balloons." He leaned forward and placed his hand on her diaphragm, letting his fingertips find the edge of her sternum and pressed into it. "Think of your lungs as water balloons being filled. Did you ever fill a water balloon?" He kept his fingers just below her sternum.

"Yes," she responded with a smile, "for my daughter's Girl Scout parties. I usually got drenched." Linda let out a quick laugh that was meant to dissipate her nervousness as much as provide some sense of understanding of his point.

"Inevitable," he retorted with a knowing smile. "So for

today and every day forward, I want you to think of your lungs as a water balloon. As you fill it the water distends and fills the balloon from the bottom up, right? Sometimes you must support it with a free hand, no?"

"Yes," Linda responded quickly.

He released his hand from her sternum and cupped it between his legs, as if testing the weight of the balloon in his palm, them raising and lowering it to give Linda a view of what her filled lungs would look like. "So when you inhale," he said, sucking in a big breathe and speaking with a measured tone, "think of the air having weight." he said, bringing his hand beneath her breasts and stretching his fingers just beneath her ribs. "The water has to drop to this level and fill your abdomen first. It might seem unnatural, but that is how you have to do it. Now," he continued, "you think of that same balloon and you want to release the air from it, but slowly, uniformly, with control. Now," he said, standing beside her and placing the edge of his palm against her sternum, "you release it slowly, evenly." He sat back down on the bench. "You try it. Put your fingers along your neck and keep your chin level with the floor."

She raised her hand to her neck and looked down to him, "Like this?" she asked, looking down at him.

Byron placed the back of his hand beneath her chin and lifted it, "Yes," he said correcting her, "but don't look down at me. If you're looking at me you're looking down." He leaned back and folded his arms again. "Some of this may seem rudimentary to you but it's important. We might get an immediate half tone just by correcting your breathing alone."

"You want me to breathe now?"

"Yes. That's it," he said. "Now, open your mouth wide, like this," he said, dropping his hand from her chin to allow her to look at the wide oval he made of his mouth. "And inhale while thinking about it. Remember," he held his finger up in an instructive manner, "your lungs are water balloons. Fill them from the bottom." He watched as she filled her lungs. "Let your belly distend to make room. It might feel funny at first but do it anyway."

"Now what?" she asked without exhaling.

"Drop your hands and fold them in front of you. Relax and exhale slowly." Linda released a slow, even stream of air through a small oval formed by her lips. "Your neck muscles are relaxed when breathing." He turned to the piano and pressed middle C. "Now," he said, "hold your neck again and vocalize to the scale as I play it."

"I thought we weren't singing today."

"We're not." He cast her a stern eye. "We are practicing breath control. You have to listen to me. Don't get ahead of me."

Linda held her neck and sang the notes he played. "Slow, steady stream of air," he said under the sound of her notes rising through the church. "If your neck is relaxed you can hear the effect of the tone on your vocal muscles, no?" He completed the scale and rested his hands again.

Linda released her neck and spun the cameo between

her fingers. "Yes, I understand what you're saying. So you think my breathing is the problem?"

"No, I think we can improve your breathing and get a better result," he said thoughtfully. "But that is only the beginning. I'm going to work you through all the fundamentals. Breathing is just one of them. We're going to start scales in a few weeks, then go on to intervals, projection, half tones, grace notes and all the ornamentation, diction, glides, all of it. It can't be rushed. Your range will increase as we clean up all these areas. But you have to be patient and trust me."

Byron checked his watch and reached into his plastic bag, setting a metronome on the piano. He looked at his watch and set the metronome at second intervals and let it continue as he spoke. "Okay, now I want to show you how to practice your breathing during the week. The metronome is set at one second intervals. You're going to fill the balloon, taking five full seconds, then rest for two seconds holding it there, and then slowly release your breath steadily over ten seconds. Can we try that?"

"Now?"

"Of course. I'm not going to have you run off and breath incorrectly all week. Just inhale for five clicks, hold for two and then exhale for a count of ten."

Linda filled her belly with a clean, even breath, watched the metronome for two clicks and exhaled evenly. "How's that?"

Byron broke into a smile at her diligence. "Well, that was good but you left too much water in the balloon. I didn't say it so it's my fault but the point of the exercise is to get an even flow of air and at the end of the ten seconds to have your lungs nearly empty."

Linda laughed and shrugged her shoulders. "Oh, well, that changes everything, doesn't it?"

Byron shook his head in agreement and clapped his hands lightly to the beat of the metronome. "Let's try again, no?"

"Sure," Linda said, repeating the exercise with precision. "Wonderful!"

"So is this all we do today, breathe?" she said through a smile.

Byron returned her smile and adjusted his glasses, "No. I think your posture needs some attention. Your shoulders are rolled forward too much. You need to square them off a bit, opens your lungs more, and your pelvis. It should be slightly bowed forward a bit." He reached to her and placed his hand on her lower back. "This muscle here, in the small of your back, it should be relaxed. You have to imagine you're a marionette" he said, raising from the bench and standing with his arms bent and suspended in air. "Your limbs are controlled by strings from above. And your hips are floating in air, levitated."

Linda adjusted her frame and allowed her pelvis to roll forward slightly. "Like this?" she asked, looking for an immediate response.

Byron smiled and pressed her hips back a bit. "No. That looks unnatural. too pronounced. It has to feel natural, like your hips are suspended, not thrust forward."

"That better?" she asked, looking forward with her chin level with the floor.

"Much better, it looks loose and natural. So this week I want you to practice breathing in and filling your lungs from the bottom. Then hold it for a second and release. Then repeat this until you get to seven seconds. Do it in front of a mirror. Don't lift your shoulders. You want to see your belly fill out with air. And don't do it on a full stomach. If your stomach is full you leave less space for the air. We want your lungs to expand. And practice your posture." He reached under the piano bench and handed her a heavy leather ball. "Do you know what it is?"

"Yes," Linda said with a knowing look. "It's a medicine ball. My dad had one in his office for his students. You want me to use this?"

"I want you to take it home and practice with it. Breath control, diaphragm strength, it all goes together. You can't do one without the other."

"I have to carry this home?"

"Well, it's not going to walk on its own, if that's what you mean."

Linda laughed and shook her head. "So what do I have to do. Hold it out, right?"

"Right, you have to hold it so you feel the muscle in your stomach pulling. That's how we strengthen it. Actually, you do a lot of walking which is very good for the abdominal muscles."

Linda held the ball out away from her body, then relaxed it back in after a few seconds. She repeated the exercise while Byron placed his hands on her stomach and pressed his fingers in. "You feel the tightness, right?"

"I do."

"After a few months you'll see a big difference." He took the ball from her and asked her to turn around for him slowly. He examined her body closely, looking at her feet and knees, each curve on the way up and the roundness of her waist. "Don't lose any weight. No diets or anything like that. The extra weight will help with the support for now. You can work on weight changes once we get your voice where we want it. Do you understand?"

"I do," Linda responded as she watched him pick up the ball and hand it back to her. "So do we do this again next week?"

"Maybe just a few minutes, it will become second nature to you soon. Next week we work more posture, placement of the pelvis, buttocks. I'm going to start you on a simple regimen. I think you need the discipline. Then we'll get into the Vaccai and the scales, intervals. Over time we'll mix it up with some simple soprano songs, some of the lovely lieder works, you know, some Shubert and Brahams, Schumann, just to keep it interesting. We can't rush it, Linda. We have to go slowly."

"Intervals?"

"Yes," he said with a raised voice and a nod of his head, "not too fast on intervals yet. You may have some trouble with them and once we start them it will be very intensive for you. But we're getting too far ahead."

Linda wasn't sure what Byron meant by that but she

521

didn't press it. "So next week we do some of this again?"

"Yes, this again. Do your exercises during the week on an empty stomach. Get yourself in front of a mirror, close, and with your eyes closed to concentrate, take in a breath and let it out slowly, evenly. You have all those mirrors where you work. That's an ideal place. It's an ancient voice training exercise. Get close to the mirror and as you release your breathe see if you can do that and not fog up the mirror when you open your eyes. That's an old technique for practicing breath control. We used to use a candle and have the student sing without extinguishing the flame. That's another old technique, but the mirror is safer. Always, always, always think breath control."

Joe Baliki sat hunched over the bar at the Deer Run Country Club. He had already exhausted the patience and wallets of several members who were inclined to provide any number of drinks to the banker who controlled the loan committee of Birmingham Savings. Maximilian Cruz, sensing the vulnerability of a compromised man, invited Baliki to join him at his table for dinner.

"So, I kept eight of the condos we put up at Stillwater Suites. My idea is to refinance them and use the proceeds for other investments."

Baliki cut his steak and stuffed a wad of meat into his mouth. "So that shouldn't be a problem. You got the condos fully rented, right?"

"Of course, leases in place, everything. I just need to know I can get a line of credit that I can draw on anytime.

You know, sometimes I've dipped into the escrow accounts but I never feel comfortable doing that. I don't want to have to beat anyone to the bank. With the bank going into play now I need the liquidity to buy stock on its way up, not just at the top."

Baliki ordered another Scotch, straight up. "The problem with the credit line is the rate changes, so you can get caught with raising rates while you're waiting for the investments payoff. I got something I can do for you if you are willing to take some risk."

Cruz pushed his plate aside and leaned over the table, nearly touching the small candle in the center. "Joe, I'm a litigator. I live with risk and uncertainty every day. What do you have in mind?"

Baliki lowered his voice and leaned in. "You leave the existing mortgages in place. You take out multiple mortgages on the condos and you just keep making the monthly payments."

Cruz's eyes darted around and he leaned back in his chair. "You mean," he asked quietly, "the bank would give me enough new money to make my investments and pay the mortgages? So the mortgage amounts would exceed the value of the real estate?"

"Exactly." Baliki sipped his vodka and smiled. "If you are confident in your investments, that they are going to pay off, I don't have any problem approving the loans."

"Isn't that bank fraud?"

"Not if you aren't defrauding the bank. If I approve the loans and the committee goes along with it then it isn't bank fraud. Besides, the point is you are making the monthly payments regularly so why would anyone even question this? And I can waive the need for appraisals. I just think it's cleaner than getting a line of credit where you have a cap on how much you can draw."

"Well, I guess it violates bank loan policy. But if you can deliver the loans, then I'm in. You see, in the condos and in the other developments I was involved in, I was a partner. And I would do all the work, have all the ideas, and then split the profits with everyone. This time I want to do it on my own. So, yes, I like the idea. When can you put this in place?"

Baliki shrugged his shoulders and smiled, "Whenever you want. Monday soon enough? Committee meets on Thursdays. I can get any approval then, signatures, loan numbers, whatever. I just need the property descriptions but we have that in the files from the existing mortgages."

"I like it. Can I have Marshall do the closings?" Cruz waived the waiter over for the tab. He pulled a cigar from his jacket pocket and tapped it on the dinner table.

"Sure, Marshall is fine. We can waive the title work so he is at no risk. Just give me a call Monday and we'll talk about how much you want to take. Then you can buy as much stock as you want. The beauty of this is that once the stock takes off you can purchase on margin. Then you basically have unlimited funds. So obviously you are aware of the proposed takeover?"

Max smirked and put the unlit cigar in his mouth, "Seems that everyone is now aware of the proposed takeover. The point is to pick up the shares before it gets too hot and the price gets bid up too much."

"But that's supposed to be how the market works. Demand causes the price of anything to rise, right?"

Max nodded in agreement then tilted his head. "Look, no one wants to compete in a true market. Everyone looks for an advantage, a market flaw that allows wealth to be made. In a true market we would be out there trying to accumulate shares of other public banks that we think are takeover targets. But that's not what is happening. The players are buying up Birmingham shares because they know the market is rigged. No one wants to compete in a real market, Joe. Everyone wants to control the market, and corrupt it if they can." Max leaned back in his chair, lit his cigar, and walked out to the veranda.

"No," Byron said sharply, looking up from the piano at Linda, then to the music before placing his hands on his thighs in frustration. "You missed the markings. You are not singing what Vaccai wrote. You missed the grace note, the G, and you went right to the F. It's like this," he said, playing it and saying the notes with deliberate emphasis, "eighth note, A, to the grace note, then G for an eighth, then into the drop to the D in a glide. You're singing the G nearly a quarter note, then dropping to the D. That's too abrupt. That is not what Vaccai wrote."

"Yes, I know I missed it, Viejo. It's just that I feel if I hit it I'll be late into the F."

Byron ran his fingers through his hair. "The discipline of

singing what is written is necessary. I can't have you improvising yet, that's for the advanced class. It must be sung exactly as it is written, at least for now."

Byron rose from the piano and walked to the center of the loft. He hesitated to collect his thoughts. "Linda," he said, placing his hand in his pocket and looking at the ceiling and into the nave, trying to contain his frustration, "how far along Vaccai did you say you got with your father?"

Linda stepped back and rested against the choir railing, facing the back of the loft as Byron turned to face her. "I don't recall," she said as if in mid-thought, "it's hard to remember that far back. I would stand by the piano and he would correct my timing and diction, but that's it. That's all I can remember, Viejo, pieces of conversations. That's all that's left," she said with a shrug.

Byron walked back to the piano and played the notes again.

"The grace note, I hardly hear it, Linda." He played it again. "But it must be sung," he said, looking at the music, then turning his eyes to her as she nervously slid the cameo over its delicate chain. "It adds richness to the piece. Besides, the next several lessons will be very difficult unless you understand this."

"What's next?" she asked, stepping off the rail and to his side as he turned the pages of the book forward, then retreated a page or two.

"The portamento. Have you heard of it?"

Linda folded her hands in her thighs and shrugged. "My

father didn't use a lot of technical terms with me. I don't know. I don't know what he was doing with me except it was beautiful and I was happy. So, no, I don't know the portamento."

Byron stepped away from the rail and circled her. His eyebrows knitted with confusion. "Didn't you say you were a voice major?"

"No. I said I was a music education major with piano as my instrument. Voice was my minor, or, I should say, was going to be my minor, but I had to drop out at the end of my freshman year because I had my daughter."

"I apologize. I think you did say that and I forgot. I thought you were a voice major. Didn't you say you sang for your jury?"

"Yes. But I wasn't supposed to sing," she said, shaking her head to correct him. "I just wanted to sing. It was a very difficult time for me. My boyfriend at the time was in Vietnam and I hadn't heard from him in months. I knew I wasn't going back to school after the first year. So I sang because I knew Il Mio Ben well. It was just something in my heart that I wanted to do." Linda raised her eyebrows a half notch and let a sad smile turn her lips down. She felt exposed. She raised her hand to the cameo and fidgeted with it. "I told you my father had polio, right?"

"Yes. You said that at one of the first lessons."

"He had polio so he would have to remind me to hold some of the sustained notes if his hands were moving on. So I still find myself cheating the sustained notes."

Byron put his hands over his face and rubbed it

vigorously. "So," he said, slapping his hands over his thighs, "maybe that's why he didn't teach you the technical terms. He taught it to you, otherwise you wouldn't have dealt with Vaccai. And you can't sing Il Mio Ben without the training. Then again, I never did hear you sing it. So how did you do before the jury?"

"I did fine. I passed. It was just a pass/fail thing. Freshman year, you know? They passed me even though I was supposed to play the piano. Just two professors were the jury. One of them, Professor York, was particularly sweet to me so she convinced the department chair to allow to let me sing instead of play the piano piece they expected. The campus was in turmoil with war protests. It was basically shut down, so I think a lot of the academic standards were relaxed."

Byron rested his hands over his stomach and asked in a quiet voice, "Is that when you stopped singing?"

"Yes," she said with a voice that quivered. "Everything sort of stopped then. I had Tori, stopped school. I never developed my voice further. There wasn't any money. I had a baby to support. That was my first responsibility. So now here it is sixteen years later and I got lucky and found you.

"You know with your voice there would have been no limit to where you could have gone. Your voice is that beautiful."

Linda allowed a weak smile to crease her face. "Thank you, but I was never interested in singing in a competitive way. At first I did it because my father took great pleasure in teaching me. He was sick and I could see how happy he was when I sang with him. Then I started to believe him, that I could actually sing. Then I started to love it, especially the love songs. I loved to stand beside him at the piano, on those warm nights in Piletas, high in the mountains, and feel the evening breeze cool my skin. I was only thirteen or fourteen, and I would sing love songs. And when I made a mistake and he would say 'piano, piano Linda, easy, easy'. He never raised his voice. I thought life would always be like that. I thought it would always be beautiful. But it's not, Viejo, life is really very sad."

Byron nodded with understanding. "So, tell me a little more about your personal life. Is your daughter's father the young man that went to Vietnam that you spoke about before?"

The abruptness of the question took her by surprise. She lifted herself off of the mahogany rail and turned her back to Byron, letting her eyes rise to the highest reach of the apse.

"No," she said slowly, allowing the word to drift out and drop the heavy truth into the nave. "No, Viejo," she said again as she turned and faced him, "He is not the father of my daughter. But..." she shook her head from side to side and let the thought pass without completing it. Then she smiled weakly and lifted her eyebrows, "Lots of sad stories today, Viejo," she whispered. She walked to the far corner of the loft, beyond the reach of the dim light and dabbed her eyes with a tissue. She lifted her head and walked to the back of the piano where her face, in the dark shadow, grew tight with intensity. She took a piece of paper from her pocketbook and handed it to Byron. "Since we're talking about sad times, Vieho, maybe you can help me. Do you recognize those notes?"

Byron studied the notes and put the paper aside. "No, I'm sorry."

Linda smiled softly and tried to keep her face from distorting with sadness. "Let's try the grace notes again, Viejo. Play the piece again."

Byron tapped around on the piano for an instant, talking as he played, explaining once again how she is to sing for a sixteenth note and then into the principal note. He tried to fill in some time to allow her to recover her voice and she sensed it.

"It's okay, Viejo. I'm ready. Play it and I'll sing it, next week we begin the portamento."

Byron placed his hands on his lap. "Oh, next week we start the portamento. Are you directing the lessons now?" he asked in an effort to break the tension.

Linda smiled and shook her head. "Oh, come on, Viejo," she said. "You know what I mean."

Byron returned her smile and nodded his head. "Yes, Linda. I know what you mean." The smile drifted from his lips. "Very soon we start the portamento. If you master the grace notes and the mordent, it will come easier. It gives the singer more freedom to express the music. When you leave a note in the mordent you'll feint your voice up or down, away from the next tone. It allows a very beautiful and graceful move into the next note when it is used properly."

530

Linda shook her head, acknowledging his reasoning. "It's okay, Byron, play the grace notes. I'd like to get through this lesson today," she said with conviction.

Byron played the piece. Linda sang through, standing beside him and noticing him anticipating errors that never materialized. When she completed the piece Byron looked at her and then back at the music, unable to offer any further instruction.

"Well, how was it?" she asked with a straight face.

"Perfect. The timing was perfect. Your diction," he said with a hesitation, "your diction we have to work on."

"My diction?"

Byron smiled at her and covered his ears with his hands. "I know. I know. I'm very tough on you. But Linda, if we're going to sit here every week and go through breathing instruction, scales, and all the ornamentation, then we have to address everything. You need to clean up your diction."

"What's wrong with it?" she asked, placing her hands on the piano.

"Sometimes it's sloppy. You can't sing like you speak, Linda. I think you just have to concentrate on how you enter a word and how you leave it. You're dropping your endings."

"Are you going to give me diction lessons?"

Byron laughed as he rose from the piano and leaned over his large belly to collect his music. "No. No diction lessons. I want you to concentrate on your breathing again. And when you sing, I want it distinct. Once again, in a mirror, even while you're at work, watch your lips, count breathes, fill your lungs from the bottom," he said, letting his hands flow down to his own diaphragm. "Then stand close to the mirror and speak with measured breathes. Your breath should not cloud the mirror."

Linda came around to the front of the piano and took her music into her arms. "What do I study for next week?

"Nothing," Byron said as he clicked the light off and they walked through the dark loft. "I want you to concentrate on your breathing and diction. Shortly I'll start you on a soprano song book that has several different languages in it, a little English, some lieder, French. I think it'll be good to get you out of classical instruction and mix it up a little."

"Will the songs be within my range?" she asked with concern.

"Of course, you have to realize that what separates a mezzo from a soprano are only a few notes. At the higher soprano range, the D, E and F above the high C, then you are really in the firmament. Some sopranos describe a sensation of their face tingling when they hit and sustain those notes. You can get up there. If you think back, when we did scales, I had you well into the soprano range and you weren't even straining."

Linda swept her coat over her shoulders and opened the doors to the grey, lifeless cold of the March afternoon. "Whatever you say, Viejo. See you next week."

"Breath control. Practice breath control," he said as she started down the creaking stairs.

"I will," she responded from the darkness.

"So what's for Jeff today?" asked Frances with an inflected tone. She glanced up as she rolled the sausages over the grill, away from the bacon fat that dripped lazily into the drain with the help of a prodding spatula. "Where's Mike today?"

"Hunting," Jeff replied in a snip."Opening day, Frances. You know he's sitting up in some tree dressed in his camouflage gear, waiting for some big buck to come strolling through, thinking he's going to fool that buck." He backed away from the grill and pivoted toward the parlor. "Give me a fried egg on a roll with bacon, Fran. That Mrs. C back there?"

"Virginia's here," Frances responded with a nod. "You want it to go?" she called out.

"Yeah."

"You don't hunt, Jeff?" Frances asked, glancing up with a twisted face and causing Jeff to step back to the grill. She held up the large knife and wiped down its blade evenly, then examined it.

"Me?" Jeff asked with raised brows, "hunt? People from Mount Vernon, we don't hunt, Frances." He laughed out loud and raised his arm, "No way." he said, axing the air for emphasis. He hesitated by Tori who was seated at the counter and tugged at her narrow braid that rested over her back. "What's up, Tor," he whispered as he continued to Virginia and responded to Frances, "Won't catch me standing in the cold waiting for some deer to come by.

Just to shoot it? And then you got to gut it right there and then drag its dead ass out of the woods? No way. Get up at three in the morning and be out there by five o'clock? I be sleeping at five, Frances. I told Mike he can keep that hunting stuff."

Jeff pulled an empty chair from Virginia's table, spun it like a top and straddled it, leaning his frame on its two back legs and balancing on it. "So what's going on here, Mrs. C?" he asked.

Virginia lifted her pocketbook from the table and set it on the floor. The contents of her coat pocket were strewn over the table. "Jeffery Scott," she said with a light smile and a quick glance up, "I hear you talking about my grandson. He's just like his grandfather. Put him in a tree on opening day and he believes he's in heaven." Virginia reached up and adjusted her scarf, turned to the mirror and fussed with it for a minute.

"Don't worry, Mrs. C," Jeff said as he touched each item on the table, adjusting the salt and pepper shaker, the sugar and the napkin holder, and fixing them in an order he thought appropriate. "Your scarf is straight up. What's all this stuff anyway? Emptying your pockets like you was being robbed or something?"

Virginia fished her hand into her coat pocket and shook her head in defeat. "Thought I had some loose change in this pocket," she said with a smirk, "but I just noticed I got a hole there in the bottom. Can you see it there?" She flipped the pocket inside out and twisted her neck, still unable to see the hole.

"I see it," Jeff said, standing bent kneed from his chair and slipping his finger through the hole, "I got my finger in it now." He gave it a sharp tug. "You feel that?"

Virginia reached over and followed Jeff's hand down to the hole. He slipped his finger out and she slipped hers in and placed the pocket back inside the coat. "Oh, it's just another job to do when I get home. The change will be sliding around the lining now. Lining's got some tears too."

"Maybe it's time for a new coat, Mrs. C."

"No," Virginia responded slowly, "I like this coat. Just have to repair it when I get some time, that's all." Virginia picked up the contents of the table and stuffed them into the other pocket. She knew her fingers, thick and gnarled with pain, couldn't handle such a fine stitch. No matter. She would try anyway in the effort of an entire morning, or an evening closed off against the world. Until then, the hole would stay.

"Yeah," Jeff said with a teasing smile. "I bet you a busy person, Mrs. C." He picked up a small pack of prayer cards and unwrapped the rubber band that was doubled around the stack. "So," he asked as he flipped through the stack, "who all these people anyway? Some kind of religious people or something?"

"Saints," Virginia said as he straightened the stack and slid it over to her.

"Saints? They do look kind of funny. You go to church a lot, don't you, Mrs. C?" Jeff asked as Frances yelled back that his order was ready.

"I try to go every day. Sometimes, if my arthritis is acting up, then I just stay home and pray. I have trouble with the steps sometimes."

"Yeah," Jeff said turning his chair back and standing beside Virginia, "them are lots of steps. It's a long way up."

"Oh," Virginia replied with an inflected voice, "going up isn't too bad. It's going down. My knees," she said, shaking her head and grimacing at the thought of the pain. "I have to go down backwards. The weight going down forward hurts my knees."

"So why don't you just stay home and pray? Ain't that good enough? I mean, if it going to hurt your knees and stuff?"

Virginia gave Jeff a sullen eye. "Well, if I do that then I'd just become a shut in. Then I'd never get out. I'd rather take the pain and pray in church."

Jeff lifted the prayer cards again and riffled them under his fingers. Then he rapped them on the table to straighten them. "Damn, Mrs. C, you do a lot of praying. What you be praying for anyway? I got an aunt that prays a lot too, but I think you got her beat," he said with a hard press on beat. "You got her beat, man!"

"Too big to fall into the hole," she said, fitting the saint cards neatly into the empty pocket. She took a long sip of tepid coffee. "You ever go to church, Jeff?" she asked, lifting the remaining cold crust of an English muffin and putting it into her mouth.

"Me?" he asked with a wide smile. "Well, when I was a kid and stuff I used to go all the time," he explained. "My mom, I grew up in Mount Vernon, and she'd get me all

536

dressed up in a white shirt and bow tie and give me a grocery bag, you know, a big brown paper bag, with a change of clothes in it and some lunch, on Saturday morning, and put me on the train to Harlem, to my aunt's house. There I'd be, Mrs. C, just me and my paper bag with a change of clothes and a little snack, on that train. Me and my sister, and she was younger than me. We didn't know anyone, just me and my brown bag on the train. I'd get off at 125th Street station and walk to my aunt's. It wasn't dangerous like it is now. Wasn't no child molesters and that kind of stuff to worry about in those days. Anyway, my aunt would take us to church. Me and my sister and my cousins. It was serious church. People be yelling and hollering. They be sweating and passing out and stuff. Got me scared, Mrs. C. Yeah, boy," Jeff said with a wide-eyed smile that recalled his young fear. "That's the only time in my life I remember being scared."

"Jeff!" Frances yelled, waving his bag over her head, "It's getting cold."

"I be right there, Frances," Jeff yelled back. "Well, I got to go, Mrs. C. So what you keep praying for Mrs. C? You never did say."

"Oh, I pray for lots of things. People I know who need help. I pray for sick people. For my son Kevin's soul and my family. For peace. I know a lot of sick people."

"So what about for you, Mrs. C? Don't you do no praying for yourself?"

Virginia held her coffee cup up to her lips and thought for a second. "I guess so," she said hesitantly, "that I can make it down the church steps because my knees hurt."

"That's it? Ain't there nothing else you want?"

Virginia smiled and shook her head from side to side. "Your breakfast's getting cold, Jeff," she responded with a wistful look in her eye.

"Something you praying for Mrs. C," Jeff said with a laugh, knowing he caught her in a ruminative moment, "I can tell by your smile. What you praying for you for?"

"For me?" Virginia asked. "I don't really pray for me. There's nothing I need, Jeff."

Jeff straddled the chair again and sat. He leaned over and closed in on her. "Now you look here, Mrs. C," he said with conviction. "I don't care about no cold breakfast. Something on your mind that you want and I ain't leaving until you tell me. I seen it, I seen it in your eyes, so if you want me to eat a warm sandwich, you just tell me and we'll be done with it. Now you going to tell me?"

"There's nothing I need, Jeff."

"So, ain't nothing you need. So what do you want? Must be something you want. Want's different than need."

Virginia rested her elbows on the table and looked directly into Jeff's eyes. He didn't smile or give any hint of weakness or diffidence. To her he was only a boy, just like her grandson Michael. It isn't right that she should tell him her needs and burden him with it. But he didn't budge and his breakfast was getting cold.

"Someday I'd like to go down to Washington. To the Wall, you know, the Vietnam Wall. I'd like to see Kevin's name and make a copy of it. You know, they let you rub it and it comes out on paper and you can keep it. That's all. Nothing else I really want. I'd like to rub Kevin's name."

Jeff reeled back in his chair. "That all you want, Mrs. C?" he asked incredulously, his voice rising and dropping in disbelief. "Someday, me and you and Mike, we'll carry you down to see the Wall. Shoot, that ain't nothing to want, Mrs. C. We'll get there. You take care now. I got to go. And I got your breakfast," he said waving his money in his fist and heading for the register.

"No," Virginia protested, reaching for her pocketbook. "I've got money here."

"I got it," Jeff called back, "maybe I get on that prayer list this way."

"You're already on it," she called to him.

Jeff walked back and stood over her table. He put on a serious look, knitting his brows tightly and squinting his eyes to a close. "What you praying for me for?"

Virginia looked up and smiled at Jeff. "One day Mike told me when you were a young man you would be hanging around 125th Street in Harlem and carrying a gun."

"Mike told you that?"

"Is it true?"

"Yes."

"Well, that's why I pray for you. That you'll be safe and stay good like you are now."

Jeff stepped away from Virginia and laughed. "So I already made the list. That's the funny thing about that praying stuff. Sometimes the people don't even know it, right?" He walked by the counter stools, spun one as he passed, and stopped at the register.

"That's right, nobody knows, just you and God," Virginia said.

"You mean me and God."

"Yeah, you know, only God and me."

"Right. Good," he said as he laughed and took his change from Frances, cradling his bag against his chest. "I think I'm confused but that's okay."

"No, No." Byron folded his hands as if in a prayer. "Your voice has to sound like it's coming right out of the bassoon. The vocal line is doubling the bassoon line if we had the score in front of us. It's a middle B smoothing right into it. Not over it. Into it so smoothly you hardly notice it. Now let's start again." He chorded the introduction again and listened for her voice to blend through his notes. He continued on, then raised his hands suddenly, as if in a mercy plea. "The grace notes. It wasn't clear enough there, in the beginning of the fifth measure. It's an F, G grace note, and then on to the barred F and E." Byron rose from the bench and stretched. "Come on now, you did all this before. Lesson eight in Vaccai, the approggiaturas."

Linda stepped closer to him and studied the music, nodding her head in agreement. "I remember. We spent a month on it." She stepped to his side and comforted herself there. "I thought I sang them. It wasn't clear?"

"You rushed through them. So, it's the F as an eighth

note, then the F, G grace note, and back to the F. You can add to the value, that's not a problem. Look, a little diversion. Sometimes it's good to have a diversion, no? Do you know the story about this composer?"

"Cataloni? No, I don't think I ever heard of him."

"Okay, so this piece, Ebben? Ne Andro Lantana. It's from the opera he wrote, La Wally."

"Never heard of it."

"That's okay, few have ever heard of it. It's not done much. But Puccini loved the music so much he named his daughter Wally."

Linda broke out in a wide smile. "Wally? Are you kidding me? He named his daughter Wally?"

"It's true. Her name was Wally. So, I know it feels natural to move over the grace notes quickly but you can't rush through it. Let's start again."

"But sometimes I feel like I'm going to run out of breath."

Byron turned and faced her. "That's because you don't trust your technique yet. You have plenty of breath left. Let's see, you're going five measures before you get to a rest. You have to trust yourself. Maybe you need to spend more time holding your exhaling in the old mirrors at work, slowly, patiently, eyes closed, with control." He turned to the piano, "From the beginning."

Linda stood beside him with her leg against the bench. She worked through the grace notes and the rest, then entered the crescendo when Byron stopped again. He didn't look at her, but played through the vocal line without talking. "There's no rest there, in the, let's see, seventh measure, there's no rest. You rested at the top of the crescendo. If you read the music you see the rest comes at the end of the decrescendo."

She shook her head without looking at the music. "I know it. I knew it when I did it because it felt natural to rest there. But that isn't what's written."

"Good. At least you recognized that. And I agree, it feels natural to come off the top and take a breath. But it's prettier and smoother to sing it as written. Let's go from the top again."

And on it went on, measure after measure, week after week, month after month, until he was convinced that after three years she had demonstrated a mastery of the vocal fundamentals, the necessary ornamentation and the range needed for the final developmental song that would - break them. It was in their third month working through the punishing soprano aria, In Questa Reggia, from Puccini's opera, Turandot.

"Stop, stop, stop." Byron stood, closed his eyes and shook his head in dismay. Linda was unable to relax despite his earlier instruction to settle down.

"You're rushing it. What is it today that you seem unable to even follow the tempo? I don't understand. It says molto lento, no? And you were not soft enough either."

Linda shook her head quietly, looking down at the music resting on the piano. "I know." She shrugged and opened her hands and said helplessly, "I don't know what's wrong today."

"I'll ask you again. Are you sure you don't want to just stop for today? We've been here for thirty minutes already and we haven't gotten through the second page. You know, some days we just don't have it. It's not a problem to stop and we can take it up next week."

Linda looked at him and tried to smile. Her face seemed frozen, as if paralyzed with fear. "No, Viejo, I don't want to stop. I look forward to this all week. I'll work through it."

"But last week you said you would be prepared to sing it through. Do you remember that?"

"I do," Linda responded softly.

Byron sat down, adjusting himself by rocking side to side for a moment. "Okay, from the beginning. Follow my lead, please don't get ahead of me."

Byron started again as the piano filled the loft and her voice entered for a few measures.

"No, no. Linda," Byron said, "there is a dotted eighth note in the third bar, then the tie begins with the sixteenth note. It's the last note of the measure, then the tie starts. You started the tie too soon." Byron turned her away from him to put some space between them.

Linda stepped closer to his side, felt his hand push against her thigh and shook her head in agreement, "I know, I felt it too. I'm anticipating the E flat." She looked down and measured the distance between them, fighting her instinct to stand closer to his side.

"Are you sure you don't want the score?" he asked, handing her the dog eared paper he stapled together.

"No, I get distracted by it. I feel like I'm reading ahead."

"Okay." Byron closed his eyes as an act of restraint, not wanting to say something he would regret or use a tone that would be offensive. "You're singing notes. We talked about this before, right?"

"Yes." Linda looked out at the dark nave and the shaft of sunlight slanting through the stained glass window above the altar. "We talked about it ten minutes ago," she said, turning back to Byron.

Byron began again. Linda stepped closer to his side and began singing perfectly, her voice soft and clear, slow and full of emotion, continuing through several measures until she had a four beat rest, and then, entering again, Byron clapped his hands and rose.

"It's supposed to be a C sharp. You sang a C natural." He handed her the music, leaving her no choice but to read it, "Again, from the top." Byron hesitated, looked at the music, and glanced at Linda. "No, let me change that. Let's begin at the key change" His voice was calm, as if he was resolved that this session was not going to produce the perfection he demanded. "Look ahead there, we have a tempo change after the eight measures, correct?"

Linda looked down at him and shook her head. "I see it. I'll sing it that way, Viejo. I'm sorry for all the difficulty."

Byron's chest heaved under a deep breath. "It's not you, Linda, it's me." He ran a clean handkerchief over his hair that was dampened with sweat. He swiveled his knees out from under the piano and faced her. "It isn't you. I'm too much of a perfectionist. But you've done so well, we have you there, just where your voice should be for this." He cast his eyes away from her, to the inky darkness of the deep recess of the loft. "Sometimes I think it's me. You know, maybe I should have steered you to some of the voice teachers at the store. They're younger, you know, maybe I'm too old to be badgering you like this."

Linda stepped towards him and patted her hand on his shoulder. "No, Viejo, I'm very happy with you. You pushed me to get to this level, even when I thought it was good enough, or when I couldn't get to the A above high C, still, you pushed me to believe that it was there, and you were right. None of those other teachers would have done that for me."

Byron lifted his eyebrows high on his wrinkled forehead and shook his head. He swiveled back under the piano. "Oh, you're wrong there, Linda. I hear some of those teachers, the female one, she's excellent. Sometimes I think I should have steered you to her. Maybe she would have been better for you."

Linda stooped down at Byron's side, placing her hand over his forearm. "Stop it, Viejo. No one else in the world would have done all you have for me. Not even a dime I paid you, nothing. Who works for nothing? No one comes to their student for three years and gets paid nothing. So what if we have some difficulty, you think it wouldn't happen with someone else? You wouldn't want my voice with anyone else, wouldn't trust them with it." Linda stood up and released her hand, "So you can just forget this talk about someone else, okay?"

Byron pursed his lips and nodded, "Okay. But I can't tell you that I won't get mad. This just gets me crazy, this notion that you can't sing this song through without any serious faults." He smiled to relieve the tension. "I don't know what it is that holds you back. I mean, this is it, this is the last performing lesson and we've been on it for three months. We were supposed to be done with this a month ago."

"So what does it matter? Is it so bad that it took a few more weeks?"

"No, Linda, it's not so bad. But there's other music I'd like to share with you but I can't until this is right. Besides, I'm not sure you want to sing this through. I mean, there is no reason for all these problems."

Linda's face contorted with confusion. "I don't understand either. I want to sing through, it's just that today nothing feels right. I told you that. And I offered to quit for today and take it up next week and you said no."

"Well, yes, I said no because I thought maybe it would work. Okay, let's try again. Just take it from the tempo marking, where the key signature changes to a major."

"Sure," Linda responded, knowing she failed to note the tempo change after the double bar.

Byron started again, pleased with her entry. They continued to the difficult full voiced hold on the B above high C when she faltered. He slammed his hands on the piano and jumped up. "No, no, no. You're rushing again," he bellowed. "It's a fermata! Enough!" he yelled, his hands flailing as he stormed away from the piano, "I've had enough!"

Linda's eyes darted over him as if they were on trackers that honed in on every twitch of his flesh. She was shocked at his anger and scared by it. She stood in silence. "We can quit for today," she said quietly.

"No," he grumbled, "it's not good enough to quit for today. Do you know what you did wrong? Do you know?"

"You're yelling at me, Viejo."

Byron exhaled loudly, the sound filling the church. He was exasperated with her. "You didn't answer me. Do you know what you did wrong?"

"I shorted the note. Is that what you want to hear, that I shorted the note? I think we should stop until next week."

Byron picked up the music and started for the stairs. "You're not ready to sing. That's the problem. I'm too old to be climbing these stairs if you're not ready. It's not the music or your voice, it's something else. But whatever it is, I can't help you with that. Only you can decide when you're ready." He started down the stairs, leaving her alone in the loft.

"Are you quitting on me, Byron?"

"No, Linda, I'm not quitting, but this can't go on. When you decide you're ready to sing this through correctly, call me. I'll be glad to come. But until then, there's no use in continuing to meet. This has to stop and it's stopping now."

Linda heard the spiral stairs creak under his weight, then listened as the interior door rocked to silence. The church was empty and quiet. She heard her own breath stutter as she tried to gain her composure. She knew he was right. She knew that she was failing him. She thought it wouldn't be apparent to him, that her failings were not technical, but emotional. She walked to the piano and sat there in peace with the silence. Then she ran her fingers over the keys and played the notes to a song she didn't know, two measures of music in an empty church, eight beats lost in an unfulfilled promise, seven notes shaded in sadness. She played them slowly and hummed them quietly then stood and looked over the broad expanse of the nave, resting her hands on the choir loft rail.

She wondered what Byron must be thinking. He yelled at her. Not corrected or criticized her, but yelled, with real anger and volume in his voice. Still, it was she who owed him an apology. She dropped her eyes to her hands and shook her head in disbelief. It wasn't his fault, but hers. She was wrong to be inconsiderate of his age, to drive him to this level of frustration. She sighed loudly, gathered her pocketbook and music, turned off the light and started down the stairs. She wasn't sure what the future held now, for even Saturday afternoons with Byron were a present and a future of sorts, at least for her. And now they were gone.

"Hey," Blake said to Tom, his young associate, "it's eight-thirty. I thought you said you had a party to go to."

Tom picked up Blake's draft copy of the Treasury Department's white paper, A Study of Intercompany Pricing. "It's okay, I told them I might not make it anyway.

I can stay. So, the plan is to get Butterfly Industries a subsidiary in a low tax overseas jurisdiction and then transfer the replacement parts business there, is that right?"

Blake shook his head in agreement, "Right, last week I was on the phone with tax authorities of several countries, talking about a negotiated tax rate of under five percent."

Tom gave Blake a perplexed look. "So, I don't get it. That's it, that's all that the sub does it collect the sales of replacement parts? And how much does Butterfly Industries charge them?"

Blake took the draft back and flipped through the pages he had marked up. "Basically, they charge cost and a small margin to cover the administrative costs. See, the whole purpose is to tie up the profits in a tax haven country. So, until they repatriate the profits of the sub to the parent, the money basically goes untaxed." Blake looked at his watch and nodded to Tom. "I want you to go. I do this all the time. You have to have a life."

Tom stood and shelved some books. "Are you sure? I really don't mind staying. It's just some of my college friends coming down. They're just going bar hopping. I can stay."

Blake waved him off. "No, you can't stay. I can handle the rest of this. We got all the good research there is to get. That's the problem with these tax shelters or proposed legislation, it's so flimsy that you keep digging, thinking there's something you missed." Blake stood and walked to the window, leaning on the ledge with his forehead pressed

549

against the glass. "You go. I insist."

Tom walked over and laid the citations down beside Blake's draft opinion letter. "I feel bad leaving you here. What about you? You have to have a life too."

Blake turned and shrugged, "This is my life."

Tom pulled his chair out and sat. "That's not good enough. I mean, some of the other associates, they told me about this stuff, that you just work all the time but, you know, I can't just leave you here. It's not right."

Blake sat and put his legs up on the table, burying his shoes among his own stacks of research volumes. "It's okay, Tom. This is what I do. You go. It's Saturday night. This is no place for you to be."

Tom got up and tucked in the chair. "Why don't you come out with us? You might have a good time. We're just going to grab something to eat and have some drinks."

"I don't think so. Thanks anyway. I'm going to finish this up. Couple more hours, I'll be done."

"Oh, man, Blake, I'll leave, but this isn't good. You need a life."

Blake smiled softly and nodded, "I know." He looked out the window and watched the street traffic far below, then turned back to Tom with the same soft smile. "I'm working on it."

Tom stood at the door, leaning casually against the frame, pretending not to be in a hurry. "Anything I can do before I go?"

"Yeah, you could do one thing for me. If you don't mind, could you put a CD on for me?"

Tom opened the cabinet doors to the sound system, turning it on all in one motion. "What do you want on?"

"It's probably in there already. Van Morrison, Poetic Champions Compose. I had it on last night."

The CD tray slid out. Tom flashed the CD at Blake. "Yeah, it's in. You want it on?"

"Yeah, thanks. But just put it on number three and then hit the repeat button."

Tom stood up and looked at Blake. "What? You want number three to repeat? Just keep repeating?"

Blake nodded in silence. His lips seemed to make an effort to smile but none came.

"Yeah," he finally whispered.

Tom programmed it and stood up without starting the player. "What's the song?"

"Nothing you know, Queen of the Slipstream."

"Never heard of it."

"That's what I said."

"Is it good? I like Morrison."

"Yeah, it's good. But to tell you the truth, it reminds me of someone. That's why I like it on repeat."

"I see," Tom said, hitting the play button and turning away. "Have a nice weekend. And thanks."

"Thanks. Have a nice time with your friends. And you're welcome."

Blake lifted his watch from the table. One-thirty. He stood and stretched, then shelved some books and yawned. He turned the lights off, finding a shadowy way to his chair where he leaned back and rested his legs along the wall-length window sill. He stood abruptly to see the night lights reflecting off the Potomac. Then he returned to his position and listened to the lyrics and closed his eyes, hoping it would happen again, the vision of her standing beside him on Elizabeth Street with snowflakes as big as medallions resting on her ivory cloche and cheeks and swirling around her face. Several minutes passed as he started to alternate between sentience and light sleep.

So it happened that her face appeared from the darkness, behind a falling snow whipped in circles and darts, spinning like frozen swatches of tulle in a slipstream caused by the traffic and wind. And he rested and waited and listened. His eyes grew heavy with sleep and he felt it again, the deepness of his breaths sending him into a rest that had eluded him for decades in his search for peace.

There she was, her face flecked in snow, smiling at him as she grabbed his arm when her foot slipped on the ice. She came in flashes, an alternating, visual percussion of blackness and brilliance. Like a lightman's signal over a moonless sea, her face appeared in alternating shards of darkness and light, in repetitive dreams that he was reluctant to wake from as Morrison's voice dug on in scat until dawn. He never heard the office door open nor saw the hall lights go on.

Norine stopped abruptly at the library door and quickly surveyed the scene. Blake was still, his head resting on his arms and his breathing audible in a fathom of sleep.

"I should have known," she commented to her husband

as she thumbed her blouse into her skirt and flicked up her sunglasses. "Imagine him worrying his mother like this." She walked to the sound system, studied it for a moment and then asked her husband to turn it off. She walked to Blake and called his name without response. "Blake," she repeated, nudging his shoulder and leaning over the table. She slid the remaining stacks of books away from him. The music stopped and the room was silent. "Blake," she said crisply, "wake up."

Blake's lips parted, "Huh?"

"Blake, wake up. It's morning. It's me, Norine. Norine and Jack."

Blake lifted his head and opened his eyes. He looked around the room slowly. "Hey," he said, squinting into the morning light, "what are you doing here? What time is it anyway?"

Norine pulled a chair out and sat beside him. Jack took a seat on the other end of the table and folded his hands. "It's six-thirty in the morning, Blake."

"Oh, I must have fallen asleep."

Norine raised her eyebrows and sided her head defiantly, "Oh, you definitely fell asleep. Your mom is worried sick. She called us a little before six. Said she's been trying to get you all night but no one answered."

Blake rested his head in his hand. His face scratched with stubble. "Oh, man, I'm so sorry she called you this early." He looked over to Norine and back to Jack who was straightening his tie. "You're all dressed up, both of you."

"We didn't know what we'd find here, Blake. You scared

the daylights out of us. We figured we'd dress and go to early services if everything was okay. You got to call your mom right now."

"Yeah, I guess."

Jack walked the desk phone over to Blake, tapped in the number, and handed the receiver to Blake. He spoke to his mom for a moment, apologized for making her worry, and handed the phone to Norine who nodded into the phone, then held the receiver out, away from her ear. "She wants to know what you were doing there all night."

"Research. Me and Tom were doing some research and it got late and I guess I fell asleep."

"He said he was doing research. Don't worry. Jack and I are going home with him, get him to clean up. Maybe take him to services with us and to breakfast."

A moment passed as Norine looked at the phone, then looked back at Blake, "No, I don't think he needs any sleep. He was sleeping soundly when we got here."

She hung up the phone and walked to the doorway. Jack stepped out behind her. She flicked down her sunglasses and pressed her skirt with her palms. "You put away your research. Jack and I will be out here waiting on you. And just what were you doing here all night anyway?"

Blake opened his palms over the table, stood and stretched with a loud yawn. "Told you, I was doing research. Doesn't it look like I was doing research?"

Norine flicked her glasses up again with a perturbed look in her eyes. She reached over and turned on the lights. "Oh, yeah, smarty, since when do you do your research in the dark?"

Blake looked at her blankly. No excuse came to mind. He buried his face in his hands and rubbed the sleep from his eyes. "It's a long story. I'll tell you over breakfast."

Linda closed the car door and stepped back. She put her hand over her eyes to block the blinding glint of sun reflecting off the store windows and squinted to read the signs above small stores lining the street. There, before the sidewalk folded up and wrapped along a steep hill thick with deciduous trees, above a store window shaded with lemon mylar to cut the sun's heat, she read the sign, 'BANKO'S HOUSE OF MUSIC.'

The wooden door was held open by a worn rope looped over a hook. The wall was full of sheet music racked like magazines. A young man with shoulder length hair tied in a ponytail picked at an acoustical guitar and disappeared behind a high counter that doubled as a work table. The aisle was wide enough only for a sideways walk, one person at a time. She stepped in, reaching her hand up over her head to guard against the dozens of guitars hanging from the ceiling, filling every inch of precious space. Turning sideways, she edged her way in where she was greeted by a flute in some degree of disassemble associated with the entrails of a clarinet splayed over the counter. A man with a crew cut and heavy glasses worked furiously at fluttering a flute key, measuring its action as he held it towards the door to see the sunlight spin through the aperture.

An older man behind the counter worked grease into a clarinet cork. An unlit cigar bounced between his teeth. He glanced at her over his bifocals. "Hi," he called out. "How can I help you?" he asked, making eye contact after wiping the grease from his fingers. "Looking for some sheet music?"

Linda moved to the high counter, reaching her arms up uncomfortably, then dropping them once again. "Hi," she responded nervously. "No. No sheet music today. I'm looking for Byron. Byron Zabusky. Is he here?"

The old man slipped his bifocals to the edge of his nose and looked at her sternly. He laid the clarinet on the counter and took the cigar from his mouth. "Are you a friend of his?" he asked as he hitched up his pants.

"Yes, I am," she responded with a slight smile. "I'm a student of his. I need to speak to him. He does work here, doesn't he?"

Wild, untrimmed grey eyebrows lifted high into the man's creased forehead. "Student?" he asked as he came around the counter. "What kind of student? I didn't know Byron gave lessons. Joe," the old man asked, looking through the door to his left, "you know anything about Byron giving lessons or something?"

Linda turned and stepped back into the narrow aisle, blocking it completely. "I feel like I'm in the way here," she said sheepishly.

The old man grabbed her arm firmly and moved her between the bodies of two hanging guitars. "You'll be all right here. Just watch your head."

The young man came around the counter with an intact flute in his hand. "Yeah, he mentioned it once. That's where he goes when he leaves here on Saturdays. Voice?" he asked as he held a guitar aside and stepped next to Linda.

"Yes," Linda said with relief. "Is he here?"

The man stepped across the aisle and handed the flute to a small girl standing with her parents in an adjoining workroom. "No. He left for the day," he said to the old man. "He'll be back Monday," he said, turning back to Linda. "Usually gets here around seven. Opens the place up. Gets here before me." He smiled courteously and turned his attention to the little girl with the flute.

"Oh, I see," Linda said, turning her head between them and the guitars. "Well, can you tell me where he lives then? It's important that I speak to him."

"You want his phone number?" the old man asked, holding the unlit cigar between his fingers and poking the air with it.

Linda squeezed her hands together nervously and bent around a guitar that turned slowly into her face. "No," she said quickly, "no, I have his phone number. I, uh, just feel that I'd like to see him. We had a disagreement, a professional disagreement, and I feel that I owe him more than just a phone call."

The old man looked at her and shook his head. "You familiar with the area?"

"A little," Linda answered.

"You know where Birchbank is?"

"No. What is it close to?"

"You know where State Park is?"

"Yes, I know that. Is it close to there?"

"Kind of, it's beyond it."

"I'll find it."

"No, that's not good enough. It's hard to explain. He lives way up in Birchbank. Unless you're familiar with the area it's easy to get lost. Very narrow road. You could use the phone if you'd like," he said turning to the wall and pointing to the phone buried among illegible notes tacked to the wall.

"No," she said with some hesitancy. "No, I'd rather speak to him in person. I'll find it if you'll give me directions."

He put the cigar back into his mouth and held it between clenched teeth. He stepped towards Linda and called the young man with the ponytail. "Kenny," he said, "show this lady where Byron lives." He turned back to Linda and stood beside her, holding a guitar back with his arm. "It's a long, narrow driveway. Not paved, lots of trees. I don't even think he has a mailbox out front anymore. You follow Kenny. He'll get you there. It's about a half an hour drive. Tough to spot the driveway." The cigar man stuck his hand out and asked, "What did you say your name was?"

Linda put her hand into his as he pumped it enthusiastically. "I didn't say, at least, I don't think I said. Linda. Thank you so much for your help. I'm a friend of Byron." Linda slipped her pocketbook off her shoulder and opened it as she spoke. She had a great, relieved smile on her face. "Can I at least pay you for your Kenny's time? I'm really so grateful."

"No, please," he said, walking back around the counter and pulling up his loose pants. "He's about ready to leave anyway and it's kind of on his way."

Linda edged her way out onto the sidewalk and waited for Kenny. She peered into the mylared window and smiled as Kenny started out to the sidewalk. "Awful crowded in there, isn't it?" she commented by way of a question.

"Yeah," Kenny said, flipping his ponytail back. "Actually, Saturday mornings are much worse. It's actually slow now. Where's your car?"

"Right there, across the street," Linda said, pointing.

"Okay," Kenny responded, pulling his keys from his pocket. "I'm parked in the back here, when I pull out just follow me. Byron lives about ten miles from here. It's very narrow, so when we get there I'll just point to the driveway and you pull in, okay."

"Okay," Linda responded, backpedaling to her car, "And thank you very much."

"No problem."

Linda followed Kenny for several miles before he turned off Route 110, passed State Park and over the railroad tracks to a narrow, winding road that had the feel of a child's roller coaster with dips and curves jumping at her every ten yards. On her left was the wooded mountain that rose steeply off the banks of the Housatonic. As they traveled further along, through fits and starts, she followed Kenny over to the edge of the road to allow cars to pass from the other direction. Summer cottages perched on cinder blocks, with dark weathered screens, snuggled along the river and the mountain. To her left an expanse of flats opened up, wooded and course. Suddenly, she saw Kenny's arm pointing to the left and then his car disappeared around a bend.

She turned into the driveway, thickly canopied with the fat, lazy leaves of August. Her tires crushed gravel beneath them in the deep tire ruts, causing the bottom of her car to scrape against the center as she make her way down the driveway. A low hanging willow branch brushed her windshield and scraped her roof just as she entered a clearing.

A small grey cape stood alone surrounded by towering birch and oak and pine. Along the back, before the mountain stretched to the end of sight, bramble skitted among wild berries harvested by sparrows and robins and blue jays and cardinals. There was no front yard to speak of, just a dusty, graveled clearing wide enough for a few cars and a turn around. Tall weeds stretched through the areas of gravel that hadn't felt the crush of a car tire all summer.

She stopped close to the front steps. A gutter hung loosely off the low roof and sprouted some grass and weeds. Towering shrubs flanking the front door masked a picture window shrouded by dingy, stale sheers. Wide swatches of crab grass spread their fat blades between broken and unevenly spaced flagstone. The front door was fully open, possibly with the hope for a refreshing breeze, with a chalky aluminum door resting slightly ajar, its screen torn and patched with clear tape that was curling off.

Linda glanced over her shoulder and turned the car off.

Cautiously, she looked around for any sign of movement, stepping out and standing by the car. Through the ripped screen she heard music, vaguely familiar, its sound swelling and filling the clearing, then retreating quickly.

The aluminum rail along the three front steps rocked as Linda climbed to the landing. She knocked on the aluminum door that shook but carried no sound. She tried shutting it, hoping that would allow her to knock with more force, but found it out of alignment and unable to close securely. "Byron?" she called out. She stood and listened before turning to the sun dappled tree tops and the shadowed road. "Byron?" she called in a louder tone, knowing her voice could not overcome the sound of the music.

She cupped her eyes with her hands and peered into the rusted screen. It was dark except for the natural light coming in from the window. She turned, stepped down, and looked back at the door. She walked back towards her car, then started along the overgrown walkway leading to the back. She bent her knees and high-stepped to avoid the tangle of brush along the path, opened the wooden side door and leaned into a large, enclosed porch. Byron was facing her, seated in a raised chair with his head resting on his arms folded over a music stand.

Along the wall to his left were metal folding chairs with instruments placed over them or in front of them. Strings and woodwinds, flutes and double basses standing in the corner. Against the back wall, laid out over two day beds, with a row of folding chairs before them, were percussions of every variety, with heads disassembled and leaning against chairs. Old tartan curtains, thin with age, blocked some of the light from the three walls of windows that opened to the outside world, allowing the music to fill the wooded mountains beyond the house.

Linda called his name again. His shirt was matted to his frame like wallpaper, wetted with sweat.

She moved to the side of the room and walked into his line of vision, stepping around the chairs and instruments. Carefully, darting her eyes back to him and then before her, she moved along the perimeter of the room.

His hair looked like he had just been called out of a shower and had no time to dry it. Sweat rolled down his cheeks and into his neck.

She kept her eyes clocking between him and the obstacles before her, feeling her way through the room until her foot caught the leg of a timpano, tipping it into the cymbals that fell into a metal chair with a loud crash.

Byron's eyes opened to a burning river of sweat. He sat up, reached over and lowered the volume of the music. He grabbed a damp towel and ran it over his face and head.

The room was quiet. Soft, golden tunnels of afternoon sun filtered in along the wall, through the thin curtains, and glistened from the brass and chrome that lay over the chairs. She turned from Byron to the timpano as she tried to set it on its legs. It rolled into the trombone on the chair in front of it, knocking it to the floor also.

"Don't bother, Linda," Byron said, running the towel over his face again. "The leg is broken. That's why it's here." Then he turned away from her and swept his arm over the room. "That's why they're all here. My entire orchestra is in pieces." He stepped away from the raised chair, turned an empty folding chair towards her and sat. A bead of sweat rolled down his cheek.

She stood in the percussion section holding the broken piece in her hand, unsure where to place it without further turmoil. "What is it?" she asked.

"That," he said from beneath another wipe of his towel, "that's the leg of the timp."

"No," Linda responded with a relieved smile, shaking her head, "not this. The music. What is the piece?"

"Oh," Byron said over belly laugh, "Marietta's Lied." He shook his head and waved a disinterested hand towards her, "Ah," he exclaimed, "the lied we never got to. Do you know it?"

"Yes, When I was a little girl, in the city, my uncle lived in the Bronx, right on an elevated line, the 3rd Avenue El. They took it down now. Anyway, I would get scared when the trains rumbled by. So my father played that many times for me, particularly the ending with the long timpani roll, he played it loudly and he would hold my fingers on the window and feel it vibrate from the sound wave and told me it was all music, the percussion, from the train or the orchestra, everything. That's one of my earliest memories."

Byron smiled broadly and nodded, "That's a wonderful memory, Linda." He wiped his face again, draped the towel over his head and rubbed it vigorously. "You have to excuse me. You caught me being Byron." He stood and placed the towel on the empty chair. "I find that piece comforting. I play it when I feel troubled. It eases me, the beautiful sound of the soprano voice, the longing she sings of, the loss she feels. It is part of the richness of the German lieder, the longing, the sehnsucht. Hard to translate it into English. It's deeper than just longing. It's, well, how do you say, meta-physical, spiritual."

Linda shook her head slowly and swallowed hard. "I'm sorry I walked in on you, Viejo. I knocked and called your name but you didn't hear me."

He waved off her comment and looked down, fatigue overcoming him. "It's nothing, Linda. I get carried away sometimes." He thought of how he must look to her, drenched in sweat, sleeping in the room full of broken and dented instruments. "You know, sometimes I conduct this broken orchestra," he said, lifting his head and tightening his lips. "Pretend is a good thing." He ran his fingers through his damp hair. "Sometimes that's all we have to get by. Do you understand that? That sometimes pretend is all we have left?"

Linda stood in the center of the room, surrounded by the instruments. She hadn't moved in minutes. She glanced beyond Byron into the living room with pictures of his family on the walls. "I do understand." She studied the room. In neat semi-circles, the instruments lay there, waiting for repair on chairs set for this purpose only. "Byron," she asked over a smile that she could not hide, "are these all yours, all these instruments?"

Byron shook his head without saying a word. He flipped some pages of the score. "Oh, no, I don't own any of these." He grinned widely. "Actually, it's really gotten out of hand since my wife died. She kept me in check. You know, women are good for that kind of thing."

Linda stepped her way through the instruments, past Byron and into the living room. "This is her?"

"Yes, that's her, with my granddaughters, just before she got sick."

"How long is she gone now? I know you told me before but I forgot."

Byron leaned over and pulled a clean towel from the top of the speaker. He ran it over his head. "Let's see," he said with some thought for what the current year was, "twenty years or so. I started taking more instruments home with me then. I listen to music, turn some screws, re-cork the valves. Fix the dents in the brass if I can. Restring violins, cellos. Whatever I can fit into the car," he said with a shrug, "I take home."

Linda stepped closer to him. His shirt was damp with sweat as was the waist of his pants from the sweat that ran down his chest and over his belly. It didn't seem to bother him.

"You were conducting before I got here? Is that why

you're so sweated up?

"Yes, but another piece, more strenuous."

"You're going to kill yourself doing that."

Byron looked into her eyes. A smiled creased his lips as he turned his palms up with restful indifference. He turned away from her and shrugged his shoulders.

"Oh, Linda," he sighed, "how do I tell you? You're still young." Then he turned back to her and rested his eyes into hers and spoke softly, as if his tone might disturb the amber tint that filled the room. "I am un viejo. When God wants me, at least he'll know where to look. You don't have to worry about me, Linda, I'm happy."

Linda looked at him and nodded, then walked along the living room wall and lined the dust off the picture with her finger. "Your wife, she was pretty, Byron."

Byron smiled proudly. "Yes, she was very pretty and a wonderful friend. She put up with a lot, as you can imagine," he said, sweeping his hand over the room.

"Didn't you tell me she played the cello?"

Byron pointed to a case against the wall. "Yes, that's her cello. She played beautifully. But," he said with an acceptance worn well over time, "towards the end, the cancer wore her down. So she would sit there, in that same chair, and I would talk to her while I fixed the instruments. And she would nod sometimes. Sometimes she would be in great pain, so I would sit beside her and say nothing so she wouldn't even have to nod. The bass against the wall, that's mine." He shrugged his shoulders and smiled, lifted his palms in benign resignation.

566

"Sometimes I still talk to her." He put his finger to his lips and offered a lame smile. "Don't tell!"

Linda stepped closer to the stand and lowered her eyes, whispering, "Never."

Byron leaned to the CD player and turned up the music so it could be heard, no longer as background but with sound that impeded conversation. "So," he said, turning back to her, "you came because you're ready to sing." He glanced up at her and flipped the score until he found his place.

Linda stepped back into the living room as she spoke. "Yes," she said quietly, "I'm ready to sing."

Byron rolled his eyes toward her. He was looking for clarity of purpose in her, strength enough to break through that which held her. "You're certain?"

Linda shook her head confidently, "Yes," she responded, without a smile or softening in her tone. "I'm sure. I wouldn't ask you to return if I wasn't. I couldn't do that to you."

Byron reached to the wall, glanced at the disk cover and handed it to her. "Number 5, In Questa Reggio. Listen to it, the great Tebaldi. Wear a dress, the formality helps." He rested his forearm over the podium and leaned over it. "Saturday?" he asked, "same time?"

"Yes," she responded, examining the disk cover as the music built to a crescendo.

"I love the recitative here," he said, smiling and pointing to the speaker, "and how the music slips back into the melody. The vocals are beautiful."

Linda smiled at his absorption with the music. He returned her smile and stepped towards her, holding out his hands apologetically, and brushed past her to the kitchen. The refrigerator door popped open, bathing his face in a dim yellow light as he poked his head into it. "I didn't even offer you a drink or anything, Linda. How about some ice water or something? Maybe something to eat? Or some soda," he asked, pulling out a half empty bottle. "It's probably flat. But ice water, would you like ice water?" He put the soda on the counter and held up the bottle of chilled water.

Linda laughed at his effort to be a host. "No, nothing, Viejo, I'm all right. I didn't come here to eat."

Byron placed the water bottle back into the nearly empty refrigerator and closed the door. "It's hard," he said with a shrug, "I don't keep anything around. I'm alone, you know, it just goes bad." He stepped by her, back to the podium. "Sorry. I don't get much company. Once in a while I invite the guys from the store up. Buy some beer and snacks. During the week I eat most of my meals out."

"It's okay, Byron, really. I can't stay anyway. I have to get back to work. So I'll see you next week, right?" she asked as she turned and walked to the door.

"Yes," Byron said, following her to the door and holding it open as she walked to her car, "three or so." Byron stepped back into the house and watched her through the rusted screen. "Thank you for coming," he called out to her as she waved before getting into the car.

"See you Saturday." She drove slowly down the rutted

driveway and hesitated at the street for a car to come over the bend. Music, faint but clear, filtered through the trees.

She waited, despite a clear road, as the heat bloomed with the sound of the soprano vocal. She imagined him standing, sweated and damp, following every note in the score. She wanted to turn back, to find him again and break into his world unannounced, to rescue him from the loneliness. But the music rested and swelled before the kettle drums rolled a sun-mottled thunder over the forested road. Glancing into the rearview mirror, she bit her lip, blinked back her concern and drove home.

Marietta's Lied filled Linda's head. She digressed from her route home and entered Route 8, northbound, from Shelton, and drove through the Valley, with the song in her head and on her lips.

She exited in Waterbury and started southbound. She thought of Byron and his description to her of the German word, sehnsucht, the longing. She longed, it seemed, for a lifetime. She bit her lower lip to keep from crying while the music played in her mind.

Route 8 was carved into the Valley, pressing lanes of asphalt that altered a hamlet's insular topography and cast its future with that of the larger world, carrying traffic through the hills and over the bed of earth stenciled by two rivers. Exit 15 careens down to the level of Hog's Island in a tight hairpin, a turn from the tree tops to bedrock in one dramatic whip, to the lowest part of the Valley.

Linda got off of that exit and rode the sweep to Main

Street, beside the flats and the vacant Farrell's plant, desolate and barren, lifeless in the stifling heat. She stopped for the traffic light and looked up and around to the majestic hills, high above the rivers, that swelled and bloomed with unsurpassed beauty. She thought of Byron's music blasting from his back porch at Birchbank and started to hum the lied. She drifted into a dream state as she lipped the word sehnsucht silently, the only German she knew. In a break from consciousness she felt levitated on the transcendent, timeless longing that she knew so well. She heard the timpani, the long roll of thunder underpinning the orchestra at the end of Marietta'a Lied. She imagined herself on her father's lap, at the window in the Bronx with his hand gently placed over her tiny fingers. Reaching up, she touched the windshield, seeing a child's hand pressed on a rattling window pane until the blast of an impatient horn startled her back to reality.

Tori stood in Janet's office overlooking the flat roof tops that lined Elizabeth Street. The verdant hills that crowned the Valley stood before her as she had never seen from that elevation. Flecks of color peeked through from peek-a-boo houses that dotted the hills through the dense foliage.

"Wow," she said softly as Janet hung up the phone, "nice view from up here." Janet grimaced and examined the nail she broke on the file fastener.

"Oh," she moaned, picking up the French tip off the floor laying a thick mortgage closing instruction file on her desk, "and I just got these nails done last night." She examined the nail again and shook her head in disgust. She straightened her skirt and looked up, "You've never been up here?"

Tori shook her head and smiled, "No. I've been on the floor but never saw the view from this side of the building.

"Really?" Janet asked, "and how long have you worked here now?"

"About two and a half years. But most of that was after school, part time and summers."

"Oh, right," Janet responded, opening a mortgage closing file and holding up a check sheet. "Well, this job is really very simple," she explained, laying the sheet on her desk. "When a closing file comes in you go down the list and check off all the forms to be sure they're all here and executed. I have a copy of all the forms in here in the order the check sheet is in."

Tori stepped to the desk, then to Janet's side. "And what if they're not?"

Janet tapped her broken nail along the bottom of the paper, reading the bold language as she spoke.

"All incomplete files are to be forwarded to the loan originator for correction," she said curtly, closing the file for emphasis, and lifting it into her arm. "You just take it right back down to the originator. It's their responsibility to have the closing attorney complete the file."

"So then I enter the mortgage data and the deed gets filed in the vault?"

"Yes. Sometimes we have to prepare paperwork for a release. Like in a refinancing, you forward the forms to processing. They match the payoff amount to the check and then approve the release. Then you pull the mortgage deed, stamp it paid and send it to the borrower with an official approval and signature."

Tori picked up the file and walked to the door. "So where do I get the files? Will someone, like, bring them to me? Do I ask someone?" she asked, leaning casually against the door frame.

"Well," said Janet walking to her chair and lifting her pocketbook to her desk. "Usually, what happens is one of the receptionists downstairs will call you." Janet ran her finger over the broken nail, preoccupied with her ruinous fate. She fingered through her bag and pulled out a nail file, then swiveled her chair out and crossed her legs. "I knew I had one in here somewhere," she said, looking up at Tori and smiling. "You all set, Hon?"

"So if it's all right I just forward it to processing and enter it?"

"Right. If all the papers are here you just put your initials on it and send it on. If you have any questions you can ask Joe Baliki. He usually likes to stay pretty close to this stuff. Sometimes, the mortgage release from another bank won't be available," she said, filing her nail and looking up at Tori on occasion, blowing the nail dust from her desk top. "But the payoff figure will be there and the title insurance policy won't list another mortgage so just forward the file. You can work right here at my desk. You'll have more room to spread the file out. And, you know, after you checked everything and make sure it's all here, just put it in the order of the check off sheet."

Tori stood there for a second, trying to think of anything else that might be important to know, putting her hands into the pockets of her sun dress. Janet's concern with her nail made Tori end the exchange without further instruction. "So how long will you be gone?" she asked, moving to the door of the office and placing her hand along the frame.

"Two weeks," responded Janet, dropping the file into her bag and swinging it to the floor. "Two weeks away from this madhouse. We just can't keep up with these closings. Mortgage lending is up twenty three percent from last year, and that was a record year. Believe me, I need some time off."

"Going to get that fixed before you leave?" Tori smiled at Janet and tugged gently on her narrow braid.

Janet blew the nail dust away and held up the finger to examine it. "Oh," she said, bringing the finger down for more work, "I get them done in Milford. I called, told me to get there before five." She blew on the nail again and shook her head, "Maybe they'll put a fake one on." She pouted her lips and shook her head again, "It'll take me a few months to grow that back."

"You don't mind wearing the fake ones?" Tori asked.

Janet placed the file back into her pocketbook. "No. Even though they make your nails look too thick. Your mom get hers done?"

Tori smiled and shook her head. "My mom? No. She doesn't even do her nails. Keeps them short anyway. My mom's very simple. Has her hands in and out of water all day." Then she thought for a second and straightened herself from the doorway. "Sometimes, if she has to dress up, like if she sings for a wedding or something, she'll use a clear polish. This way, if it starts to chip or wear, it's hard to tell. But she does her own."

"It can get expensive. You know, some women get them done once every two weeks. That saves money."

Tori nodded and raised her eyebrows. "Yeah, I guess it would. Well, have a nice vacation. Don't worry about this place. I'll try to keep up so you won't be buried when you return."

"Oh, thank you, Tori. Remember, if you have any questions don't be afraid to ask Joe."

"Okay," said Tori, turning away, "I will."

The Greek clasped the rusted railing with both hands and leaned forward. Neon yellow sunglasses swung from his neck on a knot of black shoelace. He surveyed Anson Street like a field marshal. The deep, striated canals of his face creased like supple leather as he winced into the mid-morning sun. He measured the panorama of impeding objects resting on the sidewalk and the cirrus clouds cresting thin curls over Long Island Sound. Cars standing up on skinny ratchet jacks leaned perilously as if perched on a flamingo leg. Three shopping carriages littered the gutter guarded by milk cartons stacked to serve as chairs to big bellied men in wife beaters. The Greek nodded and noted that the additional shopping carriage didn't escape

574

his count.

It's late morning, long beyond the yawn of sunrise, but a fresh day for the Greek. The August sun practiced its burning magic and lifted waves of heat from the pavement. A cigarette butt, still burning, lay in the intersection of Anson and Sixth. From the kitchen he could hear the water run as his mother tried to be heard over the swell of a motorcycle revving at the stop sign. The Greek broke into a grand smile and lifted an arm to its full extension.

"Jerry," he called out as he stood erect. "Jerry," he repeated in a conversational tone, his eyes still puffed with sleep. "That's you, Jer." Jerry smiled back and ripped away in a deafening thunder that faded up towards Coon Hollow. For the Greek, the day was just beginning to roll to a boil.

He looked down at himself, examining the sharp creases of his jeans, running his fingertip over them with satisfaction. He tugged at the oversize spread collar of his white shirt and opened up another button. He squared off his neck, planed his combed back tungsten gray hair with his palms, and lifted his sunglasses into place with an optician's care.

Lanky and spare, rakish and trim, the Greek stepped off, a drum major in denim, on a cakewalk around the Valley. Like rim shots sounding over a frosted field, he heeled the sidewalk with a clear, crisp, confident snap of his black leather shoes.

Proud and unabashed, with a percussive gait, he kicked up pebbles and ground pavement beneath every step. Past the hulking factories, mostly wasted and spent now, and the cigar store with late hours, past convents and churches, the synagogue and schools, past bankers and machinists, accountants and roofers, hookers and addicts, tenements and capes and the bungalows by the cemetery, he cinched the girth of the Valley like a sack. He greeted everyone the same way, without a break in his stride, an arm raised straight out at forty-five degrees and his hand sprung up at a ninety degree angle at the wrist, with the name of his acquaintance called out, allowing the heated excess of vice the same warmth and respect as the clergy and widows and children. Everyone knew the Greek.

Joe Baliki stepped into the mail room, laying a thick manila envelope on the postage scale and running off a meter tape. He turned to the wrapping table, laying the envelope in the outgoing basket between Tori and the young man in the mail room.

"How's everything going, Tori?" he asked, continuing on before she had time to respond. "I haven't heard about any problems with closings getting to the processors so I assume everything is okay." Baliki turned to the young man who was lifting a file into the mail cart. "You must be Dr. Miller's son," he said, sticking his hand out. "I'm Joe Baliki. I was golfing with your dad the other day and he said you were working in the mail room for the summer."

The young man released the heavy box and clasped Baliki's hand enthusiastically, grinning broadly. "Hi. I'm Fred. Nice to meet you Mr. Baliki. Yeah, my dad told me he had a bad day. Lost two balls. He hates to lose balls."

Baliki smirked. "Oh God, you'd think they were made of gold the way he cries about them. So," he continued, riffling through the stack of mail that was laying on the table, "where you going to school in September?"

"Villanova," responded Fred spritely, "to study finance." He grabbed the mail cart and started towards the elevator. Baliki followed.

"Oh, really, I have a niece that goes there." His voice trailed off into the hall. as the phone rang.

Tori stopped sorting and picked it up, placing it back into its cradle just as quickly and going towards the elevator to pick up the closing files that had come in during the morning.

"Hi, Tori," chirped Mary, seated behind the high counter on a stool with a headphone dropped to her neck, "got a whole bunch of closings for you. They all came in at once, just after lunch. I think there are eight. At least it's Friday, right, honey?"

"You're not kidding," Tori said, counting the files before loading them into her arms.

"You have to finish them before the day's over?" Mary asked.

"Well, I have to check them for completeness at least, and get the checks out so they can be posted. But it's a break to do these, gets me up from the computer for a while anyway."

Mary placed her headphones back on. "Good afternoon, Birmingham Savings Bank," she said, as if speaking to herself. "Oh," she called with her hand over the speaker, "Joe left this down here by mistake. I opened it. Looks like a mortgage deed to be filed."

Tori returned again rolling her eyes playfully, taking the deed from her and laying it over the closing files. "No wonder Janet needed two weeks off," she whispered over a smile.

The elevator stopped abruptly on the fourth floor. Fred stood before the door as it opened, his cart full as he backed away to let Tori out. "Wow, you're loaded," Baliki exclaimed, reaching in to hold the door open for Fred.

Fred pushed the cart into the elevator as Joe slipped in. "Tori, you doing anything tonight?" asked Fred as the doors closed on his cart with a loud crush.

Tori turned to him and laughed as he pushed the doors back open. Fred grinned broadly and shrugged his shoulders. "Yeah. I have to help my grandmother at the church festival until my mom gets there, around eight. Then I'm going home. Kind of tired."

Fred leaned out of the elevator holding the door with his hand. "Okay. See you. Maybe I'll go to the festival. I'll look for you."

"Okay. I'll be in the ticket booth until about eight."

"See you."

"Bye." Tori walked into Janet's office and let the files collapse on the desk. She seated herself, reaching back and pulling several closing check-off sheets from the shelf behind her.

She took the letter containing the mortgage deed Mary

gave her and reviewed it quickly for the borrower's name and the address of the property mortgaged. She scanned the deed and noted the three hundred thousand dollar loan amount before flipping it over, matching the signatures to the borrower's name typed on the deed, and putting it aside in the corner of the desk.

The closing files were set into two neat piles, allowing her to go through several of them quickly, matching the documents against the check-off sheet and turning them over as they were completed, putting them in order as she checked them off by fingering through them. She pulled the sixth file and opened it on the desk, glancing up at the wall clock, surprised it was a little after three already. She gave a thought to the festival and how hot it would be in the ticket booth tonight with the sun beating down on the blacktop parking lot and the air trapped in the food tents.

She filled out the check-off sheet, recognizing the name again. She pulled the mortgage deed and checked it off, glancing down to read the description for a second, and noticing the three hundred thousand dollar loan. She creased her forehead quizzically as she read the description again, finally placing the deed copy aside and picking up the one that Mary had given her earlier.

She set the documents side by side and reviewed them carefully. There were no differences except the date of the transaction, the loan number and the check number. Tori glanced at the clock again. She heard Joe's voice from his office as he spoke on the phone. She took the documents and walked down the stairs to the permanent files, pulling the closing file for the earlier mortgage and seating herself at her cubicle.

"Hey, Tori," said Darlene with her native South Carolina length to her words, sitting in the cubicle to Tori's rear. "Thought you'd be gone by now, being that you're in those executive offices now."

"No," Tori said, holding the word out for emphasis, "not this executive. Actually, I'm behind." She spun her chair around and stood. "Hey, Dar," she asked, leaning over the cubicle partition, "can you punch in some loan numbers for me? My terminal's down and I don't have the time to play with it."

"Sure," Darlene said, glancing up at Tori, "whenever you're ready."

Tori held the file with both hands and closed her eyes, thinking out loud. "Let's see, I want to check all the loans in this name. I seem to have two mortgage deeds, recorded on two different dates for the same property but I think I'm missing a release and a payoff."

Darlene stood and glanced at her watch. So how long was this favor going to take, she thought to herself. "Why don't I just enter the borrower's name and see what we come up with?" she suggested, hoping to move the process along.

"Yeah," Tori responded quickly as Darlene checked the spelling and sat in front of the console and typed in the name. "Try that. That should at least tell us the number of loans."

"Lots," Darlene said with the sinking feeling this would

take longer than she anticipated."Lots of loans. Should I go to the payment summary?" She entered the command before Tori could think through the question. "Current," Darlene said, looking up at Tori for direction, "it looks like everything is current."

"Yeah," Tori said with a drained voice."That's what I was afraid of."

Darlene yawned, forcing her arms back in a grand stretch. "So I don't get it. What's the big deal if they're all current?"

Tori slipped into Darlene's chair and tapped in some instructions. "See," she said slowly, clearly preoccupied with the screen and not the conversation, "I got these two deeds in today. One closed two months ago, one closed today. So why would there be two loans on the same piece of property, both for three hundred thousand dollars?"

"So," Darlene responded, setting her elbows on the partition and resting her chin on her arm, "maybe the property is worth lots of money?"

"That's possible," Tori said, tapping in a few more commands, "but I don't know." She looked up at Darlene with a serious expression. "It just seems unusual to me." She turned back to the screen. "See," she said intently, putting her finger to the screen, "there's four loans on the same property. And look at this, all in the jumbo range."

Darlene lifted her chin from her elbows and stepped to the back of her chair to get a clear view of the screen. "Check the history."

"But we just checked the summary screen and it was all

current."

"Just check again. Just for this property this time. Something's not right. I just want to make sure the loans are in the system."

Tori tapped in a few keystrokes. Darlene swiveled her head to see who else was around. The room was nearly empty except for a few clerks in a clutch of conversation across the room. The screen illuminated with the payment data of the first loan. "Current," Tori said, looking up at Darlene.

"Hit continue," Darlene demanded, hunched over Tori's shoulder.

"Current." She continued to the next loan, "current again."

"Next one," Darlene urged.

"Current." Tori turned and looked at Darlene. "How can it be, there's no payoff on the refinance? The original loan was here as well and it's still in a current status."

Darlene shook her head and raised her eyebrows. "That doesn't make sense to me." She put her hands on her hips, as if to force out some thoughts. "The vault is still open, right?"

Tori looked at her watch, "Twenty to four. Marla should still be there. She always stays late anyway."

They walked down the one flight of stairs without speaking, each thinking they must be missing something obvious that will explain away the whole thing.

"What was that, six eighteen Atlantic?" Darlene whispered to Tori although no one was in the vault.

"Uh-huh, six eighteen," Tori repeated, over Darlene's shoulder.

Darlene pulled out four mortgage deeds and rested them on the drawer. Tori took two of the deeds and compared them. "It's the same description, three hundred thousand each, four months apart." She looked at Darlene, "How about yours?"

"Same thing," Darlene responded, flipping to the signature page. "Two months apart." She turned to Tori. "They're all within the last five months, and all current. Something's not right," she concluded.

"Let's check the appraisals," Tori said, taking the four deeds with her as they went back upstairs to Janet's desk and pulled the appraisal from the file. "Three seventy," she said, looking at Darlene with confusion.

Darlene took the paper from Tori and read it herself, then looked at her incredulously. "So this guy got over a million dollars in loans on this property worth only three hundred and seventy thousand?"

Tori shook her head up and down, "Looks that way. Something doesn't seem right. But they're all current?"

"You know who this guy is, don't you?" Darlene asked.

"Sure. He's the lawyer that's doing that big case. I've seen him in here a couple of times. He's friends with some of the board members. Mostly he deals with the officers. He doesn't do a lot of closings. And the property he owns, these buildings, they can't support the loan amounts."

Darlene shook her head. "Right, he comes in a lot, but downstairs, with those other shareholders and board members."

"I know who you mean. They take Joe to lunch at Deer Run once in a while.

"Right, right," Darlene said, looking up at the wall clock. "It's time for me to go."

"Oh, you're late on account of me. Sorry, But thanks, Dar. Have a nice weekend."

"Thanks, you too. See you Monday."

Tori glanced at her watch. Four fifty. The building seemed so quiet without the normal distractions of ringing phones and workers dashing in and out of elevators or running down the stairs. Her mother expected her at the booth by five. She gathered the files and walked into Joe's office.

"Excuse me, Joe," she said, moving to the side of his desk. Biliki rose and closed his briefcase. "I was afraid you'd be gone already."

Baliki raised his eyebrows with surprise. "Tori," he said, glancing at his watch, "I was just going to check on you. I thought you were gone by now."

"I thought I'd be gone too but I'm having a problem with a closing file."

Baliki set his briefcase on his desk and stood before her. It occurred to her that maybe he was annoyed by the intrusion into his escape this late on a Friday. Maybe she should have waited until Monday. "Is something missing? Did you speak to the originator?"

She stepped to his side and laid the file down, as well as the three other mortgage notes and deeds.

"No, nothing's missing," she said, concerned now that her impression was correct since he still held his briefcase in his hand and seemed to have no intention of making this a long conversation. "These are three of Max Cruz's mortgage files. It seems that each of these loans are secured by the same property. The property is appraised at three hundred and seventy and all of them have the same appraisal showing a loan to value of seventy percent. But they're all secured by the same parcel."

Baliki released his hand from the briefcase and picked up the three notes and deeds, giving them each a quick glance. He placed them back on the desk. "Maybe these others are paid off and the paperwork just hasn't caught up with it yet. Did you ever think of that?" His tone was dismissive.

Tori stepped back from his desk and furled her brows in confusion. He seemed unconcerned and worse, annoyed. "No," she said confidently, "We checked the accounts. They're all active and current. Payments are being made."

"Who are we?" Baliki's tone was inquisitorial.

"No one, I checked the account but I had to use Darlene's screen because mine wasn't working. She was in the lobby with her sister."

"Why don't you leave this stuff with me? Max knows everyone. He's a nice guy, does a lot of business with the bank and knows a lot of people. I'll give him a call over the weekend. I'm sure it's just a clerical oversight of the releases not being prepared. You said the accounts are current, right?"

"Yes. I checked them all for this property. They're all current. But he has lots of loans that I didn't check. There could be the same problem with other parcels."

Baliki laughed and sat in his chair. He realized she wasn't going away. He had to deal with her, this spunky eighteen year old. He swung his briefcase down, "Well, I'm sure there is some easy explanation for this. The bank does a lot of business with his law firm. Besides, he owns a lot of bank stock and knows a lot of people who own a lot of bank stock. He probably has the money sitting right there in his escrow account. Maybe his secretary didn't make out the checks or something. I'll check into it on Monday. Why don't you just have a nice weekend, Tori? Been a long week for you but you've done a great job. I'll have all good reports for Janet when she gets back."

Tori gave Baliki an indifferent look. Nothing he said made any sense. Why would he have money to pay off the loans sitting in his escrow account while he continued to make the monthly payment? That's ridiculous, she thought to herself. And insulting that he would even say it to her thinking she wouldn't pick up on it. At least if he thought there was some confusion, maybe a late payment, or a payoff posted to the wrong account, that would make more sense. And who would borrow the same amount of money four times in the past five months? He hoped to confuse her, she thought. But he didn't, although maybe it's better to drop it. Besides, it's getting late. "Thank you, Joe," she said with a smile, "I do have to get going, I'm supposed to work at the festival at five."

Baliki pointed to the clock ticking along in his crystal pen set. "Well," he said with a forced smile, "You'd better be getting along. People will be lining up at the ticket booth early."

The smile dropped off of Tori's face. She canted her head, then shook it disconcertedly. She masked a fake, shallow smile, hoping to hide her anger. "How'd you know I was working the ticket booth?"

"Oh," he said over a nervous laugh, "I was in the elevator with you and Fred earlier. Don't you recall?"

"Oh, that's right," she responded with relief. "Well," she said turning and walking into the hall, "have a nice weekend."

"Thank you, and you too."

Baliki watched her walk down the hall. He opened his briefcase and took out his appointment book, pretending to busy himself as he lined out the dates he had reserved tee off times during August. When the lights went out in Janet's office he swiveled in his chair, turning his back to the hall and listened as Tori's feet clapped down the stairs.

He lifted the receiver and dialed Max's offices. "Rita," he said with a snap, Joe Baliki. Is Max still there?" Baliki stared at the clock and waited for Max to pick up. "I can't believe I caught you there at this time on a Friday."

"Just caught me as I was about to go for my second workout. What's going on?"

"We got a slight problem. We got this young girl filling in for Janet and she came across the mortgages."

"So what's the problem?"

"She keeps asking probing questions."

"You think you can distract her?"

"No," Baliki responded, "I think I confused her enough that maybe she's satisfied. But she's kind of a feisty kid."

"How old is she?"

"She's a kid, maybe seventeen or eighteen, just out of high school. But she's worked here for a couple of summers now. She's sharp. Knows what she's doing."

"So what do you recommend?"

"I don't know. She doesn't have much. Lives with her mother and grandmother on lower Main. That building that's still standing next to where River was."

"Manny's building?"

"Uh-huh, second floor." Baliki thought for a moment, then added, "I don't think anyone else lives there anymore."

"So maybe if I offer her something she'll forget it?"

"Maybe. She's a kid. She'll probably bite at anything. She's not making much here."

"If I give you the money, can you do it there at the bank?"

"I don't know. I'm a little too close to the situation here. I think she figures you're a big shot. She probably won't challenge you. I'd rather stay out of it."

"I don't mind, but how do I get her alone? She lives with her mother you said, right?"

"Yeah, yeah, and her grandmother, but tonight I overheard her say she'll be home alone after eight. Her mother and grandmother are working at the festival."

"Think I'll scare her if I just show up?"

"I don't know. She seems pretty independent You've probably seen her around here. She's the knock out with the long blond hair, kind of tall, model's figure."

"Dark eyes?"

"That's her. Her mom works at Vonetes."

"I know who you mean. She works the teller window sometimes, real pretty."

"That's her."

There was a brief silence as Max checked his watch and tapped his pen on his desk impatiently. He knew he had to act fast or maybe never get the opportunity again. Baliki could almost hear him thinking. "But," he cautioned.

"Yeah?"

"Can I cash a check now?"

"I can get it done for you. I have the window teller still open, then she has to balance out. Come up to the office and I'll go down and do it." The line went silent for a second, then Baliki asked, "What do you have in mind?"

"Five thousand?"

"Five thousand?" Baliki repeated with a raised voice, "She's just a kid. That's a fortune to someone like her. They live in a rent on Main Street. You can buy her for five hundred."

Max let a few seconds pass as he thought of Baliki's reasoning before dismissing it. "I know. But I can't take any chances. It's worth it. You see the closing price today?"

"No."

"Thirty-five and a quarter now, up another three-quarters today. So I made a couple hundred thousand just on today's rise. Five thousand is nothing. I'll tell her it's for finding out about what was wrong with my mortgages. Think she'll buy it?"

"Yeah, she might. I think I had her confused. Let her think it's some kind of timing problem for the paper to catch up, told her the money's probably in your escrow account."

"Okay," he replied confidently, "I'll be right over."

Not a week went by when Jeff strolled into Vonetes. "What will you have, Jeff?" Frances asked as she wrapped two sandwiches.

"Think I'll have a black and white, Frances, yeah, a black and white today." Jeff walked to Tori who was seated at the counter and wrinkled his forehead with concern. She hadn't looked up when she heard him talk to Frances. He leaned over the counter, reached back to tug at her braid and glanced into the mirror. She didn't lift her eyes. He turned to her and spoke quietly.

"What happened to your braid, Tor?"

"Nothing," she responded, looking straight ahead into the mirror.

Jeff sat on the stool beside her and turned so his face was inches from her ear. "Don't tell me nothing now, because every time I see you I tug it and it ain't there. So what happened to your braid?"

Tori shook her head and leaned into her milkshake. She

turned away, "I cut it."

Jeff got up and examined her hair. The cut was blunt and unnatural looking, a narrow, unbraided fingertip of hair resting two inches from the crown of her head. He studied her in the mirror and noticed darkness around her eye socket. He sat beside her again. "Yeah, so who gave you the shiner?"

Tori looked into the mirror and met Jeff's eyes. "Had an accident."

Jeff gently turned to her and pulled her face towards him.

Her eye socket was black and blue with some residual swelling. "Really," he said incredulously, "that must be the same accident that cut your braid. Must have been some wreck."

Tori turned from him and looked down. "I can't talk about it." Jeff settled himself on the stool and spoke in a whisper. "Well, you don't have to talk about it to anyone else but you going to tell me because I ain't quitting until you tell me the truth and don't bother talking to me about no accident or nothing because I don't believe that shit, you understand that. Who hit you? Your mom know? Some boyfriend hit you?"

Tori shook her head and closed her eyes. "I don't have a boyfriend."

"So that don't make me go away or nothing. I want to know what happened."

"I can't talk about it."

"Why not?"

"Because they said it's going to be worse if I say anything to anyone."

Jeff nodded his head with understanding. "So someone hit you and cut your braid and then threatened you? That what you're saying?"

"Uh huh."

"So who did it? Just tell me how it happened and why. You don't have to tell me nothing about who did it specifically."

Tori stirred her melting milkshake. "It had to do with work."

"At the bank? That work? They doing haircuts there or something now?"

Tori smirked and spoke softly. "Let's just say I discovered something was wrong with some loans and someone tried to buy me off, offered me some money to keep quiet. It has something to do with the bank stock."

"So what happened? That don't tell me what happened to your braid or how you got the shiner."

Tori breathed hard and closed her eyes. "So they offered me some money and I threw it at him and he got real mad. I don't want to say anymore. He was so mad it was like he lost his mind."

"So they punched you there, right at the bank? And cut your braid? That don't make no sense. Tell me more."

"No, it didn't happen at the bank, no one saw it happen. My eye hit his elbow by accident when I tried to get the scissors before he grabbed them. He grabbed my hair. Then he cut my braid and said it would be worse if I told anyone. So I really can't talk about it anymore."

Jeff turned to the mirror. He studied Tori's face. She looked troubled and upset. He stood and spread his hands over the counter to brace himself as he straddled the stool. "So your mother know? What she say?"

Tori shook her head. "She knows everything, and my grandmother, they know."

"You call the cops?"

"No, just better not to. I'm okay. I don't want to talk about it anymore."

Jeff stood and looked at Tori in the mirror. "Okay. But I ain't letting this go, you know. It don't make sense to me but I understand you don't want to talk no more. You go ahead and finish your milkshake, Tor. Don't worry about nothing."

"I'm holding brothers, man" the Moocher said with a confident nod. He had a manner of moving about even while seated. "Need one more, holdin' them there bros man."

Michael tossed him a card and looked to Ernie. "What do you need?" He looked up and measured the faces around the table, ready to peel off another card at the slightest hint of want.

Ernie smiled broadly. He reached up and tucked the sleeve of his T shirt to a tight roll without a hint of urgency or concern. Then he rolled the other and looked back to his cards and smirked.

Jeff's eyes darted up from his hand held close to his lap.

593

"Come on, man," he scowled impatiently, "you ain't got nothing and you know it and we know it."

Ernie didn't bother to lift his eyes. "Two," he said, laying the cards on the table so the corners snapped under his thumb. Two cards spun out at him like frightened sparrows in flight. He picked them up slowly and fitted them into his hand, grimaced with pain, and folded his hand to a neat pile. "I'm out." He leaned over and pulled a beer from the cooler on the floor. He flicked the small bits of ice from the can with a pale green towel that draped over his neck to absorb his sweat.

Jeff's forehead creased to a deep prune of bunched flesh. "Give me some of that pizza over here, Vinnie," he commanded. He slapped down three cards and complained, "Got nothing." He cast an annoyed look at Vinnie. "Gimme some a that pizza here." The sound of feet coming up the stairs caused him to shake his head with disappointment. Mike held the pizza box out over the table. "Gotta be the Greek," Jeff exclaimed, folding his cards and slapping them into the center of the table. He grabbed a slice from the box and bit it, stringing the hot cheese over his fingers and lifting it high. "Down thirty-seven bucks and now the Greek's going to disrupt everything."

The Greek appeared at the top of the stairs sporting a wide smile. He rested his neon sunglasses on his head and clapped his hands with enthusiasm. "Boys, Friday night poker with the boys." He emphasized the last two words with unaccustomed weight, bowing from the waist to impart the importance of the occasion and the company with which it is spent. His brown eyes were bright, clear memory banks full of everything he saw. "Poker time!" he said as he rocked up and clapped his hands again, "yeah."

Jeff dangled his pizza over his mouth. "Ain't poker, Greek. Stud." He ripped another bite from the slice and wiped his mouth with a balled up napkin that looked like it was rinsed in oil.

"Stud," the Greek said, darting to the sink. The world is orderly, as it should be. "The boys are playing stud. I like that."

Cut Man stood and hiked up the jeans that hung shapelessly from his waist. "Greek," he said, locking the Greek's palm into his own, "what's going on?"

"What' up with you, Cut Man, didn't see you last night. Legs must be okay." The Greek embraced him with his free arm.

"Good, Greek, real good,I slept good. My legs been pretty good."

The Greek smiled broadly, "That's good, Cut Man, real good. No more of them snake legs, right? You can sleep then, right?"

Cut Man pointed to the cooler on the floor. "Sleeping good last night, Greek." he said, sitting once again. "Have a beer."

The Greek leaned over the sink and doused his face with cold water. "No beer for me," he said to the bottom of the sink. Then he stood with his face dripping and dropped his sunglasses to his chest, letting them fall to the extent of the shoelace cord fastening them around his neck. He leaned over again and ran his water filled hands over his hair, panning it back like rolled steel.

"Greek," Michael said as he turned to him and laughed, "easy with the water. You're getting me wet."

"Mike," Vinnie asked, "you in or out?"

Michael wiped the water from his arm and turned back to his cards. He looked at Vinnie and folded them. "Ain't no use," he said, collecting the cards from the table, "just ain't." He reached into the box and lifted a slice of pizza and watched a piece of sausage roll onto the table. "Damn," he said, popping it into his mouth and wiping up the grease spot with a greasy napkin.

Vinnie laid out two kings and two eights and laughed derisively. "That's the way I like it. The way it should be. The way it should be," he repeated, stopping between each word for emphasis and pulling the money into a pile in front of him.

"Greek, have some pizza," Michael said.

The Greek pulled several paper towels off the roll that stood on the counter and wiped his face and hair, then tossed the ball into the garbage pail. "What kind you got?"

"Mootz and sausage here," Michael said, lifting the lid to verify it, "and mootz and onion here." He tapped the side of the unopened box and pointed to the opposite counter, "And plain over there, Grated cheese plain, real plain, not mootz plain."

The Greek walked to the far corner, pried open the box, and examined it. He turned back to the table. "That's real

596

plain, not mootz plain?"

"Grated cheese," Michael responded.

The Greek turned back and pulled a slice out. It drooped over his wrist as he lifted it under his mouth, leaned over the counter and took a bite. "Who orders the plain?" he garbled.

"Deal," Jeff said to Michael.

"I do." Cut Man said without turning to the Greek. "I'm on a diet. And my kids like it." Cards flew around the table.

The Greek turned to the table and stopped chewing. The slice rested in his palm as he spoke. "It's for your kids?"

"No," Cut Man responded, studying his cards.

"It's for us," Jeff said, trying to cut the conversation. "We eat the plain one last so if we don't finish it then Cut Man takes the rest home to his kids. They like it."

"So maybe I shouldn't eat this one?"

Jeff gave the Greek an annoyed look. "God damn it, Greek. We said you can eat it. If we didn't want you to eat it we would have said so." Jeff scanned the pot in the middle of the table. "You didn't put up, Mike." He turned to the Greek and scolded him, "Greek, man, you're distracting us from the game."

Mike tossed in three dollars and studied his cards. He turned to Vinnie, "How many?"

"Two," Vinnie said, somberly tossing down two cards. He shook his head. The Greek walked to Jeff's back, firmly in control of his diminishing slice.

"How's the sausage?" he asked.

"Good," Cut Man responded tersely. "I'll take two." He looked at Michael. "Two," he repeated, spinning two cards to the table, "I'll take two." He looked at the Greek and held out his paper plate, "Greek, get me a slice of onion, please."

The Greek lifted the sausage box, "Hold this," he said to Jeff, balancing it on his extended fingers. He pulled a slice of onion out and slid it on Ernie's flimsy paper plate. The plate bent and Jeff supported it with his card hand before the slice could fall to the table.

"Damn it, Greek," he laughed, "we was doing just fine until you show up." He eyed the onion slice passing in front of him. He held up his plate to the Greek, "Give me one of them, too."

The Greek stood over his shoulder and pointed to a card, "Lose it," he said to Jeff.

"Go stand in back of Vinnie," Jeff said, tossing down three cards, "he's doing all the winning."

Michael tossed three cards Jeff's way. "And I need two," he said, dealing two to himself. "Stay there, Greek, don't go telling no one my hand, stay there."

"What up in the street, Greek? What do you hear?" asked Vinnie, holding his hand up close to his face and spreading it like a peacock in full plume.

"Nothing," the Greek said, pulling out a beer and wiping the water off with his fingers, "quiet." He took his plate on the counter and turned to Vinnie. "How'd I look, man? You like this shirt?"

"Yeah," Vinnie responded, laying his cards down against

his chest and letting out a ripple of laughter, "but you got to be dying your hair man. You getting too old for those chicks, man. You know, those girls, they like you to look young, man, you know, like me, young and handsome."

The Greek slicked back his damp hair and set his sunglasses back over his forehead. He smiled widely. "Chicks like it like this. They say it looks good. They like older men," he said proudly.

"They like them mature," Jeff said, casting an eye to the Greek, "not old. Hand me a beer."

The Greek reached into the cooler and shook the ice chips off a can of beer. "They like some gray. They call me the silver fox."

Mike jumped up. "Greek," he yelled, "don't shake the cans, you're giving me a shower." He walked to the counter and pulled a paper towel from the roll.

"Sorry, man" the Greek replied, stepping to Mike and hugging him.

Michael wiped his face and laughed. "That's okay. Actually, it felt good. We need an air conditioner."

"Right," Vinnie said without looking up from his hand, "you buy it and I'll put it in."

"Forget it," Mike said, sitting back down, "we don't need it."

"Who's out?" Vinnie asked, scanning the table.

"I am," Mike said, dropping his hand to the table.

"Mike, you think I should dye my hair?" the Greek asked.

"No Greek, I don't think you should dye your hair. The

girls like you because you're cool with those neon shades. The gray hairs make you look distinguished."

Vinnie rose and pulled a beer from the cooler. "Greek," he asked, as he popped the can open, "you seen Max?"

"I seen him driving and stuff, you know, to his office, driving by and stuff, but not on the street." The Greek poked at Vinnie's hand. "You got them," he whispered. "Hold them."

Jeff looked up at the Greek with anger. "Greek," he snarled, "you better shut up, man."

Vinnie looked up at the Greek. "When you see him around last?"

"You need him?" the Greek asked.

Cut Man put his cards on the table. "Look," he said, "are we going to play cards or what?" He stood to get a slice of sausage pizza, saving the plain for the kids.

"Yeah, I'm playing, just got to figure something out." He looked back to the Greek. "It's business."

The Greek shrugged his shoulders. "I think the last time I seen Max was the night of the festival, maybe two weeks ago. Yeah, that's it," reflected the Greek, pressing his palms over his head as if to pull the memory from his brain. "That's when I seen him. Cut Man, you was with me that night. Your legs was restless or something."

"Lay down two good ones and I gets the straight," commanded Vinnie, holding his cards to his chest again.

"I seen him coming out of Manny's building with a scissors in his hand. Me and Cut Man, we was going to Club 78 when I seen him."

600

Cut Man settled into his seat and looked at Vinnie, then to the Greek. "Yeah, I remember that night. My legs were acting real bad so I wanted to walk. Think we walked the streets all night that night. Remember?"

"You owe me two cards, man." Vinnie assessed the mound of cash on the table. He looked down at his cards. "The man needs twos guys. Shooting twos bros. Hit me, man."

And then, through the oiled fingers of a gambler's pose, Mike's animated manner halted with a probing stare. "Greek," he asked, holding up Vinnie's two cards "you seen him coming out of where?"

"Give me my cards, man," said Vinnie. "Out of Manny's building."

Cut Man glanced at the wall clock. "My wife's going to kill me, man. Jesus, Mike, deal the cards."

"Give him the cards, Mike," Jeff droned.

"No, wait," Mike insisted, reeling the deck to his chest, "this is important, out of where?"

Cut Man threw his hand down and jumped up. "I got to go, man. He said he was coming out of Manny's building, for God's sake. Didn't he say that? He was coming out of Manny's building." He looked up at the Greek for confirmation.

"Sit down, Cut Man," Jeff demanded.

Mike leaned over the table towards Jeff. "Shut up and listen for a minute." He glanced at the Greek and pushed Cut Man back into his seat. "Sit down, nobody's going nowhere yet."

Jeff slapped his cards to the table. "Damn it, Greek," he yelled, and sat back in his chair, "you a god damned distraction. Don't go yet, Cut Man."

The Greek backed up against the kitchen sink. He pulled some paper towels and wiped his hands. "Out of Manny's building. He didn't stop and talk or nothing, like he was surprised to see me or something. He had scissors and an envelope in his hand and he dropped the scissors into the street before he got into the car."

Mike rolled his eyes to Jeff. "You hear the Greek?" His expression was startled and certain. "Cut Man, you seen him too?"

Cut Man shrugged his shoulders and stood to leave, "I ain't saying nothing. I don't want to get involved, man. I don't remember nothing."

Jeff held his hand out like a cleaver and sliced the air. "All right," he said calmly as he pulled Cut Man back into his chair, "all right, man, say it again because I wasn't concentrating."

"The Greek saw Max coming out of Manny's building the night of the church festival," said Michael, still leaning over the table.

"Yeah," Jeff responded slowly, "so that supposed to be a big thing or something?"

"He said he had a scissors in his hand coming out."

Jeff folded his arms over his chest and clocked his head to the Greek. "You seen him, you actually seen him come out of the building with a scissors in his hand?"

"Yeah, we was across the street, walking towards the

bridge, and I seen him."

"You sure it was him?" Jeff asked with a creased forehead, and turned to Cut Man, "You going to talk, man?"

"No, I ain't messing with Max. I said I didn't see nothing."

The Greek shrugged his shoulders with certainty. "I seen him, I held up my arm over the parked cars and said hello and he answered like he hardly wanted to." He wetted a paper towel and stuck one into his shirt to blot the sweat from his chest.

Jeff gave Michael a look of quiet resolve. It was falling into place like the tumblers of a lock. "Makes sense, don't it, Buddy?" he said to Michael, "Tori's braid gone and she ain't saying nothing, like she's scared or something."

"You talk to him?" Mike asked.

The Greek shook his head and pasted down his hair again with his hands, "No. I waved and kept walking."

"He look nervous?" Jeff asked.

"Couldn't tell," the Greek responded as he lifted another slice from the box. "It was dark."

"So what did he do," Jeff asked. "Just said hi and that's it? Didn't say nothing else?"

The Greek took another bite of pizza. Cut Man reached over and grabbed two beers from the cooler and handed one to Vinnie.

"Came around his car and got in. That's when I seen the scissors."

"When?" Michael jumped in, "Getting into the car?"

"Yeah."

"He was alone?" Jeff asked.

"Yeah."

"You sure it was scissors?"

The Greek put his slice back into the box and held up his empty hands. He reeled back a few steps until he stood against the door jamb.

"Look man," he said emphatically, leaning from the waist. "You know me a long time." His hands went to his chest for emphasis. "I don't do no drugs or nothing bad. I don't drink or nothing. But I know the streets. I know what I seen. So when I seen Max come around his car to get in I seen something shining in the streetlight and I think what's Max doing with a knife. I just keep walking, getting closer to Max. But after he opens the door I seen him and said hi to him and he says hi back and the scissors is stuck on his finger or something. I don't like nothing shiny at night."

Michael's eyebrows were suspended over his forehead as he nodded at Cut Man. "Greek, you're sure, right?"

The Greek's lips were lacquered with pizza oil. He took a paper towel, wiped his face and gave Cut Man a piercing look before turning to Jeff. "On my father's honor," he said, "Max walked out of Manny's apartment building that night."

The room was silent. Jeff's eyes clocked from Mike to Cut Man and back to the Moocher. "Where's Max now?"

The Greek shrugged. "I don't know, man." His lips knotted. "I ain't seen him since that night." He turned to the Moocher and directed his words to him. "That's the last time I seen Max. Don't think he's getting stuff from someone else. I been walking and I haven't heard nothing."

Jeff turned to the Moocher. "Where's he at now?"

A nervous look overcame him. "Now?" the Moocher asked. "How I supposed to know where he's at now, man? Who am I, that Houdini guy who knows everything and stuff? How I supposed to know where Max is at on a Friday night? Like I know or something."

"So where's Max?" Jeff asked again.

"I told you, I don't know, man. What the fuck, you think I keep tabs on Max? You seen me asking the Greek if he seen him. Why the fuck would I ask him if I know where he is?"

Jeff deadened a stare into the Moocher. He swept the table of bills and coins, sending a cascade of money over the kitchen. "Where's he hang out at?" Jeff demanded.

The Moocher leaned over the table and spread his arms open. "I don't know where the hell he hangs, man. Do I look like his mother? He calls me when he needs stuff and I get it for him. I don't follow him around or nothing, man. You talking to the wrong dude, man."

"Where you trade the stuff? Across the street?"

"Business secret, man. You know I don't tell. He don't like no one to see anything. He comes wherever I say and we do the trade or I leave the shit in there, in a spot. Nobody sees nothing."

"He married?"

"Yeah," the Moocher responded with a laugh, "third or

fourth wife or something. Don't know, I can't keep track. Word on the street is he doing so much shit he can't get it up. All his wives leave him, man. He got nuts the size of peas or something."

"He call you during the day?"

"Sometimes."

Jeff stood, reached to the wall, and handed the phone to Vinnie. "What's his number? I want to talk to him."

"Why?" Moocher snapped, hopping up from his chair and pointing at Jeff menacingly, "Can't call Max at home, man." Then the Moocher called out the Jamaican warning as a manner of a threat, "Not everything you chew on you should swallow."

Jeff slammed the Moocher back and forearmed his face against the wall. "Don't give me your fake Jamaican shit, Vinnie. Sorry fi maga dog, maga dog tun roun bite yu," he yelled, using the Jamaican insult, "I can do anything I want."

Moocher grabbed Jeff's wrist and tried to talk although only a whisper came out. "Can't just call him up at home, he's a lawyer, man. He's a big shot. He got influence, man. He's jacked, man, been doing shit a long time."

Jeff released Vinnie from the wall. "A lawyer?" Jeff repeated in an incredulous tone that ended with a derisive laugh. "That don't mean jack shit. What's his number?"

"I don't know."

"Look, man," Jeff scowled as he punched the phone into Vinnie's chest, "you might get away with all your smiling shit with everyone else but it don't work with me. Call him."

Vinnie stepped back to the far counter. "He ain't home."

"You just said you don't know where he is. I ain't playing with you, Vinnie."

"Why you need him?"

Jeff slammed the phone down. "I have some business for him. That's all. If he can answer the questions, he got nothing to worry about. You understand. And if I got to go to his house I will. What's his number?"

"He ain't home."

"How you know he ain't home if you don't know where he is?"

Vinnie leaned against the counter and screamed with his palms splayed out, "I said he's not home. That don't mean I know where he is."

Jeff unrolled some paper towels and wiped his hands. "Don't piss me off, man. It's going to be worse if I got to go to his house and do business in front of his wife."

Vinnie paused. He was distressed and trying to catch his breath. He reached to the top of the refrigerator and grabbed the phone book. "He's usually at the club on Friday night," he said without looking up. He scanned the pages, making a greasy impression on the number and dialed. "You want to talk?" Vinnie asked as the phone rang. Michael rose and rinsed his hands at the sink. He turned and dried them on a towel as he leaned against the counter and watched.

"No. You tell him you need to see him."

Vinnie cast a nervous look over the room. "I never called

him before. Not at the club."

"So," Jeff responded, "that don't mean shit." He bent over and picked up his money and directed everyone to do the same. "Game's over. Cut Man, rest of the pizza is for your kids, man. Ain't no sense getting your wife pissed and we ain't playing cards or nothing."

Cut Man slid his chair back and shook his head. "I'll wait. I'm in no hurry. I don't want to miss this. You guys don't read the papers but Max been buying up lots of the bank stock, there's been some articles on it."

"Bank stock?" Mike asked."What bank stock?"

"Birmingham Bank, papers had a few articles on it. Said speculation is that he's been accumulating Birmingham Bank stock along with some other investors."

Vinnie turned and looked at the phone as he spoke. "I need to speak to Attorney Max Cruz." He held his hand over the speaker and turned to Jeff. "What should I say, man? He's going to be pissed. My business is going to shit right here, man."

"Tell him you got to see him right now." Jeff walked to the back door and looked out, "It's dark now. He got no excuse."

"What if he don't want to come?"

"Tell him he better or we're going there." Jeff started pacing the floor. He tapped fists with Cut Man as he stepped down the stairs and clasped hands with the Greek as he followed Cut Man down. "Hey, thanks a lot Greek," Jeff called out.

"I seen him come out," said the Greek as his voice

trailed off. "Right out of Manny's building, nobody living there but Linda."

Marshall's legal research was strewn all over the library table. He was growing weary of researching every point of law from every possible configuration of argument. He was tired of repeating the same point with different words and then supporting each point with strings of citations from opinions that had no reason to ever be read. Still, it was a pivotal motion for the case and for him and Max personally. Winning this motion would turn the case into a repeat of the state and federal criminal trials. Excluding hearsay evidence against Moeller and Pollard could turn the civil case into an auction for justice, sending the negotiated settlement with the insurance company into a sprint for cover against a jury's award.

Lachlan looked up from his research. "You think Kerrington will really consider their argument seriously? I mean, don't you think it's the last thing they're throwing in just to get it on the record? They have no reason for them to be considered co-conspirators."

Marshall leaned back, balancing the chair on its hind legs as he steadied himself with his foot on the edge of the table. "No, I think they got a good chance. Karrington is not one of the boys, you know. He's not interested in the petty bantering or trying to be witty. He doesn't engage like that. He's independent." Marshall let his chair down with a slap and picked up a volume. "He's definitely taking this seriously."

Lachlan took a seat at the table and rolled up his sleeves. "I thought by now we'd have associates doing this grunt work."

"This is too important for an associate even if you had them. Anyway, that's why Max hired us as co-counsel. Shall I remind you, what did you say the damages were, just to begin negotiating?"

Lachlan let a relaxed smile splash over his face. "Sixty million, won't even talk about anything less."

"So what associate did you want to make this argument with that kind of money on the line?"

"I know you're right. There's too much at stake here. But the bank stock is going wild. Max says he doesn't have time for this detail work. He's figuring if he hits on just one of these things he'll have it made."

"So what are you complaining about? It's worth the time here to get this right, right?"

"Yeah, sure it is. Max figures if he hits both of these things, that's about twenty-five million he pockets. He figures he won't ever have to practice law again."

Marshall leaned back and laughed. "Sometimes Max is unrealistic. He thinks there is no way Kerrington would find them co-conspirators. He figures they beat two criminal trials. No one laid a glove on them. So let's say he does rule that they are co-conspirators for purposes of the hearsay exception. What does that get them? Max is thinking that no one believes Staber anyway, that he comes across as a lunatic. Talking to bees, predicting the future, knowing the head of the CIA? Max is figuring they'll laugh him out of the court."

"He's a minister, people respect that."

Marshall shook his head in agreement. "He comes across as a lunatic. And the shrinks did say he was crazy."

Lachlan grimaced. "You never know. Paint him as a nut and the jury may be sympathetic to him. His story make sense. You think this water purification makes sense to anyone? You got cash taken out of a weird little bank in Ohio that the limo driver basically traces to Staber in the hotel in New York. You got all these checks to his company for the water treatment facility and not one blueprint of that plan. Just a lousy can of lime or something that the secretary testified to. I don't care what you say, this guy can bury you and Kerrington's just the judge to do it. He's going to let it in and let the jury decide. That's his style. Besides, the Campos and Stratis report, it's credible even if we tell the jury the insurance company paid for it and how much they paid. It lays out all the subtle stuff like the cash payments and checks from obscure accounts that were rarely used. This is no slam dunk."

The black Mercedes sports car pulled into the cemetery driveway and stopped several feet before the wrought iron gate opening, resting under leafy maple shadows. The bright coin of a Cuban cigar flared through the windshield.

"Stay here, Shy. I can take care of this guy. I rather not have the Moocher see you." The humid night air seemed to thicken as he swung open the car door and left it in that position.

Max walked to the gate, raising the collar of his white designer polo shirt that seemed to burst brilliantly in the headlights of his car. He appeared gilded as he approached the gate, his muscular presence rippling under a white frame. He wrapped his hands around the fence posts with his cigar wedged between his fingers. Vinnie appeared from behind a large tree with eyes sliced by the bright lights.

"Damn, man, can't see shit," he said, putting his hand to his eyes to shield them.

Max's face was taut with anger. His eyes fastened into Vinnie's like rivets. "You're out of your mind, right? Crazy!" he said with a voice that shook with rage, "Calling me up at the club!"

"It wasn't me man," he said quickly, pointing to his left. He made me." Jeff stepped into the open from the back of a tree and walked towards the fence. He was sobered by the size of Max. He was taller than Jeff and muscular from any angle. Jeff knew then he couldn't confront Max directly.

Max pressed closer, taking a puff from his cigar and squaring his shoulders against the gate. "Him?" he asked with a snicker, pointing his cigar to Jeff, "I don't even know this guy. Who's he?"

"Don't matter who I am. I just want to ask you some questions."

"You're crazy," Max said contemptuously, turning back to the Moocher."You're both crazy." He pointed his cigar to Jeff and looked at Vinnie, still shading his eyes from the car lights. "You think I'm going to answer questions from him?" Max pivoted away, releasing his hands from the fence and started back to the car. "You called me from the club for this? You know who I got in the car with me? Shy. Your business is over man."

Shy stepped out of the car as Jeff walked forward and leaned against the fence. He knew his chance was receding with each step Max took. He grabbed the fence and put his face between the widely spaced spokes. "Hey, Cruz, man, you know what the word is on the street?" he called out with a derisive laugh. Then, with perfect Spanish inflection on the last word, he called out loudly, "Man, they say you the cabrón." He let a long belly laugh that filled the humid night. "Not the Mexican carbon, Cruz. And not the Cuban cabrón neither, man. They say, they say you the Puerto Rican cabrón, man. You can't keep a wife happy. You a trip, Cruz, you pretend to be some big man or something, but you know, man, you the Puerto Rican cabrón.

Max turned slowly and eyed Jeff hanging on the fence, doubled over with laughter, and repeating the words, 'you the carbon, man, you the cabrón.' Max walked towards the fence. Jeff stopped laughing and stood as Max got closer.

"So what you going to do, man? You think you scaring me with your big muscles or something? You ain't shit, man, nothing but a cabrón."

Max reached between the fence posts just as Jeff moved to the side. Then, with lightening speed, Jeff locked his fingers into the raised collar of Max's shirt and yanked him forward, squeezing his cheek tightly against the rusted spikes. He pressed his hot lips against Max's ear.

"Just a few questions," he whispered with heated breath."You might be the man to Vinnie here, but you ain't nothing to me."

Max burned his cigar into Jeff's forearm and grabbed the fence as Jeff pulled his arm away, allowing Max to turn and face him with noses flared in the heat.

"Just want to know why you was up at Linda's apartment the night of the festival."

Max dropped the cigar and moved his hand from the fence. He put his fingers beneath the vice of Jeff's hand that was locked on his collar. With his elbow as a fulcrum he tried to wedge himself away from Jeff. He moved his other hand against Jeff's cheek and pushed against his sweaty face. Max's mind raced back as he tried to figure out who could have seen him. "You're crazy. You don't know what you're talking about."

Jeff pulled harder. Max's fingertips dug into his face and found his eyes. Jeff released his pull and let Max snap back. Then, in a fierce wave of contracting muscle, he whipped Max back into the fence. The snap of broken bone cut into the leafy shadows as tooth shards dropped from his mouth and a heavy course of blood streamed from his eye and over Jeff's wrist, its warm river blending into a hot, slippery cocktail. Shy opened his car door and stood. "Hey!" he yelled. "hey!"

"Let me remind you, big man," Jeff whispered again between panting breaths. "You left with a scissors in your hand. You was stupid enough to take the scissors."

Max reached for the back of Jeff's head and pulled his face into the fence. "The Greek," he panted as Jeff reeled back and broke the grip, then threw him back and racked him up against the fence again, breaking his nose and sending blood flooding down his throat.

Shy reached into the car and picked up the car phone. He began dialing frantically. Michael leaned in the driver's side, rolled the cord around his hand and ripped it out, throwing it to the floor "It's between them two," he said as he slammed the door and walked to the fence.

"No," Max garbled over bloodied lips, "no."

Jeff thrust him away again and snapped him back like a rag doll, his resistance nearly gone. His jaw snapped and his face distorted in the glare of the car lights. Jeff racked him up again and again, sweat spraying over them both as blood streamed over his fists. Vinnie pulled at Jeff's shoulder without effect. "It's enough, man," he yelled desperately, "it's enough."

Jeff swung back with an open hand, sending Vinnie to the ground. Max slumped against the fence. Jeff let go of him and vaulted the lower spikes. He grabbed Max's hair with one hand and his shirt with the other and dragged his face across several rusted spikes.

"That's it, buddy," Mike implored as he wedged himself between Jeff and Max."That's it."

Jeff looked at Mike and nodded. He released Max and watched him slide down and rest on his knees, letting out pulses of moans between breathes. Mike stayed between them, fighting off Jeff's attempt to approach Max again.

"No, no more," Mike said, "you're going to kill him. It's enough."

Jeff leaned over Max. Sweat dripped from his face into Max's opens wounds, burning them further. "Don't you ever say what you going do to nobody, you understand me?" Then he delivered a fierce kick into Max's stomach, forcing the air from his lungs and dropping him to the ground. He leaned over him. "You hear me, Cruz?" he whispered. "Don't you ever say what you going to do again." Jeff stood and clasped his hands over his head to catch his breath. He bent over Max again. "Next time you threaten Linda or Tori, or if you go after the Greek, I'm going to kick your ass."

He stood and placed his hands on the fence. He rested a minute, panting and wiping the sweat from his face. He put his hands under his shirt and raised it to his face to absorb the blood and sweat. His arm bled and burned from the cigar wound. Then he looked down at Max, "Cut Man," Jeff commanded, as he pointed down and stepped back from Max, "I got some work for you here."

The Palace was quiet. Frances walked the last customers to the sidewalk and glanced up and down Main Street, then cast a wary eye up Elizabeth Street. The streets were empty except for the traffic passing through. Linda was gone for the night, having forgotten to take the dirty towels and aprons. It was unlike her to be forgetful, until the past few weeks. Frances simply picked up the load without saying anything.

She locked the door and turned off the red neon window lights. Her balled-up apron was placed in a bag along with the others. Tonight at home she would wash and dry them and return them fresh and clean and neatly folded in the morning.

Jeff sat backwards on his chair and tilted it to the table, his head cocked to the side as he concentrated on the bits and pieces of conversation Frances fed him before the last of the customers left. He tapped the edge of his hands on the table as he spoke. "So I still don't get it, Frances," he said as she made a pass behind him. His fingers and knuckles were bruised and scabbed two days after the confrontation with Cruz. He rubbed his hands and winced at the pain. "Fence did a job on my hands, man," he said, shaking his head at Michael.

"Fence did a job on everyone," Michael said with a nod. Frances returned and sat before her cold coffee. "This guy Blake," Jeff said, "he left for Vietnam and then he never comes back? That don't make no sense, Frances. And they was in love?" He gave Michael a perplexed look and turned to Frances. "It don't figure," he said, shaking his head and rocking his chair. "Make any sense to you, Buddy?"

Frances turned her cup in its saucer and rose. "Let me get more coffee." She walked to the front of the Palace. Michael drew Coke into his straw and held it there with his tongue. "I think I remember him." He shook his head disconcertedly and shrugged his shoulders. "I don't know. I remember Teddy talking to her about him once. I remember because I couldn't figure it out, what they was talking about and she seemed so serious, like, sad." He slid his soda away and let a moment pass before glancing at Jeff and then to Frances. "So who's Tori's father if he's not?"

Frances sat back in her seat. Her hands circled the coffee cup nervously. She stared down at it and closed her eyes. She turned and looked at the door, then to Jeff and Mike.

She lifted the cup and sipped it. "Well," she said, placing the cup in front of her and bringing her hands to her face, "I know you boys are close to her. You think a lot of her and Tori and she feels the same about you two, gets a kick out of your antics and the way you bicker." She turned to the door again.

"Frances," Jeff said as she turned back to them, "we ain't going to tell no one anything you say here." He hit the table lightly with his fingers for emphasis and returned his chair to its proper position on all four legs. "Not even Linda," he said, looking at Michael. "Right Buddy? We ain't saying nothing."

Michael bent his straw into a circle. "No," he said seriously, "we'll never tell nobody, never. We was just wondering about how she got a daughter and where the father is."

"Okay," Frances said, casting her eyes over them, "I know I can trust you boys." She stared down to the table. "Something happened to Linda, after Blake left," said Frances, raising her eyes to the mirror. She watched herself speak, as if overhearing a betrayal of trust and

618

continuing despite the observer. Her words came out in the quiet undertone of the telling of dreadful sins in a confessional. "I never asked her what happened." She looked at Michael and Jeff, hoping for their implicit understanding that she spoke the truth and that what she had to say is an aged mix of inference and supposition. "It was really very private, not my business. She just said to me and Teddy, we knew she wasn't herself, that she was pregnant. And that Blake was not the father. I never asked her anything more, but from the way she behaved, all upset and crying and all, I think she was forced." Frances looked at each of them and nodded as she finished. "She never said she was forced. She never said that."

"Forced?" Michael asked. "You mean like raped?" He looked at Jeff, his eyes wide with surprise of the event that he never considered. He shook his head in disbelief and repeated it "Damn, Buddy, she was raped." He held Jeff's eyes pensively. "Raped."

Jeff shook his head as if to deflect the imponderable. "You think that, right? But she never said it. But you think it?"

Frances shook her head affirmatively. Her face was etched with pain. She closed her eyes and asked plaintively, "You boys will never tell anyone, right? I couldn't hurt Linda like that."

"Never, Frances," Jeff said clearly.

"Never," Michael agreed. He looked at Frances and opened his hands with wonder. "So why didn't he come back? It still don't make sense that he didn't come back."

Frances released her hands from the cup and raised her shoulders while she opened her palms, "I don't know. He called her once, before he went to Vietnam. Called her here because she didn't have a phone at her apartment then. I guess her mother couldn't afford it. Anyway, he said he was being sent to Vietnam and couldn't come home. Everyone was going then, you know. It was a war. So she told him that she was pregnant. She thought she had to tell him, that she couldn't not tell him, you know." Frances spun the ring on her finger, running it over the resistance of her knuckle, then back again. "She said she didn't think he believed her. That's all she said. She sat on the floor behind the candy counter and cried. I remember it like it was yesterday." Frances' voice drifted off to a whisper and she took a moment to compose herself before continuing. "So Teddy, God bless Teddy, he loved her and Tori, he went over and got her up and sat her down, right there, at that table and got her some water and calmed her down. She had it tough." Frances reached over, pulled a napkin and blotted her eyes, then folded her hands with the napkin sticking out. "I don't know," she said, shrugging her shoulders, "that's all."

Jeff and Michael looked at each other in disbelief. "Who would have thought that, Buddy?" Michael said. Then he turned to Frances. "So where is he now, Frances? Did he get married?"

"Who, Blake?"

"Yeah, does anyone know where he is?" Jeff asked.

Frances shook her head and looked down at the table.

"No, he's not married. His aunt Florence comes in once in a while, so I ask about him occasionally, when Linda's not around. He's a lawyer in Washington, or near Washington, somewhere down there. She says he never got married. Says he's done very well, but never got married." Then she looked up at them and added, "Said he was never the same after he came back."

Jeff set his glass down. "Linda never tried to call him or nothing?"

Frances shrugged off the suggestion. "Oh, no, she wouldn't do that. You have to understand. She felt violated. Unclean. It's a terrible thing. I think maybe she felt like he didn't want her anymore after that. You just don't know how the mind works. And I think she felt if he loved her he would come back." Frances wiped her eyes and drank some coffee. She shook her head, "I don't know. Nobody knows."

"Was he a nice guy, Fran? I mean, was he nice to her?" Jeff asked.

"Oh, very nice," said Frances, pursing her lips and moving her head up and down. "It was beautiful, the way they fell in love. He would come in looking for her, before he knew her schedule. Then after he saw her here a few times he'd meet her after work and walk her home. She only lived down the street, the same place. Me and Teddy, we'd make them sundaes to go, sometimes sandwiches if they were hungry, and they would take the long way home, stopping at the green the way young people do when they're in love. Everything's special. That's the way they were," she said with a sad smile over her lips. "They didn't do anything, but it was all special, all the little stuff. You could just see it in her face, she would just light up when he came in."

Jeff folded his hands on the table. "So, Bro," he said with authority, "we going to Washington to see this dude."

Michael laughed and sucked down the last of his melted ice. "Yeah Jeff, right. You and me are going to Washington and find this guy and you're going to tell him he's got to come back otherwise you're going to beat him up, right?"

Jeff smiled broadly, "No, see, you don't understand. See, you think you know everything but you don't. Sometimes you just plain ignorant, Mike. Your grandmother and me, we was talking one day in here, I forget where you was, doing something stupid or something. Oh, yeah, it was a freezing morning when you was out hiding on some stupid deer. But she's sitting in here praying and stuff like that and I ask her what she wants since she prays for everyone all the time. So she says nothing, she don't want nothing, except she would like to go to the Vietnam Memorial so she could see her son's name. She said they let you make a copy of it or something. So I told her that me and you, we can carry her down there sometime, that that ain't nothing to want. So me and you and Mrs. C, we'll go to Washington and go to the Memorial and stuff and we'll go see this guy."

Michael raised his eyebrows and smirked. "Okay, when," he asked, "when we going?"

Jeff flipped his palms open angrily. "Now how am I

622

supposed to know that right now, Mike?" he sputtered. "We'll just take some time off and go. We ain't got to decide that right now. We'll go to his office. Ain't no big deal." Then he turned to Frances and asked, "So you know where this guy's office is at?"

"Well, no," Frances said, looking at both of them, "but I can find out. I can call his aunt. I can get the office address. Do you want me to call her?"

"Yeah," Jeff responded quickly, "you find out and let us know. You ain't got to call right now. But don't say nothing to Linda. I don't want her to think we be talking about her and stuff."

"Yeah," Michael added, "I don't want her to be disappointed, get her hopes up or anything."

Jeff cast Michael a disgusted look. "What you mean disappointed? She ain't going to be disappointed. She might be mad at us or something, but not disappointed. It's not like she be expecting him or nothing."

Frances looked to each of them. She remained silent but shook her head affirmatively, swallowed hard and closed her eyes. Her movement was nearly imperceptible. She spun her cup in the saucer.

"She is?" Michael asked softly.

Frances said nothing. Her head bobbed slowly, reticently. She looked down into her empty coffee cup. She had betrayed a trust. A confidence had been broken. The truth was told. She wasn't sure what they could do, these two young men who didn't know Blake and had no sense of limitations. But they thought they could do something

623

and anything was better than nothing. They were taking Virginia to trace Kevin's name. So that was enough, even if nothing else came to be. But the time was ripe. The factories had all closed. The apartments were empty, the businesses gone. Even the bank building was up for sale. She knew that Linda was running out of time. One way or the other, the long wait had to end.

The glass ceiling of the Meridian Center soared high over the polished granite floor. Like a crystal umbrella it dripped light fragments throughout the soaring lobby. Jeff, Michael and Virginia pushed through the gleaming revolving door and ambled their way to the center.

Jeff furled his forehead and winched his neck up the walls. "Damn, Bro, this is something," he said in an undertone, then turned to Virginia. "Ain't this something, Mrs. C? I ain't never been a building like this before, not even in the city."

Michael turned slowly with a dimpled smile, "Heck, man, I only seen buildings like this in pictures and stuff." He walked to the security desk tucked into a wall nook and leaned over the desk, conversing with the two security guards before turning to orient himself and waving Jeff and Virginia towards one of the three banks of elevators. "East wing, sixteenth floor," he called out as he dodged brisk walking men and women clapping their heels on the stone flooring while clutching briefcases and portfolios against impeccably tailored suits.

"One of them talking elevators, how about that, Mrs. C,"

Jeff said as they rode up. Jeff stood between the doors as Virginia stepped out to a floral rug. "Well, here we go, Buddy."

The rich gold lettering on the heavy maple double doors of the office caused Jeff to hesitate and take a deep breath. "Well," Michael said, opening the door and stepping in, "here we go. Feel like Dorothy asking to see the damned wizard." Jeff's wide smile broke into a laugh as the three of them stood before the receptionist's desk.

An older woman with a headset on looked up and smiled as she routed calls through the firm from behind a wide mouthed vase brimming with fresh-cut flowers. "May I help you?"

Jeff stepped forward and drummed his fingers on the stone counter. "Yes, um, we'd like to see Attorney Blake Teitel. We come to see him." He turned to Virginia and gave her a wink and a smile.

"Do you have an appointment?"

"No, no, we don't have no appointment. This ain't really business or nothing. It's personal. So we didn't make no appointment. It's like a surprise."

"So Attorney Teitel doesn't know you are coming?"

Jeff nodded towards Michael and Virginia. Then he leaned over the counter and rested his arms on the surface. "No, he don't know nothing. Mrs. C there, she knows him from when he was a kid. We just need to talk to him for a few minutes when he's not busy. We can wait, you know? We come a long way to see him, you know what I mean? I mean, we carried Mrs. C. down here all the way from the Valley."

The woman smiled and nodded confidently. "I'll check with his secretary. Please have a seat."

"Thank you." Jeff turned and pointed to the Queen Anne chair. "Sit down there, Mrs. C."

The woman stood and moved the flowers to the side. "Who shall I say is calling?"

Jeff turned to Virginia, then back to the receptionist. "He don't know me. Tell them it's Mrs. Cumiskey, Kevin Cumiskey's mother. He knew him. Tell him we from the Valley."

"Sure," the woman said, pointing down the hall."There's coffee and tea and cold drinks just around the corner if any of you would like it."

Michael sat beside Virginia and looked at her with wide eyes. "I don't know, Gram, I hope he remembers us. It don't look like people like us come in here too much."

Virginia's fleshy face lifted with a calming smile. "I'm sure he'll remember. How could he forget?"

Norine marched into the receptionist's area with short, deliberate strides, pressing her palm on her skirt as she approached the chair. "Are you Mrs. Cumiskey?"

"Yes."

"Attorney Teitel is in a meeting right now and I expect that will go on for another half an hour. Then he has a partner's meeting after that, but I'll tell him you're here and maybe he can see you in between."

"Oh, I appreciate that very much. I know he's very busy."

626

Norine glanced at Michael and Jeff and turned back to Virginia. "Are you all together?"

"Yes," Virginia responded, "they're with me. They drove me down here. That's my grandson Michael and his friend Jeff."

Norine stepped back and pressed her palm over her skirt. "Nice to meet all of you, I'll let Attorney Teitel know you're here."

Norine entered Blake's office as he took his phone messages and listened to her with one ear. "What's her name?"

"Mrs. Cumiskey. She's here with her grandson and his friend. They drove her here. She said she's from the Valley."

Blake hung up the phone. "Yes, yes, I know her. Her son Kevin was on the track team with my brother. He was killed in Vietnam. She's here to see me?"

"Uh-huh, and the two young men with here, they're all here to see you."

Blake looked at his watch. "What time is the partner's meeting?"

Norine checked her wrist. "In five minutes."

Blake stood and fixed the chairs in front of his desk, pulled a third one in from the wall. "Tell everyone I'll be late."

Virginia looked up the long corridor as Norine and Blake approached them. "Well, if it isn't Himself!" She planted her cane, lifted herself and wrapped her arms around him. "Look at you all grown up and handsome like that." She turned and introduced him to Michael and Jeff, asking him if he recalled Michael as a boy and explaining that Jeff was a friend as they walked down the hall.

Norine closed the door to Blake's office as they situated themselves in the chairs. Blake studied Virginia closely. She looked weary. She commented on his apparent success and he brushed it off as just a function of luck.

"So what brings you here? I don't get to see too many folks from the Valley."

"Well, you see," Virginia explained, "Jeff and Michael drove me down to see the Vietnam Memorial. I wanted to see Kevin's name and trace it so I can keep it. So they said they would drive me down here. That's why we came to Washington."

"So did you go there yet?"

"We went last night. When we got here we went right there. We saw Kevin's name and we traced it. It's very emotional. I have it here in my pocketbook."

Blake nodded in agreement and flicked his eyebrows. "Yes, it's so emotional that I've never been there. I can see it from the other side of the building. That's as close as I have ever gotten." He shrugged his shoulders and looked at Michael and Jeff, then back to Virginia. "I just can't get myself to go, you know, to put myself through it again."

Virginia nodded, "I understand."

Blake sat back in his chair and folded his hands. "So, is there something I can do for you?"

An awkward moment passed in silence. Jeff leaned forward, resting his elbow on his knees. "It was my idea to come to see you. Me and Mike, we wanted to come and see you and talk to you about Linda."

Blake leaned over the desk. "Sure," he said quietly, "why, what's happened to Linda?"

"Nothing," Jeff responded, leaning back and slicing the air with his palm as he spoke, "nothing happened to Linda. But one day, something happened with her daughter, you know, so me and Mike, we was curious about Linda, like, why she ain't been married and stuff. So we decided to go ask Frances and your name came up."

Blake took a deep breath and sat back in his chair. He looked across at the wall, then swallowed hard. "Is her daughter okay?"

"She's all right now," Mike explained. "It's kind of a long story.

"She's okay now," Jeff commented, "ain't nothing for you to be worried about. I took care of it."

Blake leaned forward, placing his elbows on the desk, "I don't know anything about Linda. I never asked my aunt about her. It was like some unwritten rule, that I never asked about her and no one ever brought her up. I assumed she was happily married. She was a great girl."

Michael turned to Virginia and responded slowly, looking to her to correct him if he was wrong. "No, no, she never got married. I don't ever remember her even going out with anyone."

Blake folded his hands before his lips and closing his eyes for a moment. "So what happened to her daughter? Can you tell me?"

"Yeah," Jeff said, leaning forward again, "we don't know the whole story but Frances talked to me and Mike after she seen my knuckles were all scabbed and stuff and my arm was burned. I guess she told Frances or something. Seems like Birmingham Savings is being bought by some other bank. There was lots of newspaper articles on it and stuff. I don't know, I guess some of these guys involved, they fighting about it. You know, that ain't nothing I followed and stuff, I just heard people talking about it. Anyway, Linda's daughter Tori, she worked at the bank in the summer, she finds out about some loans one of the guy's taking out to buy the stock or something. So she didn't want to say no more but we found out after the guy with the loans, he goes to her apartment when she's alone and he tries to buy her off, and then she got pissed and refused the money and he got mad. Then he like cut her hair. And he hit her by accident and stuff and we seen her, you know, when she's sitting on the stool with a milkshake and I go to pull on her braid and there ain't no braid and I see that she got a shiner. So I asked her what happened and she don't say nothing. Said it was an accident. So I sat next to her and she told me the details but said that he threatened to hurt her if she told anyone. So she didn't tell me the guy's name or nothing."

"So then we asked Linda when we seen her at work," Michael said.

"Yeah," Jeff continued, nodding to Michael, "we asked her and all she said was that she can't say any more because whoever did it said it would be worse the next time."

Blake leaned over his desk trying to sort out the fragments of the story. "So what happened? I'm a little confused."

"Nothing. Linda was like real quiet about it. It was like they was scared or something. We knew something was wrong but we couldn't figure it out. Then we was playing cards one night and the Greek says he seen Cruz coming out of Linda's building one night with a scissors in his hand. That's when we put it together."

"So you know who did it?"

"I took care of it."

"So they're all okay now?"

"Everybody's okay now. We was just wondering about Linda and Frances told us all about you and Linda going out and stuff before you left the Valley. So I figured while we was here we could come here and talk to you. We found out you wasn't married, neither." Jeff smiled and looked at Virginia and Michael. "Frances told us that, too."

Blake returned their smiles and raised his eyebrows, "I guess Frances knows quite a bit."

"Hey," Jeff said with another wide smile, "you know Frances. She found out the lawyers you work for, too. That's how we got here, from your aunt or something."

The conversation seemed to end for a moment as Blake took a moment to write notes on a pad. "Just wanted to take some notes about that transaction you described. I have a friend who trades stock all the time."

Jeff leaned forward and rested his elbows on his knees.

"So we was wondering why you didn't come back and stuff, seeing that you ain't married or nothing. From the way Frances said, you know, you and Linda was in love and stuff. It don't seem right that you didn't come back."

Blake sat back in his chair. He was startled at the directness of Jeff's comment, realizing they were here for that purpose. "You're right, Jeff, it isn't right. It was just a bad time for me for a long time after the war. To tell you the truth, I always imagined that her life was perfect, that she was happily married and that I was just part of the past. That's what I wanted to believe."

Virginia stuffed her babushka into her pocket and politely asked Jeff and Michael to leave the room. They looked surprised but rose, shook hands with Blake and agreed to meet Virginia in the receptionist area.

"Do you have more surprises for me, Mrs. Cumiskey?" Blake asked with a concerned look.

"No, Blake, no more surprises. This will only take a minute." Virginia patted the vacant chair next to her. "Could you sit here, Blake? I'd like that. You know," she said, looking around the room, "I've never seen an office like this. It looks like you've done very well for yourself."

Blake came around and faced her. "All this," he said with a dismissive gesture, "it doesn't mean anything, Mrs. Cumiskey. I was just trying to make a living and this is the result. I really never think about it. I just get up and come to work every day. That's it."

"I don't understand why you never got married, Blake. You must meet nice women all the time. How did this happen that you stayed single?"

Blake smiled and closed his eyes, shaking his head, "I guess I just never fell in love again. Things happened during Vietnam. For a long time I couldn't get some of the events out of my mind. Then, by the time things settled down, well, it was too late to just come back, too much time had passed. And now you showed up and I find out that the life I imagined her leading isn't it at all. The truth is that I was kidding myself. I wanted to imagine her living a perfect life because for so long I wasn't well enough to return. I had some things to resolve. I didn't want to be a burden to anyone."

Virginia nodded and turned to the door, making certain it was closed. She leaned forward and rested her hands on her knees, speaking in a soft voice with a shallow smile lifting her heavy jowls. "I want you to know that Linda doesn't know we came here today." She fixed her cane over the armrest, took a tissue from her coat pocket, and clasped her hands on her lap. "We didn't want to embarrass her or get her hopes up or anything. You know how she keeps to herself. No one knows we came, not even Frances. A few years after Kevin died, I don't know, maybe five or six years after, one day, it was a Sunday and it was his birthday. After mass when the church was empty, I called up to the choir loft and she leaned over the railing and I asked her if she would do me a favor. I told her it was Kevin's birthday and could she sing 'I Have an Angel in Heaven' for me. Of course, Linda was so gracious and she wouldn't take any money or anything. And from that day until now she still sings it for me on the Sunday closest to his birthday. She said she writes it in her calendar every New Year's Day so she wouldn't forget. I always wanted to pay her back, you know, to do something nice for her. For a couple of years I made her daughter some ceramic dolls. She always seemed so grateful, but then her daughter got big and I always told her that I wanted to do something special for her, for Linda. Until now there was nothing I could do." Virginia opened her hands with the balled up tissue resting in her palm, looking directly at Blake. "What could I give her?" she asked, shaking her head and squeezing the tissue in her hand. "So today I came here to ask you to come back to see her. I'm not asking you for her. I'm asking you to do it for me. Do you understand that? She isn't asking you to come back, I am. This is what I can do for her, to ask for something special for her that she wouldn't ask for herself."

Blake sat motionless. He eyes welled and he placed his hands over hers. "Okay," he said softly, "I understand that Linda isn't asking me to come back, that I am coming back for you."

"You won't disappoint me now, will you?"

"No, Mrs. Cumiskey," Blake answered over a deep breath that escaped as he spoke. "I'm not going to disappoint you. I couldn't live with myself." He sat back and closed his eyes for a moment. "I don't know what I'm going to say to her."

Virginia planted her cane into the floor and eased

herself up as Blake stood to assist her. "Don't worry about that, Blake. That'll come natural. You can't plan that," she said as Blake opened the door for her.

Soon after they left, Blake hung up the receiver, pressed the speaker button and motioned for Norine to take a seat. "I'm on hold for Nick. I got him on speaker. Sit down. I want you to take notes so you can get whatever he needs."

"Blake," Nick said, "what's going on? You got me on speaker?"

"Yeah," Blake laughed into the phone, "I got you on speaker so you better keep it clean."

"Hey, Nor, how are you?"

Norine sat at the edge of the chair and looked at the phone as she spoke. "I'm just fine, Nick."

"That's great to hear, Nor. Now what's going on with you two? Is this a social call or business?"

"Business, this might take a minute. You got some time?"

"I always have time for you, what's up?"

"I need information on two bank stocks in Connecticut, Great Nation Bank and its takeover target, Birmingham Bank Corp. There was some fighting going on among the board members and now the speculation is that Great Nation is purchasing Birmingham for cash. Someone on the board is supposed to be connected to someone on the state Banking Committee or something. That's all I know, just sketchy information. Anyway, I want to know if you can do some research and find out what's going on with it."

"Is this for you or one of our clients?"

"It's for me. I want to know."

"Since when are you interested in stocks?"

Blake rolled his eyes and shook his head at Norine. "I'm not. I just have an interest in this one. It's kind of a long story but I need the information. I need names of significant shareholders and officers. I can do the research but I figured you do this all the time anyway."

"I can get everything that's out there. How about the morning, is that soon enough?"

Blake's eyes lifted in wide excitement, "Tomorrow's fine. Talk to you then."

Norine opened the office door and stood in the threshold, "Oh, I have one last thing I've been meaning to ask you. You got the invitation to Myrna's son's wedding, right?"

"Uh-huh" Blake replied, making some notes in his calendar.

"I need a favor if you're not taking a guest."

Blake laid his pen down and looked up at Norine. "Sure," he said, "what do you need? I really haven't thought of who I'd bring, if anyone."

"Well, you know my great niece out in Montana, Amanda?"

"Sure. That's the one that started school late because she had some problem?"

"Right, you remember we talked about her, cerebral palsy."

"What, you think I don't pay attention when you talk about your family? She refused to be photographed in her wheelchair once she got older."

Norine laughed and thumbed her blouse into her skirt. "Right, anyway, she's applying to Georgetown. Has an interview the Tuesday following the wedding. Anyway, she won't let her parents travel with her. So we have to pick her up at the airport and she'll be with us all weekend. So I was wondering if she could come along as your guest."

"Yeah, of course she can. Does she need me to call anyone at Georgetown for her?"

"Oh, I told my sister that you have lots of connections but she said that Amanda is very independent, wants to get in on her own."

Blake nodded his head and smiled, "Okay, well, I'll talk to her during the wedding. She can make her own judgment from there."

"Oh, this is great. Now I can call sis and let her know it's all set."

"No, the capital position of Great Nation Bank is too weak to pull this off."

"So what does that mean? They didn't announce the takeover yet?

Nick laughed and shook his head incredulously. "No, they announced it. I don't know who's advising those guys but there's no way this is going to fly because it affects their tier one capital. It's a cash for stock deal. Problem is that Great Nation doesn't have that kind of cash lying around to pull this off. Even combined they don't have the cash to pull this off. Something isn't right."

"So what's the takeover price?"

"Twenty-eight a share, but the Birmingham shareholders are balking. They want thirty-four."

"Is it worth it?"

"No. The balance sheet of the target is sound. But it looks like it's priced above the fundamentals. Great Nation doesn't have the cash to do the deal even at twenty-eight. But it looks like some of the insiders and even the public have been trading on this information for a while now, months before the announcement. And the SEC is opening an inquiry."

Blake sat at his desk and tapped his fingers together. "Wow, the SEC? Are you sure?"

"I'm sure. The notice is out. I have staff that basically work at the SEC pulling notices daily."

"So what do you recommend? You have any ideas?"

"Oh yeah," Nick said as he looked out over Annapolis Harbor. He walked to the blinds and narrowed them to block the sun that streamed into the office, "I already started. We're going to short it. Going to sell slowly to keep from spooking anyone. I had one of my guys pouring over the material shareholder numbers since last night. He's like you, he likes to work. Anyway, I got an idea the big players are leveraged up to their necks. Shorts are going to win this one. They can't hold on like this once the stock drops in value and the margin calls come in."

Blake was silent for a moment. He shot Norine a look

and turned toward the phone. "Look, Nick, I don't want you losing money on this thing, right? You're doing me a favor but I don't want you to risk a lot on this."

Nick walked to the phone and picked up the receiver. "You still got me on speaker?"

"Yeah. Norine's here."

"Look, I'm going to make money on this. And I got you on as a consultant so we're going to split the profit. You understand?"

"I can put in some money. I got money lying around."

"I don't need any of your money. I'm not using client money or any investor funds for this. This is firm money. I know what's going to happen here. I've seen it before. Bunch of guys think they're going to clean up on these things. But they get bad advice, leverage themselves out, and then it collapses."

"So what can I do? What do you need, anything? I can have Norine do some stuff if you need it?"

"No, nothing. Norine can just continue to do whatever it is you two do all day. I have no idea what the hell that is, but keep doing it. I can get any information faster than you can. I'm not sure if the SEC inquiry will go too far. Several of the players are politically connected, so that may not go anywhere. But they got a bigger problem. They got to get by the State Banking Commissioner. That's where it falls short. Those guys will never approve it. The capital position after the deal is too weak, looks like there's another group shorting it too."

"Can they change the deal to a stock for stock swap?

What happens then?"

"They can try. But the big players have already bid up the price too much. They borrowed and now have to pay interest. This is not a sound deal. The investment advisors were looking at their fees instead of the deal. So the stock swap fails because these guys are already leveraged out on the cash deal. In the cash deal, selling at an inflated price, they sell their shares for cash, pay off what they borrowed, and make a nice profit. If it goes to a stock deal, number one, all the regulators look harder and they have to wait and see what the real value of the parent stock will be. Meantime, now they start getting margin calls because they borrowed upon borrowing and the underlying stock price is dropping through the floor. It's going to get ugly out there."

"So I'm just going to sit tight?"

"Just sit tight. Watch the stock. You'll see what I'm talking about. I'll send you any press releases or any other information."

Linda's face tingled. It wasn't until the last note of In Questa Reggio passed from her lips that she realized that it was the sound of Byron's piano, only the piano, that had been playing through the song. It was in her mind that she heard the strings and the woodwinds and the horns, the harp and the timpani that carried her through her limits. She turned slightly, confirming that, in the darkness of the loft, she was alone with her voice. Her chin dropped to her chest in despair and she raised her hand to her eyes.

Despite her effort to suppress it, a high-pitched cry sounded a muted peal through the nave.

Byron rose from the piano and stepped to her side, putting his hand on her shoulder and rubbing her back with tiny circles of comfort. "There, there now, Linda. I," he said in a hesitant whisper, "I don't know what it is that you are so upset about." He was confused at her tears and groping for what to say, wondering why she was so shaken at her own accomplishment. Quietly again, he spoke, searching for a reason for her sadness. "You know, Linda," he said, "life is funny. Sometimes when we reach what we have strived for there is a feeling of let down rather than joy."

She moved her hand to his and squeezed his fingers to let him know she understood his bewilderment. "I'm so sorry, Viejo," she said with a body that shook with distress, "I'm sorry for crying, but I ...." She shook her head side to side lightly without finishing the phrase.

"No, no, Linda. You don't have to explain to me," he whispered to her as she turned and buried her face in his shoulder. He held her in his arms and spoke in a whisper. "You know," he said cautiously, searching for the right words, "I don't know what happened before in your life that brought you to this moment. But our lives intersected and we shared some special hours together at this piano in this beautiful church. Maybe just an interlude, it seems now, no? But whatever it is, whatever has you so upset, it cannot be so bad. You have to always remember that this life we share, it is only a vapor, nothing more. We try to give it substance with our music, you and me, no? You take it from old Viejo, today was special. You were perfect."

Linda raised her face to Byron and brushed her lips wetted with tears to his cheek. "Thank you, Viejo. Thank you for everything." Then she wiped his cheek with her fingers and let a weak smile part her lips. "Now I got your cheek all wet."

"Oh, that's all right. You know, you're so young, I think of you as the daughter I never had. You're young enough to be my granddaughter. So if you're sad, then I'm sad too."

Linda stepped back and put a tissue to her nose. She extended the palm of her hand in a manner of resignation, "Oh, Viejo, I'm not young anymore. I used to be young, but that was a long time ago."

Byron shook his head in disagreement and as a manner of transitioning. "So, before we go any further, I want to share another piece with you. It's the Pie Jesu from Gabriel Faure's Requiem. Are you familiar with it?" Byron asked as he turned from her and sat at the piano.

Linda nodded her head in quiet contemplation. She was still thinking of the notes she wrote and the confusion of that night long ago. "No, I don't recognize the name of the piece or the composer. Is it in French?"

Byron looked at her and offered a soft smile. "No, it's a requiem. It's in Latin. Do you know what a requiem is? You're the choir director here, you aren't familiar with the requiem?"

Linda stepped back and leaned against the choir railing.

She folded her hands and dropped them to her waist. "I'm familiar with the word, but we just do songs for a funeral. Ave Marie is popular."

"So you don't know what a requiem is, what it means?

Linda smiled and shrugged her shoulders, "No, not really."

"It's a mass for the dead. It's the mass sung, each part of the mass is sung. The word requiem means rest. So the Pie Jesu is from the Faure's Requiem. It is perfectly placed for your voice, just between the mezzo and soprano range. It is right in your tessitura, do you understand?"

"I do."

"Good. Then you won't mind that I will accompany you and I want to bring in some instrumental students. It will be good for them to hear a voice like yours singing a piece like that. It's a beautiful piece." Byron leaned over and pulled out sheets of music from his folder. "I have a present for you."

Linda stepped to his side and extended her arm, taking the music and reading the title. "Visi D'arte?"

"Do you recognize the name?" he asked.

"Yes, of course," Linda responded confidently. "I've seen it written before, maybe in music books, maybe at school, or with my father. I really don't remember."

"It's from Tosca. Read the notes. Don't try to sing it, just read the notes. You have the vocal score."

Linda read the notes in a whisper until, nearly half way through, she looked at Byron and, with a puzzled expression, and asked, "Am I supposed to recognize this?

I'm not sure I know this. You said it was a gift. I don't know if I understand."

"No?" Byron said, turning to the piano, "I'm not surprised." He handed her the entire score of the opera, opened to a particular page. "The notes that you have that you wrote down, these notes," he said as he played them, "this is the aria they are from."

Linda smiled lightly and shook her head. "It can't be," she responded, looking at the vocal score once again and singing the notes. "These aren't the notes I wrote down."

Byron nodded his head and played the notes once again. "Do you recognize those notes?" he asked, "Are those the notes you wrote down?"

Linda lifted her eyes to Byron and shook her head, uttering, "Yes, those are the notes."

He turned from the piano and looked at her, resting one hand above the keys and the other on his knee. "Do you see them on the music you're holding, in the soprano line?"

Linda read several lines of music again. "No," she said quietly shaking her head. "No, I don't see them anywhere. Not even after a signature change."

Byron swiveled his legs out and sat at the edge of the bench. "Do you know what a descant is?"

"No," Linda responded with a quizzical look. "Should I?"

Byron shook his head and pursed his lips, "No, not at all. You see, you can't recognize the notes because," he said with a soft smile, "they're not from the vocal score. They are from the cello line. You see, after the first several measures of the vocal score the voice rests. It is there, in the vocal rest, that these notes are played with the vocal line coming in, layered over the instrumental line, cellos, viola, harp, bass clarinet. But the string line, the cello line in particular, at that part of the aria, is the prominent melodic line. Although this is one of Puccini's most famous arias, the voice there, for those measures, is raised in descant, in a sense, accompanying the strings."

Linda unfastened her pearl barrette and contorted her face. She was distressed again, looking as if she was approaching panic. She studied the cello line and recognized the seven notes. "But I wrote them down just as he hummed them. I remember," she said as she stood with her back against the rail and her hands holding the music limply in front of her. "I remember, I remember, I was playing and writing and I was concentrating so hard on getting the notes down that ...that ...that he stepped back and was talking but I didn't pay attention. I didn't think that was important. I was asking him the measure of each note." She stepped away from the rail and looked directly at Byron. "He said something, Viejo," she said as her eyes filled again, "he said something and I didn't pay attention. I just assumed he was humming the vocal line. All these years, I've spent a lifetime looking for those notes in a voice part and I was wrong all along." Linda put her hand to her face in dismay. "I can't believe it. I was wrong all along."

Byron rose from the bench and put his arm around her shoulder. "So your life wouldn't be any different today,

Linda, even if you had the music. No?"

"I don't know, Viejo," she said as she lifted her pocketbook from the piano and slid it over shoulder, then slipped the music into one of her song books and handed Byron the opera score. "Maybe you're right, Viejo. Maybe it's all just a vapor."

Byron turned off the piano lamp and looked at her through the darkening church. "You've been through a lot this afternoon, Linda. Maybe we should take next week off. I'll come and have lunch at your sweet shop. We'll talk about it a little, maybe start it after that. You listen to some recordings, you'll immediately understand about the descant. It's the cello line that he hummed. Now you rest your voice," he said, pausing for a moment, measuring each word carefully, straining for words that wouldn't be lost in the dusk that settled in the loft. "Are you ready to leave?"

Linda slid her pocketbook over her shoulder and clasped her music to her chest. She turned back to the nave. Her head was shaking with disbelief. "No, I think I'm going to stay here a minute, Byron. I think I just need a minute downstairs to pray." She turned back to Byron and smiled weakly. "But I'm okay, really."

Byron stepped to the rear of the loft. "Shall I wait for you outside? I'll be worried about you."

"I'm fine, Viejo, really. I'm just a little upset, but I'll be all right."

Byron reached over and pulled up an old wooden folding chair. It squealed as he opened it and creaked when he sat on it. "Where will you go from here?"

Linda tried to smile but pursed her lips instead and raised her eyebrows, "Back to work, where else?"

Byron let a comforting smile crease his face. "I don't want to intrude on you, but I don't feel comfortable leaving you alone. I think you're too upset. If you don't mind, I'd like to stay here. I won't talk and I can't see you downstairs. You can do your praying alone. Take all the time you need. I'll leave after you're gone."

Linda moved towards the stairs, able to see only the silhouette of Byron. "You can stay. It won't bother me. I can't stay long, I have to get back to Frances anyway."

"That's good." Linda perched at the top of the narrow staircase as he spoke slowly. "You go there now. Go back to your Palace of Sweets." He leaned forward in his chair, causing a sliver of sunlight to illuminate a part of his face. He continued thoughtfully, "Hold your memories in hopeful palms, Linda. Go and wait there, wait by the river for your dreams. Look into those old faded mirrors and draw full breathes deep into your belly and never lose your hope, Linda. That's all we have, no?"

She looked at him as the light fell unevenly over his face, dark but clear, a chiaroscuro profile of loneliness framed in shadow. Her brow lifted and she nodded her head slightly. "Yes, Viejo," she said with a muted voice, "that's all we have, sí."

The narrow, winding stairs creaked as she made her way down. She held her music firmly against her chest and moved to the right aisle, before the statue of St.

Anthony and Our Lady of Guadalupe. She looked up at them, ran her fingers over their toes, and stood a few seconds in deep thought. The church was empty and silent. She walked across the back of the church, stopping before the votive candles on the other side. They flicked a red hue on the marble statuary. She searched her pocketbook for change and dropped it in the coin box. She turned and stepped before the statue of the Christ raised on a pedestal. She hesitated. No prayer came to her. She was uncertain what to do. She didn't know what to say. For herself, she didn't know how to pray. She had prayed in gratitude and repentance. She prayed in adoration and love. But she had never prayed for herself. She was never without hope until now when she was left with only faith. She had never bypassed the intercessors. She was speechless and shaking. She felt her composure weakening by the second when she placed her fingers on the glistening toes of the statue.

She remembered how Byron, in his first visit to the church to tune the piano, called up to her as she leaned over the choir rail, and looked to her in amazement. He embraced the foot and commented that the marble there was polished, worn smooth by touch from supplicant's needs. She returned to the flickering candles and looked up into the eyes of the statue. Her head dropped to her chest and a pitched cry pealed through the church. Then she lifted her eyes again. A painful cry ripped from her lungs and wailed through the church. Her lips quivered as she tried to speak. Nothing came out but staccato breaths of pain and another pitched cry. Her shoulders shook. She thought of Byron and took a deep breath, letting the expanse of her abdomen soothe her. She looked at the statue again and exhaled evenly under his gaze. Still, she couldn't think of what to say. She stood in the darkened church as minutes passed, settling and ruminative.

Then her father's voice came to her. She was back on 116th Street. She remembered it clearly, the pain he tried to hide from her when his crutch slipped out on ice and he fell into the gutter and broke his shoulder. She was eight and knelt at his side, hysterical at his pain. To ease her distress, to comfort and distract her, he asked her to pray with him while they waited for an ambulance. She remembered people standing over them with concern, trying to help them while they waited. She remembered her foot over the sewer grate, frozen in slush. He held her hand while he lay there with his legs wet and freezing.

Still, he asked her to repeat after him, until she spoke it with him, in Latin. And she looked up again, into the eyes of the great Counselor, and spoke the opening lines, all that she recalled. "De profundis clamavi ad te Domine; Domine, exaudi vocem meam." 'Out of the depths I cry to thee, oh Lord; Lord hear my voice.'

She repeated it several times, each time with more clarity and confidence. 'De profundis clamavi ad te Domine; exaudi vocem meam.' Then she smoothed the marble with trembling fingers and slipped through the swinging doors.

She walked along the familiar blocks of Elizabeth Street

649

hearing nothing except the sound of her heart thumping in her breast. Her mind filled with the memories of love that slipped over her like a silk scarf, gliding weightlessly through the days and months and years and drifting into air, feathered to nothing. She looked at the lithe beech trees on the Green and noticed the delicate leaves starting to yellow with the first hint of autumn.

And she thought of her words to him, the promise of the song she denied him in a moment that was never to be revisited. She wondered if it all would have been different if she sang that night. But no, nothing would have changed except the regret she carried with her. That would have been lifted. And the promise, there would have been no promise to keep.

On a brilliant Saturday afternoon in October, Byron and three student musicians threaded up the spiral staircase with their instruments and set up their music stands in the choir loft. They were there early, over an hour before Linda would arrive for her lesson. As colorful shafts of autumn sun streamed through the stained glass windows above the altar, Byron prodded and instructed the students on the finest points of the dynamics and tone and tempo of the piece, an adagio, which they each had studied with Byron in the lesson rooms at Bankos.

"Are you applying to other schools?"
Amanda turned from him and scanned the crowded dance floor. Her Edwardian styled hat, hugging her

bobbed hairdo, was accented with a wide, autumn colored band fastened with a gold broach. The dance floor looked larger than a Kansas corn field after harvest, filled with long, elegant lines of sunlight shunting over the parquet. The centerpiece of each table was a small autumn tree with freshly fallen red and yellow leaves interspersed with bright gourds and small pumpkins. "Do you see my aunt and uncle? I know she likes to talk but she hasn't returned since before the last band break."

Blake squeezed a lemon wedge into his glass of ice water and spun it vigorously until the stirrer bent like a vaulting pole. He stood and looked around the dance floor, darting his eyes over the pockets of people grouped in clutches or walking to the bar. "I don't see either of them. Maybe they're in the lobby or something." Blake sat and turned to Amanda. He was struck by her face, open and innocent. He glanced to her hair, auburn over Irish brown, framed with pearl earrings. Her skin was peachy, smooth as fired porcelain.

He spun his ice water again until it tinkled. "How old are you?"

"Eighteen," she responded, looking directly into his eyes. "I lost a year in school when I was younger. I would have graduated at seventeen except for that."

Her blue eyes were railed with eyeliner, thickening her look to the exotica of an Egyptian Empress, as if she had studied pictures of Nephritis styling, elegant and graceful and fecund in her youth. He lifted his water glass to his lips and spoke into it. "Do you have a boyfriend?"

"Yes," she responded with eyes that darted to the dance floor again, "sort of." Then she broke into a wide smile that wrinkled her nose. "I'm not so sure."

"Oh," Blake smiled back, "and what makes you not so sure, him or you?"

She nodded her head with uncertainty. "Me, I guess."

"Is he sure?"

"I think so."

"Is that bad for him?"

"No. I like him a lot. He's real sweet and nice to me. He sits with me at lunch every day."

"Well, that's pretty certain then, right?"

"I suppose. But I have to get to know him better first. He's from a different town."

"I see. And where are you from? I thought your mom said you were from Billings?"

"Well, I say I'm from Billings because it's the closest big town, but I'm really from this little town called Roundup. It's just outside of Billings." She excused herself, craned her neck, and scanned the crowd.

"Any sign of them?"

She sat back down and shook her head. "Yes, I think I see them standing near the bar talking to another couple."

"Do you need her?"

She shook her head and arched her eyebrows. "I have to go to the bathroom. I need help walking."

Blake released his stirrer. His lips parted, speechless with concern, then he caught himself staring at her. "You need help walking," he repeated in a declarative tone.

She nodded her head and smiled. "I can't walk alone. I need to be near a railing or at least a wall to lean on. I usually bring a cane but it just attracts so much attention. I just refused to bring it."

Blake stood and glanced towards the bar. Norine was still talking. "I can take you. You're my guest, right, so I'll walk you. You just tell me what to do."

Amanda looked up at him and smiled at his enthusiasm. "Okay. It's not a big deal or anything. You just hold out your arm and I can hold on to it and it looks like we're just together. We just have to walk slower than most people." She grabbed his arm firmly with both hands and rose. Her dress fell perfectly. It was tiered with a scalloped hem and a soft, flounced cut. She blended with the tables, its coloring all autumn gold and scarlet and rust over shale.

"The bathroom is towards the bar, right?"

"I think so," she whispered as Blake pulled her chair out farther.

"That's a pretty dress," he commented as they turned from the table and she released the chair. "When we were sitting I didn't really get a good look at it."

"Thank you." She smiled broadly as they made their way through the expansive room. "My parents took me all the way to Great Falls to buy it. My mom said she wanted me to make a good impression at the interview."

They walked past the bar and the nodding approval of Norine. "Well," Blake said, "the dress is pretty, but I don't think you're going to have a problem getting in."

Amanda reached for the rail along the wall leading to the ladies room and stopped as Blake backed away. "What's that?"

Blake smiled and released her hand sending her along the rail with a steady grip. "Nothing, I'll explain later." He walked over to Norine and stood in her company, surveying the wedding. "Great wedding, isn't it?"

Norine turned to him, squinting into the October sunlight streaming through the wall length window. She snapped her sunglasses down and looked up at Blake. "Oh, it's just lovely, isn't it? So, how's she doing? I see she got you to take her to the bathroom. I'm surprised she asked."

Blake smiled and turned his back to the windows. "Well, she didn't, but you weren't available and I sensed her distress. It took her a while before she told me she needed to hold onto something."

Norine looked at Blake with a stern face, stepped to his side, and rotated him into the sun, "Did she tell you she didn't walk until she was fifteen?"

Blake frowned and lowered his brows, "What?" His answer was shallow with incredulity. "No, she never said anything about that. She just said she needed to hold onto something or someone."

Norine shook her head affirmatively. "I had to promise not to say anything to you before she agreed to attend today. Didn't talk until she was nine. And she didn't walk until she was fifteen. She wants to make it on her own and it has my sister and her parents sick with worry. But they feel like they don't want to stand in her way so, like today, no cane, no walker, nothing. Just a new dress and her own moxie. She's remarkable. Her parents wanted to come with her for the interview but she wouldn't hear of it."

Blake looked at Norine, then glanced to the hall leading to the bathroom. Norine flipped up her sunglasses and shook her head. Blake scanned the autumn ballroom, glancing at Norine with a surprised look. He turned back to the hallway. She was there, clutching the rail firmly, resplendent in her youth. She dropped her hand to her side and stepped towards them with a slow, shambling gait that cast her hemline in a pronounced counterpoint with each hesitant step.

Slowly and confidently, Amanda approached them with the earnestness of a schoolgirl, her face creased with effort over a measured smile, finally clasping Blake's arm firmly. She stood beside him and smiled broadly, assuming the style of a flapper, confident and certain, like she had just swilled from the casks of another era and appeared out of thin air. Blake had seen it before. He looked down and remembered the movement of the dress riding gently against the sway of the hip, the hesitancy of the walk, the stoic lyricism of the earnest, deliberate step. Amanda rolled her eyes to Norine. "Something tells me you're talking about me, Auntie?"

Norine turned towards the sun and flicked her sunglasses down. "Only good things, sweetheart. Are you about ready to sit down?"

"Yes. You can stay here if you like. I can walk with

Blake. He said he likes my dress."

"Of course he likes your dress. Who wouldn't? Your parents took you all the way to Great Falls to buy it, and that was after searching all over Billings. It's the material, Honey. It has weight to it, so it flows. Doesn't it flow, Blake?"

Blake smiled softly and put his hand over Amanda's. "It's beautiful."

"Hey," said Norine, raising her short, round body from her seat and clapping lightly.

"Oh, look, they're going to cut the cake," said Queen, one of the paralegals. "Myrna said it's half chocolate and half vanilla. I'm going to get me the biggest chocolate piece they cut."

"I think it's time for me to be going," he said as he stood between Norine and Amanda.

Norine strained to look up over her flipped up sunglasses. "But they haven't even served the cake yet."

"I'm going to try to catch a flight to New York," he responded as he pulled an envelope from his pocket and tapped it on the table. "Soon as this toss is done." He looked at Amanda and bent to her slightly. "Aren't you single?" he asked in feigned confusion.

She looked up at him and smiled. "Yes, but I'm not going out there, no way."

"I understand," he said, letting a breath of laughter slip through. "You're too young to be next anyway." He stooped down between them and rested his hands on the back of their chairs. "Nor, we have CPE scheduled for Tuesday, right?"

"Yes, and I expect you will be in attendance. You were the one who scheduled it at the offices, don't you remember?" She unclipped her sunglasses and laid them on the table.

"I know, the super royalty provisions and transfer pricing in international transactions. I'm pretty familiar with it. It's mostly the regulations we helped the Joint Committee write. I probably won't be back for Tuesday. I'll call you Monday."

"Sounds like you're going on vacation." Norine twisted in her chair to face him squarely. "This is only supposed to be a long weekend."

Blake sat with them again. "I'm going back."

Norine gave him a confused stare, turned to Amanda, and realized what he meant. "Now?"

"It's time."

"Okay, and what will I tell everyone at the office?"

Blake flicked his eyebrows and shrugged. "I don't know. You'll think of something." He leaned over and kissed Amanda's cheek, grasping her hand as he stood. "Thank you for being my guest today. Call me if you have any trouble with Georgetown."

"Thanks," she replied, "but I won't."

Blake drove to the Lincoln Memorial. The dwarfed encampment of the nation's capital was quiet and luminous as the October sun gilded the American Acropolis. He walked to the back of the monument and

657

stood silently, looking across the Memorial Bridge into Arlington. It was as close as he could get to saying farewell to his fallen brothers. He walked the length of the monument and took in the view of the district, then turned and walked back where he could see Arlington and thought of the gravestones, orderly, stately, and somber. He wondered for how long generations and countless thousands would continue to offer their lives for the noble dream and unfulfilled promise of the Republic. He thought of the America he now knew, failed of myth and absent of honor. History had exposed the lightkeepers as vacant of sound judgment, granting to one the kingly ability to wage war, sending to preternatural graves the innocent and the callow clothed in patriotism while shielding the privileged. Daily, in silence, the gravestones of Arlington appear like ghosts at dawn and flicker their eerie presence with inspiring uniformity. As darkness follows they recede from extraordinary view, from here, where the scope and scale of failure is often the measure of one man's ambition.

The notes floated from Linda effortlessly, as if the song, the Pie Jesu from Faure's Mass for the Dead, had been written for her voice and for this moment. The gentle strings undulated beneath and above the flawless beauty of her voice, the Latin phrase repeating calmly, comfortingly, with stately measure, 'sempriternam requiem, sempriternam requiem,' 'everlasting rest, everlasting rest.'

658

Blake closed his eyes and felt his face turn down in sorrow. The gravestones were peaceful, there in the distance, when for decades he struggled to find the smallest measure of repose. Finally, he wiped his eyes, stood down, and walked away from Arlington.

He stood near the center of the airport terminal and studied the monitor for the departure times. "Something I can help you with, sir?" the counter agent asked without lifting his eyes from the computer monitor.

Blake stepped forward and smiled politely at the young man. "Yes, I hope so. Any seats to LaGuardia left?"

"Hold on one second," the man replied, punching his last entries in. "All right," he said in a louder tone as he tapped in the destination. "Yes, plenty of seats. Shall I enter you?"

"What is the arrival time?"

A few quick punches and the clerk looked up and smiled. "How about 7:25? Can you handle that?"

Blake shook his head and responded with a nod. "Yeah, that's great."

"Round trip?"

"No."

"Okay," the agent said. "Have any bags?"

"No," Blake responded, "nothing."

The agent punched up his ticket and smiled to the screen. "Short trip?"

Blake handed him his credit card, nodded, and smiled softly, "Yeah," he said as the agent handed him the ticket, "short trip."

"You can let me off here." The cab pulled over with a screech. Blake paid the cabbie and stepped out, peering up at the two windows of the living room illuminated over Main Street. The building was otherwise dark. He walked up the stairs under the harsh light of the center hall bulb, naked, without a globe. He knocked gently and waited a moment, hearing footsteps approach the door.

"Who is there?" asked an apprehensive voice.

"Mrs. Citro," Blake responded, leaning into the wood panel door."It's me, Blake." He hesitated a moment, then repeated his name, "Blake Teitel."

The door opened the length of the chain lock and a patch of flesh appeared around dark, weathered eyes. "Hi, I'm sorry if I scared you," he said as the door closed quickly and he heard the chain fall against the door. It swung open freely to hands pressed gently against a face that had lost its youth. Her eyes sparkled in dollops of drifting dark skin that met grey hair bound in a floral tie. She looked at him standing beneath the single bulb, handsome and mature, refined in his suit. His hair evidenced glints of silver, more than flickers at his temples. He tried to smile but failed as he mustered a weak hello and extended his arms to her.

She embraced him tightly and repeated in an excited tone, "Gracias Dios, gracias Dios." Then she snapped herself back from his embrace and looked at him again, shaking her head in wonder, "I cannot believe what my eyes tell me. I knew it would happen someday but I didn't know when. But I knew, Blake, in my heart I knew you would return."

Blake blinked back tears, leaning over to kiss her cheek. "Where is Linda?"

"She is there, with Frances. You go."

He walked up the grade of Main Street, his own reflection walking beside him in the dark panes of abandoned store fronts. He stopped at the site where River once stood, looking down the fenced in area to all that remained, a weed-covered lot. Turning away, he gazed up the grade of the street, to the apex, where powerful shoulders of mortar and brick were now weak with decay and neglect, a street, dark and dead, rolled before him, a black conduit for traffic flickering by with indifferent flashes of light.

Gone was the flower shop where cut glass vases once burst with plumes of roses and carnations bundled with ribbons, poinsettia pots wrapped in red and green and tartan foil disappeared into full arms at Christmas, and long, elegant stalks of calla lilies were once interspersed with white clutches of lilies.

Long forgotten were the lace curtained windows that once framed flower boxes brimming with buds and dripping with a watering can's excess. Only the fallow grounds of unkempt earth remained where men in brilliant white T shirts once kneaded dough with forearms whitened like Kabuki actors. Across the river, beyond the triple trestles, lying flat and silent, treeless and abandoned, he saw the empty acres where the B. F. plants once stood with its hot stacks breathing dignity into the laborers' lives.

Gone. Gone, he thought to himself as he stopped and turned with a confused crease in his brow, trying to convince himself that what he recalled from a youth that expired on the fetid jungle floor existed at all, once. But it was gone and so little was familiar, except for the street grade that pulled at his lungs beneath the effort of older legs. Maybe he was lost, or just plain crazy, or he couldn't trust his mind at all. But still, Main Street, in its neglect and decay, whispered the past and moved him forward.

As he continued up the grade it occurred to him that the fingers plied gently from their death grip and the hair he stroked lovingly is just part of the calculus of his life and nothing more. And that it was his error to believe otherwise, a fault of youthful innocence. But here, close by, Virginia speaks to marble icons and soothes her pain and a voice rises to balm a mother's grief. And so, here, promises must be kept.

At the crest of the grade, with White Hills in the distance, clouds draped the far tree line and stole the moon's soft glow, but close ahead, faint at first, but growing brighter as he walked, a blanket of light illuminated a patch of sidewalk. Red neon lettering beckoned him towards a place where thoughts took him when his arms numbed hopelessly and sleep offered no rest.

He turned into the alcove and hesitated a moment as he

unbuttoned his jacket with fingers that trembled. He leaned into the door and pushed it open, stepping in cautiously and holding the door to a quiet close. "Oh," Frances said, with her eyes still on the grill and both arms scrubbing it clean. "We're closed now." She glanced up and felt her jaw slacken as her motion stopped.

"Hello, Frances," Blake said with a voice so soft it could hardly be heard. He lifted his hand slightly, as much to feel his presence as to greet her, and heard his heels click over the tile floor as he started past the stools.

Tori glanced into the mirror and clocked her eyes toward Frances. She rubbed clean the salt shaker in her hand until it squeaked, then continued her thoughts in midsentence. "So I told him that I was busy anyway." She glanced back at Frances with her jaw still slack, speechless. Tori shifted back into the faded mirror with a puzzled look. She followed Blake's every step, dropping her hands to her lap until, with celestial silence, she toed her stool into a slow orbit and watched the decades condense to interstitial space. Blake turned to her, the edge of their eyes exchanging glimpses, until the reflection in the mirror drew him beyond her spin, to the end of the candy case where he stopped.

Linda reached back and pulled the bow of her apron with a free hand, gathering it into a ball. She filled her lungs with the weight of Byron's instruction, clicked off the radio, and closed her eyes.

The Palace fell silent. No water ran into the deep sink. No dishes clacked in clean stacks against the mirrored wall. No rinse water dripped and no coffee fell into dark pools. No heavy silver doors hiding tubs of ice cream thumped to flee the impatient hands filling fluted sundaes dishes. In the absence of sound Linda felt his eyes on her, his presence near. She started a measured exhale as the seconds ticked on. Then she opened her eyes to the mirror and the volume in her lungs emptied and clouded the mirror before her. Her hand lifted cautiously to his image and his name formed on her lips. With trembling fingers she touched the faded mirror, then turned, pivoting slowly as she lipped his name again.

Blake took a step towards her, his hands reaching out. She touched her fingers to his, "Blake," she said again.

He held her hand in his and whispered her name. His eyes dropped to the floor and the tile blurred beneath him, and the candy case and the stools and the mirrors faded to a blend. He whispered her name again as he felt her fall into his arms. He held her firmly. She draped her arms over his shoulders. They said nothing, standing still in a long embrace.

Frances wiped her hands on the dishtowel and flicked the coffee pot on. She raced between the small grill and the counter, grabbed Tori's arm, pulled her off of the stool, and out the door, coatless into the chilled night and straining to look back at the embracing images in the old mirrors. No one heard the red neon lights shut and darken the window, nor the lock fall to keep the world away.

Blake pressed his cheek against her hair and reached his hand up to the back of her head, letting the silky threads fall through his hands, the pads of his fingers drinking in that sensation of touch that they longed for over countless years. He moved his lips to her cheeks and felt the soft pillow of her flesh beneath his. He kissed her softly. "I'm so sorry," he said softly.

Linda raised her apron and pressed it softly over his face, then did the same to herself, then wrapped her arm around him and whispered, "I know. I know."

Blake scanned the counter, "Where did they go?"

Linda's eyes darted around the Palace. She noticed the window lights were out and she heard the drizzle of coffee falling into the pot. "I think they left," she said with a smile. "I think Frances put the coffee on and locked us in and they left."

"The young girl at the counter," Blake asked hesitantly, "that was your daughter?"

Linda shook her head and smiled, "Yes. How did you know?"

"It's a long story."

"Her name is Tori."

Blake took her face into his palms and looked at her warmly. "She has your eyes, soft and beautiful."

Linda smiled back at him and touched her lips to his. "I can't believe you're here. I thought this would only happen in my dreams."

"You're as beautiful as the day I left."

Linda shook her head, "I'm much older. Heavier and older."

"No," he whispered as he embraced her again. "You're

prettier than I remember." Then he broke his embrace and lifted the cameo into his palm. "You wear this?" he asked.

"I only take it off when I sleep because I'm afraid I'll break the chain." With his hand in hers, she guided him to the first table. "Would you like coffee?"

"Yes," Blake responded, watching her every move.

"This is awful," she called out to him as she filled the ceramic cups and smiled over the fountains. "But how do you like it? You didn't drink coffee when you left, I remember."

"You're right." He shook his head and closed his eyes at the thought of all that had been lost, then opened them and looked around the Palace. "Nothing has changed in here."

"Oh," Linda responded thoughtfully as she returned with the coffee, "a lot has changed around here. But" she said, running her eyes to the reflection of the Palace in the back mirrors, "you're right, nothing much has changed in here." She smiled at Blake as she held up the apron and put it on the chair beside her. "I don't know why I'm carrying this around," she said as she sat across from him and smiled lamely, "I must be in a dream."

Blake rose and slipped out of his jacket, hanging it beside the wall menu. "Might as well settle in." He took her hands into his as a cloud of steam settled over his coffee. "I feel like I've waited a lifetime for this," he said through eyes that welled like spring ponds. "And if this is all I get, just this minute to sit here with you and hold your hands and look at your eyes again and watch how your lips move when you speak, if this is all I get, then that's okay. Then it was worth the wait, for just this moment when I held you close to me and felt your breath against my neck." He put his fingers to her hair and felt its silky essence fall again from his fingertips and smiled at her. "Your hair is still beautiful. Everything about you is still beautiful."

She looked at him and put a napkin to her eyes to blot the tears, then wondered through a whisper as she kissed his hand, "How do we begin?"

A moment passed silently, then his palm brushed her cheek and he raised his other hand to her face and caressed it, "I don't know," he whispered, "did we ever really end?"

She breathed hard, then pulled his hands to her face and cried, "What happened?"

Blake leaned his face into hers and wept with her, without restraint or reservation. Time passed without measure and the faded mirrors absorbed the event into memory.

"Are you all right?" he whispered to her finally.

"Yes," she said, and raised her eyes to his and smiled over a wet face. "Our coffees are cold."

He smiled back at her, pulled several napkins from the holder and offered them to her. "That's okay, there's more. I have nowhere to go." He rose and dumped the coffees into the deep sink and refilled them.

"How did you know I was here?" she asked, as she lifted the cup to her lips.

Blake settled back into his chair and smiled,

anticipating her surprise. "Your mom told me."

"You saw my mom?" she asked with a surprised expression.

"I took a cab from LaGuardia. I saw the lights on so I had him let me off. I knocked and she answered. And we kissed and hugged and she said you were here. So I walked up."

"Did Frances say anything when you walked in? I was going to turn off the radio. I didn't hear anything."

Blake held his cup to his lips and laughed. "No. Her jaw dropped. I think she was in shock. So where's Teddy, playing cards at the club?"

Linda shook her head from side to side and touched Blake's hand. "Teddy died, Blake, in seventy-eight. It was a peaceful death. One morning Frances went to wake him and he was gone."

Blake looked at Linda with disbelief, then spoke softly to her, as if narrating the contents of an old photo. "I remember, the night before I left, he hugged me and told me not to be a hero. Told me to come back. I remember asking him to watch out for you. I feel like I let him down." Blake lowered his head, closed his eyes. "You know, being away this long, you always think of things as they were. I just always pictured him sitting there," he said, pointing to the center table, "with The Sentinel and reading the obituaries out loud."

"He was great, Blake." Linda's face was serious, her head nodding slightly, as she looked into her coffee and rubbed the cup with her fingertips. "Through the worst days," she explained, "during the pregnancy, and right after Tori was born, they were so good to me. Making sure I was all right, feeding me until I was ready to burst." A sad smile pulled her lips as she remembered Teddy wrapping sandwiches for her or serving Tori at her favorite table that he would set for her. "Once Tori started school, he would wait to make sure she ate and they would play games until my mother picked her up after work." Linda looked up at Blake and smiled through watered eyes as she continued. "He would carry string around in his pockets and they would play cat's cradle and laugh and get silly together." And the smile dropped from her face and she held his eyes and said, "He said that you would be back," she said as she squeezed his hands and entangled their fingers into a web of flesh, "that something must have happened, but someday you would come back."

Blake looked away from her and tightened the lock of their fingers. He closed his eyes and remembered the blinding flash that cut through the blackness of the jungle floor. He remembered the illumination flair that sent foreboding shadows over a face that was only half there. He shook his head slowly and opened his eyes and leaned back in his chair, "He was right." Blake looked away from her again, recovering his voice, "I'll explain it all to you, someday." Then he touched her hands and asked, "Tell me about Tori."

Linda cocked her head to the side and let a relaxed smile fan across her face. "She's eighteen and she knows more than her mother," she commented over a laugh.

"She's a freshman in college, a good student, plays piano better than I do. We have our differences. She's a fighter. But she's very good to her grandmother and Frances."

"You seem very proud of her," Blake said gently. "No boyfriends?"

Linda's eyebrows bounced with enthusiasm. "Not right now, thank you. I'd like her to get through college. She had a few in high school but nothing serious."

"She's a beautiful girl," Blake said, pushing his coffee to the side.

Linda nodded affirmatively and looked down at the table, then returned to Blake's eyes. "She is," Linda said without inflection, "I want her to be a good person as well."

And so it went, the two of them, beneath the lights of the Palace that burned brightly, long into the dark hours of the morning, burning later and longer than ever, fingers interlaced like imbricate roofing, the woof and the warp of their flesh tightening and loosening, planishing decades into hours, great distances into inches, evanescing the past into the present.

And after many hours, Frances and Tori and Linda's mother walked up Main Street in the early morning chill while the rest of the Valley slept. They tapped on the window and entered the Palace of Sweets with warm embraces and wet eyes, and the long mark of the metronome came to a close.

It's Christmas Eve morning in the Palace of Sweets, just a few months after Judge Karrington found that Hunter

Biller was a co-conspirator for evidentiary purposes and ruled that Protection Mutual and Coast Indemnity didn't have to pay off on the policy because Biller participated in the arson. A grey sky hung over the Valley like old tulle rolled in loose balls. Hoary tree limbs, spare and severe in their retreat from winter, rose along the crown of the Valley. A week ago the State of Connecticut Banking Commissioner disapproved the Great Nation Bancorp takeover of the Birmingham Bancorp and the stock price of Birmingham collapsed, drowning Maximillian Cruz in an ocean of debt and margin calls. The December air was damp and bone-chilling.

Frances tightened the wrap of her white cardigan sweater, fighting off the chill that greeted her with each swing of the door. She stood, prodding the eggs and bacon and toasted rolls and muffins, and melting a bit more butter under them on the sizzling, snapping grill.

Fresh coffee streamed in a hot drizzle as she turned and answered the phone with her cheerful 'Vonete's Palace of Sweets' tone and jotted down the order, then rapped the grill with her spatula. She stood there, glancing out the decorated window and exchanging greetings and smiles to the frosted faces and cold hands that arrived to stand and pivot before the little grill, perch on the worn leather stools, and spend an hour of warmth in the Palace.

The early crowd was in and situated already. Carm, Dougy, Izzy and Louie, in tractor hats and fire station gear were seated on stools. Joe, who is behind the counter wearing an unshaven face with a thicket of unruly grey hair sprouting from a navy watch cap that he plopped on top of his head like a limp sock, held an advertisement from Valley Oil and read it.

"Says here they going to guarantee this price for the season," he said, pointing to the ad, his hunter's vest hanging unzipped at his sides and his lips collapsing into each other because he 'just got plain sick of them dentures anyway.' "Gettin' back to this price though, I'm gonna call them and see if they'll guarantee it like they say. Can't trust them oil companies," he clamored on, waiting for someone to respond with something more than smiling indifference. He took a fresh towel and dried the dripping breakfast dishes, holding them in his hand, and eyeing the counter.

"Thought you were going ice fishing?" Carm asked, stuffing the last bit of toast into his mouth.

Joe rested the dish towel against his stomach. "Too many guys up there already," he ranted, shaking his head and smiling a toothless grin, "I go up to Pink House Cove later. These other guys get cold and go home early. They don't know the fish like I do," he said with a wink. He lined the fluted sundae dishes along the shelf backed by the faded mirrors. "Them same guys were telling me the deer hunting was going to be bad this year. But they don't watch like I do. You got to watch the acorn mast. It was a good mast this year, you know, plenty of acorns. Especially from the white oak, they had a big mast. Deer are set for the winter. They put on the pounds. Them guys don't know what they're talking about."

Blake sat at a table in the parlor area with his back against the mirrored wall, a hot coffee twirling a halo above his lips. He looked up from his newspaper and smiled as Joe ranted on.

"What's the latest?" Joe asked as Cut Man thumbed through an old Evening Sentinel and Dougy flipped the page of one of the New York papers.

Cut Man glanced over the page and shrugged his shoulders. Dougy nodded his head, then pointed to one of the column headings in dark print. He glanced up into the mirror and caught Cut Man's eyes.

"Hey, I got one for you here." He fingered the words as he spoke, "Says here that the scientists found the top quark."

Cut Man put a perplexed look on his face, "Says they found what?"

Dougy read from the headline and spoke slowly, "Says they found the top quark, in Illinois. Scientists found the elusive top quark at the Ferni National Accelerator Laboratory."

Cut Man looked up at Dougy's mirror image and let go of his aged Evening Sentinel. He took a bite of his fried egg sandwich and lifted his shoulders. "Really, at the Fermi Lab?" he said with a puzzleded look, "I didn't even know they were looking for it."

Joe looked up and racked the remaining sundae dishes. "Yeah," Joe responded in a surprised tone, "I didn't even know they were looking for it neither."

Izzy turned from the stool and threw on his heavy coat

that nearly blanketed him. He reached back and felt the firm mold of the shoehorn in his back pocket, then adjusted his snap brim cap and seated it smartly over his eyes. They will come in today, legions of feet, in pairs, he thinks, in need of flavor and color and size and feel. And his shoehorn will slide them and guide them and pop them with smooth dexterity and compliments. And patience, unperturbed patience.

He fastened his last button and looked up at Frances, catching her eye, and she asked over a satisfied smile, "Okay, Izzy, what'll it be today?" In her inflection, enthusiasm spiraled over the wash of dishes in the deep sink. She tapped the grill for good measure and waited for his response. He stood and raised his arms slightly for effect. A resonating baritone of I'll Be Home for Christmas surfaced among the clanging phone and the belly pop of the two handed registers, turning his head to the parlor and the smiling into the mirrored images at the counter.

Linda took the table orders, heaping mounds of whipped cream in hot chocolate and watched the delight of children as they lingered before the giant candy cane in the window and stuffed their names into a box for the drawing at noon. Joe the fruit and vegetable man leaned into the door with a full case of oranges balanced on his shoulder that Frances rejected, "You order the jelly beans yet, the ones from Chicago?"

"Yeah, yeah, we got the order in all ready." Frances turned, lifted the phone to her ear, and shrugged her shoulders, "It's not even Christmas yet."

"And what about the marshmallow chicks, them too?"

"Hold on, Judy," Frances said, placing the phone against her thigh. "Yeah, but not them little ones, the other ones, Easter Chicks from Staten Island or Brooklyn, somewhere down there. That's the kind you like, right?"

"Yeah," Joe responded enthusiastically, "them are the ones. You got it. I'll be back with another case of oranges."

Frances shook her head at Linda and put the receiver to her ear. Linda glanced to Blake, shook her head, and smiled. She spooned fresh whipped cream into the piping bag and walked among the tables, topping off the hot chocolates with a dollop of freshly whipped cream. Blake returned her smile and took measure of the treasure that surrounded him.

"Food and entertainment," Izzy called out as he laid his money at the counter, "all for the same price. Got to get you a cabaret license, Fran," he said with a dapper nod as he held the door open to Main Street for others to slip in.

They come here, you know, still, to the Palace of Sweets. They come in worry worn and life beaten. They come from what is common and unremarkable but satisfying, with wide eyes and full hearts, feeding from the quenching fountains and warm grill and rich cream. They come here, all of them do, finding the restful interludes that baste their lives, holding the fabric limp until the cloth is whole and the garment is complete, until, in one unforgettable moment, the waft of the hem sails gracefully against the movement of the flesh, in a walk they call dance.

675